First
of the
Tudors

Joanna spent twenty-five years at the BBC writing and presenting for radio and television. Her first book, *Rebellion at Orford Castle* was a children's novel set in East Anglia. This was then followed by *Island Games* and *Dubious Assets* and published under the name of Joanna McDonald.

Gripped by Shakespeare's historical plays, Joanna originally began researching King Henry V's 'fair Kate' as a schoolgirl and the story of Catherine de Valois and the Tudor genesis has remained with her throughout life.

Joanna Hickson lives in Wiltshire and is married with a large family.

Follow Joanna on Facebook or Twitter @joannahickson.

BY THE SAME AUTHOR

The Agincourt Bride
The Tudor Bride
Red Rose, White Rose

First
of the
Tudors

JOANNA
HICKSON

HARPER

Harper
An imprint of HarperCollins*Publishers*
The News Building
1 London Bridge Street
London SE1 9GF

www.harpercollins.co.uk

A Paperback Original 2016
1

A catalogue record for this book
is available from the British Library

ISBN: 978-0-00-813970-4

Typeset in Adobe Caslon by Palimpsest Book Production Ltd,
Falkirk, Stirlingshire

Printed and bound in Great Britain by Clays Ltd, St Ives plc

MIX
Paper from
responsible sources

FSC
www.fsc.org
FSC˚ C007454

For my gorgeous granddaughter
Lyra Joanna
Second of the Ashtons
Conceived, gestated and delivered
Along the same timeline as
First of the Tudors

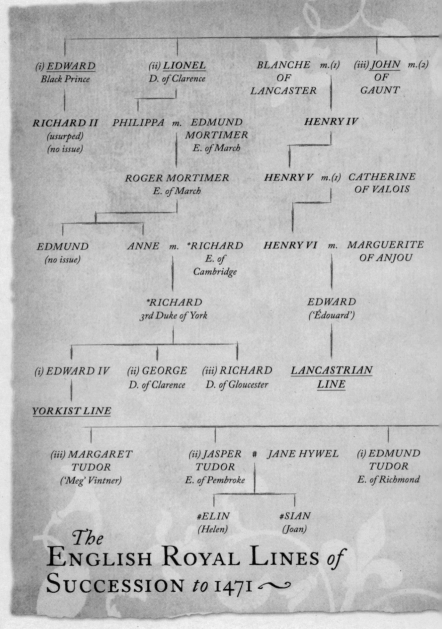

(i) EDWARD
Black Prince

(ii) LIONEL
D. of Clarence

BLANCHE   m.(1)
OF
LANCASTER

(iii) JOHN   m.(2)
OF
GAUNT

RICHARD II
(usurped)
(no issue)

PHILIPPA   m.   **EDMUND
MORTIMER**
E. of March

HENRY IV

ROGER MORTIMER
E. of March

HENRY V   m.(1)   **CATHERINE
OF VALOIS**

EDMUND
(no issue)

ANNE   m.   ***RICHARD**
E. of
Cambridge

HENRY VI   m.   **MARGUERITE
OF ANJOU**

***RICHARD**
3rd Duke of York

EDWARD
('Édouard')

(i) EDWARD IV

(ii) GEORGE
D. of Clarence

(iii) RICHARD
D. of Gloucester

**LANCASTRIAN
LINE**

YORKIST LINE

**(iii) MARGARET
TUDOR**
('Meg' Vintner)

**(ii) JASPER
TUDOR**
E. of Pembroke

JANE HYWEL

**(i) EDMUND
TUDOR**
E. of Richmond

#ELIN
(Helen)

#SIAN
(Joan)

The
ENGLISH ROYAL LINES *of*
SUCCESSION *to* 1471 ～

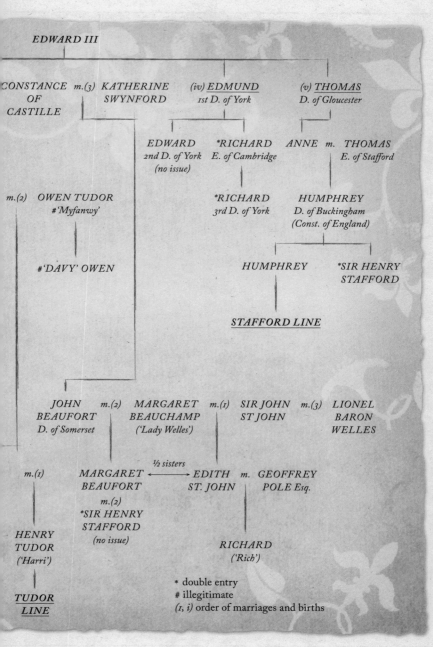

EDWARD III

CONSTANCE m.(3) KATHERINE (iv) EDMUND (v) THOMAS
OF SWYNFORD 1st D. of York D. of Gloucester
CASTILLE

EDWARD *RICHARD ANNE m. THOMAS
2nd D. of York E. of Cambridge E. of Stafford
(no issue)

m.(2) OWEN TUDOR *RICHARD HUMPHREY
#'Myfanwy' 3rd D. of York D. of Buckingham
(Const. of England)

#'DAVY' OWEN HUMPHREY *SIR HENRY
STAFFORD

STAFFORD LINE

JOHN m.(2) MARGARET m.(1) SIR JOHN m.(3) LIONEL
BEAUFORT BEAUCHAMP ST JOHN BARON
D. of Somerset ('Lady Welles') WELLES

½ sisters
m.(1) MARGARET ←——→ EDITH m. GEOFFREY
BEAUFORT ST. JOHN POLE Esq.
m.(2)
*SIR HENRY
STAFFORD
(no issue)

HENRY RICHARD
TUDOR ('Rich')
('Harri')

TUDOR
LINE

* double entry
# illegitimate
(1, i) order of marriages and births

ENGLAND
(MIDLANDS)　⚔ Maxey

⚔ Kenilworth
Northampton ●　⚔ Bletsoe
✂　　● Bedford
Banbury　(SOUTH)

St Albans ✂
　　　London
Windsor　(Westminster)
Reading ●　⚔
　Woking　Greenwich
⛪ Clarendon Palace　(Placentia
　● Southampton　Palace)
　　　　　Dover ●
　　　　　　Calais ●

North
Sea

FLANDERS

River Thames

Boulogne ●

The Channel

Honfleur ●
　　● Rouen

● Paris

FRANCE

River Seine

● Chartres

River Maine

River Loire

⚔ Angers　Tours ●

● Nantes　⚔ Chinon

PART ONE

Brothers to the King

1451–1453

I

Jasper

Westminster Palace & London

FLASHES OF IRIDESCENCE GLEAMED like fireflies in the gloom of the small tower chamber. I stared at the river of fabric as it settled in graceful waves across the bed. It was the intense blue of a noon sky, yet it glittered with the gold of midnight stars. 'Do you think she will like it?' Edmund asked.

I took a deep breath, hesitating to prick my brother's bubble. 'Yes – and no,' I said.

'What do you mean?' Indignation raised the timbre of his voice. 'Jesu Jas, a gown fashioned of such fabric would make any female feel like a queen!'

My hackles rose. I hated Edmund calling me Jas and had told him so on numerous occasions, yet still he persisted. It was a boyhood nickname and we were no longer boys but squires in the service of the king, soon to become knights. My name was Jasper. I had stopped calling him Ed on the day we came to court.

'But she is not a queen and there are sumptuary laws. Our sister could be royally fined for wearing a gown made from such fabric. You know its use is restricted to royalty, archbishops and the effigies of saints.'

I touched the cloth, admiring its shimmer as the slight movement stirred it into life; it was soft and sinuous under my fingers. I imagined the deft fingers that had wound the fine gold wire around the warp fibres with infinite skill and patience. Edmund was right; wearing it would make anyone feel illustrious. Cloth of gold! Just how had Edmund come up with the huge price it commanded?

Edmund drew himself up to his six-foot height. 'The daughter of a queen may wear what she likes. They would not dare to fine her.'

Exasperated, I flicked the fabric so that it rippled, like a sudden flurry on a calm lake. 'Your head is in the clouds, brother. Come back to earth. Our sister lives in Tun Lane, London. Nobody knows what we know. In her world she is not Margaret, just Meg, and she is about to marry the man of her choice who is not a prince but a lawyer. She will be a wife and, God willing, a mother. She is happy, with a warm home and enough money for her needs. Whatever you dream for your own future, do not wish it on her.'

Irritably Edmund twitched the length of fabric into his arms, gathering it in like a shield against reality. 'I know what she is – what she has chosen to remain – but she is still the daughter of a queen, the granddaughter of a king, and I *will* give her the honour of royal raiment, even if she never wears it.'

I shrugged. 'So be it but you have wasted your money.

And do not dare to reveal her true birth by so much as a whisper at the wedding or you will win Mette's enduring wrath – and mine too for that matter.'

My brother paused in his careful folding of the cloth-of-gold. 'Mette – is she still alive then?'

Unlike me, Edmund no longer went to The House of the Vine in Tun Lane where our sister had lived since the death of our royal mother fourteen years ago. In recent years he had acquired what I considered an exaggerated sense of rank and the refuse-strewn back streets of London offended him.

'Of course she is alive. You know she is. She always asks after you, as does our sister.' Mette was Meg's foster mother, the faithful servant into whose care our own mother had entrusted her little daughter on her deathbed, hoping she might enjoy the happy childhood she herself had not known. Our mother was one of many children of the sixth King Charles of France and the ravages of the king's madness had had consequences for them all in the fierce struggle for power that resulted. Now Meg was to marry her foster brother William, who had recently qualified as a lawyer at the Middle Temple. A spring wedding at St Mildred's church.

'And what do you tell them?' Edmund asked as he laid the cloth on top of his chest, which stood next to mine against the wall in our chamber in one of the many towers of Westminster Palace.

'I tell them you are well. That is all.'

Edmund's chest was filled with apparel of every kind. I had wondered before how he managed to afford such finery since he received the same royal pension as I did. I presumed he must be winning at dice or frequenting the moneylenders of Lombard Street, like many of our fellow squires. I hated debt and could do without fashionable clothes, preferring to buy harness and armour if I had any spare funds but I did quite envy the dashing figure Edmund cut about the court.

'You *are* coming to the wedding, are you not?' I added. My query contained a note of anxiety for Edmund could be unreliable.

'Of course I am coming. I would not miss a feast.' A smile revealing perfect teeth lit his dark features – another advantage he enjoyed, my own smile being marred by a chipped front tooth, the result of an unhappy collision in a joust. 'What are you giving her?'

I felt the blood rush to my cheeks. A tendency to blush was one of the drawbacks of having red hair and a fresh complexion. There was no reason to feel ashamed of my gift, yet I knew Edmund would think it niggardly. 'A hogshead of ale.'

'Ale?' He was incredulous. 'You are giving them *ale*?'

'Yes, the traditional Bride Ale, strongly brewed and flavoured with herbs and honey, for all the guests to drink their health.'

Edmund grimaced and flicked back his glossy hair. 'Oh well, I daresay there will be wine as well. After all, their name is Vintner. There are plenty of wine merchants in the family.'

* * *

Meg and William Vintner were married at St Mildred's church in the London ward known as the Vintry, the same church that had witnessed the nuptials of his parents more

6

than twenty years before. As the bride and groom stood in the porch making their vows, I studied the face of the woman who had brought them both up. Mistress Guillaumette Vintner, known to close friends and family as Mette, was now a matron of sixty-three years, stout and wrinkled in her wimple and veil to which, on formal occasions such as this, she added a widow's barbe to mark her lone status since the death of her husband Geoffrey several years before. They had enjoyed seventeen happy years of marriage before he had succumbed to congestion of the lungs and once or twice I saw her gaze wander wistfully off towards the churchyard where he lay buried. The bridegroom, their only son William, had been what she called their 'autumn leaf', the last fruit of their fertility before the sap began its winter retreat, and no one could have been more delighted than Mette when the relationship between William and Meg changed from the affection of siblings to the attraction of adults. Probably Geoffrey had foreseen their future together too before he died. Somehow it seemed inevitable. Meg had been Queen Catherine's secret bequest to the woman who had been her wet nurse as a babe and whom she had come to regard as a true mother.

Owen Tudor stood beside Mette. Father to Edmund, Meg and me and still handsome, with his silver hair and ruddy complexion, he had travelled from the Welsh March for the occasion. I knew he still practised regularly with sword and bow, which kept his physique that of a man ten years younger than the fifty he had lived and I admired him for it. Nor did he appear to have lost any of his ability to charm the ladies; more than once he caused Mette to blush and smile at his whispered comments as the short ceremony progressed. He also aimed a sly wink at Edmund and me, which I returned but which made Edmund hiss through his teeth. I think my brother would rather it had been our mother, Queen Catherine, who survived to attend the wedding, instead of the Welsh squire she had married in secret and to whom she had borne four children. Edmund was the eldest. Our younger brother Owen, the child born shortly before our mother passed away, was now a monk at Westminster Abbey and had taken another name.

Edmund's wedding gift was wrapped in plain linen and draped over his shoulder. He was clad in a bright green damask doublet lined with scarlet, the sleeves dagged and his hose parti-coloured, one leg white and one yellow. The sight had attracted startled glances as we walked from the inn to the church.

'Why do they stare like that?' he had grumbled. 'Have they never seen dagged sleeves?'

'It might be your legs rather than your arms,' I responded. 'A short doublet and hosen like that are rarely seen in London streets.'

'And no wonder,' he declared, stepping gingerly over small piles of animal droppings and rotting vegetables. 'I thank Saint Crispin that I thought to wear bottins rather than shoes.'

After the wedding Mass we walked in procession to Tun Lane, behind a group of beribboned minstrels who rivalled Edmund for colourful apparel and played merry tunes to set the mood. A spectacular array of wafers and pastries was laid out in the panelled hall at the House of the Vine and we were promised a feast of roasted meats when the banquet began. As I kissed the bride and groom and wished them well I noticed that my hogshead of Bride Ale stood in pride of place below the salt, ready for folk to fill their jugs at will. Meg thanked me warmly for it and while other guests gathered around the barrel Mette took me off to sit with her by the hearth. People were taking their places at the cloth-draped boards decked with spring garlands and their flowery scent vied with the smell of yeast and herbs as the ale flowed. Casting a scathing glance at the hogshead, Edmund wandered off to find some wine to drink.

'That was a very thoughtful gift, Jasper,' Mette said, 'just what every wedding needs to get the conversation flowing. It is so good to see you – and Edmund too of course, although I barely recognized him. I must say his taste in clothes has taken an exotic turn!'

I laughed at that. 'Still not mincing your words then, Mette? Of course at court Edmund's style is hardly remarkable. It is mine which stands out as being rather bland.'

The old lady perused my best blue doublet with its grey coney trimming. 'You both look as you choose,' she commented tactfully. 'And I hear the king favours sober dress. Are you still happy at court? Not swamped by the ceremony or daunted by the protocol?'

'No, we have our duties and the company is fair. Plenty of other squires to spar with and the food is good.' I grinned at her. 'Better than at the abbey!'

After our mother's death, our parents' marriage became known and our father had been imprisoned for contravening the Marriage Act. Edmund and I had found refuge with the nuns at Barking Abbey on the Thames outside London, living among a group of young royal wards being educated there. Only when our half-brother, King Henry, reached his majority was our father released and we were brought into Henry's own household, where tutors and instructors were engaged to prepare us for knighthood, a process which was now approaching its conclusion. It had been a change of lifestyle much appreciated by both of us.

Mette's rheumy eyes crinkled. 'Ha! I can imagine. And damsels? Does the queen keep a charm of goldfinches in her solar to delight the young men at court?'

'She does, but none outshines her. It must be owned that Queen Marguerite is dramatically beautiful. They say that her dark eyes and skin are inherited from her Spanish grandmother.'

Mette sniffed and leaned forward to speak in a confidential whisper. 'And that does not endear her to the English, especially as she has not yet produced an heir to the throne. As your mother knew only too well, in a queen beauty is no substitute for fertility. Besides Queen Marguerite is actually French, whom the English dislike even more than the Spanish, or the Welsh for that matter.'

'Which is the very reason I am careful to avoid revealing my doubly unpopular origins.' I shot her a wry look. 'You are French, Mette. Have you found the English much prejudiced against you?'

Her smile was reassuring and rather nostalgic. 'No, but I live very quietly now. Your lady mother did though – very much so; but then if she had not she would never have married Owen Tudor and retired into obscurity – and you would not have been born.'

'Did I hear my name? Are you gossiping about me, Madame Mette?' My father had approached the hearth and with his usual gallantry removed his rakishly feathered hat, bowed over Mette's hand and kissed it.

She responded with a broad smile and a raised eyebrow. 'From what I hear you do not need me to spread gossip about you, Master Tudor.'

My father looked affronted. 'Now what are they saying in the city? None of it will be true of course.'

I pricked up my ears. Unless invited to attend the king, our father wisely avoided the royal palace these days, but when he was in London I often met him in one of the taverns clustered around Westminster Hall, where the courts of justice sat. Any rumour Mette had picked up would have come through her lawyer son William.

She gave Owen a stern look. 'They say you are making the most of your new appointment as King's Forester in North Wales; working your way through the poor widows of Denbighshire.'

Owen gave a loud hoot of laughter and his deep brown eyes, so like my brother Edmund's, danced with delight. 'I told you there would be little truth in what you heard. Is it likely that I would take up with any *poor* widow, Mette? I may have dallied with one or two rich ones – nothing more I assure you.' With a polite display of reluctance he released her hand. 'But you have no refreshment I see. At the risk of heaping more fuel on the flames of rumour, let me play your cupbearer and bring you a draught of the Bride Ale.'

Mette accepted his offer with alacrity and watched him cross the floor on his quest. Turning back to me she murmured confidentially, 'After all, why should he not seek consolation where he can find it, Jasper? He is still a handsome man – but there is no woman alive that could ever fill the space in his heart left by your beautiful mother, so sadly taken from us, we all know that.' As she spoke I spied a nostalgic tear escape her eye. She went on, 'I see her face every time I look at Meg. I cannot think why the world does not recognize the truth of her birth. And yet I thank God it does not.'

I cast a glance at the bride and groom standing in the centre of the room, pledging their love in a shared cup. At twenty-one William Vintner was an affable and good-looking young man. Only a few weeks younger than Edmund, he was quick of wit and slow of ire, neither tall nor short with a sturdy build, curly brown hair and rosy, clean-shaven cheeks. He bore a strong resemblance to his genial father, a man I had greatly admired, but his beard did not yet sprout thick enough to warrant letting it grow as Geoffrey Vintner had. I was less than a year younger than William and in our infancy at Hadham Manor he, Edmund and I had been close playmates, but my brother seemed to have forgotten that. Out of the corner of my eye I saw Edmund leaning elegantly against the hangings, alone, sipping from a horn cup, his gaze sweeping the other guests with an unfathomable expression. He had yet to congratulate the young couple, or give them his gift.

Our sister was slim and fair with delicate features, deep blue eyes and a countenance of doll-like sweetness, which I knew concealed a strong will and a generous nature. If it were true that she closely resembled our mother then I cursed the weakness of my memory, which retained no clear image of Queen Catherine to compare her with. I had been six when she rode away from Hadham Manor, never to return. Only six years old when our lives turned upside down, and while I could remember every detail of the island in the River Ash where we three little boys had played at knights and outlaws, to my deep regret I had no recollection of the lovely face of our mother – the fifth King Henry's widowed queen and Owen Tudor's late and much lamented wife. I knew that somewhere in Windsor Castle there was a portrait of Catherine de Valois, painted when she was a princess of sixteen and sent to the conquering King Henry as a marriage-bait, but as yet I had not found it.

Mette was enjoying her ale, raising her cup to the bridal pair, when Edmund moved out from behind a knot of guests, ushering a servant who carried a joint-stool and spread it open to place it before the bride and groom in the centre of the hall. On it, with a ceremonial bow, my brother laid his wedding gift, still wrapped in its protective linen shroud. The room hushed expectantly as he stepped forward to kiss his sister, then, taking a proud stance beside the stool, he cleared his throat to speak. Although my stomach lurched with dread of what he might say, I thought what an impressive figure Edmund made despite the garish nature of his clothing, darkly handsome, with all the grace and sinew of a noble horseman.

'Like all here, I have come to wish the bride and groom health, wealth and happiness in their life together. This gift is for the beautiful bride, so that she may array herself like a queen and show the world her true worth.'

With a deft movement he pulled off the linen wrapping and flung the exposed cloth-of-gold across his raised arm in a dramatic flourish. Beams of light falling through the open hall shutters reflected off its folds and illuminated the faces of the surrounding guests, who stood open-mouthed at the spectacle. Edmund's expression was one of triumph as he anticipated Meg's response.

She cast a troubled glance at her new husband, whose brow creased in concern at the threat of revelation contained both in the shimmering fabric and in Edmund's words. Apart from the Vintner family, Owen, Edmund and I, no other guests in the room had any notion of Meg's true birth and it was the family's intention that it should remain that way. Edmund's gift and his style of presentation had rendered the secret more fragile than ever.

After a pause Meg stepped forward and gathered the material off her brother's arm, laying it carefully over the stool, from which it hung in liquid folds, pooling on the floor like molten metal. Her gauze veil, secured by a coronet of spring flowers over her fair, profusely curling mane of hair, frothed around her smiling face as she dropped Edmund a graceful curtsy.

'Thank you, Edmund,' she said, and stretched up to kiss his cheek. 'It is a fabric of spectacular beauty – a vision of heaven in fact – and, with your permission, I shall donate it to the Queen of Heaven herself, to fashion a gown for the statue of the Virgin in St Mildred's church, in gratitude for her blessing on our marriage today.'

Beside me I heard Mette release a long sigh, as if she had been holding her breath. Then her familiar chuckle cut through the tension, which had begun to pervade the room. 'Saint Nicholas be praised! We have a bride with brains and beauty and will have a shrine to the Virgin to rival any royal benefice. For such a gift the Holy Mother will surely grant this marriage happiness and fertility.' Applause rippled from the crowd as she turned away, rolling her eyes at me and adding under her breath, 'That piece of cloth would have bought a new bed and all the hangings – but luckily I have given them that.'

Edmund strolled over to us, bending to place cool lips on Mette's cheek. 'Meg does you proud, Madame Mette. Your William is a very lucky man.'

'They are a happy pair, Edmund,' she responded emphatically. 'Long may they remain so!'

2

Jane

Tŷ Cerrig, Gwynedd, North Wales

THE SOUND OF THE watch-bell always caused a bustle in the house. It meant either trouble or visitors, sometimes both. The cheese-making would have to wait. I took off my apron and sent Mair the dairymaid to discover what all the clanging was about, while I sped out to the brewery to draw a jug of ale. Whoever was arriving, refreshment was bound to be required. By the time I had taken the ale to the hall and set out some cups Mair returned to tell me that three strangers on horseback were trotting up the road from the shore. Strangers were a rarity at Tŷ Cerrig.

'What is it, Sian? What is happening?' Face crumpled from sleep, my stepmother appeared through the heavy woollen curtain that divided the solar from the hall, although the word 'mother' seemed hardly appropriate for a girl who had seen only three more summers than me; that is to say, seventeen.

'Strangers arriving,' I said. 'I was just going out to see.'

Her face fell. 'Oh. Must I go and greet them?'

She was pregnant; very pregnant, her belly taut and round, only days from delivery and suffering from swollen ankles and shortness of breath. It would not be good for her to stand in the yard while men and horses milled about and dust flew.

'No Bethan, you stay in here. Sit down and wait. Whoever it is will come inside eventually. Father will be there by now and I will go out. You can pour the ale.'

Visibly relieved, she waddled to the large wooden armchair that stood by the hearth. 'Yes. I will do that. I will wait.'

Bethan was sweet but she was a simple soul. Her marriage to my father had taken us all by surprise the previous year, being only eight months after the sudden death of my mother, to whom he had been wed for nearly twenty years and who he had unquestionably loved and respected. But Bethan was an heiress, the only child of a neighbouring landholder. The match had been made and a contract drawn up with a view to securing both her future and ours. It was a sensible arrangement for she had known my father from childhood and trusted him and we all knew her well and understood her disability, brought about by a slow and difficult birth, which both she and her mother had only just survived.

I glanced around the hall to check that it was ready to receive guests. A peat fire smoked lazily in the hearth, beside it an iron cauldron seethed steadily, containing the evening pottage. With regret I calculated that I would have to wring the necks of a couple of chickens if guests were staying, unless they came bearing gifts.

Outside, I had to shade my eyes against the sun which still stood high in the May sky. The warning bell had brought my father Hywel and two of my brothers, Maredudd and Dai, from the sheep pens where they had been checking the month-old lambs before their spring release with the ewes onto the high moorland grazing behind the house. Sheep dogs were yapping at their heels but on curt orders from their masters they dropped to the ground, crouched and silent, as four horses clip-clopped under the farmyard gate-arch. Three of them were mounted, the fourth was a laden sumpter led by the foremost rider.

My father gave a shout of welcome and stepped forward to grab his boot. 'Ah, glory be to Saint Dewi, it is you Owen Tudor! You are very well come to Tŷ Cerrig.'

The long-legged man who swung down from his horse immediately drew my father into a bear hug and slapped his back heartily. 'It has been too long, Hywel, but at last I have brought my sons to meet their Welsh kin.' He turned to the two young men who still sat their horses and switched to English. 'Edmund, Jasper – get down and greet your cousin Hywel Fychan. You probably do not remember him but I expect he remembers you, eh Hywel?'

He was a good-looking man, this Owen, whose Welsh was fluent but tinged with a foreign lilt. However, the sons who obeyed his command to dismount were of a great deal more interest to me. At first sight they seemed of similar age but judging by the way the darker one took the lead as if by right, the redheaded son was the younger. Both tugged off their felt hats and made respectful bows and while the elder was receiving another of my father's generous hugs, the gaze of the younger wandered in my direction. I felt an unexpected rush of pleasure as his face creased in a chip-toothed smile. I shyly returned the smile.

'I remember two small boys who were often up to mischief,' said my father when the greetings were done. 'But now I see two young men who may create more.'

Owen laughed heartily. 'You can say what you like, Hywel, because they will not understand you. I am ashamed to say they have no Welsh. I thought if I brought them here they might learn a few words and something about farming. Only one generation from the land and yet they know nothing!'

'My boys will see to that,' declared Hywel, beckoning them forward and switching to English so that Owen's sons might understand. 'This dark Welsh ram is Dai and the one with the light hair is Maredudd, my eldest son. He looks like his mother, do you not agree? Sadly she went to the angels at the start of last year.'

'Agnes is dead?' echoed Owen, making the sign of the cross. Clearly he had known my mother well for his expression became shadowed with regret. 'May she rest in peace. I am very sorry to hear that.'

My father frowned fiercely. 'Yes, it was a great loss. She gave me two daughters and three sons and then died from a fever; who knows why? I have a new wife who is about to give birth so we are praying all will be well with her. Come inside now and meet her. Her name is Bethan. Mind your head.' He caught sight of me as he ushered his cousin towards the low door of the house. 'Oh, this is my younger daughter Sian. The elder one is married and lives away now.'

I bobbed a curtsy as they passed me and Owen paused to smile and bow, repeating my name in his mellow voice before ducking under the lintel. The two younger men stopped and greeted me politely. The first followed immediately in his father's footsteps but the one with the bright hair and the chip-toothed smile lingered before me. 'Sorry, I did not catch your name. Mine is Jasper.'

Why did I have to blush? Having three brothers I was used to boys and these cousins were surely no different to them? 'It is Sian,' I said.

'Shawn?' he repeated, inaccurately. 'Is that a Welsh name?'

'Yes, I suppose it is. My mother was French and called me Jeanne but everyone here calls me Sian.'

He still looked a little puzzled. 'Oh I see. So that might be Jane in English? Will you forgive me if I call you Jane?'

I found myself telling him I would; yet even as I said it I knew it was not true. My name sounded harsh and plain in English – but then he endeared himself to me once more by saying, 'My mother was French too.'

'Yes, mine was your mother's companion at one time. I am sure my father will explain it all.'

He nodded and paused to gaze around him. 'It is very beautiful here. Believe it or not it is my first close-up sight of the sea and I find it quite breathtaking, so wild and empty!' His grin was apologetic but he turned his face to the land and went on, 'And I like the way the stone walls make patterns on the hillsides. We rode through the mountains yesterday and they were truly awe-inspiring. I have seen nothing like them in England.'

His enthusiasm for my homeland made me garrulous in return. 'I am so glad you think that. I do not know how long you will stay but very soon we will be moving the sheep up into the hills. We walk them to the high pastures and sleep out under the stars. Perhaps you might join us?'

Jasper shrugged. 'My father seems to take it for granted that we will stay for a while but tell me honestly, do you have room for us?' His gaze swept the facade of the house and he looked doubtful.

Whatever kind of accommodation this Jasper was accustomed to, his question indicated that it was much grander than the sturdy stone farmhouse before us. My grandfather Tudur Fychan had built Tŷ Cerrig in the reign of the fourth King Henry, after English soldiers had run him off his lands during Glyn Dŵr's rebellion, when half of Wales had risen against the English occupation. On that dreadful occasion they had put his family's timber-framed house in Ynys Môn to the torch and in due course, when my grandfather Tudur at last managed to establish a new home on land in the foothills of Yr Wyddfa, he proudly called it Tŷ Cerrig – House of Stone – to show that he had built a place that would defy the flames. But it was just two floors: the lower one was a byre and a dairy and the upper floor was where we all lived. All the outbuildings, barns, stables, brewery, kennel and latrine, were made of timber. My father Hywel came back from England with his French wife to take over the family farm when Tudur Fychan died before I was born.

I quickly dismissed Jasper's doubts. 'Oh yes, there is plenty of room at this time of year. Now that the cows are out in the fields and the byre is scrubbed clean, the boys sleep downstairs. Fresh straw makes a good pallet.'

He laughed. 'It is probably considerably cleaner and more comfortable than some places we have lodged in during our journey.'

I gestured through the door, towards the steep ladder-stair

that led to the family quarters. 'Shall we go up? There is refreshment ready.'

He glanced back at the horses. Maredudd and Dai were walking them towards the stable.

I understood his concern for his mount. 'You do not have to worry. The boys will see to them and bring in your saddle-bags.'

He nodded. 'I am sure they will. I was just remembering that there is a brace of hares in one of the bags. My father did some hunting while we were crossing the high moors yesterday. He is a crack shot with his bow. In this warm weather they will be ready for eating.'

I smiled happily, for this meant the chickens were reprieved and our egg supply preserved. 'We will roast them this evening,' I said. 'I will see to it. You go on in and meet your hostess.'

'I feel as if I have already met her,' he said, gazing at me earnestly and making me blush again, 'and I look forward to the rest of my stay, however long or short it may be.'

I went off to search for the hares with a spring in my step.

* * *

We ate outside in the soft evening light, eleven of us around the long board used for harvest feasting. Even Bethan managed to clamber down the stair and sit with us, smiling happily and saying little but looking bonny in her best blue gown, laced at its loosest. My youngest brother Evan, a cheeky dark imp of eight, had been sent to the neighbouring farm across the valley to bring Bethan's parents, Emrys and Gwyladus, to meet the three Tudors and we all squeezed onto benches and stools, with the big wooden armchair brought down from the hall and packed with cushions for Bethan. Beyond the farmyard wall the ground sloped towards the west, giving us a fine view over the vast sweep of Tremadog Bay and, in the far distance, the dark humps of the Lleyn Peninsula, Gwynedd's westernmost arm. As the sun dipped below the hills the sky turned from pink to ochre, gold and red, reflecting off the sea and turning the bay to a fiery crucible. Such long, stunning sunsets were infrequent here and we made the most of it, the men draining a cask of father's treasured malmsey and talking on well after the last of the pottage had been scraped from the cauldron and the bones of the hares tossed to the dogs.

'It is a pity that Gwyneth is no longer here with us,' Hywel said to Owen as I brought baskets of dried fruit and bowls of cream to dip it in – a rare treat, because most of our cream was made into cheese for winter. 'Perhaps you remember her as an infant, Owen? She was our firstborn and lived with us at Hadham when Queen Catherine was still alive. She married two years ago to a man from Ynys Môn – or do you call it Anglesey now that you are an English gentleman?'

Owen smiled, his teeth showing impressively few gaps. 'It depends who I am with, Hywel. Did she marry a relative, another descendant of the great Ednyfed Fychan, Steward to the Prince of all Wales?'

My father's teeth did not make such a fair showing. 'It would be hard not to in that part of Wales, would it not? She is living in the Tudur family heartland now, taking us back where we would be still, had our fathers not supported Glyn Dŵr.'

'Oh you are not going to start telling tales about the good old days before the great rebellion are you, my father?' cried Maredudd, well lubricated by the wine. We were all speaking English, although some were more fluent than others in the language of our conquerors. 'And give our guests a chance to crow about the Lancastrian victory at Shrewsbury!'

I cringed inwardly. Maredudd was the salt of the earth and as solid as a doorpost but tact was not his strong point. Fifty years ago there had been a battle at Shrewsbury in the Welsh March when the present king's father had slain the famous knight Hotspur and put an end to a rebellion led by my father's ancestor Owain Glyn Dŵr, who had subsequently fled to the wilderness of Yr Wyddfa.

Owen's brow creased alarmingly. 'Why would my sons crow about a disaster that befell their father's godfather?' he cried, flushed and perhaps also a little excited by the rich malmsey. 'Glyn Dŵr was a great man and a learned one. Not a man to be denigrated in my hearing.'

Edmund selected a dried plum, unperturbed. 'I fear I know nothing of all that,' he told Maredudd, dipping the fruit in cream as he spoke. 'Our tutors taught us only ancient history.'

'And poetry,' added Jasper in an apologetic tone. 'Now if you were to ask us to recite some Virgil one of us might oblige.' He looked pointedly at Edmund but his brother ignored him, chewing contentedly on his plum, perceiving no need for a tactful change of subject. Jasper clearly did and turned to me to provide it. 'What were you telling me, cousin Jane, about walking the sheep to the high pasture?'

Before I could answer Maredudd spoke up from the fire, on which he was heaping more windfall branches gathered from the nearby woods. 'We were hoping to start out tomorrow but perhaps you have changed your mind now, Father?'

Hywel glanced across at him and frowned. 'No, I have not. We need to start tomorrow to be back in time for Bethan's baby. We cannot leave any later.'

'Surely Bethan is not going with you!' exclaimed Edmund, clearly alarmed at the thought.

I hid a smile behind my hand and my father roared with laughter, while Edmund reddened with chagrin. 'No, no!' Hywel exclaimed. 'Of course not! Do you think we are Irish gypsies to birth our cubs in the bracken? Gwyladus and Emrys will stay here with Bethan and we will not be away more than two or three days. The babe is not due for a sennight yet.'

I glanced at Bethan then, realized she was drooping in her chair and decided I should take her in before she fell asleep. When I stood up I was surprised to see Jasper follow suit.

'I will light your way, Jane,' he said, reaching for a lantern.

In the end we had to half carry Bethan between us, so sleepy had she become, and I decided it would be best to move one of the pallets from the byre and lay her down on the floor of the dairy, thinking that if she needed to relieve herself in the night, as she often did in her present condition, she could simply wander outside to the latrine. When I had finished making her comfortable and she had fallen into a deep sleep I found Jasper waiting for me on one of the stone benches built against the front wall of the house, the lantern at his feet casting his honest, open face into mysterious shade. The moon had risen, spreading its pale light across the open expanse of the yard and turning the shadows inky black.

He patted the bench beside him. 'Please sit with me a while, Jane. Our fathers talk too much of times gone by. I would like to learn about your life here and now. I think Bethan cannot be much help in the house. She seems a little – simple, or am I being unkind?'

I bit my lip. We did not like to discuss Bethan's condition with strangers but although he had no Welsh and clearly knew nothing of our ways, I discerned a warm heart in Jasper, which gave me confidence in his discretion. After all, however many times removed, we were cousins – family.

I sat down, careful to leave a respectable distance between us. In the moonlight he looked younger, more like one of my brothers than an esquire of the king's household, which I now knew him to be. 'No, you are not unkind, sir; you are perceptive. Bethan *is* simple but she loves my father and shares his bed willingly. It is not her fault that she has no great domestic skills. She cannot cook or make bread or cheese, although she can churn butter if you stop her at the right moment. She cannot recognize one herb from another or remember their properties and she cannot tell a mark from a groat. But when she is not great with child she can weed the vegetable garden, milk the cows and goats, feed the poultry and collect the eggs; she loves to tend the orphaned lambs and calves and if I set it up for her she can turn a spindle for hours.' I gave him a cheerful smile. 'So you see she is far from helpless, and there is also Mair who is our dairymaid, who lives in the village by the shore and fetches and carries and makes the pottage.'

The sound of the stream that ran fast-flowing through

the wooded vale beside the house filled the silence between us agreeably. The vale and the stone-walled fields surrounding the policies were all bathed in milky moonlight. 'Our grandfather chose well when he built here,' I told him. 'The stream gives us milling-power and clean water, we have wool for weaving, grain to make bread and ale, and fat for lamps and soap. The sheep give us fleeces to sell to the monks, we have fish in the sea, meat on the hoof and crops in the fields. Between us we make most things we need and I keep the accounts and the recipes. Our household works quite well. You will see if you stay a while.'

'I suspect that it works because you toil from dawn to dusk, Jane. And where and when did you get an education, which you clearly have?'

'That was due to my mother. She spent her girlhood in a convent and taught us all to read and write and reckon. I am trying to ensure that Evan learns now but it is not easy, especially at this time of year when he is needed on the land. In winter it is easier to keep him at his letters. Our mother intended him for the priesthood but I cannot imagine that happening now. He is bright but not at all bookish.' I knew I was talking too much but the words just seemed to spill out of me.

Jasper screwed up his face and shook his head in exasperation. 'I feel I should remember your mother. Her name was Agnes was it not? But tragically I cannot even picture my own. Edmund says he can but if so he does not describe her very well. He makes her sound like a royal doll, which I am sure she was not.'

I felt a stab of pity for him. My memories of my mother were so vivid that sometimes when I was quietly sewing I felt she was sitting at my shoulder. 'My mother always spoke of yours as an angel. There is no doubt that she was beautiful, whereas mine was like me – I think homely is the word.'

Jasper gave a derisive snort. 'In my vocabulary homely is a polite word for ugly – and that you are not, Jane! I would say that comely is the proper word – or pretty – certainly attractive! With sweeping eyelashes like yours how could you be anything else?'

I dropped my head, hoping the white glare of moonlight would disguise the sudden colour that rushed to my cheeks. Compliments did not flow freely in our family and my reaction to Jasper's was involuntary and regrettably rather gauche. 'Not beautiful anyway,' I muttered, clenching my hands together in my lap.

He made another dismissive noise. 'Huh! I do not think beauty always begets beauty, Jane. Look at Edmund and me for instance. He has our father's bronze good looks, whereas I am blessed with ginger hair and ruddy cheeks. My mother called me Jasper after the dark-red bloodstone in her ring and I imagine she thought the name, like the gemstone, would bring me luck. A younger son always needs luck, does he not?'

With his fresh, freckled complexion and brilliant blue eyes, which even the moon's glare could not bleach, I wanted to say that he appeared more than comely to me but shyness prevented it. Instead I said, 'You remember that much about her anyway.'

'No, I do not remember that; Mette told me.'

'Who is Mette?'

'A very bright and forthright lady who knew both our

mothers well. She is an old lady now but in some ways you remind me of her.'

Regrettably I have a mercurial temperament and abruptly my mood changed from shyness to indignation. 'I remind you of a blunt old lady? Well, thank you indeed, sir!' I stood up and made him a sudden curtsy. 'Please excuse me, it is time I chased Evan to bed.'

I knew I was being rude to a guest but I could not help myself and left him frowning. Moments later I heard footsteps behind me; his voice in my ear sounded contrite. 'I said bright, not blunt, Jane! And Mette is probably the woman I admire most in the world.'

It was not until later, curled up sleepless on my pallet by the hearth, that I appreciated the compliment hidden in Jasper's words.

3

Jasper

The Royal Progress; Westminster & Greenwich

Sweet jane's bonny features were to become a recurring image in my mind throughout the year that followed, particularly those long, sweeping eyelashes shading her deep brown-velvet eyes. Certain memories made particularly vivid returns. In blessedly balmy weather we had shared the rustic delights of shepherding Hywel's flock of sheep up to the high pastures and the picture of Jane, in a straw hat and long boots, with her skirts tucked up and a shepherd's crook in her hand, made frequent visitations in my quieter moments. Later, on our return to Tŷ Cerrig, I had witnessed her handling the birth of Bethan's baby, when she chased all the men out of the house and set about supervising the midwife, cheering the mother and reassuring the grandmother, all with seemingly unruffled efficiency. And meanwhile I managed to pick up a few words of Welsh, at least enough to identify a *mab* from a *merch*, which is to say a boy from a girl. I had little experience of females of any age but the sight of this smiling fourteen-year-old *merch* emerging from the front door of the farmhouse to present her father with his newborn daughter remained with me for months, inspiring comparison with church images of the Madonna and Child.

Walking our horses to the field one day Edmund had been scornful of my friendship with Jane, pointing out to me that a relationship with a Welsh farm-girl, especially one whose grandfather had been outlawed for rebelling against the crown, would not be one to mention at court. 'Enjoy her company while we are here, Jas, bed her if you will, not that beds seem to abound in this part of the world, but for pity's sake keep silent on the subject of Jane when we return to Westminster.'

I worried about Edmund's attitude towards females. He did not seem to have absorbed any of the rules of chivalry drummed into us during the lessons on Arthurian legend, which the king had insisted should be part of our preparation for knighthood and which laid particular stress on respect for women. Edmund was always careful to impress our tutors with his grasp of Latin verse and philosophical texts but his moral code was that of the alehouse.

I angrily rejected his implication that I had lecherous designs on Jane. 'The only bedding I have done here is strawing down the horses, brother – and for pity's sake will you please stop calling me Jas!'

'Temper, temper!' he cried. 'What does plain Jane call you then? Rust-head?'

'No, but I will tell you what she calls you. Pretty boy! You frightened the sheep in your bright red doublet and yellow hose – you should have left them in London.'

'And you should leave those mud-coloured rags of yours in Wales,' he retaliated. 'Along with your Welsh words and your bumpkin shepherdess – Jas!' He had to dodge under his horse's neck to avoid my bunched fist.

When we did return to court, however, it was not our clothes or my language which sparked a bout of teasing from our fellow squires but the tanned faces we had acquired after three months in field and saddle, weeks which we had both greatly enjoyed, no matter how much Edmund protested that he had stagnated in the 'rural backwaters' as he called West Wales.

But there was no prospect of a return to Wales. Memories of Jane were all I was ever likely to have, for now that Edmund and I had both reached our majority our brother the king often summoned us into his company, significantly more than the other household squires. I suspected that this was due to prompting by Queen Marguerite, who seemed to relish the notion that we were first cousins; her father's sister, Marie of Anjou, was also our aunt by marriage, being queen to our late mother's brother, King Charles VII of France.

'But we cannot make anything of this in the court,' she warned privately, in what I considered her rather charmingly broken English, 'because King Henry is still *le Roi de France*, however successful are the armies of our Uncle Charles in Normandy and Maine.'

It was a moot point. According to the peace treaty that had married our mother to Henry's father, he was officially king of France as well as England. But his commanders were gradually and ingloriously losing the vast swathes of French territory conquered by the fifth Henry and the peace of the realm was seriously threatened by hordes of displaced soldiers who, having settled in Normandy and Maine with their families, were now forced to flee the invading armies of King Charles and return to England, where many of them roamed the shires, homeless, penniless and desperate, stirring up trouble. This series of military setbacks had also drained the royal coffers and caused a dangerous split in the ranks of the English nobility. Earlier in the year the king's distant cousin, Richard, Duke of York, who publicly lamented these failures, had been banished from court for bringing an army to London, demanding to be given command of the French wars and named as Henry's heir.

It was Queen Marguerite who told us that she and the king were going on a Royal Progress and Henry desired that Edmund and I accompany them, not as his household squires but as his brothers. 'Henry will dispense justice to all the poor people who have been robbed and attacked by these renegades from France,' she explained.

This was undoubtedly an honour, intended to give us an intimate knowledge of our brother's duties and beliefs. We were to lodge near the royal apartments and share the private solar.

I learned a great deal during that Progress about the way the king's justice was dispensed, and discovered the enormous discrepancy between those nobles who were actively involved and compassionate overlords and those who dealt with their tenants at third and fourth hand, often using unscrupulous methods of extracting their rents and revenues.

I also found out a great deal about the king and queen themselves. They treated each other with unfailing courtesy but little apparent affection; the private time we spent with them significantly lacked laughter or casual exchange of the kind I expected between two people who had been joined in matrimony for more than six years. In fact, I felt there was a constant, underlying tension, which puzzled me. Of course love was no prerequisite in a dynastic marriage such as theirs but Henry scarcely seemed to notice that Queen Marguerite was undeniably lovely, with an exotic beauty and a graceful figure that elicited furtive but appreciative glances from most of the young men about court. He refrained from any comment on her dress or appearance unless he thought it too elaborate or excessively extravagant. He himself dressed more like a cleric than monarch despite Marguerite urging him to adopt the bright fabrics and brilliant jewels she considered appropriate to the royal state.

She sought our support in this endeavour. 'The people expect splendour of their king, do you not think? Edmund – you must agree for you are always *á la mode*. Perhaps you might advise his grace on what the nobility are wearing? I notice that the hems of the young courtiers' gowns are getting shorter, their hose is more colourful and their jewellery more lavish but I cannot persuade Henry to adopt this style. He dresses as if every day were *Vendredi Saint*.'

Nevertheless Henry continued to avoid splendour, even when attending the opulent feasts provided by our hosts during the Progress, all of them anxious to please their sovereign, hopeful of obtaining some reward. These occasions provided opportunities for dancing and masking, when many young male courtiers chose to display their physiques, stretching their hose tightly over their thighs and exposing more leg than would be wise in cold weather. King Henry certainly enjoyed a mask, especially if it was based on a biblical theme but his habit was to retire to his private chamber before the evening entertainment became too boisterous.

Usually and much to Edmund's vexation, he asked the two of us to retire with him. Henry then chose to drink small ale and talk over the events of the day, such as the judicial cases he had heard at the local assizes or a visit he had made to a religious shrine. As strains of dance music drifted through open windows, Edmund's feet would start tapping out the rhythm, while he strove to preserve an expression of rapt interest in the king's discourse. I confess that I was often guilty of this myself and reminded of the countless times our greybeard tutors had droned on about the Rule of St Benedict or the writings of St Gregory while beams of sunshine beckoned us outdoors to the joust or the hunting field.

Henry's cousin and chief counsellor Edmund Beaufort, Duke of Somerset, joined the Progress for its final days during a stay at Reading Abbey. We shared our brother's evening ale as usual and on this occasion so did the duke, a man well known to us. We had good cause to pay him full attention. As a young man, with less status and influence than he commanded now, Edmund Beaufort had proposed marriage to our mother, the dowager Queen Catherine, but the royal council had vetoed the match. Subsequently he had discovered her clandestine marriage to Owen Tudor but agreed to keep it secret and stand godfather to their first son who was named Edmund in his honour. Ever since then he had proved a staunch friend to us and so his presence that evening was highly significant.

The abbot had surrendered his Great Chamber to royal occupation; a huge vaulted and panelled room in which even King Henry's substantial travelling bedstead looked like a campaign cot. All the doors and windows were closed and the heat of the summer day lingered stiflingly beyond the dusk so that I longed to loosen my collar and open the front of my doublet, under which my shirt clung to me, damp with sweat. The duke and the king sat in carved oak armchairs in front of the empty hearth, two cushioned stools placed before them.

After we had been invited to sit in the king's presence it was the duke who spoke first. 'His grace is grateful for the company you have both afforded him during this Royal Progress. He is much comforted by the unflinching loyalty of his two brothers, to him and to his queen, and he has decided that the time has come to show you his favour.'

At this point King Henry lifted his hand to indicate that he wished to speak and Somerset fell silent. Edmund and I exchanged glances and I spied a gleam in my brother's eye, which resonated with the increased beat of my heart.

'My lord of Somerset is right,' the king began. 'Lately we have felt the grave responsibilities of monarchy weighing heavily on our shoulders and although we can share some of this with our queen and our loyal officials and councillors, it has occurred to us that you, our beloved brothers, who share our royal blood and show us so clearly the love and loyalty which naturally bind us, should be brought within our close circle and raised to a rank which reflects your true status. Therefore it is our desire and intent to create you, Edmund, Earl of Richmond and you, Jasper, Earl of Pembroke. It is our hope that the necessary arrangements can be made for these honours to be conferred by Christmas so you may be ceremonially installed on the

Feast of the Epiphany, when gifts are presented in celebration of those brought by the Magi to the newborn Christ. This will be my gift to you.'

At the end of his speech Henry held out his hands, psalter-width apart and smiled expectantly at us, whereupon both Edmund and I sank to our knees before him. Exerting his seniority as usual, Edmund placed his hands between those of the king and spoke the time-honoured oath of fealty, which every nobleman learned by heart.

'Sire, I am your liegeman in life and limb and truth and earthly honours, cleaving to you above all men, so help me God and the Holy Dame.'

King Henry leaned forward to accept Edmund's kiss on his cheek and then turned to me, his hands once more outstretched. I felt them encompass mine, his palms surprisingly dry on my sweat-slicked fingers. The same oath left my lips in a voice that shook with emotion. As I moved to give my brother the kiss of fealty I caught the unmistakable odour of incense clinging to his clothes, pungent evidence of the hours he spent daily, praying in church or shrine.

He rose, obliging us to follow suit and his broad smile was unfamiliar but warm. 'I feel God's benison descending to salute our brotherly union,' he said. 'I will let his grace of Somerset explain the details of your advancement but I hope you will not neglect to give thanks to our Lord and His Holy Mother for their bountiful blessing; and now I will retire to the abbot's chapel to seek God's guidance on tomorrow's assizes. I am told there may be hanging matters involved. I wish you both good night.'

In the absence of a chamberlain, I strode to the door to open it for him, making the guards on the other side jump in surprise and bring their halberds hastily to vertical in salute. As Henry walked out he already looked lost in his own thoughts, his head bowed over clasped hands, like a monk making his way to the midnight Office. As I closed the door Edmund came up behind me and flung his arm around my shoulders.

'How is it with you, my lord of Pembroke?' he cried with undisguised glee. 'Now we are truly brothers to the king!'

I returned his embrace with equal enthusiasm but a stern Somerset stepped forward, urging caution. 'Not yet, not yet, young sirs!' He waved an admonitory finger, his grey beard jutting forcefully. 'His grace bid me warn you to keep this news to yourselves until the formal announcement is made at court. There are legal documents to prepare and land grants to be drawn up. These will take time but meanwhile you can give thought to your crests and coats of arms. The heralds will be made aware of your impending ennoblement and you can also begin to order your robes and livery from the royal tailor. All are used to keeping such secrets. The king plans to make the announcement at Christmas and belt on your swords at the Tower of London on the Feast of Epiphany, as he told you. Meanwhile I offer you both my hearty good wishes and look forward to welcoming you to the ranks of England's mighty earls.'

* * *

On our return to Westminster Palace we found we had been allocated quarters close to the king's private apartments, a move that fuelled a spate of court gossip, whether Henry and Somerset liked it or not. Our new chambers were light and airy, boasting elaborate furnishings and casement windows overlooking the Thames, diamond-glazed instead of merely shuttered. Each had a separate guardrobe with a latrine draining into a moat washed clean by each high tide, a welcome privilege, indicative of very high status. Between these chambers lay an anteroom where attendants and visitors might await admittance. The apartments were on the same floor as those of the king, but the sweeping stone staircase was reserved for his use and we accessed our rooms by a narrower and steeper spiral stair. Queen Marguerite and her ladies were housed in a separate wing of the palace, linked to the king's apartments by a private gallery, where handpicked and trusted members of the royal guard kept discreet watch, despite little sign that it was a path well trodden.

Behind the closed doors of our new chambers Edmund and I were fitted for our coronets and mantles of state. We had been granted funds to extend our wardrobes and for once I was grateful for Edmund's familiarity with fabrics and fashions, being woefully ignorant on such matters myself. However, King Henry planned a joust in our honour following our installation, and then the boot – or more accurately in this case the sabaton – would be on the other foot, for it was I and not Edmund who knew the best agents from whom to commission new armour, having made a study of the latest developments in military design. Until this time, as yeoman squires of the king's household, we had been provided with standard ready-made body-defences and so for me it was a proud day when I stood in a hot, noisy workshop off Cheapside to be measured for my first custom-fitted attire.

Edmund was less enthusiastic. 'What can it matter

whether I have the latest hinges on my helmet's visor,' he demanded, 'as long as I can readily open and close it? My chief concern is the shape of the sabatons. The style of a noble knight is judged by how much of his foot extends through the stirrups when he leans back to aim the lance. I definitely want sabatons with the longest possible points.'

The kneeling armourer paused in the act of measuring Edmund's calves for greaves. 'As an earl you are permitted to wear them twice the length of your foot but I must warn you, my lord, that if the points are too long, the foot will not readily be released in the event of a fall from the saddle,' he cautioned. 'It is a dangerous fashion.'

'So fashion can prove deadly if you are dragged by a galloping charger, Edmund,' I remarked scathingly, adding more seriously, 'You should heed the man's advice.'

My brother eyed me scornfully. 'A knight who expects to fall can expect to lose. Nothing demonstrates cowardice more than stunted sabatons.'

In my opinion, foolish risk-taking in jousting and fighting demonstrated nothing but idiocy, but I recalled it was I, not Edmund, who had been lucky to receive only a chipped tooth as a result of a jousting accident and so in the interests of maintaining good brotherly relations I shrugged and, leaving the armourer to pursue the argument, wandered off to examine my surroundings.

Like most noble English knights we would have the individual pieces of our armour made to our measurements in Germany where they had perfected the steel-rolling process. They would then be fitted and altered as necessary in London workshops like this one. I watched perspiring apprentices scurrying between three forges where the master armourers worked. There was barely a moment of silence as they hammered expertly at the many separate items that formed a knight's 'attire': breastplates and backplates, greaves and gauntlets, cuirasses and vambraces and all manner of joints and swivels, buckles and bracers. The mingling of heat, sweat and noise formed a miasma, which I found exhilarating, stirring images of jousts and tournaments and the heady prospect of action on the battlefield. There were shutters at either end of the premises, which even in this late autumn season stood wide open, allowing what breeze was to be found in the narrow streets of the city to carry away the poisonous fumes from the red-hot forges. I leaned against one of the supporting pillars and admired the skill of the finishers working at benches along the walls as they engraved and stamped distinguishing designs into the metal before polishing it. As a squire I was thoroughly familiar with the order and attachment of one gleaming element to another when I fitted them to a knight's body and felt a thrill at the thought that soon I would be able to appoint my own squires to perform this onerous task for me.

Christmas that year was held at the Palace of Placentia at Greenwich, whither the court moved en masse two days beforehand, travelling downriver on a convenient morning turn of the high tide. Still officially serving as the king's Squires of the Body, Edmund and I accompanied King Henry and Queen Marguerite on the royal barge from Westminster, enjoying the thrill of the slide under one of the narrow arches of London Bridge as the water churned through to escape into the wider reaches of the Thames beyond.

King Henry had inherited the palace and park at Greenwich from his uncle, Humphrey, Duke of Gloucester five years previously and it was a particular favourite of his, due to the celebrated library his cultured uncle had amassed there. It was Queen Marguerite who had renamed it Placentia for its green and rural setting – though it lay only a few miles downstream. The contrast with Westminster's tightly packed streets and buildings was magical; an oasis, and like the outgoing tidal waters of the Thames, the queen yearned to escape from the confines of urban life upriver. Besides, hunting was one of the few pastimes Henry and Marguerite had in common and there were great chases to be had in the vast enclosure of Greenwich Park. As the oarsmen made swift work of the long meander around the north bank mudflats, I sniffed the salty tang in the air and prayed that the crisp, calm weather would persist and give us some magnificent Christmas sport.

It was King Henry's decree that on the Eve of Christ's birth his court should be unsullied by too much eating, drinking and merrymaking, such as had been common during previous reigns and still persisted in many noble houses. So after a long celebration Mass during the morning, there was a decent meal of three courses accompanied by a limited quantity of wine and small ale, consumed while choristers sang beautiful but plangent psalms, and prayers and Gospel readings were heard. Afterwards a troupe of mummers performed a Nativity play dressed in gorgeous traditional costumes kept in the royal Wardrobe for use on this one night of the year. It took place in candlelight as darkness fell outside and was an unexpectedly moving experience. When the shepherds fell to their knees in awe at the choir of angels, enthralled by their soaring voices and twinkling jewelled wings I felt a surge of nostalgia, recalling nights spent under the stars with Jane Hywel and her brothers while embers from the camp fire rose into the dark sky and my father played his harp and sang stories of ancient Welsh legend.

It was at the conclusion of this play, as the applause died down and a hum of conversation started, that King Henry chose to have his big announcement made to the court. He did not do it himself but, appropriately enough, through the services of his Richmond Herald, who began by sounding his trumpet for silence.

'My lords, ladies and gentlemen of the king's court and household, hear your gracious sovereign's will. In so far as his grace's uterine brothers, Edmund and Jasper, have gained their majority, it is his royal highness's desire to recognize their legitimate descent from his beloved and much lamented mother, the right royal Queen Catherine, consort to his glorious and right royal father King Henry the Fifth of England. Therefore the honour of knighthood shall be bestowed on them and in addition the king's beloved brother Edmund shall be created Earl of Richmond, a royal honour and title held in abeyance since the death of his grace's uncle John, Duke of Bedford, and the king's beloved brother Jasper shall be created Earl of Pembroke, a royal honour and title held in abeyance since the death of his grace's uncle Humphrey, Duke of Gloucester. As blood brothers of the king, they shall be granted precedence over all other nobles of the court save the royal dukes. This is the king's solemn intent and shall be accomplished with full ceremonial at the Tower of London on the Feast of the Epiphany.

Hear ye the will of your sovereign lord Henry the Sixth, King of England, France and Ireland!'

The trumpet sounded again and there followed a pause while people digested the content of the herald's announcement, and then suddenly our fellow squires surrounded us, clapping us on the back and uttering cries of surprise and congratulation. This tumult was brought to a halt by two royal pages calling for precedence and pushing our friends aside to clear the way for Queen Marguerite, who appeared before us, beautiful in her glittering Christmas array, and favoured us with a smile that almost outshone her jewels.

'May I add my felicitations to those of your companions? Our court will be much enhanced by the ennoblement of two such worthy gentlemen and his grace the king will greatly appreciate your good counsel and company. But, *mes presque-seigneurs*, I wish to be first to retain your services as my partners for the first two dances at tomorrow night's Christmas Ball. I trust there are no ladies of the court to whom you have already pledged yourselves.'

Brilliant though her smile was, it offered no indication that she would give way to any prior pledge we might have made. Queen Marguerite did not bestow the honour of a dance lightly and certainly did not expect it to be refused. Edmund made a swift bow and left her in no doubt. 'I would be honoured and enchanted to be my queen's partner,' he said gallantly. 'In fact I would walk barefoot over broken glass to take your hand, Madame.'

The queen's brows rose in surprise. 'But then you would be in no fit state to dance, sir,' she said. 'And the first tune is always a lively one.'

I made my own bow of acquiescence. 'Then I hope the second may be long and slow, your grace,' I murmured.

She gave me a quizzical glance. 'Do you indeed, Master Jasper? Then you had better have a word with the musicians. I look forward to tomorrow, *Messires*. Again, my congratulations.'

Her damasked cloth-of-gold train swept the floor as she turned away.

4

Jasper

The Palace of Placentia, Greenwich

IGNORING THE SUMPTUARY LAWS – again – Edmund
chose to wear a purple doublet for the Christmas Ball
although he called it violet.

'We are royalty,' he retorted when I questioned this. 'The
king confirmed it last night. We are "in the purple".'

'We have not yet been knighted or belted,' I persisted.
'You will be considered presumptuous.'

'Bah! I do not care what people think. The colour suits
me and I will wear it. I guarantee the queen will compliment
me on my choice.'

To ensure that his appearance attracted even more attention he wore the same yellow hosen that had frightened the
sheep in Wales. The belt slung around his hips was set with
amethysts and the doublet was trimmed with something
that looked suspiciously like sable, which was in the same
sartorial category as purple, but Edmund claimed it was
marten.

My own appearance was probably unremarkable beside my brother's but I was pleased with the belt I had found, studded with stones of polished green agate to match my emerald green doublet with cream-panelled sleeves and with my parti-coloured hose of dark red and blue. The barber had trimmed my hair and shaved my cheeks smooth and I had bathed in lavender-scented water for the occasion.

Mellow with food and wine from the feast, I stood aside to observe Edmund lead the queen onto the floor and tried to steady my nerves at the prospect of doing the same in my turn. Judging by her dimpled smiles, Queen Marguerite was delighted with the nimble-footed Edmund, and I feared my ability on the dance floor would not match his, despite much effort on the part of a French dancing master.

However, I forgot these qualms as my attention was drawn to the charming sight of a tiny girl with long dark chestnut hair, which swung as she danced and was held off her perfect little face by a slim gold circlet. I recognized the man she danced with as one of the king's household knights who rejoiced in the name of Sir John St John but it was the girl who caught my interest. Her pink gown was trimmed with pearls and figured with gold daisies, and the bodice was cut straight across her chest in the fashion ladies adopted to show off the swell of their breasts. But this girl was too young for breasts. She could have been no more than ten years old and I wondered what she was doing at court at such a tender age; then I forgot my curiosity, absorbed in the gracefulness of her dancing. Erect and straight-backed, her small feet seeming barely to touch the floor, she danced the *estampie*, a lively French dance involving intricate stamping steps as the name implied, that built to a crescendo of energetic jumps and whirls. The girl's slender body began to sway and leap with supple strength, keeping perfect time as the pace increased, completely at one with the music, smiling all the while, a sweet, secret smile as if delighted with the place it took her to. The girl's demure presence seemed dominant in the dance; she was always in the right position, yet she seemed unaware of who took her hand or with whom she turned but danced as if she alone were on the floor. Even the queen's glittering and glamorous figure was outshone. I could not take my eyes off her.

'Congratulations on your impending ennoblement, Master Jasper; I see you are enjoying my daughter's dancing.'

I turned in surprise. At first glance the woman who stood beside me appeared to be an adult version of the same girl, except her hair was hidden under a black turban headdress studded with jewels and her gown was a darker pink with old-fashioned trailing sleeves. She stood as slight and straight as her daughter but her face was wrinkled and faintly mottled.

I made her a bow. 'You have the advantage of me, my lady, in that you know my name.'

'I am Lady Welles but my daughter's name is Beaufort, Lady Margaret Beaufort. Her father was the first Duke of Somerset, the present duke's late brother.'

The music raced to a climax, accompanying my moment of enlightenment. 'Ah – the Somerset heiress,' I found myself saying and then wished I had not.

Lady Welles frowned. 'Indeed. Most men measure her worth by her estates but I thought you had discerned something more. You did not appear to be counting her fortune as you watched her.'

'She is very young,' I said, feeling the accursed blush creep up my neck. 'But even so, yes, there is certainly something remarkable about her.' The music crashed onto its final chord. It was over, and the dancers made their acknowledgements. I bowed politely again to Lady Welles. 'Forgive me, my lady, but I am obliged to the queen for the next dance. I hope we meet again.'

Walking away, I cast a last glance at Margaret Beaufort as her partner escorted her from the dance floor. She was not in the least out of breath. Suddenly I wished it was her rather than the queen that I was pledged to dance with, naively believing that so young a girl would not judge me or compare me with my brother. She appeared to be a creature of the air rather than the earth, reminding me of one of the hovering angels illuminating my psalter.

As I had anticipated, the next dance was a slow one. Edmund had performed all the leaps and kicks demanded by the *estampie* and now I was able to relax into a *bass*, performed to a largo given by a piper and a solo singer. It began with alternate men and women holding hands and circling in a series of short and long steps first one way then the other, interspersed with graceful individual spins and regular changes of position through the centre, couples forming the spokes of a wheel and turning back and forth. The moves were intricate but the pace was slow, the intention being for the dancers to show off their balance and posture rather than their stamina. Happily there was little opportunity for conversation as we weaved across, around and between each other, passing with smiles and nods, until the dance ended and we found ourselves once more with our partner for a final bow.

'Thank you, brother,' Queen Marguerite said, raising her hand in mine ready to be escorted from the floor. 'That was a pleasant, easy dance. You and your brother are not in the least alike are you? Neither on or off the floor.'

I wondered where this was leading and if I was about to receive an unfavourable comparison with Edmund. 'Well, we are close in age, your grace, but not twins, as you know,' I replied.

'No, you are not.' She gave me a sideways glance. 'Edmund is a charming companion – witty and amusing – but I know which brother I would prefer as a father to my children.'

Alarmed by this extraordinary remark, I swallowed hard, wondering if I had heard her right; then I managed to gather my faculties enough to smile and make my response. 'You mean our brother the king obviously, your grace.'

Her lips pursed and her voice dropped almost to a whisper, so that I had to bend my head to hear her. 'The king *will* be the father of my children of course, when God permits it, but we have waited a long time as you cannot have failed to notice. Too long.'

Conversation all around us effectively prevented her words reaching any ears but mine; even so the blood rushed to my cheeks and I suddenly felt hot all over. The subject seemed far too intimate for such a public situation; too intimate for discussion between us at all. Instinctively I glanced across at King Henry on his throne, removed from the dancing and conversing with the Duke of Somerset, who perched beside him on a stool. As we drew nearer Queen Marguerite tightened her grip on my hand and drew me to a halt. We stood isolated in the respectful space preserved between the energetic activity of the dance floor and the raised dais with its royal presence, alone in the midst of many.

The queen took a deep breath and locked eyes with me. 'We have been married nearly seven years and I have been a true wife to him only as many times. How can Henry imagine we will ever give England an heir? Yet it is not him the people blame, it is me. You can help me in this matter, Jasper, I know you can.'

I felt the room spin around me. Could I trust what I was hearing? Was the queen actually suggesting that I might get her with child? I could not believe this was what she meant but I perceived deep desperation in her dark eyes. Outwardly she was the glamorous, twenty-one-year-old Queen of England but inwardly perhaps she was still the girl of just fifteen who had married a king, with no one to turn to for help in achieving the one thing she must to fulfil her life's purpose. Except now she had chosen me. What could I say? What *should* I say?

My throat constricted and I swallowed again. 'I am flattered that you think so, your grace. It will always be my intention to serve you but in this matter I cannot immediately see how.'

She squeezed my hand again and turned to glance at King Henry who, alarmingly, was gazing straight at us with a puzzled look on his face. 'No, I can see that you do not,' she said, suddenly flashing me a dazzling smile, 'but perhaps you will give it some thought. It is a matter of some importance that the kingdom has an heir. I asked my lord of Somerset's advice but he is still thinking about it.' She aimed her social smile at the king and he turned hastily away. 'For now, perhaps you might get Henry to enjoy himself a little?

It is Christmas and people like to see him laugh at such a time. Now you may take me back to the king.'

Queen Marguerite's ladies materialized as if from nowhere and helped settle her voluminous skirts between the arms of her throne. The king half rose to greet her return and the Duke of Somerset took the opportunity to slip away in the direction of a servant who was circulating with a flagon of hippocras.

'I enjoyed the dance you did with Jasper, my lady,' King Henry said. 'It was very graceful, but the first dance was a little – err – vigorous was it not? Rather undignified for a queen.'

Queen Marguerite smiled blandly and ignored the implied criticism. 'Your brother is going to procure some hippocras, my liege. I think a *digestif* might be good for all of us.'

She looked at me and moved her eyes meaningfully in the direction the duke had taken and I needed no second bidding, quickly commandeering the servant's flagon before sending him off to fetch sweetmeats as well. As I poured the wine into the cups set out on a table between the two thrones the musicians struck up again. It needed surprisingly little persuasion on the part of the queen for Henry to accept a measure of the sweet, spiced hippocras and I obeyed his invitation to take the duke's vacated stool. In due course the servant provided a heaped platter of almond wafers and the three of us nibbled and drank as we watched the dancing.

Fortified with the heady wine, Somerset had taken to the floor with his niece Margaret Beaufort, and Queen Marguerite was quick to remark that they made an odd couple.

'I am reminded of the story of the ogre and the little maid my nurse told me when I was a child,' she said. 'Do you know it?'

She held out her cup, which I hastily rose to fill, and it was the king who answered.

'I cannot allow you to call Somerset an ogre, my lady!' he protested, looking shocked but amused at the same time. 'He is a man of culture and refinement.'

'Perhaps, but his appearance has become quite craggy. His niece is a pearl, however. There must be forty years between them. I would wager that she considers him an ogre.' Marguerite took another good gulp of wine. 'Do you not agree, Jasper?'

I nodded and smiled and offered sweetmeats. The hippocras was working quickly. 'I am surprised to see a girl of such tender years at court,' I remarked. 'Young ladies do not usually attend until they are marriageable.'

Out of the king's line of sight Queen Marguerite was nodding in his direction and making urgent pouring movements. King Henry put down his empty cup and I leaned behind his throne to refill it. She nudged it towards him and smiled encouragingly. To my surprise he picked it up and drank again. The whole occasion had taken on a bizarre, carousing quality and I began to wonder if I had imagined what had passed between the queen and myself only minutes before.

'The king invited her mother to bring Lady Margaret to court,' Marguerite revealed.

'I wanted to take a look at her,' Henry said, his eyes following the girl as she glided through the intricate steps of another dance. 'She was contracted in infancy to the

Suffolk heir but Somerset suggested that I have the match annulled.' I thought I detected a slight slur in his voice.

'Did he?' The queen sounded astonished. 'He surely can't want her for his own heir – they are too closely related.'

'No but she is fatherless and his niece and he thinks she could do better. Young Suffolk shows little promise, neither in arms nor intellect.' Henry gulped more wine and nursed his cup, his eyes on his new protégée. 'She certainly dances well.'

This observation surprised me further. It was always understood that Henry disapproved of dancing and yet it seemed that he might have been watching Margaret Beaufort just as intently as I had.

'Will you now make her a royal ward, then?' the queen asked.

Henry cast a glance at me over the rim of his cup and swallowed another gulp. 'No. I thought to give her as ward to Edmund and Jasper,' he said and I nearly choked on my wine. 'She can go on living with her mother of course but in the meantime the revenues from her estates will supplement their incomes nicely. Edmund's Richmond holdings are not vast and some of your Pembroke estates are tied up in legal wrangling, Jasper, so the Somerset lands will provide you both with enough immediate funds to establish your new households.'

'Your grace is more than generous,' I spluttered. 'You have already shown us immense favour.'

A wry smile lifted one side of the king's mouth. 'It might seem logical for the Duke of Somerset to hold the lands that pertain to his title but that would not work in the present political climate. I was content for him to assume the dukedom after his unfortunate brother died but if I grant him the lands as well, the Duke of York will find more cause to accuse me of favouritism. No, I wish my brothers to have them and they shall.'

It occurred to me that he would never have confided these thoughts had he not freely partaken of the Christmas spirit but I was certainly not going to argue with him. Being recognized as the king's nearest relatives was likely to prove a costly business and any grant of extra funds was welcome.

A bold household knight appeared beside the queen's throne and, with a deep bow, begged the favour of a dance, which she graciously conceded. Henry took the opportunity of her absence to suggest that he and I retire to his private chamber. 'I have more to discuss with you about the Somerset wardship, Jasper. Send a message to Edmund to join us – and order more hippocras,' he added, standing and signalling the alert heralds to lower their instantly raised trumpets. 'We do not need a fanfare. Let the merrymaking continue without interruption.'

I collared a page to carry out the king's orders and we made our exit from the great hall via the privy door at the back of the dais. A cloister and a stairway led to the royal apartments and King Henry walked there in silence, giving me an opportunity to ponder my extraordinary conversation with the queen. Had she actually hinted that in a desperate attempt to conceive an heir to the throne I might take her husband's place in her bed, or had she made a cry for help of another kind? The first possibility appalled me. I had found little opportunity to sow wild oats, my life being governed in recent years by tutors and masters at arms, and had no reason to think that I would be any more successful at procreation than Henry. And, far more importantly, beautiful though Marguerite was, the very notion of cuckolding my brother went against every Christian principle those greybeard governors had been so careful to instil. I decided to cling to the idea that the queen's true intention had been that I should use brotherly privilege and every ounce of tact I possessed to encourage Henry to try a little harder and certainly more often in the queen's bed, if not for his own satisfaction, then for the benefit of the kingdom. As a waiting chamberlain threw open the door to the royal chamber I took a deep breath and made a vow to seize the moment, hoping Edmund would not arrive too soon and interrupt my efforts.

The sharp winter cold of the open cloister seemed to have dispelled Henry's slight slur and so when the fresh supply of hippocras arrived I quickly poured another measure, which he showed no hesitation in accepting.

'I find warm spiced wine an excellent soother of the stomach after the over-indulgence of Christmas fare,' he confessed a little sheepishly, taking a chair beside the glowing fire. 'Please tell me if I begin to appear inebriated, Jasper. I so dislike drunkenness in others.'

'There is never any question of you appearing anything but sober, my liege,' I assured him.

Henry leaned closer, his brow creasing in concern. 'It is not necessary for you to address me so formally when we are alone, Jasper. I like to think that in circumstances such as this we can converse freely together as brothers. And please sit.' He waved at the chair on the opposite side of the hearth.

I sat. It was now or never. I wet my lips with the hippocras and gave a nervous preliminary cough. 'Thank you, Henry; if I may call you Henry, sire?' How foolish that sounded but he gave me an encouraging wave and so I ploughed on. 'Forgive me for asking but I wonder whether your promotion of Edmund and me and your interest in Margaret Beaufort may have come as a result of concern at your own isolation? The throne must be a lonely place when you do not have close family, whose loyalty you can rely on.'

At this point Henry's attitude became avuncular rather than brotherly. 'For a young man you are very perceptive, Jasper. Yes, I have certainly felt the lack of relatives of the kind that many of my nobles seem to rely on in large numbers. That is why I have come to value you and Edmund so highly.'

I took the plunge. 'Of course there would be no such lack if you and the queen were to have a family of your own . . .'

My words hung between us like feathers caught in an up draught, hovering weightless, before their slow, hesitant descent into meaning. Henry resorted to another large gulp from his cup. Then, after due consideration and yet more alcoholic encouragement, his response came like a bolt from the blue. 'Was this what you were talking about with Marguerite after your dance together?'

In future it would be hard for critics of his reign to persuade me that Henry was always an arrow short of a full quiver. 'No. Well yes, indirectly,' I stuttered. 'She told me how happy she was that you were favouring your brothers and mentioned how much she regretted you having no children of your own as yet. She seems to think that the people blame her for this.'

Henry's brow creased deeply and at first I thought it was

in anger. I steeled myself for his reprimand but instead he drained his cup and then replaced it with careful deliberation on the table. 'She obviously already trusts you with her confidences, Jasper, and I am going to do the same,' he said. 'And what I am going to tell you must never be repeated to anyone, not even your brother and certainly not Marguerite. Do I have your word on that?'

The solemnity of the moment was striking. I pulled from beneath my doublet the reliquary I wore: it held a trace of the blood of Saint Thomas Becket and had been given to me for protection by the Abbess of Barking when we left her charge to begin our training as knights. The saint's sister Mary Becket had been a nun at Barking and had received the martyred Archbishop's bloodstained garments following his murder at Canterbury Cathedral. They had become an object of pilgrimage to the abbey and the tiny scrap of bloodstained cloth that the abbess had snipped from them was my most sacred and treasured possession. 'You have my oath on holy Becket's blood, my liege.'

What he saw in my eyes seemed to satisfy him. 'Good. Then I will reveal to you that I have never liked the process of procreation. It does not come naturally to me as it does to other men and my late lamented confessor, Bishop William Ayscough, encouraged me to steer my energies instead towards the worship of God and his saints. Like Saint Thomas, the bishop was also murdered by evil men you know, outside one of his own churches after he had celebrated Sunday Mass. He was like a father to me.' He faltered, as though there were a lump in his throat.

I risked a supplementary point. 'And he was the priest who married you to the queen. Did he not speak as well of the obligations of the marriage contract? Even I, though not yet wed, am aware that between man and wife there is a debt each owes to the other in the marital bed. Is it fair, or even legal, to fail your wife in this debt and expose her to the unjust censure of your subjects when no heir is conceived?'

I was not sure if Henry heard me because he only asked if there was more wine in the flagon. He put the cup to his lips the instant it was full, and it occurred to me then that perhaps an inebriated husband was exactly what Queen Marguerite had in mind when she suggested that I get Henry to enjoy himself a little. Certainly I was not entirely sober myself.

'Women are strange creatures are they not?' my royal brother mused, nursing his cup fondly in both hands, as if anxious not to let it out of his sight. 'Their conversation is all of material matters; who should marry whom, how great will be the dower, of which fabric shall a gown be made. They have little concern for their souls and much for their bodies. Marguerite is no different. I find I cannot bear to use her body in the necessary way to bring about a child when she responds the way she does, with such enthusiasm. Why can I not just take her quietly and discreetly and then return to my prayers?' He stared deeply into the dark wine, pondering his next words. 'When I was your age I knew nothing of such things. In truth I know little now and wish to know less. I told your tutors not to let you become corrupted by loose women and feckless companions. They are the ruin of many a young man. I hope you are keeping yourself pure and unsullied, Jasper.'

I stared at him, hearing a maudlin tone in his voice and

wondering if he ever really enjoyed himself. I felt a twinge of irritation, combined with a surge of affection for this intelligent yet strangely innocent man who seemed to have become old before his time and who, as a result, had never truly experienced human love. How could he be our mother's son, the child of a woman who had refused to submit to the restraints imposed on her and had secretly loved and married the man of her choice, a lowly Welsh squire? Our mother had craved happiness and fulfilment, and she had also greatly loved the children who were the result of this reckless passion. I had disappointingly little memory of her face but I vividly recalled her fragrance and the warmth of her embrace. It was a tragedy that this cold and pious Henry could not remember the joy of his mother's love. It would be so much the better for Queen Marguerite if he did.

'But achieving the honour of fatherhood, Henry, implies no impurity. Perhaps if you were to try to please your wife a little more often you would find that her enthusiasm is a measure of her sense of duty,' I suggested, suddenly careless of whether I angered him or not. 'I know I look forward to finding such a wife myself in due course. Surely every man does.'

The maudlin tone persisted in Henry. 'But how would I do that, Jasper? Please my wife I mean?' His pale, greenish-blue eyes pleaded across the hearth, like those of a trembling hound.

It was probably the wine talking but I said the first thing that came into my head, brother to brother. 'Put God to the back of your mind for an hour or so, Henry, and concentrate on her. You are a man after all. And she is beautiful, you know.'

There was a scratching on the door and it suddenly opened to allow the entrance of the queen, escorted by Edmund. Henry and I both jumped as if caught in some act of petty larceny and Marguerite's gaze went immediately from the cup in her husband's hands to my expression of startled guilt. Her delighted smile caused Henry's jaw to drop in amazement.

'Blessed Marie, we have discovered a den of iniquity, Edmund!' she cried with glee. 'Shall we join it?'

5

Jasper

The Tower of London

EDMUND AND I KNELT on the stone floor before the high altar. Our long white tunics and red cloaks represented the body and blood of Christ. Dark shadows obscured the vaulted ceiling and arched aisles of the Chapel Royal of St John the Evangelist at the top of the ancient keep in the Tower of London. The overnight vigil was observed by every candidate for knighthood, other than those dubbed on the battlefield or during a campaign. I had begun by dutifully reciting all the prayers and psalms I knew by heart, repeating them under my breath so as not to intrude on Edmund's orisons, but as time went on and the shadows began to play tricks, my mind strayed sinfully.

I found myself thinking about why Henry's attitude towards the stirring of the flesh was so different to mine. How was it that he abhorred the very idea of sex and even shied away from the beautiful woman he had married? Did he not feel the same lustful urges that I experienced and constantly struggled to control? From banter with my peers I knew that if the temptations of the flesh were the devil's work then Lucifer was a busy fiend, for all the young squires in the royal household were in his grip; this thought caused me a wry smile. So why was Henry different? At thirty-one he was hardly an old man. In ten years' time would I too have retreated into monkish chastity and arid dreams? It was not a prospect I relished.

I glanced across at Edmund, whose knees were doubtless suffering as mine were, but his eyes remained closed. I wondered if he prayed. But I did not think it could be God or the Virgin or any particular saint that was sustaining him. Perhaps like me he was considering his sins, itemizing them so that he could make a full confession in the morning. As he rarely managed to resist a weekly trip across the river to the Southwark stews I calculated that his time spent with the priest might be longer than mine; unless of course, as he often boasted, he genuinely did not consider it a sin to cross a whore's palm with silver. Queen Marguerite had been right; although close as brothers, Edmund and I were very different.

One of the candles on the altar guttered and I was glad of the excuse to stand up in order to light a fresh candle from the failing one. I rubbed my kneecaps briskly as I stood. In the flaring of the new flame the pristine steel of our swords cut across my eyes and the gleaming crests of our shields leapt out between them, strangely close. The leopards and lilies of England and France emblazoned there, the very emblems of the royal arms, felt dream-like, but in the sudden brightness Edmund had opened his eyes and reality resumed. Mindful of the presence of the priest who sat sentinel in the choir stalls behind us we did not speak but Edmund aimed a wink at me and slightly lifted the hem of his white tunic. Hidden beneath its folds was an embroidered prayer cushion, one of those laid out for ladies who used the chapel. He had managed to sneak it past the priest and it was clear that his knees were nothing like as cold, cramped and bruised as mine. There were times when I had to admire my brother's ability to bend the rules but on this occasion I could not help thinking that keeping vigil before an altar on the eve of knighthood, when honour and integrity should actually count for something, was not the right time to cheat the system.

Perhaps it was to escape the fierce pain that knifed up from my knees when I knelt again that repressed images leapt to the fore to tease my carnal senses: Jane Hywel's shy smile and dancing brown eyes, along with one or two of the more voluptuous court damsels and, entirely inappropriately, Queen Marguerite. So much for my contemplation of the vows we were due to make during the knighting ceremony. But one of the vows was to respect and protect women, so I tried to reflect what that was about. Many knights of my acquaintance seemed to think it applied only to a woman of their own nationality, class and affinity and every other woman was fair game for seduction or ravishment. Personally I did not consider them untouchable, as Henry seemed to, but nor did I consider any woman fair game, as Edmund unquestionably did; not that it seemed to make him any less popular among the livelier members of the queen's entourage. If his own boastful accounts were to be believed his charm had won him many a conquest.

As the long night drew on I found inappropriate matters intruding more and more. I wondered if my father felt any pangs of jealousy that his sons had found favour with the king more readily than he had himself and speculated that Henry's bias against Owen Tudor might arise from his monk-like abhorrence of the fleshly love that had brought us into the world. I also made several important decisions concerning the nature of my household and the administration of my estates but the future of my spiritual life was regrettably still unconsidered by the time the dawn light began to filter through the stained glass. However, at least I had managed to stay awake, unlike Edmund who had twice jerked from a doze on the verge of toppling off his smuggled cushion. Fortunately for him, the sentinel priest also succumbed to slumber on his misericord, as his snoring revealed, and Edmund took the opportunity to return the cushion to its prie dieu on his way to relieve himself. I too visited the latrine shortly after and found on returning that the chapel had begun to fill with our sponsors and those members of the court who had been invited to share the ceremony of our knighting, which would begin with a solemn Mass.

While the choir sang a plangent introit we were at last invited to rise from our knees to take seats beside the altar, facing the congregation. From this viewpoint I spied our father tucked away at the back, his habitually cheerful expression replaced by one of mingled pride and awe.

King Henry and Queen Marguerite occupied a prominent position at the front of the church. Beside them was the Lord Chancellor, the venerable Archbishop of Canterbury, Cardinal John Kemp who, in due course, was to give a sermon on the responsibilities and duties of knighthood, a singular honour and one that could only have been commissioned on our behalf by King Henry himself. A significant absentee was the Duke of Somerset, for reasons that became clear as the day wore on. After the Mass we made confession and then followed the king and queen in solemn procession to the great hall. There our knighting and investiture would take place on the royal dais, with a crowd of invited courtiers gathered on the floor below.

We made our solemn vows of loyalty, honour and religious observance kneeling before the king who then officially dubbed each of us with a blow to the shoulder, requesting us to rise as Knights of the Realm and of his Household. His words were the signal for an ear-splitting fanfare of trumpets, to which we rose. As gleaming spurs, symbols of our knightly status, were attached to our shoes I felt a surging sense of duty, as if in one bound I had leapt from youth to manhood, a feeling that was immediately and doubly reinforced moments later when we were invested as earls. Richmond Herald announced our new titles, whereupon the earls of Warwick and Wiltshire stepped forward to buckle ceremonial sword-belts around our hips, and the king slid our gleaming swords of office into their scabbards. The two powerful earls, both stony-faced, then completed the ceremony by displaying the new shields painted with our crests, which were based on the royal arms and proof of our precedence over all other nobles, including them, with only the dukes our equals. The leopards and lilies of England and France brought the enormous significance of our elevation into sharp focus and receiving the shield from the hands of the king I felt tears spring to my eyes. I planted a fervent kiss of loyalty and gratitude on his coronation ring.

Heraldry is a precise science and I had chosen the golden martlet as my differencing device because it was one that had been used by previous earls of Pembroke. The martlet also signified a younger son; one who stood to inherit no estates but had achieved honour through merit and service; for that reason Edmund had also chosen it, alternated with fleurs de lys to indicate his seniority in our French mother's second family. Heraldic limners depicted the bird as a swift without feet to signify its habit of apparently constant flight, seeming never to land, an appropriate metaphor for our quasi-royal status as brothers of the king but not contenders for the throne. Years later I was to see that this constantly airborne emblem was a personal augury, indicating a restless future of which I was, as yet, blissfully unaware.

To my consternation, as I left the king's dais, I found my father kneeling before me and kissing my hand. 'My lord of Pembroke, you have my undying loyalty. My sword and my bow are yours to command. How proud your mother would have been to see you ennobled at the king's side, where you belong.'

I urged him to his feet, hastily blinking back a fresh welling of tears. 'Do not make me weep, Father, I beg you, or King Henry will regret his action. It is strong allies he requires, not milksop weaklings!'

Owen Tudor made a derisory noise. 'Bah! A man who weeps at triumph will also laugh off failure. What is your next move, Jasper, now that you have land and income? Marriage perhaps? Children to found a dynasty?'

The saturnine Earl of Warwick had followed me from the dais and overheard my father's queries, adding his own sardonic observation as he passed by. 'That must surely be the king's expectation, considering his own lamentable lack of an heir.'

Warwick's lengthy stride had carried him out of earshot before I could protest at his offensive remark, but Edmund had also overheard Owen's questions and had his own response. 'A dynasty is certainly my intention,' he said, 'and I know precisely who will suit my purpose in that regard. Already Henry has all but given her to me.'

'Aha, and who is that?' Owen enquired. 'A rich widow perhaps?'

'A widow?' Edmund's eyebrows knitted in distaste. 'I think that is your territory, Father. No, I have the wardship of the Somerset heiress. Marriage to her and the income from her considerable estates will perfectly serve my purpose. Besides she is a Beaufort with direct royal descent. I shall make it clear to Henry that she pleases me.'

Already rattled by Warwick's uncalled-for remark, I could barely disguise the further outrage I felt at my brother's bald assumption that he would marry Margaret. 'She is only nine years old, Edmund!' I pointed out. 'And I would remind you that her custody and estates are to be shared between us. You do not have sole rights in the matter.'

Edmund cocked an eyebrow at me. 'After her yourself are you, *younger* brother?'

'I have no intention of marrying a child,' I snapped, 'and nor should you.'

Anxious to forestall an argument, Owen tried to intercede. 'Steady my sons! It is hardly worth coming to blows over something that will be decided by the king anyway.'

Edmund ignored him. 'She will not be a child much longer. Besides she has older married half-sisters and in those circumstances a girl learns the facts of life very quickly.'

'And you would know all about that I suppose!' The biting sarcasm I had injected into this remark made Edmund flush with anger but a blast of trumpets brought an abrupt halt to our rapidly escalating quarrel. The commanding voice of the royal usher proclaimed the start of the feast. 'By Your Leave my Lords, Ladies and Gentlemen – to your places!' We turned on our heels, parting to take our seats at the high table.

It was at this point that the reason for the absence of the Duke of Somerset, who was after all Edmund's godfather and might have been expected to attend, became clear. With no dukes present, as premier earls we might be seated on either side of the king and queen, while the Archbishop, as head of the Church hierarchy, was placed between the royal couple. It was a relief to find that Edmund was shown to a position on Queen Marguerite's left, four places away from where I was seated to the right of King Henry.

During the first course, a series of fish and vegetable dishes served with sauces coloured blue and white to honour the livery colours of the House of Lancaster, I noticed that Lady Welles and her daughter had been seated only a few feet away at a reward table on the dais, among other high-ranking guests. I had observed her from afar, but as yet I had not actually met our new ward and between courses I took the opportunity to wander over to speak with her and her mother.

When her mother had introduced us I addressed her. 'I hope you are not disappointed to have my brother and myself as your new guardians, Lady Margaret?'

Her eyes had been demurely studying the floor but now

they flashed up to my face, revealing whites the colour of skimmed milk and spectacular slate-grey irises that were speckled like a peregrine's breast. Her reply was unexpected. 'When the king told me about the wardship he said I could choose whether I wished to stay with Suffolk or go to you. I do not think he really meant it though, because he made you both sound so admirable that it was clear he wanted me to choose you.'

'However, Margaret kept his grace waiting,' said Lady Welles with more than a hint of pride. 'She asked if she could sleep on the decision, which gave her time to consult with me and the rest of her family.'

I made the girl a grave bow. 'I am proud that your consultations led you to choose us, my lady.'

Her responding smile displayed a trace of mischief. 'Oh it was not the consultations, my lord. I was still undecided at bedtime and so I prayed to St Nicholas, the patron saint of young girls. He sent me a dream in which I encountered a fierce dragon – and lo and behold not one but two knights rode to my rescue. After that it was easy.'

I returned her smile. 'Do you often have such vivid dreams?'

'No. That is why I knew it was the right thing to do. The dragon is the symbol of St Margaret.'

'It was very obliging of both saints to come to your aid,' I said. 'I will remember to thank them in my prayers.'

A fresh blast of trumpets announced the arrival of the next course and I hastened to ask for the honour of being her partner when the dancing commenced.

Her curtsy was graceful and dignified. 'If my mother permits it.'

Lady Welles did so and we all returned to our places at table as roasted boar and swan were carried shoulder-high into the hall. King Henry refused wine and sipped at his usual cup of small ale looking weary as he ate achingly slowly and in silence. I waited for his page to bring him water to wash his hands before broaching the subject uppermost in my mind.

'May I ask your grace if it is your eventual intention to make a marriage between Edmund or me and Lady Margaret Beaufort?'

It took several moments for his distant gaze to focus and I wondered where his thoughts had been. 'Actually I have sent a letter to Rome asking for the Holy Father's opinion on the matter,' he said. 'Like me, Lady Margaret is a great-grandchild of King Edward the Third and carries a line of succession to the throne. She could pass her claim to any son she may have, so much care must be taken in the matter of her marriage.'

'The Beaufort claim is very tenuous though, is it not, my liege? Your royal grandfather confirmed the legitimacy of his Beaufort half siblings but an Act of Parliament barred them from the succession did it not? Surely the York claim is stronger? But of course none of this will be of any consequence when you and the queen have a son.'

Henry's brows knitted at the mention of the York claim and his frown deepened further when I referred to the possibility of a royal heir. 'I am glad your tutors taught you the law and history of England so well, Jasper, but Margaret Beaufort is young yet. Let us leave consideration of her marriage until the pope makes his ruling.'

This was not exactly what I wanted to hear but at least

there would be no immediate betrothal. I would be able to enjoy dancing with Margaret, knowing that if Edmund were to press the king on an imminent marriage he would get nowhere.

As I followed the steps of a stately gavotte, I found it hard to take my eyes off my partner's slender form. Even in the rather severe grey gown they had dressed her in that day she still managed to remind me of a graceful falcon gliding between tall trees as she wound her way between the other dancers in the set. The more I saw of Margaret Beaufort the more she resembled the Honoured Lady of Arthurian chivalry and the more I saw her as a potential wife, one day. There seemed to emanate from her a noble grace, which entirely outshone the lush temptations offered by other ladies on the floor.

* * *

A few days later we had each received a written summons to attend the Royal Council. 'I cannot contemplate sitting around a table with a bunch of greybeards discussing the king's finances,' Edmund grumbled. 'I must look to my own affairs and that means inspecting the meagre estates as yet granted to me. I will leave tomorrow for Leicestershire, as planned.'

'It is our first summons from the king, Edmund – an honour. He will expect us to attend.' Despite my warning I understood his wish to visit his new estates. I, too, wanted to go to Wales but a series of disputes over lordships connected to the Pembroke earldom were hampering my possession of many of its manors. I had to wait for the Council to settle these.

'You have business there anyway, Jas, so you can keep me up to date with what happens and make my excuses. There is no need for us both to go.' Edmund flashed one of his disarming smiles, slapped me on the back and departed, leaving me irritated but resigned.

As it turned out the retrieval of the Pembroke lands was achieved without difficulty and no comment was made about Edmund's absence. He returned in time to take his seat with the Lords and hear the petition read in which the king publicly proclaimed us as his brothers, although since we were related through our mother and bore only French royal blood, we were barred from any succession to the English throne. Once passed, the same Act of Parliament also established that our earldoms were not just for life but could be inherited by our legitimate male heirs. I should have been a proud and happy man, had it not been for Edmund's muttered remark after hearing the Act read.

'Well, if a son of mine can inherit my earldom of Richmond, it surely follows that he can also inherit his mother's titles and honours, including any line of succession she may have to the English throne.'

PART TWO

The Tudor Earls

1453–1459

6

Jane

Tŷ Cerrig, Gwynedd, North Wales

SINCE OUR PATHS HAD last crossed, Jasper Tudor's life had been transformed – and so had he. When I hurried nervously from the house to confront the troop of armed and mounted men approaching the farmstead up the track from the shore I failed to recognize him, at first. I should have been prepared since I knew from the songs the bards sang around the local farms and lordships that the cousins who had slept on the straw in our byre two summers ago had now been declared the king's closest kin and created the foremost earls in the land. Nevertheless, when Jasper rode under the gate-arch, bareheaded but wearing gleaming armour, on a warhorse trapped in blue and silver and leading an entourage in what looked like royal livery, my jaw dropped.

He did not wait for a man to run and hold his horse but flung his steel-clad leg over the pommel and jumped from the saddle with eager assurance. 'Jane! It is Jane is it not?

You have grown taller and even lovelier than when we last met.' He bent over my hand before raising his head and pressing his lips briefly to mine. It was a common enough greeting between family members but I must have looked shaken because he stepped back at once with an apologetic expression. 'Oh, have I offended you? I crave your pardon. I thought we parted friends. And we are cousins are we not?'

I saw with an inner smile of relief that, earl or not, his cheeks had flushed. An inability to hide his blushes was one of the things I had liked about him, and the way he cocked his head enquiringly to one side instantly recalled the unpretentious young man I had known. I gave a little laugh and shrugged. 'Distant cousins, yes – and no, you have not offended me. We heard you had become Earl of Pembroke but did not expect a visit this far from your earldom. Welcome back to Tŷ Cerrig, my lord.' Remembering my manners I dropped a low curtsy.

He urged me to rise, his colour deepening. 'I am still not used to ceremony,' he confessed. 'I came to see my cousin Hywel on a matter of business but it is an added bonus to find that you are still here, Jane. I thought you might be married and away by now.'

Not knowing how to respond to this remark I averted my eyes and cleared my throat. 'My father and brothers are in the fields but I have sent word and they should be here directly.' Seeing the dozen or so men still mounted behind him and awaiting orders I added, 'Will your retinue take refreshment? We have bread and ale and water for the horses.'

'Thank you yes, they will be glad of that, but fear not,

they have no need of lodging. They will find it in the town.' He signalled them to dismount. I noticed that most wore mail-armour under their livery and swords on their belts, while the remaining few were obviously servants, armed only with small blades. Their horses were damp with sweat and it looked like they had been moving fast, as if through potentially hostile territory.

'They may be welcome trade at the Abermaw inns but there are always empty barns on the farm at this time of year,' I said. 'We would not turn them away.'

A lad came forward to hold his master's horse. 'There are water troughs over yonder,' Jasper told him, pointing towards the stable block. 'And tell the captain to send a couple of men up to the house to collect refreshments.' The youth touched his forehead in acknowledgement and led the horse away but Jasper called after him. 'And bring my saddlebags to me.'

'I will, my lord.'

By now Bethan had emerged cautiously with Nesta. The little girl was clutching her mother's skirts, scared by the sight of so many horses and men, but Bethan was smiling and nodding, delighted in her simple way to see Jasper again. 'Give you good day Jasper,' she said with a little bob.

He strode forward and sent her into a flurry by kissing her hand. 'Bethan, looking as beautiful as ever and blessed again I see.' His sharp eyes had noticed her swollen belly. 'God protect you, and the little one.' He squatted down and ruffled Nesta's curly mop of bronze hair. She stared solemnly back at him, her dark eyes enormous. 'Oh you are a brave girl,' he said, smiling. 'Most children I speak to immediately start yelling.' He glanced up at me. 'So this is the newborn babe you brought into the world the last time I was here?'

'Well, the midwife helped a little,' I said, 'and Bethan helped a lot, obviously!'

'What is your name?' Jasper was still squatting at the infant's level.

'Nesta,' piped the little girl.

'It is a Welsh form of Agnes. Bethan loved my mother.' For some reason I felt it necessary to explain why the offspring of a second wife should be named for the one who had preceded her.

'Agnes is in heaven,' my stepmother said in her guileless treble. 'She looks after my Nesta.'

Jasper straightened up. 'It is a pretty name for a pretty girl,' he told Bethan.

At this moment my father and my brother Maredudd strode around the corner of the house, wiping hands mired with sheep grease on their smocks. Hywel bent his knee to Jasper respectfully. 'I was told the Earl of Pembroke was here,' he said. 'You are welcome to Tŷ Cerrig, my lord.'

Jasper urged him to his feet, clasping his shoulder in warm greeting. 'I thank you, cousin Hywel. I hope you and your family will always think of me as Jasper,' he said. 'Indeed I hope I may rely on the continued friendship and support of all my Welsh kin.'

'The Earls of Pembroke have not always found favour among the Welsh,' Hywel observed, edging himself free. 'Especially here in the north.' I could sense an uneasy tension about him and groped for a valid reason.

'The Earl of Pembroke has never been a Welshman before,' responded Jasper swiftly, turning to Maredudd, who had followed our father's lead and set his knee to the ground. 'Cousin Maredudd, I give you God's good day as well. We parted friends two years ago. I hope nothing has changed.'

My brother's attitude was less wary. 'Not as far as I am concerned, Lord Jasper, but my father pays the king's taxes and does not like the way they are spent.' This revelation earned him a fierce frown from Hywel.

'Ha!' Jasper pulled Maredudd to his feet. 'Nor does the Duke of York. Does that make you all Yorkists now? I confess I dislike the way the country is splitting between Lancaster and York. I myself favour a united front and peace with France and intend to work towards that end.' He turned to Hywel. 'As for the taxation, I have something to discuss which may ease your troubles on that score. Jane offered refreshment. May we talk over a mug of ale?'

The atmosphere shifted as my father remembered his duty of hospitality. 'Of course, my lord, let us go in.'

Before climbing the steep stair to the upper hall of the farmhouse, Hywel and Maredudd stopped to strip off their malodorous smocks in the empty byre, replacing them with clean homespun tunics and washing their hands in water drawn from the cistern barrel outside the dairy door. Meanwhile I poured ale and Bethan fetched loaves from the morning's batch of bread and a cheese from the store-cupboard, before retiring behind the solar curtain with Nesta.

Jasper accepted a full mug from me and took a long swallow while I opened the shutters, letting light into the dim hall. 'I must say that a draught of your fine ale is very welcome, Jane. We have been in the saddle since daybreak.' He sat down in the big hearth chair I indicated. 'I am going to ask your brother Maredudd to join my household at Pembroke. Do you think he will accept a position as my squire?'

With a sudden surge of jealousy I realized how much I would relish the opportunity of escaping the confines of Tŷ Cerrig. The world outside was unknown to me, an unexplored land, and likely to remain so. 'I cannot speak for my brother but if it were me I would jump at the chance,' I said. I placed two trestles in the middle of the room, then Mair helped me fit the board across them.

Jasper watched us lay out the cheese and bread and begin to cut wedges. 'Would you really like to leave Tŷ Cerrig, Jane?' he asked with thoughtful surprise. 'But how would your father manage without you? He has other sons to work the farm but no one else who can run the household as you do.'

I made no response because at that moment my father and brother entered the hall. Maredudd was hauling a pair of large and obviously heavy saddlebags, which he set down beside Jasper. 'Your lad brought these up to the house,' he said. 'They feel as if they are full of gold.'

Jasper laughed and stood up, putting his mug down on the board. 'They carry the parts of my armour that I am not wearing. Could I ask your help in removing the rest? I am sure I will not be needing it here.'

He watched keenly as Maredudd set about undoing the buckles that secured the various elements of armour he had considered necessary for protection on the road. I had no idea what any of them were called but I was surprised to hear Maredudd name each piece as he removed it, obviously impressed. 'This is beautifully made, my lord. Fits you perfectly,' he remarked, placing the last item on the pile of gleaming steel. 'It must have cost a great deal. Shall I give it a rub before I put it in the bag?'

Stripped to tunic and hose, Jasper looked considerably more comfortable. 'Not now, thank you.' He shook his head and went to pull his chair up to the table but Maredudd was ahead of him, placing it at the centre of the board and pushing it in as Jasper sat himself down. 'Perhaps later, after we have all spoken a little together. And let us eat while we talk. I confess I am hungry.'

I went to replenish his supply of ale and fill cups for my father and brother, who drew up a bench opposite Jasper. I found it strange to see my father take a subordinate position at his own board and it brought home to me the new gulf in rank between our Tudor cousin and us. I could see that Hywel was chafing silently under the inferior position.

'Please sit with us, Jane,' Jasper said unexpectedly. 'If you can spare the time.'

I glanced at my father, received his curt nod of approval and slid onto the bench beside Maredudd. As I did so I remembered the rest of the men waiting for refreshment outside and reached out to cut another, much larger wedge off the big cheese wheel. I handed it to Mair and told her to draw some jugs of ale and take them with the cheese and several loaves down to the stables. 'Do not linger down there gossiping,' I charged her. 'Get straight back to the dairy.'

'There should be men waiting below to collect the victuals,' Jasper said.

Far from looking grateful, garrulous Mair frowned and left the hall muttering under her breath, the heavy hunk of cheese held in her apron. I guessed that a flirtatious exchange with the men at arms would have provided her with a week's supply of gossip.

For a short time the three men drank and ate without speaking and I nibbled at a crust of bread and picked at the morsels that had crumbled off the cheese. Jasper was the first to break the silence.

'As you all appear to know already, my brother the king has granted me the earldom of Pembroke. When I was last here at Tŷ Cerrig I had not expected any such honour and I confess that running such widespread estates is a daunting prospect. There is already an administration in place but I am now in the process of appointing a household and retinue, people I can trust and who will serve me honestly and loyally. That is my main reason for coming here, apart of course from renewing old friendships and family ties. So Hywel, the position of Steward of Pembroke castle is available, which I offer to you if you feel you could combine it with your farming activities.'

He paused and we all looked expectantly at Hywel. As far as I knew few Welsh citizens held an office as high as steward, especially of a castle as important as Pembroke. I had never been there but I was aware that it was a major stronghold, one of a ring of fortresses built around the perimeter of Wales to preserve the English monarchy's grip on the principality and defend it from outside attack. For the last two hundred years a succession of royal relatives and favourites had been installed as overlords of Pembroke and in return for its revenues had been expected to defend the south west shores of Wales from incursion, as well as dispense justice and keep the peace among the native population. I guessed that Jasper would be the first to try and achieve this with a foot in both camps – as the son of a Welshman and the brother of the king. It would not be easy and my father's carefully worded reaction offered evidence of why.

'I am grateful that you should consider me worthy of the honour, Lord Jasper,' he said gruffly, 'but with regret I must decline. Since your last visit, sadly my wife's father, Emrys, has died and I have assumed control of her lands as well as my own. I would be unable to devote the necessary time to administering a castle of the size and importance of Pembroke, to say nothing of overseeing its estates in your lordship's inevitable absences. I hope you will forgive my refusal and accept my apologies.'

In deference to Jasper's presence we were speaking English and I was impressed by my father's diplomacy in wording his rejection so tactfully in a language that was not his native tongue. I knew that Welsh had been his only language until he followed his cousin Owen Tudor to England to serve Queen Catherine, but since then, with my mother's help, as well as English he had acquired a smattering of French. This and his comprehensive grasp of land-use would have made him a very suitable candidate for the job of Pembroke's seneschal.

Jasper seemed undaunted by his response. 'I cannot say I am surprised by your answer, Hywel,' he said. 'You are right to put the needs of your family and farms first. My condolences on the death of your father-in-law but congratulations on what I am sure you hope will be another son. However, even though I cannot count on your services, I trust you will retain an attachment to my affinity and that I may call on our family ties should the need ever arrive.'

By that I took him to mean military support in time of trouble and it might have been a cue for Hywel to offer his oath of allegiance but my father made no move to make it. Instead he nodded slowly and acquiesced rather half-heartedly. 'I would not ignore your call, cousin,' he said. 'And I wish you well in your endeavours.'

His tone implied that he did not believe success was very likely but again Jasper chose not to notice. 'Thank you, Hywel. I know you will be anxious to return to your sheep but there is one other matter that I must place before you. I would also like to offer Maredudd a position as a squire in my retinue. I realize this would take him away from the farm and from his roots but I am hoping that the opportunities it would offer him to expand his horizons and learn new skills will sway your decision and that you will allow him to go.'

Hywel turned to look at his son, who had become pink with excitement. Like me, Maredudd was obviously keen to explore the wider world. 'Remember that you were permitted to follow Owen Tudor to England, Father,' he said breathlessly and in Welsh, before Hywel could speak. 'I too need a chance to spread my wings and Dai is growing more capable by the day.'

Hywel replied in the same language, while Jasper glanced from one to the other trying to fathom what was said. 'I do not forget my service to Queen Catherine and the advantages it brought me, son, but I cannot afford to lose your labour on the farm unless the rich new lord pays for your absence so that I can hire a man to replace you. Ask him.'

Maredudd shook his head, scowling. 'No, you ask him. He says I can only go if you say so.'

Jasper looked at me, one eyebrow raised in query. Torn between loyalty to my father and a sudden urge to support Jasper, I found myself opting for the latter, mainly due to what I considered to be my father's discourtesy in using a language that he knew his guest did not understand. Learned at my mother's knee, my French was fluent and I knew Jasper had learned his the same way, so I decided to present Hywel with a taste of his own treatment, knowing he could only follow simple French, spoken slowly.

'They are arguing about money.' I said quickly to Jasper. 'My father says he cannot afford to lose Maredudd's labour unless you finance someone to replace him. In other words he wants you to pay him for the privilege of taking his son away. You could call it extortion.'

To my surprise Jasper grinned and responded in equally swift French, causing both my father and brother to glower in frustration. 'I would not call it that. I was going to offer compensation anyway but they started gabbling away to each other and I did not like to interrupt.' He switched to English and turned his smile on Hywel. 'Now that I know what you were talking about let me put your mind at rest, cousin. I confess that it would be of great comfort to me to have a family member among my close companions but of course I would not take Maredudd away from the farm without offering you some form of financial compensation. Once I know that he is willing to swear allegiance to me we can talk money – preferably in a language we can all understand.'

He fixed my brother with a searching, sapphire gaze, speaking with a new solemnity. 'If you are to become one of my squires of the body, Maredudd, an oath of allegiance is essential. I have seen your interest in armour and your skill with the bow, and I know your honesty and enthusiasm, but are you prepared to put your hands between mine and swear to serve me, Jasper Earl of Pembroke, faithfully and to the exclusion of all others? Without that solemn oath we cannot continue.'

Judging by his expression Maredudd was experiencing inner turmoil. He was acutely aware of our father's ambivalence towards this Tudor cousin, half-brother to an English king, whose Lancastrian forefathers had within living memory brought ruin and deprivation to Wales. To swear allegiance to Jasper now might in the future mean having to abandon his natural allegiance to his father. In an agony of indecision Maredudd frowned fiercely at me, seeking my opinion and I responded with an almost indecipherable nod. I hoped God would forgive me for disloyalty to my father, but I could not believe that the attributes I discerned in Jasper – honour, integrity and a sense of justice – could set a bad example to my brother or lead him into actions that were incompatible with his family obligations.

After another moment's hesitation Maredudd slipped around the table, went down on one knee and placed his hands between those of the new Earl of Pembroke.

* * *

Looking back I can see that this was the start of a subtle change in my own sense of duty and at the earliest opportunity I sought out Maredudd, anxious to gauge his true attitude towards Jasper. Shortly after pledging his new allegiance, he and Hywel had gone back to the sheepfold so it was not until near dusk that I spied him from the hall window, alone and bare-chested, standing over a pail by the dairy cistern. Knowing that he would once more be covered in sheep-grease, I took soap, rough linen rags and a jug of hot water from the hearth kettle and carried them down to him.

He was appreciative but puzzled. 'This is an unexpected kindness, sis,' he said, immediately making use of all three items, scrubbing at his hands and arms. 'Any particular reason?'

I dragged a milking-stool from the dairy and sat down. Maredudd was nearing his eighteenth birthday and I noticed how muscular his torso had become since I had last seen him shirtless during the previous year's sheep-walk. 'I wondered how you felt now that you are Lord Jasper's man,' I replied. 'What did our father say to you?'

His teeth gleamed in the twilight. 'Probably the same as you are about to say now.'

'You do not know what I am going to say,' I protested.

'I can guess though. You are going to accuse me of disloyalty, of abandoning my blood ties.'

I shrugged. 'If that is what our father said I am not surprised, but it is not what I would say.' Maredudd paused in his ablutions, one eyebrow raised in query. I continued, 'I asked how you felt with your hands between Jasper's while you made your oath of allegiance. Did you feel as if you were betraying your family?'

'No, I did not because I regard him as family. His father and mine are of the same blood and becoming a squire in Jasper's retinue is a means of improving my status. I do not want to remain a yeoman farmer all my life, as our father obviously does.'

At this I detected a hint of scorn in his voice and I could not let it go unchallenged. 'I think he regards himself as a gentleman farmer and sees a wider picture. As a boy he heard the stories of Glyn Dŵr's rebellion and his own father's struggle to rebuild his life and he blames the Lancastrian kings. Jasper is brother to a Lancastrian king.'

'Half brother,' Maredudd corrected me. 'And the other half is Welsh and our blood relative. He straddles the two nations and so can I. Perhaps Lord Jasper is *Y Mab Daragon* as some bards sing. Perhaps he truly is the Son of Prophecy come to restore the pride of the Welsh nation. People are beginning to think so.'

I had always seen something special in Jasper Tudor but it was not that. My reasons for favouring him were more personal, more heartfelt than lodged in legend, but I was not going to reveal my heart to my brother, who would only mock me for it. 'Who are these people?' I asked. 'Ruffians and hotheads from the Abermaw taverns?'

Maredudd shook his hands and drops of water flew in all directions, some of it sprinkling my face and cap. 'There is a poet,' he said defensively, grabbing a dry towel he had draped over the dairy door. 'His name is Lewys Glyn Cothi and he is a farmer's son like me but he has the bard's gift of song. He is making a name for himself among the local gentry and I have let it be known that he would be welcome here.'

'Really?' Bards travelled the country singing and reciting legend, verse and polemic of varying literary, musical and political merit. We had never received a visit from one, Hywel being uninterested in such 'riff-raff' as he called them. 'When will he come, do you know?'

'As soon as he gets wind of Lord Jasper's presence I should imagine,' said Maredudd. 'Bards like to sing for people with money and influence and at present they do not come any richer or more influential in Wales than the Earl of Pembroke.' He aimed an entreating smile at me. 'Be a good girl, Sian, and fetch my best blue doublet. I do not like to parade through the dairy half-dressed in front of Mair – it gets her far too excited. By the way, I hope the fact that you are loitering down here does not mean that supper will be late.'

Incensed by this lordly attitude I picked up the pail of warm water, now containing only tepid dregs, and threw them at him, soaking his braies. He objected loudly and made fruitless efforts to dry himself off but I ignored him, declaring, 'There will be no supper until our father and Lord Jasper have finished talking about money in the hall. But I will fetch your doublet, my lord Maredudd –' I bobbed him a sarcastic curtsy '– if you fetch the cask of wine Jasper says his men unloaded earlier. It should be down at the stables somewhere. It seems Father wants to toast your departure!'

In fact, Mair was no longer in the dairy but I could hear footsteps descending the steep stair from the hall so I dumped the pail in the stone sink and hurried to see who it was, hoping to encounter Jasper. Sure enough he was striding out of the farmhouse entrance as I scurried up behind him.

'Lord Jasper, I was hoping to catch you.'

He spun around, smiling. 'Jane – never far away!'

'You will stay here with us I hope – not ride off to Abermaw with your entourage.'

'Your father has just invited me. He offered to vacate the

solar in my favour but I said that a pallet on the byre floor would be perfectly adequate, as it was before.'

'Oh good,' I said with relief. 'That means I can sleep in the hall as usual. I will start supper directly. We have some little birds that Evan netted this morning.'

'You are never at a loss, Jane, are you?' he remarked, fixing me with his laughing blue eyes. 'I think you could victual an army in a desert. If you were a man I believe I would make you Steward of Pembroke Castle.'

I felt my knees become suddenly unreliable and clutched at the doorpost for support, inwardly ordering my wayward female instincts to behave. This charming, snake-hipped, copper-topped cousin might once have been within my reach but now that he was a belted earl he had soared way above it. I might look and I might yearn but I told myself sternly that I had to keep my feelings under control, like the household I ran so proudly.

I managed a balanced curtsy and a modest bow of the head. 'And I would gladly serve you, my lord,' I said.

7
Jasper

**Clarendon Palace, Wiltshire; Dinefŵr Castle,
South Wales**

WE HAD BEEN TAKING a break at Clarendon Hunting
Lodge during another royal progress when the sick-
ness came on. The king had enjoyed a good day's sport: he
was weary but cheerful after a strenuous day in the saddle.
Queen Marguerite was close to giving birth, an event Henry
awaited with joyous trepidation. The child must have been
conceived, I secretly congratulated myself, within weeks of
our hippocras-fuelled Christmas tête à tête. But Henry's
contentment on that evening in Wiltshire was to be short-
lived. An urgent letter was brought for his immediate
attention just before supper was due. I noticed that as he
perused the letter his body seemed to shrink within his
doublet, his face drained of colour and his eyes grew wide,
the lids blinking frantically as if his mind could not comprehend the contents of the page. I rushed forward to catch
him as his knees buckled, the letter falling to the floor . . .

My first thought was that the queen had suffered a stillbirth but as I frantically loosened the neck of Henry's

chemise I was vaguely aware that someone had snatched up the letter and was muttering details from it. 'Disastrous defeat in Gascony . . . army routed . . . Shrewsbury killed. Jesu save us – France is lost!'

Terrible news indeed – the room erupted around me – but my chief concern was Henry's extreme reaction to it and for several heart-stopping moments I feared he was dead. I searched desperately for signs of life. 'Send for the Physician!' I yelled over the confusion, patting my brother's chalk-white cheeks and putting my fingers under his nose to check for breathing. Bending closer, I detected a sigh of air escaping from his nostrils and began to breathe more steadily myself. Whatever fit or apoplexy the king had suffered he was not dead, it was his sovereignty over France that had suffered a fatal blow.

England's defeat by French forces outside a town called Castillion added the loss of Aquitaine to that of Normandy, Maine and Anjou, and with it the city of Bordeaux and the all-important wine trade. The dreadful realization of the almost total loss of his father's glorious French legacy seemed to have robbed Henry of his wits; somehow his mind had become frozen and refused to function. His doctors over the coming days were utterly perplexed, unable to offer any remedy except for the usual cuppings and bleedings, which achieved little other than to render him more feeble and listless. He ate and drank if nourishment was put before him but was otherwise unresponsive and had to be guided from room to room, apparently unaware of where he was or who was with him. After extensive discussion within the Royal Household, we took him in a closed carriage to the security of Windsor Castle, where I left him in the care of two long-standing and faithful servants and hurried to Westminster to call an emergency meeting of the Privy Council in the king's name.

I could have done with Edmund's support at this time but he had taken himself off and left no word as to where he had gone and so I was alone in attempting to arbitrate between the Duke of Somerset and the Duke of York, who exploited the absence of the king and all the force of their superior age and rank to pursue their private war. Somerset insisted on keeping to the king's policy of peace at all costs whereas Richard of York, a soldier as much as a diplomat, had always favoured pursuing an aggressive military policy, admittedly with an impressive past record of success, which fed his lip-curling disdain for Somerset, whom he held entirely responsible for England's ignominious loss of France. York's habit in Council was to bully his way through an argument, whereas Edmund of Somerset had been accustomed to gentlemanly debate, relying on his close relationship with the king to drive his point of view. With the king indisposed and the queen in confinement awaiting the birth of her child he floundered under the lashing of York's scathing tongue. I found it impossible to mediate in a poisonous debate that triggered bitter exchanges and further widened a rift between the two dukes that seemed likely never to be closed.

As the meeting disintegrated and York departed in red-faced fury, his parting words to me were delivered with unwarranted spite. 'Well, you tried, young Pembroke, but you would do better watching your own back. While you played nursemaid to your witless half-brother, your full flesh and blood was plotting to cut you out. Next time you see

Richmond, ask him where he has been. I guarantee you will not like the answer.'

Later that day I was still seething over the sneering laugh that had punctuated York's parting jibe, when my brother Edmund burst into the Westminster Palace armoury where Maredudd was helping me into the old hauberk I wore for my daily arms practice. 'Ah, here you are, Jas! God's greetings, brother. You may offer your congratulations to a married man – well, as good as married anyway.'

My already low spirits plummeted further and I stared at him, speechless. He cackled – there is no other word for it. 'Ha ha! Do not tell me you still harboured hopes for Margaret yourself? She was always meant for the eldest you know. We make the perfect combination – I am handsome and royal and she is rich and willing. Well, why wouldn't she be? Willing, I mean.' He spread his arms wide to display his undeniable charms.

'Perhaps because she has good taste.' My voice grated from my constricted throat. Edmund was right. I had harboured high hopes for Margaret, had even broached the subject again with Henry before his malady took hold but he had given no hint that he had already granted the marriage to Edmund.

My brother shrugged. 'I will allow your sour grapes because I understand that you are a bad loser but there will be another rich bride for you, Jas.'

I raged inwardly. As if riches were the only reason for coveting Margaret! At this juncture my thoughts were of a murderous intent.

'How about Elizabeth of York?' he added. 'You can be sure that her father will endow her well. Or the Earl of

Warwick's little sister, Katherine? There are plenty more like Margaret Beaufort.'

I had turned away, hiding my dejection in the rattle of chainmail as Maredudd hauled the hauberk over my head. Edmund was wrong; the delicate and graceful Margaret Beaufort could not be outshone in my estimation and definitely not by a daughter of York. In hindsight, I had put Margaret on a pedestal and allowed myself to see her as my perfect honoured lady and me as her gentle knight. I had been captivated by her elfin charm and her engaging manner but I think I can truthfully state that my thoughts had been entirely chaste. She was too young to be the subject of lustful urges but pure fascination has an equally strong pull and in Margaret's case I doubted if I would ever be entirely free of it.

After my mauling at the Royal Council and Edmund's devastating betrothal my instinct was to get away. It was a long ride to Pembroke, across half of England and the widest part of Wales but I took with me only a small troop of mounted retainers. I wanted nothing like the long column of guards and courtiers, cooks, clerks and house-carls, such as accompanied the king on his interminable progresses. Long-suffering Henry bore the tedium of these cavalcades with saintly forbearance but I insisted that my tight-knit retinue covered at least thirty-five miles a day and preferably forty, depending on the terrain and the weather conditions. However, having crossed the Severn by ferry below Chepstow, we rested two nights at my nearby castle of Caldicot so that I could meet the constable and inspect its demesne and defences.

Caldicot manor had been part of our mother's dower lands

so King Henry had thought it fitting to add it to my lordships, but until this visit I had not realized what superb hunting was offered by its extensive parkland and made a mental note to come back at a convenient time and take advantage of it. On the other hand the castle itself was a disappointment. It had been built to monitor the river traffic on the lower Severn and to enforce Norman rule in the area and as such it was a very basic fortification consisting of a moated curtain wall around a large bailey, a ramshackle old keep, a gatehouse and a random trio of defensive towers, all of which were in a state of neglect. I deduced that it could probably just about withstand a siege and provide a refuge for local farmers and their stock but its domestic arrangements offered little comfort for any noble companions I might wish to invite for the excellent hunting and wildfowling. I resolved to have plans drawn up for improvements.

From Caldicot we took the high route through the Black Mountains, avoiding Glamorgan in the southernmost part of Wales, where I knew trouble was brewing. The pugnacious Earl of Warwick was in violent conflict with one of his Lancastrian cousins over the lordship of Abergavenny and was also disputing possession of Cardiff Castle with the Duke of Somerset. I had already learned at court that where Warwick disputed mastery it was best not to venture, unless you had a troop of lawyers at your side and an army at your back. Moreover there was a convenient string of lordships and manors belonging to Welsh gentry located in the green rolling hills further north, where comfortable accommodation might be obtained and useful connections made. I was eager to introduce myself as the new Earl of Pembroke and to seek their counsel and advice.

As it transpired, although the servants in each house we visited hosted us generously, only one of the landholders was in residence, but my meeting with Gruffydd ap Nicholas at Dinefŵr Castle was a fruitful and fortuitous one. When I was at Tŷ Cerrig, Hywel had described this powerful clan leader as a warmongering old rascal with questionable morals and no respect for authority and I found this to be true in many respects; he was ageing and boisterous, with a bald pate, a grizzled beard and a loud voice. However, even on this first brief encounter we somehow established a rapport that made nothing of the forty-year difference in our ages and the fact that his English was badly mauled by the loss of his front teeth in a skirmish. My foolish attempt at Welsh almost prompted an apoplexy on his part but after a few false starts I managed to get the hang of his lisping English.

'I have sons of about your age, Lord Jasper,' he told me jovially. 'Thomas and Owain, and there is never a cross word between us – as long as they do exactly as I tell them!' His laugh was like the crackling of a log fire, cheerful and warming, but the steely glint in his grey eyes revealed his iron will. I was to learn that arguing was the sport he and his sons relished most and quickly came to the conclusion that I would prefer to stand beside him rather than confront him on a battlefield.

'I have heard that you are a patron of the arts,' I remarked early in our meeting, 'and that you hold festivals here at Dinefŵr.'

I had found his favourite subject. 'Yes indeed, in the spring we held an eisteddfod; at least that is what the bards called it. There was singing and music and poetry; performers came from all over Wales. It lasted two weeks and they ate and drank me out of all supplies, but it was worth it for the entertainment and the comradeship. They held a competition to see who could deliver the best praise poem and there was even one to you, Jasper Tudor!' His laugh boomed out again. 'It was soon after you had been made Earl of Pembroke and I suppose the bard thought it topical. It was not strictly a praise poem but then he knew next to nothing about you – ha, ha!'

I was astonished. 'I would like the name of the man who did that!' Maredudd had told me of the Welsh tradition of poets declaiming long and effusive eulogies to their chosen heroes and had mentioned one in particular. 'Do you know of a poet called Lewys Glyn Cothi?' I asked Gruffydd on impulse.

His face creased into smiles once again. 'Do I know him? Of course I know him and a spirited declaimer he is. What is more he is here. He often calls in when he hears I am at Dinefŵr. He has gone off somewhere just now, probably gambling or wenching, but he will be back at dinnertime. He always is. How did you hear of him?'

'My Welsh squire told me about him. Was he the one who delivered the rather lacklustre praise poem about me?'

Gruffydd cogitated, stroking his beard. 'Now I come to think of it, I believe he was. What a coincidence! Shall we ask him to sing it for his supper tonight?'

The prospect of this clearly delighted him but I quailed at the idea of hearing an inaccurate list of my imagined attributes aimed at me in a language I did not understand. 'I do not think so, thank you, but I would like to meet him and perhaps he might sing someone else's praises?'

The venerable Welshman sucked his teeth. 'You will have

to get used to that sort of thing, my lord, now that you are Earl of Pembroke. Believe me it can be useful. The spread of a praise poem around Wales can bring men rushing to your banner.' He spied a lean figure striding across the bailey towards us. 'Aha, here is the man now.'

I had imagined a bard to be an old man with a wild grey beard, rather like my elderly host, but Lewys Glyn Cothi was no more than a decade my senior and his hair was russet brown, his beard neatly clipped. He wore a long hooded tunic of undyed wool, rather like a monk's habit, which he tucked up into his belt when walking, of which he did a great deal as he wandered from manor to manor, seeking gentry rich enough to patronize his poetic skills. A plain baldric crossed his chest from which hung a leather scrip containing his worldly goods, which as far as I could tell on greater acquaintance consisted chiefly of pen, ink and paper. Had he been a harper like my father, I imagined his instrument would have been slung on his back, but instead a rolled-up cloak or blanket was in its place. His well-worn canvas boots had wrinkled into folds at the ankle and the exposed skin of his face was weathering into fine cracks.

On hearing my name he instantly flung himself at my feet, and began kissing the hem of my doublet. 'Lord Jasper! *Y Mab Daragon*! You have come to Wales, just as I prophesied. My cup runneth over!'

Nonplussed by this gushing enthusiasm, I was temporarily struck dumb, but Gruffydd spoke for me. 'God's nails, Lewys, anyone could have prophesied that! The man has been made Earl of Pembroke. He was bound to come sooner or later. The question is, what prompted all that verbiage you spouted about Lord Jasper's courage being that of an ox and his colouring that of the Red Dragon? How did you know he was a ginger-top? And why are you calling him the Son of Prophecy? He has barely set foot here and has no grasp of our language.'

'That does not signify, Gruffydd,' the bard assured him, stubbornly refusing to rise. 'He is *Y Mab Daragon* because he can trace his bloodline back to Llewellyn the Great, Prince of all Wales.'

Gruffydd snorted. 'Well so can I, for that matter. Most of us can if we try hard enough. Get up, man, for Dewi's sake and let us go and broach the barrel. There's a cask of Bordeaux wine waiting. The situation in France being what it is, we should drink it while we can still get it but I fear my bibulous sons will have lowered the level already. Come, Lord Jasper, I want you to meet them.'

The 'old rascal' proceeded to lead us up the steep steps to his great hall at a pace reminiscent of a mountain goat. Gruffydd's hair might have been sparse and his beard grey but he did not lack energy or muscle. I imagined him still being capable of taking on a dozen men half his age on the battlefield. As he had predicted his two sons, Thomas and Owain, were already supping cups of the rich Bordeaux wine and laughing together while servants spread cloths over the boards for the coming meal.

'I like to eat with my household in the old fashioned way,' their father told me. 'They need a hot meal at the end of a hard day's toil.'

'You are a good master, Lord Gruffydd,' I said, raising the cup he had thrust into my hand. 'Many gentlemen take their meals separately these days.'

'We do not call my father Lord,' Owain corrected me. 'He is a proud Welshman and the English kings do not create Welsh lords.'

'Lord Jasper is the exception to that though, Owain!' cried Lewys, his tone rising and falling with excitement. 'He is a lord *and* a Welshman.'

'Oh, is that so Master Poet? If he is a Welshman, why are we all speaking English?' Both Owain and his younger brother Thomas were the image of what Gruffydd might have been thirty years before, solid and broad-shouldered with dark hair and complexions and a blunt manner. He clapped the bard on the shoulder and grinned. 'Ha, I got you there did I not, my friend?'

Lewys bridled. 'He has not had the advantage of a Welsh education as you and I have, but if Lord Jasper's father is a Welshman then he is as Welsh as you and I.'

This subject was quickly dropped because Gruffydd and his sons were more interested in probing for details of the king's illness. I tried to keep information to a minimum but they were only too aware that control of the country had been slipping from King Henry's hands long before his mind went blank.

'The leading families of Wales are dividing into two camps,' Gruffydd observed grimly. 'I have always supported the Lancastrian kings but there are more chieftains than ever now who openly side with York, especially the Marcher gentry like Herbert of Raglan and the Vaughans of Tretower. You must be careful who you trust, Lord Jasper.'

Knowing better, I took his pronouncement of undying loyalty with a large pinch of salt but nodded sagely. 'I know that Warwick and York have joined forces over their territorial disputes with Somerset but I am trying to remain neutral. Actually I believe York is holding his fire until the queen's child is born, waiting to see if it is a boy or a girl.'

'Waiting to see if he can press his demand to be proclaimed heir to the throne you mean,' chortled Thomas. 'How he must be hoping that babe is a girl!'

'Or even better born dead,' added Gruffydd. 'There are rumours it is not the king's child anyway.'

In defence of my brother I could not let that pass. 'Do not be misled by Warwick's mudslingers,' I protested. 'Many a marriage does not produce an heir for years and then suddenly succeeds. The Yorks were also subject to such groundless slander around the birth of young Edward of March.'

Gruffydd wagged a finger at me. 'Be careful, my lord Jasper – fences make uncomfortable seats. When you have to jump down on one side or the other remember that William ap Thomas – or William Herbert as he calls himself now that he has adopted English ways – is a slippery customer. Did you call in at Raglan on your way here?'

'I did but he was not there. I met his wife though – Lady Anne. She is a strong and lovely woman.'

'Aha, like me you appreciate a lush and fertile female,' nodded Gruffydd. 'William did well there. But she is a Devereux, a family well tied to Ludlow. York's son Edward is their idea of an heir. He may only be eleven years old but he is Warwick's cousin and already tall and strong. Marcher folk like the Devereux clan think the lad's golden hair is spun from sunbeams.'

Lewys came out of his apparent trance. 'That is a good metaphor Gruffydd ap Nicholas. I may use it one day.'

Gruffydd grunted. 'Not while I am listening, you thieving bard. Not if you want your dinner.' He glanced irritably around the hall and raised his voice so that the rafters shook. 'And where *is* dinner! Someone kick the cook up the arse. I am hungry and so are my guests.'

8

Jasper

London and St Albans

WHILE I WAS ABSENT in Wales the feud between Lancaster and York reached boiling point in London, fuelled by the Duke of York's unceasing campaign to be proclaimed King Henry's heir, and by the constant drip of innuendo from Warwick's scandalmongers, suggesting an adulterous relationship between the queen and the Duke of Somerset. York's demands to be named Henry's heir were halted temporarily when Queen Marguerite was delivered of a healthy boy at Westminster Palace, but the slanders proliferated once more when King Henry failed to recognize the child as his heir.

At Windsor the little prince had been placed in Henry's arms but the king's face had remained expressionless, his grip flaccid. If not for the swift reaction of the nurse in catching him, the infant would have tumbled to the ground. Several subsequent attempts were made to secure the king's attention but with equal lack of success. In the absence of the monarch's approval, the boy was hastily baptized Edward after the canonized English king known as the Confessor, whose shrine was in Westminster Abbey, while Parliament agreed to the appointment of the Duke of York as Protector of the Realm. Within weeks York had his rival Somerset confined in the Tower, charged with treasonous negligence for the loss of France under his command. As a royal duke he was housed in the palace rather than the prison but he must have heard the crowds of Londoners, stirred up by Warwick's agents, yelling for his head.

By Christmas however the queen had emerged from her confinement and the king recovered his wits enough to acknowledge his son and heir and resume his rightful place on the throne. With power back in royal hands the Duke of Somerset was released from the Tower and the Duke of York relieved of his post as Protector. The Lancastrian star should have been on the rise again but sadly Henry's malady soon returned and when Marguerite petitioned Parliament to allow her to rule as interim Regent for her infant son they rejected her outright and reappointed the Duke of York as Protector. A fresh flood of pamphlets now turned the people of London against the queen, stirring those who believed their poison to march on Westminster declaring the baby prince to be no son of the king's but sired either by the Duke of Somerset or the Earl of Wiltshire. Marguerite took her son and fled downriver to Greenwich in fear for their safety.

Meanwhile my brother recovered again and dismissed the Duke of York, who disappeared in fury to Fotheringhay. Bravely in my opinion, Somerset returned to Henry's side and decided that the court should move from a hostile

London to the Lancastrian heartland of the Midlands. In May I brought my retinue from Pembroke to join the large escorting army deemed necessary to protect the royal family on their journey north.

Queen Marguerite rode beside the litter that carried her eighteen-month-old son, but once we had cleared London she let him sit smiling on the pommel of her saddle, waving at passers by. The Earl of Wiltshire and I were invited to ride beside her and it was during this time that I learned the details of Henry's mysterious malady.

'It strikes when it will, out of nowhere, Jasper,' Marguerite explained. 'There is no warning and apparently no remedy, and when it passes, after days or even weeks, it leaves him a little more depleted each time. My Édouard must grow quickly if there is to be a king on the throne who can hold England together, for I fear Henry will steadily become more unfit for the task. It is hard enough now to get him to concentrate on matters of state. James here knows how difficult it is to get him to understand the Treasury papers he has to sign.'

I glanced across at James Butler, Earl of Wiltshire, who rode knee-to-knee with the queen at her other side. He was close in age to Marguerite and had always been about the court in one way or another, particularly in the queen's company, but his prominence had been but lately achieved. During York's Protectorate Wiltshire, like Somerset, had been sent to house arrest in the Tower, ostensibly for crimes committed during disputes over his estates in the west country, but he had been swiftly released when the Protectorate was ended and promoted to the office of Treasurer of England. I realized that since then Marguerite had come to rely on his counsel a great deal and for the first time I discerned the roots of the scandal spread by the London mudslingers. Wiltshire was the kind of handsome, dashing figure that King Henry would never be and the favour Marguerite showed him was enough to set tongues wagging both in and outside the court. Remembering Marguerite's veiled proposal to me a few years before, I even found myself looking for signs of Wiltshire's blond good looks in the little prince but saw only his mother's dark eyes and colouring.

'Prince Edward seems to be doing his best to grow at a rapid rate, your grace,' I responded. 'He is already threatening to take the reins of your horse I see.'

Marguerite gently removed her son's chubby fist from her mount's reins and bestowed a kiss on the dimpled knuckles. 'Yes, it cannot be long before he will need his own pony. I must tell you though, Jasper, that I prefer the French pronunciation of his name – Édouard.'

'Then it shall be as you wish, my lady.' I bowed acquiescence but could not help thinking how badly this would be received in the ranks of England's xenophobic soldiery.

'Prince Édouard has the makings of a true French "chevalier", do you not agree, Jasper?' declared Wiltshire, endowing my own name with a French polish that put me uncannily in mind of my mother. 'It will not be long before he is riding at the head of his army.'

'Well there is no likelihood of his father taking command,' said the queen, her tone distinctly flat. 'I may have to acquire a suit of armour myself.'

'Let us hope such a thing will never be needed, your grace.' The brilliance of the smile Wiltshire flashed at her then would have lured a cargo ship into a smuggler's cove and I began to find his celebrated charm somewhat overwhelming.

I showed my own chipped tooth. 'No, where we are going, my brother will have the peace and security he needs to make a full recovery.'

With her free hand Marguerite made the sign of the cross. 'To that very end, I intend to make offerings en route, at St Alban's shrine,' she said. 'Henry has much need of the martyred saint's protection.'

However, when we arrived in St Albans we received the unwelcome news that an army led by York and Warwick was blocking our way north. Shocked, the queen hastily took Prince Édouard to the shelter of the abbey while the Duke of Buckingham, who as Constable of England was in command of the king's escort, immediately sent heralds to negotiate with the Yorkists. Meanwhile the rest of the escorting nobility rapidly deployed their retinues in defensive positions. There were no walls around the town of St Albans, which had grown around the famous abbey shrine. Wiltshire and I took our men to the north bar, where people and goods entering and leaving the town paid their tolls. But despite it being the access to Watling Street, which was the highway on which we planned to continue our journey, we could see no sign of hostile forces.

'They are playing hide and seek it would seem,' Wiltshire grumbled. He had intended to wave the king's standard, which he had the honour of carrying, boldly in the face of the opposing forces, to make them aware that they would be committing an act of treason by attacking the king's person. King Henry himself was stationed in the town's central Market Place with Buckingham and his bodyguard. 'If it has no purpose here I must take the standard back to the king,' he said, beckoning his squire to bring his horse. 'You take over command of my men, Jasper.'

'I will but you should know that I have no experience of battle, only the theory . . .'

'There you are then.' He cut me off, re-mounted and shouldered the standard. 'Just apply the theory and all will be well. I doubt if there will be conflict anyway. Buckingham's orders are to avoid civil war and so it will likely be a repeat of York's march on London three years ago – all bluff and bluster with his heralds conveying spurious declarations of loyalty and of bringing the people's grievances before the king. York and Warwick will be forgiven and we will all continue on our merry way.'

I very much hoped Wiltshire was right but I watched him ride away with serious misgivings. Our captains were lingering by the bar awaiting instructions and I had little notion of what to tell them but did my best to hide my inexperience by issuing orders to establish a hidden defence, using the network of lanes and alleyways off the main highway to deploy the troops where they might spring a surprise on any incursion. Soon after the men had concealed themselves, banners displaying the Duke of York's Falcon and Fetterlock and the Earl of Salisbury's Verteagle began to emerge from the suburban gardens of the houses lining the roadway beyond the bar. It appeared that York and Salisbury had had the same idea of concealment but their troops were now mustering to make a rush for the centre of the town.

I bid my herald give the signal to emerge and confront

them and at the same time loud shouts and trumpet calls sounded behind us and I heard the unmistakable whoosh and thud of arrows finding their mark. I realized with dismay that the Yorkists had split their army and that while his allies kept us occupied, Warwick was moving in on the Market Square from the east. We were caught between the two forces. In the absence of Lord Wiltshire it would be impossible to command on both fronts and so I had no choice but to turn my back on Warwick's attack and order the men to engage the troops approaching rapidly from the north.

The clash of forces in the town confines was bloody and confused. Having decided there was no room for cavalry in the narrow streets my troops were all on foot, while York and Salisbury's retinues were mostly still mounted, giving them an initial advantage. Although my vanguard tried bravely to bring down the enemy's horses we were forced off the main highway and back into the narrow lanes. Wiltshire's soldiers, without their commander, soon melted away into the shadows but I called together my own men and led them through backstreets and alley-ways in order to bring support to Buckingham and the king in the Market Square, which seemed the only thing I could do. Although I knew there had been several casualties I prayed we were not leaving any dead behind us, only to find when we got there we were too late. Buckingham had been felled and was lying wounded on the cobbles with blood seeping from under his helmet and King Henry and his bodyguard were surrounded. Both the Earl of Warwick and the Duke of York were there already in force. Clearly we had no option but to lay down our arms. There was no sign of Wiltshire or the royal standard.

The battle, if it could be called that, was over. While York and Salisbury had barged their way through my unsuccessful defence of the north bar, Warwick's attack from the east side of the town had taken the king and the royal guard by surprise and I was to learn that during the brief hostilities key Lancastrian leaders had been singled out and killed by Warwick's men, including the Duke of Somerset, the Earl of Northumberland and Lord Clifford. But to my immediate consternation I noticed that the king himself had been wounded by a Yorkist arrow, the shaft of which was still protruding from the back of his neck.

I stepped forward and offered my sword to York, and then my support to my brother. As soon as he saw me the look of fear and bewilderment left Henry's eyes and he leaned heavily on my shoulder. 'Ah, Jasper, it is you. I think I need the services of a surgeon.'

The duke nodded agreement. 'Yes, Pembroke, take his grace for treatment. The monks will know where to go but my men will escort you.' He signalled to a sturdy knight who was hovering nearby and gave him whispered instructions. Monks were already beginning to emerge nervously from the abbey with offers to assist the wounded and it was one of them who led us, unarmed and surrounded by a considerable Yorkist escort, to a tanner's workshop, assuring us that it would have the tools necessary to remove the arrowhead without causing more damage. And God be praised, the monk was right; King Henry's injury proved to be only a flesh wound, which was successfully treated and bandaged. The arrow had missed any vital blood vessels but

I was greatly impressed by the courage and stoicism Henry displayed as the brawny tanner wielded his hefty pincers so close to a vulnerable area.

Meanwhile the Duke of York had been making hasty arrangements for dealing with the other casualties. By the time we returned to the Market Square Buckingham had been taken away for treatment and my men had been relieved of their arms and corralled together in a dejected group in one corner. York bowed punctiliously to King Henry and informed him that he and Warwick would escort him back to London. No mention was made at that time of the death of Somerset.

'But I wish to go to Kenilworth with the queen,' Henry protested, gripping my arm tightly as if fearful he might be wrenched away from me. 'Tell him, Jasper – we are going to the Midlands. I do not like residing at Westminster or the Tower.'

'The queen and the prince may go north if they wish,' said the duke firmly, 'but the people expect their king to be in London. We will make sure that you are comfortably accommodated, sire, have no fear.'

Henry turned beseeching eyes on me but I shook my head. There was no future in arguing at the point of a sword. And so the royal family was separated, apparently with the worthiest of motives. The king rode into London beside York, while Warwick led the procession, bearing aloft the Sword of State in hands which only hours before had sent the Duke of Somerset into the hereafter. The people who cheered them through the streets were in no doubt as to who was now in control of the kingdom.

When Henry was finally told of Somerset's death the

shock sent him into such a state of grief that he would not have been capable of ruling anyway. I wondered how Marguerite had taken the news when she heard it, far away in the Lancastrian castle-in-the-lake that was Kenilworth. She must have been distraught that she had lost both her favourite counsellors; Somerset to Warwick's sword and Wiltshire to self-inflicted exile in Flanders, where he had chosen to take refuge rather than face York's vengeance. The royal standard had been found propped up against a hovel in a dark alley and most of Wiltshire's armour was dragged out of the River Ver, which ran through the town. Some monk claimed that the fleeing earl had given him a mark for his habit to use as a disguise.

As for me, the duke chose not to take offence that I had fought against him at St Albans. 'You are the king's brother,' he said. 'I hold family loyalty in high esteem.' He went so far as to call me back to the Royal Council, even though I warned him that my prolonged absence from Pembroke would leave crown property in West Wales vulnerable to Gruffydd and his sons. This was where York's ulterior motive showed, for his response was to favour my brother Edmund, who had not been at St Albans, and appoint him as the king's Lieutenant in South Wales, with orders to bring Gruffydd to heel. Shuddering at the prospect of Edmund destroying all the diplomatic advances I had made with the 'old rascal' and his sons, I went to Henry to protest but it was immediately clear to me that my royal brother was still reeling from Somerset's death.

With his household scattered he had been accommodated at the Bishop of London's palace and I found him pale and timid, barely clinging to sanity. 'Edmund's appointment was the Duke of York's idea, Jasper,' he whispered. There was still a fresh scar on his neck where the arrow had so nearly severed a vital blood vessel. 'He is very angry about our royal dignity being disparaged in Wales. I thought it best not to argue with him.'

In making my response I swapped my usual cheerful tone for what I hoped was a gently persuasive one. 'I understand completely, my liege, but on this occasion I believe second thoughts are needed. Highly as I know you regard Edmund, I submit that he is not the man for this task. He makes no secret of the fact that he does not like the Welsh, which must seriously affect the chances of successful negotiations with the local chieftains.'

Henry frowned. 'But he is Welsh himself and the appointment has been made public. It cannot be changed.'

I tried not to sound exasperated. 'You are the king, Henry. If you believe an error has been made then you can cancel the appointment.'

He shook his head vehemently, as if trying to eject a buzzing insect from his ear. 'No. No, I will not do that, Jasper. I cannot.'

Reluctantly I let the matter drop. A time was to come when I would wish that I had not.

9

Jasper

Bletsoe Castle, Bedfordshire

F IVE MONTHS AFTER THE regrettable clash of arms at
St Albans, Edmund and Margaret stood before the altar
in the chapel at her mother's castle of Bletsoe in Bedfordshire.
It was a cold day and the bride's blue and silver mantle
embroidered with the Beaufort portcullis swamped her small
frame; a jewelled circlet secured her long dark hair. She was
twelve and a half years old and dwarfed by Edmund who
stood tall and magnificent and twice her age, at his physical
and fashionable fittest. During our two-day ride from
Westminster to Bletsoe, I had asked him why Lady Welles
had agreed to the wedding while her daughter was still so
young but he informed me gleefully that Margaret had more
or less demanded to be married.

'She says her prayers have been answered. I think she is
somewhat in love with me.'

The look of smug satisfaction on his face stung me to
anger and my right fist developed a sudden desire to make

contact with his chiselled chin, which I resisted only with difficulty. 'But you must not bed her until she is older, Edmund.'

Edmund gave a noncommittal shrug, avoiding my gaze. 'That rather depends on Margaret. Lady Welles confides that her daughter has flowered – a rather coy euphemism I think – but it does imply that both nature and the law deem her ready for *de*flowering.' He turned to face me then, delighted with his own coarse wit.

I swallowed an explosion of wrath and fought to keep my voice steady. 'She is not though, Edmund, is she? And you know it. You only have to look at her. She is still a child. Where are the breasts? Where are the womanly curves? And apart from anything else, whatever the Church's rule on canonical age, conception would endanger Margaret's life and that of the child.'

At this Edmund lost his temper. 'I have had enough of you lecturing me, Jasper! I will be responsible for my wife's health and her wealth and I will brook no interference from you or anyone else. If you cannot contain your jealousy then I suggest you stay away from us. You insisted on coming to the wedding and now I demand your solemn oath that you will make no more mention of canonical age, consummation, conception or any other word beginning with "C".'

My brother's outburst made both our horses shy and when I had controlled mine I held up my free hand in capitulation. 'All right, Edmund, you can calm down. I have said my piece. You will hear no more from me except to ask what you might like for a wedding gift. I assume you would turn your nose up at a hogshead of Bride Ale?'

This reference to our sister's simple wedding nearly five

years before revived his sense of humour. 'Ha! You assume right. No yeoman Bride Ale will be served at my wedding, Jas. Lord Welles keeps a well-stocked cellar and I intend to drink a number of toasts in fine wine to my sweet Margaret and several more to the fortune I shall receive as lord of her considerable estates.'

He was goading me. Edmund would receive all the income from the Somerset estates but only when they had become true man and wife. Until then we held joint custody and he would continue to share the revenue with me. Although this additional income was useful to me, not for one moment did I want him to think it was the reason I was urging him to delay consummation.

'Do I take it then that a vat of wine would be more welcome?' I said. 'I know an excellent vintner in Tenby who imports direct from Brittany, outwitting England's losses in France.'

'That would be most welcome, brother. Have him deliver it to Lamphey Palace. Our fellow Privy Councillor, Bishop de la Bere, has agreed to let me use it while I am acting as the king's Lieutenant in South Wales. He was kind enough to suggest that a newly married man needed somewhere comfortable to enjoy his new bride.'

With a sly smile he watched my jaw work hard to keep my lips sealed. The Bishop of St David's country retreat at Lamphey was rumoured to be where members of the Welsh clergy went to forget their priestly vows of celibacy, poverty and obedience. It was a beautiful hall set deep in parkland full of game and its plentiful ponds and orchards yielded fish and fruit to tempt the most discerning palate. It also happened to be located only a few miles from Pembroke

Castle. Their honeymoon playground would be right under my very nose.

I glared at him, unable to summon even a glimmer of a smile in return. 'God has dealt you some fine cards, Edmund,' I said. 'But these are uneasy times; I hope the Almighty shows you how to play them wisely.'

* * *

When the wedding celebrations reached the dancing stage at Bletsoe Castle, I stood among the crowd of applauding guests watching Edmund lead his new bride onto the floor. As the minstrels struck a slow rhythm the newly married couple clasped hands and began to turn together and Margaret's admiring gaze at her new husband sparked a conversation between two people standing behind me.

'I trust you will look at me like that when I lead you out at our wedding next year, Edith.' It was the voice of a young man, light and teasing in tone.

'And I hope you will have transformed your appearance and perfected your dancing enough to induce me to do so, Geoffrey,' came the reply, in a soft female voice.

Edmund swept his bride up into his arms and twirled her around and she laughed delightedly. I was glad to avert my gaze in order to identify the speakers, although I had already guessed that the girl was Margaret's older half-sister, Edith St John and her companion was also known to me. Geoffrey Pole had been a squire in the king's household at the same time as Edmund and me. He came from a well-to-do Anglo-Welsh family and I had encountered him once or twice while attending to business in West Wales, where he held minor royal offices in Haverford and Carmarthen, towns not far from Pembroke. Word at Westminster tipped him as an up and coming courtier and from their brief exchange I gathered that he was betrothed to Margaret's sister.

When I turned, Edith had the grace to blush. 'Oh I crave your pardon, my lord of Pembroke. I had not realized it was you, but I hope you know that I was not disparaging your brother of Richmond; rather comparing his magnificence to my betrothed's lack of it.'

Geoffrey Pole, a tall man of perfectly acceptable but unremarkable appearance, did not seem at all offended by her veiled insult. 'Pay no attention to Edith, my lord. Her sense of humour may be inclined to sarcasm but she is kinder than she sounds. It is terrible what jealousy can do to a maid.'

'And what maid would not be jealous of a sister who has netted an earl when she herself can only aspire to a squire?' I might have been embarrassed to witness this apparent slight if it had not been for the young lady's playful sideways glance at her betrothed, which revealed more about her true feelings for him than her words.

I entered into the spirit of her mood. 'It is not unheard of for a squire's son to become an earl,' I pointed out. 'Like myself,' I added with a bow, 'and like my brother there on the floor, whom you call magnificent. Nor should we forget that your sister is the daughter of a duke and an heiress to boot; attributes liable to outshine the indisputable beauty of a mere knight's daughter!' This time my bow was aimed at Edith and with her slim full-breasted figure, high cheek-bones and playful blue eyes my compliment was not misplaced.

She countered with a graceful curtsy, giving me a mischievous sideways glance. 'At the risk of being called a loose woman, I suddenly find my interest swerving from one brother to the other! Let me return the flattery, my lord, by saying that you seem a great deal more approachable now than you did when standing supporter for your brother of Richmond in the chapel, at which time you gave a very good impression of an approaching thunderstorm.'

For a moment I was taken aback, concerned that I should have given myself away to this sharp-eyed observer, but Geoffrey came to my rescue with a cheerful man-to-man comment. 'He looked as any man is bound to do when witnessing his brother's descent into matrimony. I hope my brother will show similar fellow-feeling when we stand before the priest, my sweeting.' He planted a gentle kiss on his betrothed's hand. 'But I think it is time we claimed some of the limelight for ourselves by joining the bridal couple in the dance. That is a sister's obligation is it not? I hope you will excuse us, Lord Jasper, temporarily at least.' I watched them make their way onto the floor and reflected how much more appropriate this pairing of equals seemed than the one my brother had just made.

A break in the dancing brought my first opportunity to converse with the bride, while Edmund was occupied with her mother. In the warm crush of bodies in Bletsoe's crowded great hall Margaret had discarded her fur-lined mantle to reveal a gown of gold satin figured with a pattern of marguerites and trimmed with seed pearls, a clever double play on her name. Her hair swung down her back, long and free in the tradition of maiden brides and a pearl collar clasped her smooth neck. She presented the perfect image of a duke's daughter.

'I hear you are to start your married life in the Bishop's Palace at Lamphey, Lady Margaret,' I began. 'I have been there and it is truly a green and pleasant place set among lakes and trees. I am sure you will find much to delight you.'

Margaret regarded me solemnly. 'It is kind of Bishop de la Bere to lend it to us but I believe he does not go there himself, or even to Wales, surprisingly. I suppose as Almoner to the king he is much involved in Council affairs.' I detected a note of disapproval in her young voice at the notion of such an absentee shepherd of his flock.

'Yes, the king is very conscientious about his charitable responsibilities,' I said. 'The bishop is kept very busy.' She was such a serious little soul. I supposed that marriage for a girl of any age was a serious matter and for one of only twelve, however well she disguised it, must surely be a daunting prospect. 'Lamphey is a secluded palace and I am sure Lord Edmund will be much taken up with official business. I hope you will not be lonely. Will you take some ladies with you, to keep you company?'

'Master Pole, my sister Edith's betrothed, has arranged some companions to attend me and Edith herself will stay with us until after Christmas. My lord Edmund says the apartments at Lamphey are particularly comfortable. Also I am told that Wales is a land of music so I think we shall be cheerful and I will not be short of books, for there is a fine library. But thank you for your concern.'

'If I may, I will visit you when I return to Wales. It is a pleasant ride from Lamphey to Pembroke and I hope you will also consider visiting me.'

Her smile was like a flame bursting from a dampened

fire. 'I will certainly do so, thank you. We are brother and sister now are we not? I hope we can be friends.' She gestured at the cleared floor, where wedding guests were gathering for another dance. 'I come from a large family and we are used to many merry celebrations. My lord Edmund says he hopes God will grant us many children.' She shot me a sideways glance and her grey eyes sparkled with mischief. 'I told him he should not make me blush.'

I took a deep breath to steady my heartbeat. She had showed me a flirtatious side that I had not suspected. She might have been young but she was not ignorant and she would be conscious of her duty to supply a Richmond dynasty. I could only pray it would be later rather than sooner. How I wished she had told him he should not make her rush.

I extended my hand and returned her smile. 'I look forward to sharing some of those merry celebrations. And now, would you honour your new brother with the next dance, my lady of Richmond?'

10

Jasper

Pembroke Castle & Lamphey Palace

'I F YOU ARE RIDING to Caldicot, my lord, you might assess the situation at Carmarthen on the way.' Geoffrey Pole made this suggestion as we passed under the inner gate at Pembroke Castle and set out across the wide expanse of the outer court. Geoffrey and I were the same age and as a result of his Easter wedding to Margaret's half-sister Edith we were now brothers-in-law and he was a frequent visitor and valued adviser. I appreciated his unassuming nature and quick wit and found his local connections very useful.

'Why, what have you heard?' I asked. Strictly speaking, since Edmund had been sent to Wales, being a royal castle Carmarthen was no longer my responsibility and I had not intended to stop there on my journey to Caldicot Castle, where last-minute preparations had to be made for the hunting party I was planning for the end of May – its precise date timed to coincide with Margaret's thirteenth birthday.

As always, Pembroke's outer court was busy. Geoffrey dodged around a courier's horse being led off to the stables before replying. 'If you remember, while he was Protector the Duke of York made himself Constable of Carmarthen Castle. Well, the appointment has never been reversed, and now York has instructed his ally, William Herbert of Raglan, to claim the castle on his behalf. Old Gruffydd ap Nicholas swears he will take it himself rather than see Herbert's men in there, which leaves the present deputy constable in a cleft stick. He does not know who is his master, whether to defend the castle for the king or surrender it and if so, to whom.'

I cogitated, pursing my lips before replying. 'Strictly speaking it is Lord Edmund's responsibility to exert royal authority and secure Carmarthen for the king, but as yet he has no army at his command.'

Geoffrey sucked his teeth. 'Even if Lord Edmund were to issue an array I do not think he would have much success recruiting men. He does not have the support in South Wales that you do.'

An involuntary oath escaped me. 'Jesu what a mess! If I raise a force to defend Carmarthen, York would be within his rights to accuse me of treason, considering his name is still on the statute roll as constable.'

We had reached the south wall of the outer court and the site of my half-built new mansion nestling in the lee of the South Tower, and close to the Great Gatehouse. If Pembroke was to be my main home I needed somewhere more sheltered and comfortable in which to bring up the family I hoped to have. Previous earls had occupied the Solar Tower in the inner court, which was exposed to every wind that blew off the Pembroke estuary.

I wanted to pick Geoffrey's brains on the subject of local craftsmen for work on the interior, after the roof was on. But Geoffrey was still talking about Carmarthen, his voice lowered to a confidential level. 'Perhaps I could suggest to Gruffydd privately that he move his men into Carmarthen before Herbert arrives. He will be only too keen to do so and then at least you would know that the castle was secure for Lancaster.'

It was my turn to scowl. 'Herbert will not stomach that surely! There will be war – or at least a siege.'

'Yes inevitably, but by then Lord Edmund will have had time to acquire a commission of array from Westminster. If he recruits in England he will have more success. The process can be set in hand while we are at Caldicot.'

I clapped my companion on the back. 'That is a splendid idea, Geoffrey! You are a cunning politician and a superior tactician. Now, be so kind as to demonstrate your knowledge of the local craftsmen. Who shall I get to turn this house into a palace?'

I intended that its main windows would overlook a private garden courtyard formed against the curtain wall, turning its back on the noise from the vast outer court and the cold winds from the north and east. Geoffrey laughed and scratched his head, surveying the empty shell of the new residence, the rising walls encased in their surcôte of scaffolding. 'How long before you expect the roof to be on?'

'They work fast,' I said, drawing his attention to the network of wooden walks and rails where a team of masons could be seen laying ashlar; tramping the stones up on a great treadmill crane. A thatched shelter to our right was the workshop where apprentices were mixing mortar and the master mason was consulting a design scratched out on the clay floor. 'Master John assures me it will be watertight by the end of the summer.'

'So you will want the interior finished by next spring perhaps?'

'Well, I would ideally like the house to be ready for Christmas but I do not expect miracles.'

Geoffrey grimaced. 'It sounds to me as if you do but I happen to know an excellent fresco artist who will travel far and fast for good money. I have no idea where he is at present but I can track him down for you.'

Indeed, I had a hankering for bright murals above the warmth of panelled walls. I went on. 'Do you also chance to know of any woodcarvers working in Wales?'

'No but I know a man who does and coincidentally his name is Gruffydd ap Nicholas.' Geoffrey rubbed his hands and grinned at me conspiratorially. 'I think I might manage to kill two birds with one arrow.'

I clapped him on the shoulder again. 'Well if you achieve that before coming to Caldicot, Master Pole, I will award you the first stag of the week!'

* * *

I decided to call at Lamphey Palace on my way to Caldicot, as I had done a couple of times since Edmund and Margaret's wedding. On those occasions Edmund had not been present, off on some royal business, and I had enjoyed some time with Margaret and her young lady friends, girls from local gentry families who came and went and kept her amused through the long winter months. On this occasion I discovered that my brother was in fact in residence. I sent

Maredudd with my horse to the stables while I made my way to the inner gatehouse, which led into the palace's private domain. Beyond its arch was a garden, which in the balmy May weather was already verdant with spring growth. It ran under the wall of the impressive hall where Margaret had entertained me on previous visits. But before venturing further I stopped inside the arch to speak to the porter, who wore a monkish habit, although I knew him to be a lay member of the episcopal household.

He recognized me and came out of his lodge to make me a bow. 'My lord of Pembroke, welcome. I believe my lord and lady of Richmond are in the garden making the most of this fine weather. Would you like me to send someone to announce your arrival?'

'No, thank you.' I wagged a negative finger, put it to my lips and winked at him. 'I will seek them out myself and surprise them. The garden is not that large after all.'

The porter looked a little doubtful but said nothing and bowed himself back into his lodge. Stepping out into the bright sunlight I paused to get my bearings, blinking and temporarily blinded. On one side the garden was divided by straight gravel paths with tidy herb beds, and on the other side small trees and shrubs were arranged in clumps with winding walks between which visitors might wander and lose themselves. A green retreat, laid out for the bishop to take the air, commune with nature and pray. But the sounds emanating from within the bushes were not the sounds of prayer.

I stood in the dappled shadow of a path where branches met overhead forming an emerald tunnel. Suddenly Margaret appeared in a brief flash of blue silk, running across the path a few yards ahead of me, too quickly to register my presence. In her wake she left the echo of laughter, then her voice sang out through the bushes. 'Catch me if you can, sir, but you will not!'

'Oh yes I will, my lady, and when I do – watch out!' It was Edmund, striding across the path further along, clutching a jewelled cup and snatching a sip from it as he went. He, too, did not see me.

I hesitated, uncertain what to do. A few seconds later I heard my brother's voice again, raised in triumph. 'Got you! You are a naughty girl, Margaret Richmond. What made you think I would let you read your book when I am here to play with you? Anyway, what are you reading? Whoops, it is heavy. Ah. *The Romance of the Rose*. Now why would you need to read about romance when it stands here in front of you, yours for the taking?'

From the tone of his voice I suspected that Edmund was slightly tipsy but obviously not sufficiently to offend Margaret because the infectious giggle I had first heard erupted once again. 'Be careful! It is borrowed from the bishop's library, although I am not sure a priest should be reading such a work. There, I will put it down on the bench and you have my full attention. Mind you don't sit on it!'

Now I knew that Edmund had drunk freely, possibly of the strong Rennish wine I had provided as a wedding present, for there was a coaxing note in his next words and I heard a slapping sound, as if he had sat down and patted his thigh. 'You could sit on my knee and whisper words of love in my ear.'

There was a rustle of silk as Margaret evidently complied

and asked teasingly, 'Which ear shall I speak to first, my lord? This one – or this one?'

'Oh, my lovely lady, never mind my ears . . .' Edmund said and for several long seconds there was silence.

At this point I decided it was time for me to leave. Whether I liked it or not my brother and his wife had every right to behave as they wished, having reason to believe they were alone together in their own private garden. Whatever might be the outcome of this encounter, it was none of my business. I made the sign of the cross to dismiss the evil demon that sat on my shoulder, tempting me to announce myself and spoil their fun, but it was not without a sense of foreboding that I turned on my heel and crept from the shadows back into the sunshine. Anyway I would be seeing them shortly at Caldicot.

II

Jasper

Caldicot Castle, Monmouthshire

Aᴌᴌ ʜᴀᴅ ʙᴇᴇɴ ǫᴜɪᴇᴛ at Carmarthen when I passed through the town on my way to Caldicot to complete the arrangements for the hunting party. The gatehouse mansion had been renovated and I now considered it offered enough luxury to satisfy the most discerning taste. I intended to lodge the two married couples there: Margaret and Edmund and Geoffrey and Edith, while my father and I would take chambers in the East Tower, which flanked the other end of the Great Hall, where we would gather each evening after hunting to eat some of the product of our exertions and be entertained.

Minstrels and mummers were already camped around the bailey. Soon Owen would arrive – he had promised to bring his harp – and so would the bard Lewys Glyn Cothi who was to sing some of his latest poems.

Margaret and Edmund rode over from Lamphey along highways that foamed with hawthorn blossom, and it seemed to me, as Margaret emerged from the shadow of the gate-house arch into the bright sunshine of the bailey, that she was the Spirit of Spring personified, in a vivid green riding kirtle with cream lace at the neck and wrists.

She rode astride and I helped her dismount as the horses carrying the Richmond retinue continued to clatter over the drawbridge behind her and Edmund. As she swung her booted leg over the saddle and I smiled inwardly at the sight of a pale pink ribbon threaded through the lace trim on the hem of her chemise. Anyone who had not seen the pink ribbon would have put her age at fifteen or sixteen but I knew she remained a young girl underneath.

'I am so looking forward to our week of sport, Lord Jasper,' she enthused. 'Edmund told me there is excellent wildfowling on the Severn marshes and I have brought my favourite merlin in the hope of seeing her bring down a snipe.'

'All shall be done to make your stay perfect, my lady,' I said, bowing over her hand.

Edmund had left his horse to a groom and come up behind her. His first words were ominous. 'You will have a task to make mine perfect, brother, thanks to that ruffian Gruffydd ap Nicholas. Have you heard his latest outrage?'

'No. Has he made a move then?' I asked, knowing he spoke of Carmarthen.

'More than a move by Saint Michael! Only two days ago he actually managed to take Carmarthen Castle. He must have had inside help because his men just seemed to walk in unopposed. I need to talk to you about this, Jasper.' Edmund made a grim face at me over Margaret's head.

I nodded agreement. 'We will discuss it later. Geoffrey

should be here soon with Edith; it will be helpful to hear what he has to say on the matter. But now I am sure Lady Margaret needs to rest after the journey. Let me show you to your chambers. They are in the gatehouse, where I have recently made alterations and refurbishments. I trust they will meet with your approval.'

'It will be hard to match Lamphey Palace,' remarked Edmund as he preceded me into the new covered stair that led to the apartments above the gate-arch. 'Bishops certainly knew how to live in the old days.'

Margaret called from higher up, 'We are here for the sport, Edmund, not for the luxury of the furnishings.'

Edmund rolled his eyes at me over his shoulder. 'You wait until you are married, brother. A man must brook such female contradiction in the interests of marital peace!'

I offered him no sympathy. 'I cannot believe your lady wife makes any complaint against you, Edmund, no matter how much you vex her.'

Margaret's laughter floated down between us. 'You are right, Jasper. My lips are raw from biting them!'

The unmistakable affection in Edmund's responding chuckle surprised me. I had never seen such an ardent expression on my brother's face and with the incident I had overheard in the Lamphey garden still fresh in my memory it both delighted and troubled me because while I rejoiced that Margaret was happy, I still had this nagging dread of her falling pregnant too young.

Nevertheless I had given them separate bedchambers and their quarters were divided from those allocated to Edith and Geoffrey by a shared solar. When I showed the other pair up a short time later Edith immediately ventured off to find her sister. Both ladies had brought female servants and Geoffrey jerked his head at Edith's to make her disappear.

'We came here via Carmarthen,' he revealed immediately she had left, 'and I found Gruffydd already installed in the castle without any exchange of fire. He had simply told the garrison that he would burn the villages of each and every one of them if they did not return to their wives and children. All thirty trooped out of the main gate and the deputy constable went with them. I cannot imagine how he will explain himself to the Duke of York but that is his problem.'

'And what of William Herbert?' I asked. 'He will not take this lying down.'

'No, I think not and according to my last report he was in Hereford with his brother and two thousand men. So he must be planning to make a move but before he does it seems likely that there will be a council of war with York at Ludlow.' Geoffrey as always spoke like the strategist he was.

At this point Edmund arrived and grasped Geoffrey's shoulder in greeting. 'Good to see you, Pole. I need your help.'

Geoffrey grinned and made him a bow. 'Always happy to be of service, my lord. I do not need to ask for what.'

Edmund made an exasperated noise. 'What am I to do with that bastard Gruffydd and his meddling sons? I cannot have them thumbing their noses at the crown like this. The next thing we know he will declare himself Prince of Wales and the queen will never let me hear the end of it.'

'I should think not, now that Parliament has conferred

that particular title on her son,' Geoffrey agreed. 'Why do you not send to her for instructions?'

Edmund's brows almost disappeared under the rim of his draped velvet hat. 'What, deal with a female? Definitely not! I shall write to the king.'

'It amounts to the same thing,' I said with a shrug. 'These days Queen Marguerite reads all his letters and deals with most of them. However, you might get a commission of array and then at least you can recruit an army. It will take a siege to get Carmarthen back.'

'But that will take months,' Edmund complained. 'Has no one got the ear of the Gruffydd creature? I just need him out.'

Geoffrey shook his head. 'In my opinion you need do nothing, my lord. If you wait a month or so William Herbert will do the job for you. Even you do not hate Gruffydd more than Herbert does.'

'But Herbert is York's toady. He will not return Carmarthen to royal control will he?'

I intervened again. 'Now that the queen – I beg your pardon, I mean the king – has dismissed York from the Council, sooner or later the office of Constable of Carmarthen will go to someone else – probably you, Edmund. Then you can legally demand the withdrawal of whoever is in there.'

My brother threw his hands in the air. 'Yes but will they go? Holy Mary save me from Wales! Where nothing is straightforward and no one obeys the law.'

I slapped him lightly on the back. 'Never mind that now – write to the king then let it go for a few days and enjoy the hunting. Wait and see what transpires.'

He flashed his famous smile. 'Good idea! What have you got planned for us tomorrow – boar or stag?'

'I thought Margaret wanted to go hawking,' I said, intrigued to get his reaction to this suggestion.

For a moment Edmund hesitated, considering. Then he shook his head. 'No, the falconer told me her merlin is not sharp. He needs to starve her for another day to be at her best. Besides, Margaret likes a good gallop as much as anyone. Let her follow us after the stag.'

'As you like Edmund, but I must tell you that I promised Geoffrey the first kill.'

He glowered at Geoffrey. 'Hmm. I could pull rank of course.'

I feared that good-natured Geoffrey was about to accommodate him when Edmund's brow cleared and his smile shone out again. 'But I find I cannot. Only make it a clean kill, Master Pole, if you please. My wife does not like a bloody mess.'

Geoffrey swept him a bow. 'Have no fear, my lord, my arrow will go straight to the heart of the hart.'

Edmund groaned.

The sound of a horn announced another arrival and so I left them. It was my father, who had encountered the bard Lewys a few miles up the road walking in the same direction and taken him up behind him on his palfrey.

'This mendicant said he was coming here,' Owen said as he drew rein. 'I thought it unlikely but then he started spouting some lines in Welsh, singing your praises, so I decided he must be telling the truth.'

Like a grey eel Lewys slid his skinny frame down from behind the high back of the saddle and adjusted his baldric before retaliating. 'This ancient mercenary told me he was your father but it was only when I spotted the harp-bag slung from his saddle that I was forced to believe him. The damnable instrument has been bashing me in the backside ever since.'

I laughed. 'This sounds like good ammunition for a bardic battle. I will start you off after dinner, Harper versus Poet. I am glad you have had an opportunity to get to know one another.'

Lewys hunched his bony shoulders. 'Well, I am familiar with the back of his head anyway.'

Owen dismounted and as ever I admired his nimbleness, being generally of the belief that a man past fifty should be old and weak of knee. 'And I will know this sing-song bard's voice anywhere,' he retorted, 'and take evasive action.'

'You can start right now then,' I declared, detecting the start of a love-hate acquaintance. 'Lewys you are in the West Tower with the squires – over there.' I pointed to my right. 'And you, my honoured father, are with me in the East Tower – all the way over there.' I indicated the far end of the building that held the Great Hall. 'Is that far enough apart? Refresh yourselves and come to the Great Hall when the dinner horn sounds. Oh, and I would ask you to speak English while you are here, for the benefit of Lady Margaret, our guest of honour, whose birthday we are celebrating.'

* * *

Our first evening began quietly with the aim of conserving our energy for the chase the following day. Owen and Lewys made their first attempt at a bardic battle but surprisingly both managed to agree that their efforts needed further work. A more polished performance was promised for later in the week. Music from the minstrels kept us cheerful through the meal and then Margaret and Edith retired early, leaving the men to gather round the hall fire and bemoan the state of the country over another flagon drawn from the cask of Breton wine I had acquired from my new vintner.

As is the way of the world we did not stop at one flagon and cloudy heads the next day meant the men of our party were quite relieved that the hounds took a good hour to flush out a stag. However, when the horn finally sounded the chase I was astonished at Margaret's horsemanship. Eager for the scent, she rode her small dapple-grey palfrey in the same way that she danced; lightly, with delicate touches of her heels on the mare's flanks and soft, coaxing hands on the reins. I kept a close eye on her and she did not falter or fall behind. I had assumed that she would have more desire for the chase than for the kill but she stuck with the pack, keeping her nimble little horse in the wake of our larger, stronger steeds by taking a more direct line through the trees and undergrowth. She reminded me of a woodland hawk after its prey, swooping under low branches and between close tree-trunks where heavier, bulkier creatures could not go. When the hounds eventually held the stag at bay against a steep rock face she was a close witness to the despatch of our first quarry.

It was a fine, mature animal, velvet still soft on its half-grown antlers, which it lowered and flicked menacingly at the baying and snarling pack of hounds surrounding it. The huntsmen stood well back as Geoffrey Pole quietly dismounted, unslung his bow and walked forward, gravely saluting the panting stag, whose attention was concentrated on the dogs rather than the calm man with the long bent stick. Sunlight shining through the wind-tossed canopy dappled the scene in a moving pattern of light and shade, distracting to any marksman, but I watched in admiration as the capable squire nocked a barbed arrow, took slow and careful aim and shot the beast straight through the heart as he had promised. Edith caught up with us just in time to view the kill, hand over mouth and eyes wide, then she dismounted as the stag sagged to its knees and hit the ground. Walking proudly up to Geoffrey she kissed him on the lips, an embrace he returned with victorious gusto. At this Margaret smiled and dropped her reins to put her hands together in delight.

The sounding of the hounds rose in a crescendo as huntsmen beat their way through to the stag, sliced out its entrails and tossed them away for the dogs to fight over. I turned to check Margaret's reaction to the bloodiest part of the proceedings, and found that Edmund had already urged his mount alongside hers and they were both clapping, he with slow applause and she with childish enthusiasm.

'Oh, that was well done, Master Pole!' the girl cried. 'A deft and swift dispatch.'

'Praise from the expert, Geoffrey,' Edmund told him. 'You may not be aware that my lady has witnessed more kills than she has years. She is truly a Diana.'

Margaret giggled, a sound that was to become a familiar accompaniment to the week's activities. 'Only in some respects, my lord,' she said, reaching out to lay an affectionate hand on her husband's arm. 'Diana was a virgin goddess and I am a married woman. Besides, I would never turn

Master Pole into a stag, even if he did find me bathing naked in the woods.'

I was too stunned at the implication of Margaret's denial of virginity to be surprised at her knowledge of Roman mythology and I squirmed as I detected a note of lust in Edmund's responding chuckle. 'If he did I would set the dogs on him myself,' he declared, leaning from his horse to slide his arm around his wife's waist and whisper something in her ear that made her blush.

I realized then with intense regret that I had allocated too many chambers to Margaret and Edmund. I turned my face away, for rage though I might against my libidinous brother, there was nothing I could do except pray for a substantial delay to any pregnancy.

The hounds found scent twice more that day and I thanked the rules of etiquette that I could not assume the honour of the kill because I was bound to cede it to Edmund and Owen as my guests. Had I been obliged to aim an arrow at a cowering stag my anger might have caused my aim to wander unforgivably.

I did not speak with Edmund alone for several days. I kept busy with my duties as host, which I could have delegated to Maredudd, who was more than capable of taking some of the responsibilities off my shoulders, but I was grateful to be occupied arranging minstrels and huntsmen for the pleasure of my guests. Had I found myself alone with Edmund before I had simmered down, I feared I might have said something I would regret, something that might also have lost me the friendship and respect of Margaret. Finally I confronted him as he emerged from the mews in the hour before Margaret's birthday feast, the final event of our hunting party.

Edmund was grinning broadly and eager to confide the reason for his being there. 'Come and see what I ordered from London, Jas. My falconer has just attached them to Margaret's favourite merlin.' He put his arm around my shoulders and led me back into the wooden lean-to, which served as a mews for the hawks. Margaret's little merlin Elaine was dozing on her perch, tired after bringing down a variety of birds during the day. 'Take a good look at her, Jas. Do you notice anything different?'

I inspected the little hook-beaked raptor that had earlier stooped so magnificently on partridge, snipe and redshank. Only a blind man could have failed to notice the new jewelled bells attached to her legs; even in the dim light of the mews they glowed with the viridescent gleam peculiar to large emeralds, the birthstone of those born in May. I gave a low whistle and Elaine lifted her hooded head, suddenly alert. Her feet shifted and the bells jingled. 'Phew! That is a costly sound, my lord of Richmond. Are we to assume that you have come into some money?'

He pressed his finger to his nose, nodding. 'Those Somerset estates are yielding good revenues, so why should their lady not enjoy the benefits? The bells are Margaret's birthday present. I am having the bird brought to the dais later.'

Edmund did not notice my silence; he had barely stopped smiling since we entered the mews and now he grinned from ear to ear. He was happy because, now he had taken her virginity, he had got his hands on her money!

'How much in debt are you that you could not wait to seduce the child?' I demanded to know bitterly.

My blunt accusation wiped the grin from my brother's

face. He grabbed my arm above the elbow and marched me out of the door, his voice harsh with ire. 'Jesu, what kind of a question is that? A man cannot seduce his wife, Jas. Just as he cannot rape her, in case that is what you are going to accuse me of next.'

'It may not be called rape but it amounts to the same thing,' I hissed, wrenching my arm free.

We were both trying to keep our voices down but our faces were only inches apart in open confrontation. I could feel his spittle on my cheeks as he enunciated his words with furious emphasis. 'There is – was – no question of force, God damn you! It was Margaret's decision; she came to me willingly and has done so a dozen times since. She loves me as you have observed and it is patently obvious that you are green with envy. But do not allow your jealousy to lead you into thinking that an evil deed has been done here. This is married love, Jas. Get over it and go and seek your own.'

I, too, was irate beyond maintaining any semblance of calm. 'Perhaps you did not force her but you are responsible for her, Edmund. If she dies in childbirth it will be your fault. You are her lord and husband and you have acted like a beardless youth who has no control over his base instincts.'

'Why should she die? I hope she does become pregnant!' he retorted.

I gasped. 'I cannot believe I am hearing this! Look at the size of her – she is tiny. Not only Margaret but the child could die as well.'

He shook his head violently. 'I do not believe that. Girls are made to have babies. However, you are right in one respect and one respect only, it is *my* responsibility and not yours. It is you who are acting like an interfering old woman. I told you before – stop meddling in my life and get on with your own!'

Just as he had done a hundred times during our youth, Edmund ended the argument by shoving me in the chest and striding off, determined to have the last word. And as I had always done on those occasions I let him go, but this time I vowed I would do exactly as he had demanded. When they left Caldicot the next day I would wave them goodbye and from then on I would leave Edmund to sort out his own life – and forget Margaret Beaufort.

12

Jane

Tŷ Cerrig & Pembroke Castle

I HAD NEVER RECEIVED a letter from anyone before and I held the folded square of paper in trembling fingers. I did not recognize the smudged imprint of a bird in the wax seal. 'Who is it from, Maredudd?'

Maredudd had just arrived, alone, and was busy unhitching a pannier from his sumpter. 'Who do you think? Lord Jasper of course. I do not play the courier for anyone else.' He slung down the heavy basket. 'There are gifts in here and I have gold for our father in a body purse. I do not know how much but I tell you, it has been uncomfortable riding and sleeping with it wrapped around my waist.'

'He will be glad of it,' I said. 'It has not been a good year on the land.'

'I suppose it is further "compensation" for me being away from here as Lord Jasper's squire,' said my brother. 'I will give it to him at supper, when I have changed – is there a fresh chemise I can wear, Sian? I stink of crowded hospice dorters.'

'I will leave one of father's by the cistern. Make sure you wash before you put it on – and in case you have forgotten, let me remind you to use a pail, the cistern water must remain clean.'

Of course he knew the house rules and I smiled at the rude hand signal he made at me under his horse's neck. His last visit had been at harvest time. Since then Gwyladus, Bethan's widowed mother, had come to live with us, and my father had taken on two farm workers, which meant two more hearty appetites to feed. It was only early December and I was already worried that our stores of grain and salted meat would not last until next summer. Not forgetting the three infants (so far!) my stepmother had borne. Housekeeping did not get any easier at Tŷ Cerrig.

I held off opening the letter until I had unpacked the pannier – a cone of sugar, crocks of honey, a wineskin (mead, I later discovered), and packets of dried fruit, rice and spices. Exulting in this sudden and delicious plenty, I placed the empty pannier and a clean chemise beside the dairy cistern downstairs. Back in the hall, I still resisted reading the letter; I stirred up the fire, swung the pottage cauldron over it, lit a lamp, and only then sat down in my father's carved black oak armchair with the letter in my hands, my fingers cracking the wax of the smudged bird seal. The writing was spidery but at the same time words were cramped closely together to fit on the page. I made slow progress but as I read my heart was wrenched, first one way and then another.

To Jane Hywel of Tŷ Cerrig in the county of Gwynedd, North Wales
I write to share with you the dreadful news that my

brother Edmund died in Carmarthen Castle a few days ago. We had heard only lately that he had been held prisoner there since August, when he was captured leading an attempt to regain it for the king. As Earl of Richmond, Edmund should have been ransomed immediately but news of his capture was kept from us, and from Margaret, who is now his widow. For he lies in Greyfriars Church at Carmarthen and I know you will join me in praying for his soul.

William Herbert, who holds Carmarthen illegally, claims Edmund was taken by the plague but my agents report no evidence of plague in the town. I am determined to discover the truth of his untimely demise.

His countess is bereaved and alone at Lamphey Palace. I write from Kenilworth where King Henry has made me her guardian and ordered me to take her to the safety of Pembroke and so I have entrusted this letter to Maredudd in the hope that you may agree to ride with him and join us there as soon as possible. Lady Margaret, although mature beyond her tender years, will have need of a sympathetic female companion to advise and comfort her and I can think of no better person than you for such a sensitive position. Maredudd also carries a letter to your father requesting his permission to let you leave as soon as possible. I feel sure that in the circumstances he will find it in his heart to allow you to come to Lady Margaret's aid, if only for a few months.

Written in haste and in the hope of greeting you soon at Pembroke, I am your faithful friend and cousin,

Jasper.

I was still reeling from the import of this letter when feet sounded on the ladder stair and my father's voice reached me, calling my name. Hywel entered the hall, closely followed by Maredudd carrying a full wineskin. He wore the clean chemise but the grubby body purse he had unwound from his person and draped over his shoulder spoilt the effect. I stood up, relinquishing the armchair in which my father always sat, unless outranked. 'Ah yes, Maredudd said you also had a letter.' He thrust another letter at me, similar in shape and seal to the one I had just read. 'What does this one say?'

My father's patience, to say nothing of his eyesight, was not up to deciphering Jasper's scrawl. I took the letter across to the window and opened the shutter, allowing sufficient light for me to read without the aid of the lamp.

Again I read the tragic account of Edmund's death, this time aloud but it was told in words meant for my father and therefore less emotional in their effect on me. The last paragraph was cunningly aimed at neutralizing two of my father's chief anxieties, money and the smooth running of his house. I felt the blood rise in my cheeks as I read it.

'I am conscious that you will be reluctant to lose the loving help and presence in your household of your daughter but I can think of no other person to match her as a source of comfort, advice and protection for a lonely and bereaved young lady. In recognition of this I have entrusted Maredudd with the pension I agreed when he took service with me and a supplement which I hope may serve as some compensation for the temporary absence of Jane from your house, so that she may use the

skills she has learned at Tŷ Cerrig to care for young
Lady Margaret and help her through this terrible time
of grief. I beg you to pray for my brother's soul. In haste
and with high regard, your bereaved cousin Jasper.'

A tense silence pervaded the room as I turned to close
the shutter against the chill wind. In his chair, chin propped
on fist, my father was deep in thought. Maredudd hoisted
the heavy linen purse from his shoulder and dropped it over
the arm of Hywel's chair not occupied by his elbow. The
outlines of a series of coins were visible along its sweat-
stained length.

'There is the Earl of Pembroke's gold,' my brother said.
'I have not counted it but it feels like a tidy sum.'

'It feels like selling my soul,' growled Hywel, fingering
the purse. 'He is buying my children.'

'No, Father,' I said hastily. 'Lord Jasper is kin and mourning his brother and the lady is in great need at this time.
As he says, it is fair compensation. I will not be gone forever.'

'And you and Bethan are not doing a bad job of replacing
us,' observed Maredudd bluntly. 'Little Nesta is only five
but she already milks the goats and feeds the hens. And
Gwyladus can run a house just as well as Sian. She and I
will leave in the morning.'

Hywel glared at us from under beetled brows. 'The day
I take orders from you Maredudd will be the day your great
lord knights you – which I would guess is never. Both of
you, put out the board and hold your tongues until I have
counted the coin.'

When we had placed the board on the trestles, he upended
the purse and the gold coins cascaded onto the polished

wood. Then began the counting with King Henry's head moving, coin by coin, from one pile into another, Father calling out the tally as he did so.

'… eighteen, nineteen, twenty.' He looked up at us, eyes wide in undisguised amazement. 'Twenty crowns – that is two knight's fees! Lord Jasper values your services very highly it seems.'

'Could it be the value he puts on his sister-in-law's health and happiness?' I suggested slyly. 'The Countess of Richmond is young at present but she is an important lady, a cousin of the king. It may not be wise to refuse this opportunity to be of help to her.'

Hywel grunted, his fingers playing with one of the coins; then he piled them up into four columns and shoved them to one side. 'Let us eat,' he said, glancing across at the sideboard where Maredudd had put the wineskin 'When I have broached the contents of that, I will make my decision.'

Jasper had judged the compensation and the content of the wineskin shrewdly and Maredudd and I were on the road to Pembroke at dawn the following day. The excitement I felt at the prospect of finally seeing something of the world alternated with my dread of meeting the person I would be serving.

I knew almost nothing of Lady Margaret but Jasper had once told me about when he first met her at court and his account had disturbed me because he had given the impression, intentionally or not, that he thought the sun beamed from her noble backside. In my perverse way I had concluded that such a paragon of virtue was quite likely to be a pain in that part of the anatomy, the sort of pain I was now literally suffering due to prolonged and unfamiliar contact with the saddle. As my fingers also froze to the reins in the icy wind, I began to wonder if the big wide world was where I wanted to be and if a blue-blooded countess who was also a spoiled brat was someone I wanted to serve. Nor did I hold out much hope that the present Jasper Tudor would be the same smiling and likeable person I had found so appealing on his first appearance at Tŷ Cerrig five years ago. Would he still be so charming and easy now that he was installed in his earldom and lord of all he surveyed? The nearer we got to Pembroke the greater my misgivings grew.

Having at last turned away from the coast, we wended our way for several days through mountain passes and green valleys, staying at inns and hospices and finally finding hospitality at Carew Castle, despite the absence of its lord, who was one of Gruffydd ap Nicholas's sons. I had found Carew daunting with its soaring turrets and high walls but that was before I set eyes on Pembroke the following day. During our journey some of the churches and abbeys we rode past had amazed me, but I had never laid eyes on anything to compare with the huge and fearsome edifice that was Pembroke Castle.

Viewed across an expanse of rippling water, it crouched like some gigantic monster on a steep rocky promontory, its mighty lime-washed towers and battlements appearing to grow out of the pale rock beneath, as if it was rooted in the earth itself. It looked like a man-made white mountain, indestructible, impregnable.

I had to clear my throat to find my voice and ask Maredudd weakly, 'Is that the entrance?' pointing to a huge arch in the base of the cliff that appeared to be the maw of the monster. A cluster of boats and people on the mud flats in front of it might have been its prey.

My brother laughed. 'No, that is the great cavern. A natural cave connected to the castle by an inside stair and used for landing and storing supplies and armaments. The main gatehouse is around the other side and leads from the town straight into the outer ward. First we must cross the bridge.' He indicated a stone structure arching over the narrows where the River Pembroke flowed into its estuary.

I took a deep breath to steady my beating heart. 'If I were Lady Margaret arriving here I think I would be terrified.'

'Yes but you are a farm-girl and she is a countess; she has lived in castles and palaces all her life.'

I had thought that gaining admittance to the castle would be a slow process but as squire to the earl Maredudd's face was familiar to the guards and our business easily stated. We trotted on past the high barbican wall, through the echoing tunnel under the gatehouse with its two open gates and raised portcullises, and into the vast Outer Ward. My brother had told me the castle was presently very quiet but the noise and bustle we found inside was greater than any I had ever experienced and the maze of buildings ranged against the enclosing walls of the ward beyond made me think how quickly I would become lost if I were left alone here. Later I discovered that each structure gave out clues to its identity, a wheeze of bellows and clang of hammer, the barking of dogs and the whinny of horses, the tantalizing smell of bread and the warm whiff of malted grain. On the far side of the ward I could see vegetable and herb gardens laid out in the shelter of a large, square tower. Turning left from the gatehouse we skirted a substantial, newly erected stone house, roofed in slate and partly encased in wooden scaffolding. Intricate decorative carving around its imposing entrance and some elaborate gargoyle gutter-spouts indicated a dwelling of some distinction.

'What is it?' I asked Maredudd.

'Lord Jasper's new mansion,' he replied. 'He says the Solar Tower has too many echoes and draughts. This house even has a special room with a stone tub for bathing. He wanted to be living in it by Christmas but that is not going to happen now.'

Beyond this new building lay a long range of stables where we finally dismounted and handed our tired horses to a groom. Then Maredudd led the way to a lofty battlemented dividing wall and through another huge gatehouse as if we were entering a castle within a castle.

'This is the original stronghold,' Maredudd explained, 'constructed by the Normans to keep the troublesome Welsh out of their lives. They are still trying to do that but we are testament to the fact that they have not succeeded.' He shot me a triumphant grin. 'Because here we are!'

The same cold sea-breeze that had plagued the first part of our journey from Abermaw now struck again, swirling about a vast, round tower-keep and howling through a tunnel where a curved stone staircase led upwards.

'This is the old keep,' my brotherly guide revealed. 'It was built by the famous knight Sir William Marshall when he was Earl of Pembroke. The base is twenty feet thick.'

I craned my neck to peer up at its many narrow arrow-slit windows. 'It looks truly sinister,' I said with conviction.

'No need for you to worry, females are not allowed in the keep.'

'Good. Where will I be living then?'

'I have no idea. Wherever Lady Margaret is lodged I suppose. Lord Jasper had a big new window added to the Solar Tower so perhaps she is quartered there.' We had rounded the keep into a more sheltered courtyard, where he pointed to another outside stair set against a plastered building. 'That is the entrance.'

'Good, for I am so cold now that I cannot feel my toes.'

'I believe you are getting soft, sis,' chided my brother. 'I was told we will find Lord Jasper here.'

'Did your informant happen to tell you if Lady Margaret was also here?' I enquired sharply, sensing he was keeping something back.

Maredudd smiled slyly. 'Yes, he did and she is.'

I could have strangled him. I was frozen, filthy from the road and saddle-sore, in no fit state to meet a countess on whom I wished to make a good impression. 'I will need to visit a latrine before I meet her,' I insisted.

'Well I am sure Lord Jasper can supply one of those.'

I clenched my teeth and sighed. Lord Jasper might be able to supply one but would I have the nerve to ask him?

13

Jane

Pembroke Castle

A CHAMBERLAIN TOLD US to wait in the anteroom and entered the solar to announce our arrival. I only had time to remove my gloves before Jasper came out to meet us. I was shocked by his appearance. There were deep shadows under his eyes, his hair was unkempt and his jaw stippled with several days' stubble. He looked as if he had not slept for weeks.

'Jane! Thank God you are here.' I thought he might be about to embrace me but then he checked himself and took my hands instead as I dropped him a curtsy. 'It is so good to see you.'

He did not release my hands immediately when I rose and I was conscious that mine were rough from work but his felt just as worn and his doublet looked as if it had been slept in. He was far from the grandiose nobleman I feared he might have become. 'I am very sorry about Lord Edmund's death, my lord. It must have come as such a shock to you. I have been praying for his soul as you asked.'

'Thank you, Jane. From what the priests tell us of purgatory I believe the dead need all the prayers the living can offer.' He turned his attention to my brother. 'And thank you for bringing her to Pembroke, Maredudd. Did your father need much persuading?'

'No more than your gold was able to supply, my lord,' my brother said dryly. 'Gold speaks louder than words when times are hard and they are hard at present.'

Jasper nodded and his next words were music to my ears. 'You must want to refresh yourself, Jane.' He beckoned to the girl who had entered the room with him. She was about my age and dressed very similarly, her hair covered by a plain linen coif. 'This is Lady Margaret's maid, Alice. She will show you the way.'

'How is Lady Margaret, my lord?' I asked.

A haunted look swept his face and he shook his head, sighing. 'Not good. She needs you, but you will see for yourself. Go with Alice now and I will speak with Maredudd. When you return I will take you in to meet her.'

In a connecting tower Alice stood sentinel while I made use of one seat of an intriguing double latrine. A wicked image of past earls and countesses seated sociably together inspired an inappropriate giggle, which I hastily smothered. But to confirm its use by the rich and privileged, next door in the garderobe I found a water-jug, bowl and soap with a brush and hand mirror nearby – luxuries of which I took full advantage, removing my coif, washing my face and hands and brushing my hair before replacing it. When I followed the maid back to the anteroom I felt considerably more presentable.

Maredudd was gone when I got there. 'He will be back

for supper in the hall in an hour.' Jasper told me. 'There are refreshments in the solar if you are hungry and thirsty in the meantime. Come now and meet Lady Margaret.'

She sat beside a blazing fire wearing a black veil and enveloped in dark furs, her head bowed over her clasped hands as if in prayer. She looked tiny, almost shrunken, lost in the high-backed armchair, and when she raised her eyes I noticed they were swollen and bloodshot and her cheekbones were blade-sharp. Jasper introduced me, whereupon Lady Margaret struggled to her feet and her fur mantle fell back to reveal a swollen belly that seemed grotesque on her childish frame. I judged that she was at least seven months pregnant.

I was quick to disguise the horror I felt with a smile as I slowly approached, took her right hand gently in mine and placed my left on her elbow. The action was instinctive because she looked as if she was about to fall over. I tried to keep my voice level. 'I hope I can be of service to you, Lady Margaret. First of all, I think you should sit down again.'

'Yes, I do feel a little dizzy,' she confessed, allowing me to lower her back into the chair. 'I am *enceinte* you know.' I found her use of the French word quaint and rather touching.

'Yes, I can see that. If you are dizzy perhaps you should eat something. In your condition a little and often is the best way.' The bony feel of her arm had shocked me.

Curiosity flickered in her inflamed grey eyes. 'How do you know that? Are you a midwife?'

'No but in recent years I have helped my stepmother through three pregnancies so I do know something about

157

it.' I caught sight of a tray of wafers and sweetmeats on a table nearby and picked it up. 'Why do you not nibble at one of these? I am sure you would feel better.'

She looked at the titbits as if she thought they might poison her. 'Oh, do you think so? I am not very hungry.'

'Perhaps not but I expect your baby is.' I smiled again and pushed the tray nearer. 'You must eat to nourish him.'

She frowned and a look of irritation crossed her face. 'How do you know it is a boy? I am sorry, I have forgotten your name.'

'Jane,' I said, deferentially providing the English version. 'It is Jane. And I do not *know* that your baby is a boy, my lady. I just do not like to refer to a human soul as "it".'

Almost without appearing to realize she had done so Lady Margaret took a wafer and nibbled at it, nodding. 'I agree with you. It does not seem right. But the priests say that a child is not a Christian until after baptism. If not a Christian how can it have a soul?'

I hesitated. Arguing Christian doctrine was not something I cared to do. Although only a girl, this highly educated aristocrat probably knew much more about it than I did. I glanced at Jasper for help but he too appeared nonplussed. 'I think that is a question you should ask your confessor, Margaret,' he suggested at last.

'But I do not have a confessor,' she said sadly. 'Lord Edmund said he was applying to the pope for permission to appoint one but I do not know if permission came because he . . .' Fresh tears rushed from her eyes and she covered her face with her hands. 'I am sorry, I do not mean to weep.' Her words were muffled and her shoulders shook. Alice hurriedly supplied her with a kerchief.

To give Lady Margaret time to recover I took the opportunity to scan the room. It was spacious and elegantly furnished, hung with colourful tapestries and scattered with bright silk cushions that caught the rays of the setting sun shining through the oriel window. A large tester bed stood at one end, heaped with quilts and pillows. Jasper was hovering behind Margaret's chair, regarding me helplessly. Judging by his distraught expression he was close to tears himself.

'I think it might be better if Lady Margaret were in bed,' I suggested when her sobs eased a little. 'She is obviously exhausted.'

Jasper made a hopeless gesture with his hands. 'She says she cannot sleep.'

'Nevertheless she needs to rest. I think that if you leave us, my lord, together Alice and I will be able make her comfortable. Perhaps some gruel could be ordered for her, made with beef bones preferably.'

Lady Margaret raised her head. 'No beef. It is Advent. I am fasting.' A shuddering breath punctuated each burst of speech.

I rolled my eyes at Jasper who shrugged again. He clearly had no idea how to tackle such female resolve.

'The Church does not require pregnant women to fast, my lady,' I said, crossing my fingers. I had no idea if it was true but my mother had told me this once and she had a convent education. 'If you wish we can call a priest to confirm it.'

Margaret's hands dropped from her face and she stared at me, as if testing my honesty. Then she nodded and, wiping her eyes, said in a small voice, 'Very well. I will go to bed and I will try to swallow some gruel.'

An hour later, when she had been installed in fresh linen sheets, propped on soft pillows and had consumed a bowl of delicious-smelling gruel, her inflamed eyelids drooped shut and she slept. I sent Alice to find Lord Jasper.

'You are right, my lord,' I told him, having left the maid in my place beside the bed of our mistress and sat down with him in the anteroom. 'Lady Margaret is very distraught. She should not be left alone.'

'She should not be pregnant,' he said angrily. 'God knows I greatly mourn my brother's death but were he still alive I could kill him. He should not have consummated his marriage so soon. It was tantamount to murdering her. I fear she will not survive.' On a smothered sob he sank his head in his hands.

Only the distance between our chairs prevented me taking his hand to comfort him. It was clear to me that he cared deeply for the girl. He had looked at her as if he would like to throw himself at her feet, offer her anything her heart desired, bring her the moon on a platter if only it would relieve her pain, if only it would make her smile. I did not know what obsession looked like but I instinctively knew that Jasper was obsessed, and the great change in his appearance was due to this. I was to learn that the nobility called this courtly love. I considered it senseless folly.

I summoned my rallying tone, the one I used for Bethan when she was in labour. 'Take heart, my lord; I do not believe she will die. We still have time to calm her distress, feed her up and teach her how to bear a child. It will not be the first time a girl of thirteen has given birth and it will not be the last. But she has obviously been mourning alone for too long. Before you brought her here she must have felt abandoned and terrified. Does she have no family of her own to support her?'

'She has a large family but they are scattered all over England. Her mother, Lady Welles, is apparently unwell and unable to travel and her sister Edith is about to give birth to her own first child. At court we only heard of my brother's capture a month ago, then a ransom was raised and we expected him to be released imminently. News of his death came as a terrible shock. Margaret needs someone practical and kind like you to befriend her, Jane. You were the first person I thought of . . .' He leaned forward beseechingly. 'Just tell me what you need and I will provide it.'

* * *

Slowly Lady Margaret regained her appetite and recovered some of the energy and vitality I remembered having at her age, although of course I had not been pregnant nor had to contemplate the fearsome prospect of giving birth. I believed it was this fear that drew her so frequently to the castle chapel. She heard Mass every morning and only missed a second Mass in the evening if she was feeling particularly tired. Her faith seemed to sustain her and she derived great solace from ordering her days according to the Church calendar. When she was not in the chapel she read books or sewed tiny chemises and embroidered a beautiful baptism gown and coif for the baby in fine silk thread. Her needlework was immaculate and she designed her own patterns. Jasper was right; she was a gifted girl but she was also a proud one. I was not used to being treated like a servant and frequently I found being in her company like treading on hot coals.

'You should come to Mass with me, Jane,' she said one morning as I helped her into her fur-lined boots in order to cross the Inner Court to the chapel. 'You neglect your duty to God.'

Because I was kneeling at her feet I managed to hide my irritation. It was only when she was in chapel that I had time to attend to the other tasks I had assumed in the household. Jasper had no wife or chatelaine to oversee the domestic arrangements. In general the castle was a male enclave; sentries patrolled the battlements, guards manned the gates, male cooks and scullions sweated in the kitchens, grooms and huntsmen staffed the stables and kennels and archers and men at arms practised their skills incessantly in the outer court. Only in the brewery and the laundry were any women employed and they did not have the manners or the training to be of any use in a lady's solar. I had quickly realized that more female staff were needed as cleaners and tire-women if I was not to become exhausted and Lady Margaret was to be attended in the way to which she was accustomed and on which Jasper insisted. So he had asked the steward to seek out some suitable candidates from among the women of the town and for the first week I was busy interviewing them and inducting those chosen. This had been done while Lady Margaret attended Mass, along with the routine tasks of changing bed linen, ordering meals and obtaining potions and salves from the Pembroke apothecary.

Luckily Alice was of a similar age and mind as me and we worked well together. She always accompanied her mistress to the chapel, for which I was grateful. The Church required attendance once a week and I adhered to that, with confession at Easter and Christmas but otherwise my prayers were said privately and usually in bed at night.

I tied the laces of Lady Margaret's second boot before looking up. 'I believe God knows what my duties are, my lady,' I said, swallowing my impatience. 'And as long as you have Alice to go with you I am satisfied that you are well attended.'

She frowned and took my hand to pull herself out of her chair. 'It is not my soul or Alice's I worry about, Jane, it is yours.'

'Perhaps you will honour me with your prayers for my soul then, my lady, for I feel sure He will listen to you. Now do you have your psalter?'

* * *

Jasper had booked the services of a Pembroke midwife, a bossy but motherly soul called Mallt, who had been recommended by his steward's wife because, apart from having some experience with very young mothers, she also spoke fluent English. Lady Margaret had an abhorrence of revealing any personal physical details which made it hard to estimate when her pregnancy had started and therefore when it might end. Between us, the midwife, Alice and I decided that she should enjoy the Christmas celebrations and begin her confinement at Epiphany.

I had suggested to Jasper that the apartments of the West Hall would be the most suitable for the lying-in. It was in a far corner of the Inner Ward, tucked between the chapel and the original curtain wall of the old castle. It seemed a peaceful place, quiet and shadowy and sheltered from the cruel north wind, well removed from other buildings and occasionally used for accommodating visiting ladies. I thought it ideal for the purpose because Margaret would be able to hear Mass through the door that linked it to the chapel.

But Jasper shook his head. 'No, I do not like the West Hall for the lying-in. It might be fine for the waiting time but not for the actual birth. Do not mothers often cry out loud? And might these cries not be audible during Mass?'

He looked embarrassed to be mentioning this aspect of childbirth but I chided myself that I had not thought of it. 'You are right. Although anywhere in the castle is probably the same, is it not?'

'I have an idea,' he said suddenly. 'My new mansion will be finished, except for some of the interior decoration and we can delay that. You have not yet seen inside but I deliberately planned for the solar block to have a blank wall onto the Outer Court for privacy and it will baffle noise as well. We could install Margaret there and close it to everyone except appointed ladies. All it needs is furnishing and some thick hangings and rugs and it will be quiet and fresh and clean. A new house, perfect for the birth of a new life.'

14

Jane

The Mansion, Pembroke Castle

COCOONED IN HER NEW and shrouded lying-in chamber Margaret barely noticed the snow that came soon after Epiphany to cover the courts of Pembroke Castle under a white blanket. Those of us who ventured out found the exposed stairways treacherous with ice and the cisterns and pumps frozen solid but in the mansion fires burned constantly and somehow Jasper managed to obtain enough wood for fuel to be delivered to us daily. Only women were allowed in the mansion and fortunately a female cook had been found, a Pembroke woman of gentle birth who was only too willing to leave her family to their own devices for what seemed an exorbitant sum but it had to be owned that the dishes that emerged from her kitchen were delectable, despite the scarcities of winter. Although excluded from her company, Jasper gave orders that anything she wanted Lady Margaret must have. She had sophisticated tastes and relished sauces made with copious quantities of costly

165

nutmeg, pepper and cinnamon. Jasper himself rode a mule – not wishing to risk the legs of his precious horses – over the frozen track to Tenby to fetch fresh supplies of spices, embroidery silks and herbal remedies. With her books and needlework, music from a female harper and gossip from anyone who would provide it, the expectant mother remained tranquil and calm.

'He is kicking, Jane,' she said to me from time to time. 'He is a lusty boy. Just here.' She would place her hand over a particular spot on her ever-expanding belly. Then one day, instead of a kick, she felt something else.

'Oh, oh Jane! He is coming. Quick, I must lie down.' Margaret suddenly heaved herself from her chair and threw off the woollen wrap that had been tucked around her.

I looked down, expecting to see tell tale signs that her waters had broken but could spy none. 'Are you sure, my lady?' I asked, offering her my arm. 'Did you feel a pain?'

'Not a pain as such but there was a definite twinge – just here.' She put her hand to the small of her back. 'Should I lie down? I do not want him to fall to the ground.'

At that moment I wondered if perhaps it had been wrong not to explain the process of birth in more detail but she had shown remarkably little curiosity and we had not wanted to disturb her with warnings of how much pain and effort would be required before her precious baby saw the light of day.

'No, that is not necessary yet. It may be a false alarm. Perhaps you have a cramp. Would you like to walk a little?' I suggested. 'It can do no harm to stretch your legs. The baby will not come after just one twinge.'

'How many twinges will it take?' Her brow creased in a

frown and she fixed me with a questioning stare. 'I was with my mother when she started to bring my stepbrother John into the world. I remember the midwife began counting between the pains. They would not let me stay but it did not seem very long before we heard his first cry.'

I had learned something of Lady Welles's history: she was on her third marriage and had given birth to at least eight children prior to John, her last child. 'Babies take their own time, my lady, but the first one usually takes longer than the rest. Come.'

With her small hand tucked into the crook of my elbow we began our slow progress towards the door. It was hung with a heavy curtain and Alice held it back to let us out. I had encouraged Margaret to walk a little each day but because of the snow we could not go outside, exercise was restricted to the hall, a few steps from the lying-in chamber. The hall was magnificent, half-panelled with carved oak, which extended into an ornate mantelpiece over the hearth, where a fire was kept constantly burning, and lit by three mullioned windows looking out over the new garden court. At night these windows were shuttered but at present the wilderness of white outside reflected bright light through their diamond panes and we paused on entry to blink until our eyes adjusted. Slowly and carefully we walked the length of the hall, stopping to peer through the distorting glass at the curious striped tracks made by iron-hooped pattens across the garden paths and the plump white cushions of snow that topped the dark battlements on the round tower across the court.

'What is that tower called, Jane?' Margaret asked. 'We see it every day but I have never known its name.'

'I do not know if it has a name; it is just part of the castle defences and used by the knights and archers.'

'Perhaps Lord Jasper will name it for my son. He does not have a name yet either.' She suddenly clutched at my arm. 'I felt another twinge,' she whispered. 'Is that all right?'

I smiled reassuringly. 'Yes, my lady. If it is not a false alarm they will come at intervals, which will get shorter by degrees, but there is no hurry. Do you feel strong enough to walk a little more?' Looking for distractions I glanced up at the spectacular ceiling. It was crosshatched with dark oak beams, the rectangles between them plastered and painted with heraldic symbols. I pointed upwards. 'I believe those are the coats of arms of Lord Jasper and his relatives. Can you show me your Beaufort badge?'

This took her mind off her twinges for a few minutes while we wandered about the big empty room, gazing upwards, scanning the various images. She reeled the devices off as we went. 'There in the centre are the royal arms, the leopards and lilies, and around them King Henry's antelope, Queen Marguerite's swan and the Prince of Wales's three ostrich feathers. And then there is the red rose of Lancaster and the fleur de lys of France – and are those not Jasper's golden martlets? I do not recognize that one with the three helmets; perhaps it is his father's device but does Owen Tudor have a coat of arms? Ah, there is the Beaufort portcullis and next to it – oh! – is the flowering mount of Richmond.' This last brought tears to her eyes and she turned to me, her face crumpling. 'I wonder if my dear lord knows that his child is coming? I wish he were here to see his son born!'

Although I made soothing noises I regretted that the sight of the Richmond device had defeated my attempt at distraction. It also troubled me that Margaret was so fixed on the child being a boy but considered that now was not the time to admit any doubt about the gender. Another twinge caused her tears to spill more freely and I abandoned any further attempt to extend the walk. Once she was settled back in her bed I sent a message to Jasper that the labour had begun, the midwife should be summoned and the wet nurse warned.

For many hours there was little or no progress. I had only Bethan's births to compare it with but Mallt assured me that all was well. 'Young girls' bodies have to adjust to the process of opening up,' she said. 'Muscles must stretch that have never stretched before and it will hurt.'

Margaret heard this. 'How much will it hurt?' she asked anxiously. 'I am getting pains but they are not as bad as when I sprained my wrist. Will it hurt as much as that?'

Mallt smiled at her kindly. 'It is a different sort of hurt, my lady. You must pray to your patron saint to help you bear it. You are fortunate to be called Margaret for it is she who aids all women in childbirth and particularly those who bear her name. Very soon I will rub your belly and thighs with my special oil, which smells of roses and it will ease the pain.'

'I like the scent of roses. I must be strong so that my son is strong,' said Margaret, becoming breathless as another spasm started.

'We are certain that it will be a boy then, are we?' Mallt sounded sceptical. 'Have you dangled a gold ring over your belly? And did it swing north-south for a boy?'

Margaret was beyond making any comment in return but I spoke for her. 'Lady Margaret has always felt that she was carrying a boy. She does not believe in old wives' tales.'

Mallt chuckled. 'Old wives' tales you call them, do you? Let us try it shall we? And then soon we will see whether the ring is right.' She pulled a length of ribbon from the bosom of her gown and revealed a gold ring attached to it. Holding it over Margaret's belly, she stilled it with her other hand and when she let it go it slowly began to sway to and fro. Mallt watched it for several heartbeats before making her pronouncement. 'East-west. The ring says it is a girl.'

I saw Margaret's eyes widen in protest and took her hand. Her fingers crushed mine and I shared her pain.

Mallt confined the ring once more to her bosom then asked gently, 'Did you confess your sins before your lying-in, my lady? That always makes everything easier.'

Relieved as the pain subsided, Margaret managed to croak, 'I did but it seems a long time ago. Should I do so again? Shall we send for the priest?'

Mallt looked shocked. 'Oh no, my lady, that would never do. Childbirth is women's work. Now that your labour has begun it is doubly bad luck to let a man enter the chamber. We women will all work together and with God and St Margaret's help we will welcome a new life before morning.'

However, when I went out into the great hall to meet with Jasper at dawn I had nothing to report. My expression must have revealed my deep concern because before I could open my mouth he burst into speech. 'Oh Jane! Is she still labouring? Is there no sign of the child yet?'

'I fear not, my lord. She is brave but getting very tired and no wonder.' As I spoke there came a muffled cry from the lying-in chamber, which crescendoed into a long, agonized moan, enough to tear at the hardest heart.

Jasper gasped. 'Lord save her! Can she survive such pain?'

'Have courage, my lord!' I said, cutting short our discussion in order to return to my mistress.

The midwife had instructed me fetch the birthing chair, which had remained out of sight until the appropriate time so that Lady Margaret would not be disturbed by its curious shape. I bent and picked up the chair from where it had been tucked away in a corner near the door to the lying-in chamber, staggering a little as I found it heavier than I had expected.

Jasper stepped forward to steady me and rapped on the door for entry.

I whispered to him, 'Keep praying, my lord, and do not despair. We are doing all we can.'

The labour went on hour after hour. Poor Margaret felt exposed and vulnerable in the birthing chair, perched on its back ledge and racked with pain. I pointed out how she might grip the arms and push and the position would allow the baby to arrive more easily and not fall to the ground and so she agreed to bear it, at least for a while. But at length she no longer had the strength to grip and we lifted her back to the end of the bed where the midwife could tend to her while she lay back, exhausted, on pillows.

'Is there any sign of the head?' I asked Mallt in a whisper, after she had felt under the bedcovers for what seemed like the hundredth time.

She nodded. 'I can feel the crown but it is all too slow. The babe will die if I do not help.'

At that moment Margaret let out a piteous moan, which escalated into a full-blooded scream as a new and prolonged contraction tore at her fragile body. Mallt called for a light as she ripped off the top quilt and tented the sheet beneath, thrusting her head under it. I held a lamp near so that its light shone through the white linen.

Tense minutes passed. It did not seem possible that Margaret could have the strength to scream any louder but then she did and moments later a red-faced Mallt emerged from under the sheet . . . to my horror, her hands and the sheet were covered in blood. 'I have had to cut her,' she said. It was then that I realized with horror that the midwife's long thumbnail was sharpened like a blade.

I stumbled away, gulping for air as my mind filled with dreadful and bloody images and the lamp nearly dropped from my hand. Trembling violently I set it down and then another prolonged groan filled the room and Mallt's urgent cry called me back to sense and duty.

'Jane, bring a towel quick – I have the babe!'

15

Jasper

Pembroke Castle

I SPENT THE SEEMINGLY interminable period of Margaret's labour kneeling before the altar in the Pembroke chapel. In the freezing small hours of the morning I begged God to spare Margaret's life, even over and above that of her child and I realized with an appalling sense of guilt that my motives were as selfish as Edmund's ever were. I wanted her to live because if she died it would be my fault for letting Edmund get his own way as he had done all his life. I should have fought harder for her, persuaded King Henry that I, not Edmund, should marry her because I would care for her wellbeing so much more than he. I felt I had spinelessly abandoned her and now, if she lived, I would be forced to abandon her again because by marrying Edmund, whether the babe lived or not, she had become my sister and I was forbidden by the laws of consanguinity to marry her, as the mother of my brother's child.

On the third day of Margaret's ordeal Jane came at dawn

– she found me prostrate before the Holy Rood, my face wet with tears. She knelt and touched my shoulder. 'Is she dead?' I asked, my voice a croak.

'No, my lord, but she may be close to death. She has lost much blood and is insensible, but the child is a healthy boy.'

I hauled myself up onto one knee, my head swimming. 'Close to death you say. How close?'

Jane looked as pale as death herself and shook her head. 'I do not know. There is also the ever-present threat of fever. Your prayers will be needed more than ever.'

'Oh dear God Almighty, save her!' I cried, turning back to the altar and making the sign of the cross. 'What does the midwife say of her condition?'

'She says Lady Margaret is lucky the baby is small, though he is strong. Nevertheless he should be baptized as soon as possible.'

I ran my hand over my face, trying to remove all sign of my tears. 'Yes. I will alert the priest and then we will bring him here.'

Jane brought the baby out of the lying-in chamber with a lace-trimmed chemise over his swaddling and a beautifully embroidered coif tied over his head so that all I could see of his features were crumpled red cheeks, a small, straight mouth and tightly-closed, rather puffy eyes. Knowing that his mother lay at death's door seemed to rob me of all feeling for the child. He was my nephew but I could summon no sense of kinship.

Then the midwife carried him wrapped in a thick woollen shawl through a crowd of curious servants and soldiers who greeted the newborn with blessings and applause as we walked past them to the Inner Gate and the castle chapel.

At the font I undertook the godfather role and passed the baby to the priest.

'Who names this child?' he asked.

'I do,' I answered, realizing that I had no idea what name to give him.

Then all at once it came to me, perhaps as a way to induce in myself some sense of family connection, and as I made the declaration the list of Welsh patronyms ran fluently off my tongue. 'His name is Owen – Owen ab Edmund ap Maredudd ap Tudur.'

* * *

'A fine name for a Son of Prophecy!' declared Lewys Glyn Cothi in his lilting Welsh-accented English. The poet had appeared at the castle gate at noon as if he knew by magic that the expected child had been born. His intuition had also brought him on foot through a fall of snow from Haverford in time to join me at dinner. 'This young Owen is descended from Cadwalladr and the great Princes of Wales, just as you are yourself, Lord Jasper. The prophecy says that one such called Owen will raise the red dragon standard and become our saviour. We call him *Y Mab Daragon*!'

'That is bardic nonsense!' I said, irritable from lack of sleep. 'As far as I am concerned he is named for his grandfather.'

'It does not matter if his name is Thomas, Dafydd or Harri,' the poet persisted. 'It is his lineage that matters and this little Owen has it.'

'I still think his mother should have been consulted about the name, my lord,' Jane said. I had invited her to join us although she was about as interested in her food as I was in mine.

'His mother is at death's door,' I snapped. 'Otherwise of course she could have named him herself.'

'I am sorry I did not ask her for a name before she fell into a faint,' Jane snapped back. 'She was crying out to Saint Margaret to save her from the pain and suddenly she was unconscious.'

'You have all suffered a momentous birth,' said Lewys, pausing in his rapid consumption of a bowl of fish stew. He went on soothingly, 'Some sleep will bring you peace, and you will recover, just as the babe's mother will.'

As the eccentric bard had foretold, by the following day I felt considerably better, and more so when Alice came to say that her mistress was awake and had asked for me. I had no place in the lying-in chamber, I knew that, but I blundered in there like a charging bull, before any protective female could deny me entry. Margaret was no longer awake and the sleeping face that confronted me from the pillows was terrifyingly pale but the cowering nurse told me this was a good sign. 'It means there is no fever,' she said in a whisper. 'My lady is very weak from loss of blood but if the fever stays at bay she will slowly recover her strength.'

'And the baby?' I asked, glancing at the cradle, set as close as was safe to the hearth. A young and rather bosomy lady dozed nearby – the wet nurse I deduced – but Jane was nowhere to be seen. I assumed she had retired somewhere to sleep off her exhaustion.

The nurse smiled. 'Her son has been feeding well and seems strong.'

At the sound of voices Margaret stirred and opened her

eyes. 'Lord Jasper, he must be baptized,' she said immediately, her voice weak but insistent.

I knelt down beside her. 'God be praised you are recovering, Margaret. You must not worry, he has been baptized already.'

'Yes, so I heard.' Her head rolled from side to side on the pillow in agitation. 'But he must be baptized again. His name is not Owen. Lord Edmund wished his son to be called after his brother the king. His name is to be Henry. Also Bishop de la Bere agreed to be a godfather but he will need a proxy.' The effort of making even this short speech drained her strength and her eyes closed again.

I was not sure if the Church sanctioned second baptisms but rather than embarrass the chaplain who had performed the first one, I decided to ask Father Richard Warren, the vicar of St Mary's church, which lay beside the castle gatehouse. I considered the first to have been an emergency baptism and the names I had spoken spontaneously given to ensure the child's place in heaven and the priest made no objection. The baby was dressed once more in his beautiful chemise and baptismal coif and wrapped up against the snow-cold air. Once more I performed my role as godfather to Owen Tudor's grandson and this time under the statue of the Virgin in the Pembroke church, with Steward Dŵnn standing proxy for Bishop de la Bere, Edmund's wish for his child's name to be Henry was fulfilled. As if in confirmation of the correct choice of name the baby gave a loud sneeze when the Holy Water ran off his brow, proclaiming that this time the Evil One had left him.

* * *

Later, when back at court in Kenilworth, I witnessed Henry's delight on hearing that Edmund's son had been named for him, and I regretted my initial instinct to call the babe Owen. While the Tudor connection might be important in Wales, in England the boy's interests would depend on his connection to the Lancastrian throne. I must do my best for him.

I had been obliged to return to court as soon as the thaw came. I heard from Jane often, the baby thrived and Margaret's health slowly improved. The letter I received towards the end of February informed me that at last Margaret had recovered enough strength to move from her bed to a chair but it would be well into March before she would be fit to emerge from her confinement.

I was pleased to see that in the peaceful and safe environment of Kenilworth my half-brother had recovered his physical health, although perhaps had not returned to full mental capacity. But I was able to discuss with him the appointment of a commission to enquire into Edmund's death and the need to make arrangements for his widow and son.

The king announced at the next meeting of the Great Council that he would confer the vacant Richmond title, which was a royal honour, on his nephew Henry Tudor, our late and much-lamented brother's son.

Then he went on, to my surprise, 'However, the boy's mother is still a minor, too young to have his custody. We will grant that to his uncle, the Earl of Pembroke, with an allowance for his keep from the Richmond estates and the bulk of their revenues reverting to the crown for the time being. The title Countess of Richmond will remain with

Lady Margaret, as will the Somerset estates, and we will find her a suitable marriage as soon as the mourning period has elapsed so that they may be well supervised.'

Later the king explained his intentions further. 'As matters stand in the realm at present, Jasper, I cannot grant you the full revenue from the Richmond estates during your ward-ship of young Henry, because it will stir resentment among certain of my nobles.'

'I am sure his grace does not need to spell out which noble in particular,' remarked Queen Marguerite tartly. Seldom far from her husband's side, she seemed to have taken the place formerly filled by the king's successive favour-ites, the Dukes of Suffolk and Somerset, whose deaths she had deeply mourned and blamed on one man alone, the man whose name did not pass her lips.

I nodded and observed casually, 'We have not seen his grace of York at court since the Protectorate ended. Has he other business? Perhaps his duchess has produced yet another child to add to their plenteous family?'

Marguerite's lip curled. 'You are perceptive, Jasper, but at least it is another girl. I keep telling the king that he should send the duke back to Ireland. Children do not thrive there they tell me.'

I acknowledged her cold smile, knowing that her real hope was that one of Ireland's notorious bogs would swallow up Richard, Duke of York completely. 'And how is the Prince of Wales, your grace?' I asked. 'He must be three by now – practically a knight!'

'Édouard is well, thank you. The Kenilworth air suits him.' This time the queen was the one to choose an apparent non sequitur. 'I find it interesting that your sister-in-law chose to call her son Henry, rather than Edmund after his sire.'

'I believe it was his father's greatest wish, if he had a son, to name him after his brother, Madame. Perhaps he thought it a small but enduring way of expressing his gratitude to the king.'

'A small way as yet,' Marguerite observed dryly, 'but the boy will grow, if he is healthy. Is he?'

'Yes, so I am told, but Lady Margaret and her son have yet to emerge from her confinement. It was a lengthy birth and fraught with danger for them both. I thank Almighty God daily for their deliverance.'

'Lady Margaret is so very young,' King Henry broke in, frowning. 'We must find her someone wiser and less head-strong than Edmund for her next husband.'

I could not argue with that. Nevertheless the thought of Margaret re-marrying caused me pain I found hard to conceal.

'What do you think of Buckingham's younger son, Sir Henry Stafford?' This bolt from the blue came from the queen. 'His elder brother still suffers grievously from wounds he received defending the king at St Albans but at least he has a young son to inherit the dukedom. The Staffords are a powerful family and staunch Lancastrians and the king and I think Sir Henry would make a good husband for Lady Margaret. He is a kind and considerate man, still young enough to father a family and he would be a worthy lord of the Somerset estates. Do you know him?'

I had to clear my throat to release my strangled voice. 'Yes, Madame, I too fought at St Albans, if you remember.' Sir Henry was not a regular at court but I recalled him as a good reliable knight and a gentle, unassuming man who was unlikely to use marriage with the Somerset heiress to elbow him to the forefront of power, a situation that would clearly suit Queen Marguerite in her assumed role as the king's mouthpiece.

'I think you should consult with Buckingham before you return to Pembroke, Jasper.' Queen Marguerite voiced this as an order rather than a suggestion. 'Sir Henry and Lady Margaret are second cousins so a papal dispensation will be needed.'

'I could not commit Lady Margaret without a meeting between them,' I responded, bristling under her brusque tone. These days I found it hard to detect in Marguerite the alluring teenager who had married the king.

Henry roused himself to exert his authority. 'Let them meet,' he urged, 'as soon as she is strong enough. I will have the Chancellor apply to the Holy Father for a dispensation. Nothing will be lost if it is not used.'

I had no choice but to comply. By the end of March Margaret was able to ride and we stayed at Caldicot for the promised meeting, which took place at the Buckingham manor of Ebbw, only a short distance away. Little Harri was left with Jane and his wet nurse at Pembroke and on the journey Margaret was constantly fretful about the separation and understandably nervous at the prospect of meeting Sir Henry Stafford.

'I really do not wish to marry again,' she declared more than once. 'I would prefer to go back to my mother or stay with you at Pembroke.'

I hated having to deny her. 'It is the king's wish, Margaret, and your mother agrees with him. You know that a young lady like you needs to be married if she is not to take holy vows. It is to protect your estates, but I promise it does not have to be to Sir Henry Stafford if you do not like him. Whoever it is to be, I will make sure it is not until next year. Meanwhile you are very welcome to stay at Pembroke, both you and Harri.'

Although this seemed to mollify her a little, she was still peevish. 'I do not like Henry being called Harri. I have told Jane but she still does it.'

'It is the Welsh version of Henry and not a bad name to carry. Harri of Monmouth, the victor of Agincourt, was possibly the greatest Lancastrian of all. And it distinguishes your son from other English Henrys – like the king and your potential new husband for instance,' I said. 'When Harri is older he can use his grown-up name if he wishes.'

'When he is older the world will call him Richmond,' she said proudly. 'I am grateful to the king for granting him his father's title, if not his estates.'

'They will come later, when he is older, I dare say.'

Margaret shrugged. 'I expect you are right.' Clearly unconvinced, she sat her palfrey as proudly as a princess, her back ramrod straight, but so soon after her confinement she was using a side-saddle for comfort.

I did not like to tell her at this stage that her marriage would not bring about a change in her son's custody. When she went to live with her new husband, whether it was Sir Henry or another, she would not be taking Harri with her, for his care and upbringing had been assigned to me.

16

Jane

Pembroke Castle

'WELL, WHAT DID YOU think of Sir Henry, my lady?' Lord Jasper had made it clear to Lady Margaret that despite royal enthusiasm for the match with the Duke of Buckingham's younger son, it was entirely reliant on her consent. I believed he might secretly have been hoping that she would refuse it. Having heard her praise Lord Edmund so highly I too thought she might have done so. Therefore, her answer to my question surprised me.

'He is nothing like my dear Lord Edmund of course – a little older and not as handsome – but I liked him, Jane. At first he was very quiet and let his father do all the talking but while Jasper and his grace of Buckingham were discussing terms and contracts Sir Henry kept glancing at me and smiling, just a small twitch of the lips and twinkle of the eye, so that I found that I could not wait to talk to him and to hear what he had to say.'

'And you liked what you heard?'

She looked a little sheepish, as if her memory of their conversation still surprised her. 'Yes, I did. His voice is low and musical and he asked me what I liked to do, what entertainments and games I enjoyed and it turned out that his favourite pastimes are very similar to mine. He likes reading and hunting and hawking and even dancing, just as I do. And he is also devout, attending Mass daily and favouring St Catherine and St John the Baptist in his prayers. Although I am so much younger than him, I felt we might be kindred spirits – is that not astonishing?'

Privately I thought that the prospect of becoming lord of the Somerset estates would be good reason for any younger son to be charming, especially when the widowed heiress was lively and attractive, but I nodded agreement. 'Yes, it certainly is. But you say he is not handsome?'

Margaret pursed her lips. 'Not exactly, but he is pleasant looking and he dresses well – not extravagantly but elegantly, favouring muted colours, his doublet not too short and not too long.'

I laughed at this detail. 'He sounds the perfect gentleman,' I said.

She frowned a little. 'Not completely perfect. I do not like his beard. It is dark, like his hair, but he wears it trimmed into forked points. It makes him look like the Duke of York.'

I sucked in my cheeks. 'Not good on a Lancastrian. But still, perhaps a clever wife could effect a change.'

She gave me a sly smile. 'Exactly what I thought.'

'So have you agreed to marry him?'

The smile vanished in a solemn nod. 'Yes I have, but not immediately. Lord Jasper told his grace of Buckingham that

I needed time to mourn Lord Edmund and recover from Henry's birth. The wedding will be at the beginning of next year. There will never be another for me like Lord Edmund but I understand that I must have the protection of a powerful family and the duke was very reassuring on that point. I think I have done the right thing.'

It was almost a question, and her eyes sought mine. I had not met Sir Henry Stafford so I could hardly make an informed comment but at the same time I had no wish to sow any seeds of doubt in her mind. 'I expect you have prayed for guidance, my lady, and been led to make the right decision,' I said. 'You will have won the approval of the king and in the Council the Duke of Buckingham will be able to serve your interest.'

She sighed, her mask of self-assurance still slightly askew. 'Yes, I think it will be all right. I hope it will. Anyway a lot can happen in a year.'

* * *

As Jasper put it, as he had no wife to act as chaperone and counsellor for Margaret, it would be 'improper' for him to remain at Pembroke while Margaret lived there. He said, 'Now that she is betrothed to Henry Stafford there must be no hint of a stain on her character.'

'But you are her legal guardian,' I protested. 'How can there be any scandal attached to you both living under the same roof? Also I am here as chaperone.'

He shook his head. 'I mean no disparagement, Jane, but you are young and unmarried and do not have the status to be a guard against scandal. However, you are the best friend Margaret could have and an excellent governess for little Harri and I do not want to import a stranger into the household, a lady from court, for instance. Until the wedding, I will make my headquarters at Tenby. It is only a few miles away. I will not be abandoning you.'

I said nothing but thoughts raced in my head, the most pertinent being that it was not Lady Margaret who required protection from slander but Lord Jasper who needed removal from the object of his hopeless attachment.

He took my silence as evidence of affront. 'Please do not take offence. I wish to confound the gossips, not to upset our friendship, Jane.'

I wondered how he would react if I blurted out that I did not want his friendship, I wanted what he felt for Lady Margaret, except that if he gave it to me it would not be hopeless. Instead I merely asked, 'Where will you live in Tenby, my lord? I believe the castle there is ruinous.'

He looked relieved at my acceptance. 'Yes, it has been neglected for years and I am working with the Tenby Guilds to reinforce the town's defences. I will be renting a house from the Mayor, Master White, who is also my vintner. He and his fellow merchants have made Tenby a flourishing port and feel the urgent need of increased fortification, especially against incursion from the sea – by pirates and the French.'

'Well, before you leave us perhaps you would make arrangements with your Master of Hawking,' I said. 'If you remember you promised Lady Margaret that she could continue learning the skill and offered to let me join her lessons.'

Jasper smiled triumphantly. 'I have not forgotten and Thomas Falconer has instructions to begin them, for you as well, whenever Margaret is ready. But I have a favour to ask you in return. I need to improve my grasp of Welsh if I am to have any chance of negotiating properly with Gruffydd ap Nicholas and his sons, as I will have to over the summer. You would make the ideal teacher, Jane, if you would spare me the time.'

As spring warmed and blossomed, Lady Margaret flew her own merlin, Elaine, resplendent with emerald bells, whilst I was allocated a bird from the castle collection. Elaine responded with alacrity to the sound of her owner's voice, whereas my 'hawk of the day' was invariably temperamental and I began to yearn for one of my own. Lord Jasper rode over from Tenby regularly to attend to castle business and to get his tongue around some useful Welsh phrases. On one of these occasions we happened to meet in the mews when he came to visit his peregrine, Arthur, who was sitting out his moult.

It was then I learned from Jasper that the peregrine and the merlin are the prerogative of earls and countesses and the reason I was only ever allowed a goshawk was because that is the yeoman's bird. 'Actually you should be grateful,' Jasper said, 'in my experience the gos is the wilier hunter and will fill your game-pouch more quickly.' Seeing my mulish expression, he went on, 'Besides, Jane, you will never get Master Falconer to allow you to break rules that emerged from the mists of time, and you must not cross him. I pay him more than my Treasurer and I cannot afford to lose him if I am to play Pembrokeshire's overlord convincingly.'

'Why did you agree to let me learn falconry with Lady Margaret then, my lord, if you knew I would always be at a disadvantage?' Perhaps Arthur was sensitive to my petulant tone for he suddenly bated off Jasper's fist and flapped wildly upside down until his master managed to restore him to his dignified upright stance. Even though he was hooded, the falcon assumed an injured air, averting his head from my direction.

Jasper stroked Arthur's breast and whispered a few consoling words to him before turning back to me, his brow creased deeply in a frown. 'Is anything the matter, Jane? I have explained about the hawking protocol, surely it cannot simply be that?'

He was right and more perceptive than I had given him credit for. His manner was gentle, full of concern and we were close together in the twilight of the mews. I had spent so many years keeping my feelings to myself, disguising them from the world and above all from him. His face was inches from mine, his soft, full lips curved in a half-smile and his bright blue eyes wide with enquiry. Arid years of unfulfilled longing rushed in on me and my control snapped.

'No, it has nothing to do with hawking. It is simply this.' Impulsively I went on tiptoe to kiss him. I felt his instinctive, startled surprise at the sudden contact change gradually to eager acceptance and there was a long moment of spine-tingling pleasure while our lips remained fused and I believed my heart might burst. Then I felt his withdrawal, not with a sudden jerk but with a reluctant, almost apologetic removal of consent.

We broke apart and for several silent moments we gazed at each other, the space between us filled with unspoken questions and then his sandy lashes dropped over his eyes. 'No, Jane, this cannot be,' he said hoarsely. 'I am sorry.'

I had no intention of begging but nevertheless I could

hear the agonized pleading in my response. 'Why can it not be? We are not such close cousins that it is forbidden, we are both free and I have loved you since the first time you came to Tŷ Cerrig. You cannot deny that you find me attractive and you know that you can never have Lady Margaret.' His eyes flashed at the mention of her name and I continued hurriedly. 'I do not mind if you do not love me now. Later you will. We would be happy together, I know it.'

He rubbed his forehead distractedly and then bent to take both my hands in his. This time he did not allow his gaze to leave mine. 'I do love you, in my fashion. But this has nothing to do with love, Jane. It has to do with honour – and dishonour. Marriage between us is impossible. My brother the king would never permit it.'

'Why would he never permit it?' I knew I sounded desperate and I hated myself for it but, regardless, I had to scratch at the wound that was already bleeding. 'I am of common stock I know, but that same stock was good enough for King Henry's mother – your mother – and she was a queen. Why should he deny you what he allowed her?'

'He did not allow her – she married without permission and it is only because King Henry is a forgiving monarch and our mother is dead that he has overlooked her transgression. He would not do the same for me. Besides I owe him my loyalty and compliance, simply because he has chosen to recognize me as his brother.'

'But he has not acknowledged you out of kindness. He has done it because he needs you. Apart from his wife and baby son you are the only close family he has. You are his knight champion. The gauntlet on his hand, always ready to fend off his enemies. He will not disown you if you follow your heart.'

'Perhaps not but he will no longer trust me.' Jasper sighed and cupped my chin in his hand, gazing more deeply into my eyes. 'I am not a free man, Jane, but that is of my own choosing. You must believe me when I say that I will never betray his trust. I will always support and defend my brother the king as long as I have breath in my body.'

'And what if he never gives you permission to marry?' I was losing heart. The look in his eyes told me I had made a mistake in revealing my true feelings for him.

He shrugged and dropped his hand, leaving me bereft. 'Then I shall die without issue. I may do so, even if I do marry. It is all in God's hands.'

I wanted to tell him that I would love him and give him children without the sanction of marriage but I did not want to hear the word 'honour' again. I had heard enough of Lord Jasper's thoughts on that subject.

17

Jane

Pembroke Castle

T HE FEAST OF ALL Souls came and went and Harri loved the guising and the games we played to scare the evil spirits away. Maredudd dressed up as an imp, his face blackened with ashes, and leapt through a flaming ring to flee, capering in fear at the sight of a wooden crucifix decorated with evergreens, causing the nine-month-old infant to laugh and clap his chubby hands. In Jasper's new mansion the gloom of the lying-in chamber was a distant memory; it had become our playroom, with colourful hangings and cushions, rugs on the floor and a guard before the fire to prevent accidents. Harri had been weaned onto bread messes, vegetable pottage and ewe's milk from a special cup and the wet nurse had returned to her home in Pembroke.

November rain and gales howled in, sending us all to seek warmth around the hearth and tell each other ghost stories. Lord Jasper's couriers brought letters and Lady Margaret maintained a regular correspondence with Sir

Henry Stafford. His latest missive held news of the wedding.

'We are to be married on January 3rd at Maxstoke Castle,' she said, looking up from reading it. 'Oh that is a pretty place. I went there once with my mother. It is only two days' ride from Bletsoe.'

I looked up from my sewing. 'And will your mother come to the wedding?'

'Possibly not, I think she may hold Christmas in Lincolnshire. But you will come I hope, Jane. And Jasper too, of course.' Margaret pouted a little. 'What a shame Henry does not yet walk or he could have stood beside me as my supporter.'

I smiled at the thought. 'He will not be one year old. A little young perhaps.'

'I have been meaning to ask whether you will continue as Henry's governess after I am married, Jane? It would be so good for him to have someone familiar there while he accustoms himself to new surroundings.'

I bit my lip, considering. I was very fond of baby Harri and I admired his clever, accomplished young mother, but did I really want to go to live in England? Indeed did I want to leave Pembroke, to which Jasper Tudor would surely always return while he remained its earl? But how could I remain in his household if there was no little Harri to look after and no Lady Margaret to attend?

I prevaricated. 'Of course I would be honoured to remain with you and Harri but it might involve some negotiation with Lord Jasper, to whom I have sworn allegiance; and with my father, who expects me back under his roof when my task here comes to an end.'

Margaret did not consider these hurdles to be of any consequence. 'I will speak to Jasper,' she said, tucking the letter from Sir Henry away in the casket she kept for the purpose and locking it with the key she wore on a gold chain around her neck. 'I think he will not deny me.'

But on this matter she was wrong. During his next visit to the nursery when I mentioned Lady Margaret's offer Lord Jasper's expression immediately darkened and he left me, tossing an odd remark over his shoulder as he left. 'Do not pack your saddlebags yet, Jane.'

The next thing I heard was a wail of dissent from the solar and Lady Margaret's voice raised in anguish. 'No! That is not possible. It is not right. I will not allow this! You can stop it, Jasper, I know you can.'

Jasper's low, murmured response was indecipherable but Margaret's shrill retort was clearly audible and very revealing. 'The king can say what he likes. He is only Henry's uncle. I am his mother and I am not leaving Pembroke without my son.'

I caught my breath. I knew Lord Jasper had been made Lady Margaret's guardian after Lord Edmund's death but had custody of her son also been granted to him? After their marriage Sir Henry would assume charge over his wife but he would not automatically take custody of her son, especially when the boy was of the blood royal. I understood enough of court procedure to realize that ultimate responsibility for his care resided with the king, who had the power to delegate it wherever he chose. I also knew for a fact that it had never entered Margaret's head that it might not be granted to her.

Harri was having a nap when Margaret rushed into the

nursery wearing her green riding kirtle, a hat and boots. 'Can you find your brother for me, Jane?' she demanded, for once not considering the slumbers of her precious son. 'The Marshall will not allow me to take my palfrey out alone.'

I put my finger to my lips and ushered her gently out of the nursery. 'Why now, my lady? It is nearly dinner time and threatening rain.' I peered at her more closely. 'Have you been crying? What is the matter?'

She brushed my questions aside. 'Never mind that. I am angry. I need air and I need speed. Riding clears my head. Perhaps you would come with me too, Jane? Alice can watch the baby.'

'If you wish it but neither of us goes without a cloak.'

I fetched two cloaks from the guardrobe and pulled on my boots, also stowed there. On my return I said, 'Maredudd will be at arms practice still and he will not be pleased to miss his dinner.'

Margaret did not quite stamp her foot but she became dauntingly haughty. 'Tell him to fetch some food from the kitchen on my orders. Do not be long. I will see you both in the stables.' Snatching her cloak from me, she ran off down the nearby stair.

With a sigh I hastened to carry out my errands, thinking I had never known Margaret so forceful. She had shown an amazing ability to exert her will. Was this the effect of royal blood in the veins I wondered? I found Alice and sent her to the nursery and set off in search of Maredudd. As I had predicted, he was not best pleased at the prospect of missing the main meal of the day. 'What ails her?' he complained, glancing up at the dark mass of cloud gathering in the north sky behind the Great Tower. 'It is hardly the weather for riding out.'

'Something Lord Jasper said has made her angry. She is headstrong and wants to ride fast somewhere. Where do you suggest?' We were striding across the Outer Ward in the direction of the stables.

'I suppose we could head along the river towards Lamphey. It should be more sheltered there.' As we passed, fragrant steam belched from the door of the castle kitchen and Maredudd nudged me in its direction. 'I have been training since first light. Fetch some food, sis. I cannot do this on an empty stomach.' I had forgotten to pass on to him Lady Margaret's order that *he* should get food from the kitchen and now could not bring myself to mention it.

The head cook hated women in his kitchen. 'Keep out!' he snarled at me. 'You will curdle the sauce!'

I ignored him and ran through to the bakery. The pastry cook was more amenable and tossed several pasties into a linen bag when I explained my errand. 'Bring the bag back!' he ordered but smiled as he handed it over.

I had not been long but when I got to the stables there was no sign of Lady Margaret or Maredudd. The duty groom gave a shrug and reluctantly set down the barrowload of horse dung he was wheeling out to the midden. 'My lady was in a hurry,' he said. 'She said you should catch them up.'

'Is there a horse I can take?' I asked. A glance down the line of stalls did not reveal a saddled mount.

The groom shook his head. 'No women allowed to ride out alone. Not without the Marshall's say-so and he went to the hall for his dinner.'

I glared at him. 'So how am I to catch them up?'

He shrugged again and bent to raise the barrow's legs. 'No idea,' he said rudely and trundled it away under the stable arch, leaving me seething and anxious. There was nothing else for it; I would have to tell Lord Jasper.

By the time he had mustered a posse of men, all grumbling about going on a wild goose chase unfed, the rain had begun to fall in torrents. Although I had pulled the hood of my cloak well down over my brow I could feel the sting of the raindrops on my cheeks.

'Margaret will be soaked,' Jasper fretted. 'What can have possessed her to go off like this? Thank the Blessed Virgin that Maredudd is with her at least.'

It was not until we were trotting past St Mary's church and down the hill to the river that I plucked up courage to ask, 'What did you say to her earlier, my lord? She was very upset by something.'

A guilty look crossed his face and he glanced about to see if there were other ears to hear. 'Perhaps I should have told her this before but I did not want to give her too long to brood over it. Young Harri is to stay here at Pembroke. The king wants me to oversee his upbringing.'

My suspicions were confirmed. The mighty power of the crown was removing Lady Margaret's little boy from her care. There would be no argument, no right of appeal, no consideration of a mother's feelings. However hard she railed against it, racing through the wind and rain to vent her feelings, at the end of her ride nothing would have changed. Lady Margaret Beaufort was to go to her new husband as an unencumbered bride and someone else would raise the child she had nearly died to bring into the world. It was a *fait accompli*, tantamount to abduction.

'Oh dear God,' I said, my voice shaking with fury. 'I should think she will want to ride and ride and ride until she drops.'

A look of horror drained all colour from Jasper's rain-washed cheeks. 'Oh no, we will find her. We *must* find her. Are you sure they headed this way?'

'Well that was Maredudd's idea and she might see Lamphey as some kind of refuge. What else have we to go on? At least she is not alone.'

'I will never forgive myself if she comes to any harm,' he yelled over the sough of the wind in the trees lining the course of the Pembroke River. Raising his arm, he called an order and the whole posse broke into a canter along the well-worn bankside trail. 'St Margaret preserve my lady of Richmond!' Jasper shouted into the gathering gale. 'A cask of wine to the first to sight her.'

We found them several miles further on, where the river curled around the outskirts of Lamphey village to flow under a bridge into the demesne of the bishop's palace. Lady Margaret was lying prone among the exposed roots of a willow and no man could have been more relieved to see us approach than Maredudd, who leapt up from her side and grabbed Jasper's bridle.

'God be praised you have come, my lord,' he cried, his teeth chattering. 'It was a tree root – Lady Margaret's horse tripped.'

Jasper swung down from the saddle, not waiting to hear more. I followed more slowly, careful to pull my skirts over the cantle before jumping down; we did not need two unconscious women lying in the rain. Jasper had thrown himself to his knees beside Margaret, hands clasped, eyes closed, his lips moving in prayer. It was as if he could not bear to look on her and find her dead.

'She is stirring, my lord,' I said, dropping down to lay my hand on the girl's brow. I could see her eyelids fluttering and put my mouth to her ear. 'Can you hear me, my lady? It is Jane.' Her eyes flew open, full of alarm and she tried to rise but I firmly pushed her down. 'No, no. You must stay still until we see if you are hurt. You have had a fall. Can you feel any pain?' The hood of her cloak had fallen back and drips from the branches above were splashing on her face. Her hat was missing; I felt carefully around her head and neck to see if there was any blood and sighed with relief to discover that it was only water soaking her hair.

'My shoulder hurts,' she said, shrinking from my touch. I noticed that her arm was caught underneath her body and I eased it very gently clear. She cried out but not in agony. 'That is better,' she said. I saw her skirts move as she tested her legs. When she spoke again, her voice was hesitant but remarkably calm. 'I – do not think anything is broken.'

I heard Jasper expel his breath in a long sigh. 'Jesu be thanked,' he murmured and stood up, turning to his men and re-assuming command. 'Someone find Lady Margaret's palfrey. Maredudd, go to the palace and tell them we are bringing her in. The Infirmarian can prepare a bed and she can rest overnight. Jane, you will stay with her. Can she walk, or should I carry her?'

'Help me up, Jane,' said Lady Margaret, gingerly raising herself but noticeably saving her right arm. With her left hand, slowly and carefully I hauled her to her feet and she immediately turned her back on Lord Jasper. 'It is just my arm that hurts. I can walk, thank you.'

The earl dashed moisture from his face; it may have been tears, it may have been raindrops. Frowning despondently at her averted back, he said, 'I will come with you to the palace, Margaret, to make sure they look after you.'

I supported her at her waist as she put her good arm around my shoulders. 'That will not be necessary, my lord. Jane will take me.' Her voice sounded hard and uncompromising, her raw resentment at the custody arrangement painfully evident.

We lay one night at the bishop's palace but Lady Margaret would not stay longer. She said it held too many memories of Lord Edmund and I understood her wish to get away, especially as, apart from the wrenched shoulder and a few bruises, she had been lucky – or else she had divine protection. When she rose the following morning her first action was to go to the palace chapel and thank St Margaret for preserving her from serious injury. The palace servants had dried our outer garments and the gale had blown itself out. Maredudd rode over from Pembroke on a pillion saddle and she travelled back behind him at a sedate pace. On the road we met Lord Jasper coming to check on her condition but once again she averted her gaze and answered him only in monosyllables.

The earl turned his horse to ride beside me, his distress at Lady Margaret's snub very evident. 'Do you think she will ever forgive me, Jane?' he murmured. 'I did not want wardship of Harri but the king and the queen both insisted.'

I sympathized but did not say so. From what I had heard of Queen Marguerite's determined grasp on power, I suspected Harri's custody had been her idea. If he was reared far away in Pembroke, his drop of royal blood would be forgotten and the court would regard her own small boy as the uncontested heir to the succession.

'Surely her resentment will pass, given time,' Jasper persisted, his gaze fixed on Lady Margaret's back.

'I would not bank on it,' I said, sensing the fierce anger and distress somehow radiating from her rigid shoulder blades.

When, later in the month, I agreed to remain in charge of Harri's nursery at Pembroke I begged Jasper not to tell Margaret until the last minute – but inevitably she guessed and demanded to be allowed to take Harri to spend Christmas at her sister Edith's home near St David's. She also asked Edith and Geoffrey Pole to escort her to her wedding. She now wished neither Lord Jasper nor me to attend it. Christmas at Pembroke was a melancholy feast and two days after our unhappy festivities we rode to collect Harri from his mother, before she set out for Maxstoke and her marriage.

Perhaps Edith had talked her sister round because at least Lady Margaret's anger towards me had softened when we met at Haverford Castle, of which Geoffrey Pole was deputy constable. He took Lord Jasper on a tour of the defences while Lady Margaret, Edith and I played with Harri and watched him eat some curds and honey to fortify him for the onward journey.

'I know Henry will be safe with you, Jane,' Margaret assured me, refusing as always to use the name Harri. 'But I insist that you to write regular letters telling me of every new tooth and of course when he takes his first steps. Edith and I thought it might happen over Christmas but although he stands if you hold his hands he has not yet stepped out independently.'

Her eyes misted as she contemplated missing this important milestone in her son's life so I hastened to reassure her that I would not only write but also attempt to draw him standing freely on his feet. 'Although I am not the most talented artist, it must be said,' I added with a grimace. 'When I drew Lord Jasper's peregrine, if you remember, you thought it looked more like a pigeon.'

I detected a moment of uncertainty at the mention of her brother-in-law, as if she was about to pass comment and thought better of it, so I took a chance. 'He feels just as wretched as you at the separation, my lady. It is not his choice but I am certain he will be like a father to Harri. It would greatly ease his anguish if you were able to forgive him, or at least acknowledge the awkwardness of his position.'

For an instant I thought I had made a dreadful error in taking Lord Jasper's part. She was after all a fourteen-year-old girl, not an experienced woman, aware of the Wheel of Fortune's erratic turns.

At this moment Edith chose to intervene and spoke frankly, as only an older sister could. 'Geoffrey believes Lord Jasper to be the best man ever to be granted the lordship of Pembroke and the best ambassador Wales could have in the English court. If anyone can teach a boy how to become a man of honour and worth it is he. Your Henry needs a role model to guide and advise him and, lacking his own father, his uncle is the perfect choice. It is the inevitable fate of a noblewoman to lose authority over her sons at a young age but at least you can be sure that Jasper will never let him forget who his mother is. Leave him with good grace, Margaret, and go and have more children with your new husband.'

Harri crawled to where his mother was sitting and pulled himself up on her skirt so that he stood before her, unsteady but smiling triumphantly. She laughed and swung him up onto her knee, hugging him tightly. Then she shifted her gaze to her sister and let it rest thoughtfully on her for a moment before nodding reluctant agreement. 'You are right, Edith. I should be grateful that it is Lord Jasper and not some total stranger that the king has chosen to be Henry's guardian. He will never allow my son to forget me because he loves me as much as Lord Edmund did.'

Clearly I had been wrong to think Lady Margaret too young to understand Lord Jasper's position. Inside that gracefully inclined head resided a firm belief that God's Will would be done – and an exceedingly sharp insight.

When the time came to bid farewell and mount up, I stood ready to move forward and take Harri from his mother's arms. But instead of giving him to me she kissed her infant son firmly on his lips and told him gently, 'Now go to your Uncle Jasper, Henry, and be a good boy.' As she passed him over she smiled bravely but I could see tears welling in her eyes. 'Take care of him, my lord.' Her voice broke on the words. I could not see Lord Jasper's expression but I watched Lady Margaret go on tiptoe to kiss him too. It was a kiss of forgiveness. 'Remember, he is my beloved son.'

'I will never let him forget it,' he said.

18

Jasper

London & Pembroke Castle

THE KING WAS BACK in London. I was crammed among a crowd of crimson-robed peers at the foot of the altar steps of St Paul's Church, where King Henry sat, crowned in state on a gilded throne, lost in the purple folds of his ermine-trimmed mantle. Five hundred candles lit the cold, cavernous setting, but the atmosphere in the chancel was oppressive and my companions as tense as the strings on a gittern. Beside the king stood the Archbishop of Canterbury and the Bishop of Durham, propped on their ornate croziers, the gold thread glittering on their lavishly embroidered copes and mitres. Fumes belching from censors swung by over-enthusiastic acolytes hung in clouds around us as one by one, willingly or unwillingly, dukes, earls and barons queued to make their vows of peace before God and king.

In the two months since King Henry had summoned his leading nobles to a Great Council at Westminster the city had become a cauldron of contention. Anticipating conflict, leading lords had come accompanied by huge private armies and antagonism between the two main affinities had festered so fast and so violently that an edict was issued, ordering supporters of York to reside within the city walls and supporters of Lancaster to stay without. Armed royal guards had been placed at the gates to keep the two sides apart.

Principally, the Lancastrians accused the Yorkists of murder by the assassination of prominent Lancastrian peers during the confrontation in St Albans three years previously. After weeks of argument the Archbishop of Canterbury had managed to negotiate an agreement, which involved the payment of vast sums by the Yorkist leaders in compensation to the embittered Lancastrian heirs of the dead. But no one really supposed that, even if it was paid, money alone would assuage the vengeful anger of the young Duke of Somerset, the Earl of Northumberland and their hot-headed ally Lord Clifford, who had all lost their fathers. No one that is except the king, who genuinely believed that the service of reconciliation at St Paul's would mark an end to animosity and herald a new era of goodwill. After making their vows, leading members of the two warring affinities were to walk hand in hand through the streets to reassure the citizens that peace had been restored among the great and powerful of the realm.

Hiding my misgivings, I had spent an awkward morning closeted with my brother and Queen Marguerite, trying to decide on the order of this procession. 'You and the queen will lead it of course, my liege,' I proposed.

But Marguerite disagreed. 'I think the king should lead it alone. It was he who instigated the peace council and he who managed to persuade the lords to agree terms.' She placed her hand admiringly over her husband's arm. 'I will never know how you succeeded, my lord, especially as far as the Duke of York is concerned.'

Henry appeared gratified by her praise. 'I prayed and the Almighty heard my prayers,' he declared. 'And the Archbishop had a lot to do with it. But you know I do not like to walk alone, my dear. I need my queen at my side.'

She was sympathetic but adamant. 'Yes, my dearest lord, but on this occasion I think you must be brave. If you walk alone in the van it will be clear to the people that their king understands their longing for peace and is entirely responsible for controlling his barons. You must receive the gratitude of your people. Besides, I believe it is my penance to walk hand in hand with Richard of York who, as you know, I consider a treasonous thug and a threat to your throne.'

'Is everyone to walk with their arch enemy then?' I asked in surprise. 'Is that wise, or even possible? Surely we cannot ask the Duke of Somerset to walk with the Earl of Warwick? The man who killed his father at St Albans? He will never agree.'

Marguerite drew herself up, jaw jutting. 'If I can walk with York, young Somerset can walk with Warwick. Heaven knows I mourned his father's death as much as anyone but it was Richard of York who led an army against the king. By taking his hand I will be forgiving his treason, the gravest of all crimes. Whereas Somerset will only be forgiving an act of war.'

'Marguerite is right,' insisted King Henry. 'We must show a united front to our people. As St Matthew wrote in his gospel, "A kingdom divided against itself is brought to desolation".'

'So the order of precedence is to be suspended is it?' I persisted. 'Because if the Earl of Warwick is to walk hand in hand with the Duke of Somerset, he will have to go ahead of the dukes of Buckingham, Exeter and Norfolk in the procession.'

Henry and Marguerite exchanged enquiring glances then nodded in unison. 'Yes,' said the queen. 'Peace must prevail over precedence.'

There seemed no point in further argument. 'So be it, but I would not like to be the one to explain that to the dukes.'

I detected a hint of malice in her smiling response. 'Well that is a pity, Jasper, because I believe you are the one best placed to do so, since you will be ceding your pre-eminence among the earls to Warwick. To soften the blow you can stress that it is only for this one, exceptional occasion.'

One did not refuse a royal command and Queen Marguerite had made plenty of these lately without any reference to the king. I cast a quizzical look at Henry for confirmation but he ignored it.

'Tomorrow is the Feast of the Annunciation,' he said, making the sign of the Cross. 'The day that Love was conceived. We shall call our reconciliation "Loveday".'

Whatever he had chosen to call it, I could feel little love emanating from the column of disgruntled courtiers who followed the king down the nave of St Paul's. King Henry may have been radiating joy as he led his 'Loveday' parade but behind his back the forced smiles of his fulminating barons gave little indication of a sudden blossoming of brotherly love.

As we spilled out into the gloomy churchyard at the top of Ludgate Hill, canopied by a heavy blanket of dark clouds,

I had a sudden vision of the wide, clear skies over Pembroke Castle and Jane Hywel striding out in her purposeful way across the Outer Court towards the herb garden. When I blinked the image faded but I was left wishing I were there, in Jane's congenial company, rather than setting off towards Temple Bar feigning happiness among a column of noblemen who were probably as fervent as I in wishing that they were somewhere else. The muted cheers of the crowd indicated that they, too, had little faith in the message of Loveday.

The king and queen departed from London as soon as possible and I was glad of the excuse to join their escort to Berkhamsted Castle. 'Stay faithful, Jasper,' Queen Marguerite urged me as I took my farewell the next day. 'I am worried about the king's health. He is heading for another breakdown; I know the signs. So I am taking him back to Kenilworth.'

Bending over her be-ringed hand, I thought she looked magnificent but also alarming. I wanted to warn her to be careful not to further alienate the Duke of York but thought better of it. It was too late. She knew as well as I did that Richard of York had been totally unimpressed with the 'Loveday' attempt at reconciliation. He had taken his six hundred retainers back to Ludlow where he would be nursing his resentment and keeping close contact with his allies. And working in the king's name, Marguerite would be doing the same at Kenilworth. Her next words confirmed my conclusions that peace between York and Lancaster was a vain hope. She had embraced the Lancastrian cause and would do all she could to advance those lords who did the same.

'Steer your Welsh chieftains away from York, Jasper, and I will see that they receive their reward. We need those sturdy soldiers to fight for the crown when the time comes. And come it will, of that there is no doubt. Henry refuses to see the danger but I will make sure we are ready to secure the throne for my son and I will rely on you to bring Wales to its prince's aid. Will you do that, Jasper?'

I looked into her dark, almost black eyes, burning now with zeal, and thanked God I had resisted her suggestive hinting when she had thought she might never conceive a child with the king. Yorkist propaganda still questioned the paternity of her son, Prince Édouard, but at least it named others as his sire and not me. Yet I could not help admiring Marguerite's strength of character. York might scorn the weakness of my timorous half-brother but in the queen he faced a fearsome adversary.

'My loyalty to the king is undying,' I said, dropping to my knee. 'And it extends to his wife and son. I am his to command – and yours, my lady – and always will be while I live, as God is my witness.'

'I have said it before, Jasper, you are the king's gauntlet,' the queen said, placing her hand on my shoulder. 'He needs you like he needs me. We will never betray his trust, you and I.'

* * *

With a profound sense of release I took the high road to Pembroke, accompanied as always by Maredudd and a handful of men at arms. I held to my belief that moving fast and with few men was safer than being surrounded by a large retinue and in fine weather we made good time, crossing the River Severn at Gloucester less than three days later. However, we did not cease watching our backs until we had put the castle of Raglan well behind us. Since Edmund's death I would never trust William Herbert of Raglan.

As we drew nearer to my own estates I felt for the first time a sense of going home. I had not set foot in Pembrokeshire until four years ago but now I realized it had acquired that status in my mind. 'Home', where a man could rely on the warmth of a hearth and a friendly welcome. I had sworn lifelong loyalty to my brother King Henry but that did not make his palaces places where I felt comfortable or even secure. The royal court simmered with schemes and conspiracies; jealousy and rivalry thrived and honour fought hard to survive. I could understand why Henry sought refuge whenever possible in churches and abbeys, peaceful havens of prayer and contemplation, where God was a constant presence, but I did not seek that kind of solace. I wanted human friendship and the comfort of knowing I could trust my companions. I glanced across at Maredudd and under-stood that in him I had found these things and perhaps even more in his sister Jane. As Harri's nurse and a valued member of my household, she was part of what made Pembroke my home. But then, all at once, a sudden recall of her kiss in the mews sent a rush of blood to my cheeks.

My experience of females had mostly involved the more adventurous young ladies of the court, some of whom were rather obviously keen to draw a new earl into their net. But, unlike my brother Edmund, I stopped short at harmless flirting, to avoid any and all complications. I discovered after his death that he had not confined his sexual exploits to the Southwark stews. His accounts revealed that he had been obliged to pay substantial sums to daughters of minor gentry, who had been hastily married off to others, to disguise the results of his philandering. This was not information I would ever wish to reach Margaret's ears, but it was no wonder that his debts had mounted beyond control.

Jane had only kissed me once – other than a kiss in greeting as friends do – but that had been enough to tell me that she was nothing like those eager court fillies with ulterior motives. At first I had considered my response to her kiss no more than an automatic reaction, a stirring of the blood, but then what had she said to me? 'I have loved you since you first came to Tŷ Cerrig.' And what had I said in reply? I could not remember my exact words but I recalled their gist with a sense of regret that churned inside me. I had flatly rejected her. Gabbled something about honour and keeping the king's faith and she had gone quiet; had been quiet ever since. Yet she was still there in my life, still caring for little Harri, as if nothing had happened. I wondered, did she still love me or did she see me as the fool I was beginning to regard myself?

We reached Pembroke at dusk. Long shadows stretched out from the lofty castle walls to meet us as we crossed the bridge over the river and rode up the hill to the barbican. There were guards at the gate and on the battlements but the Outer Ward was quiet, the rest of the garrison and household no doubt in the Great Hall, filling their bellies. Maredudd drew rein outside the entrance to the new mansion.

'Shall I take your horse, my lord?' he asked, breaking into my thoughts. 'No doubt you will be wanting to visit your nephew before bedtime.'

I had forgotten that sunset signalled the end of the day for an infant such as Harri. 'Yes, thank you, Maredudd. And tell the steward I will take supper here, not in the hall. You are welcome to join me if you will.'

Maredudd grinned as he took my courser's rein. 'Thank you, my lord. I will see that the kitchen sends enough food. I expect you are as hungry as I am.'

Actually, my appetite seemed to have vanished as I climbed the mansion steps for the first time since Margaret's departure; I pictured the domestic scene awaiting me, little Harri playing with his toys on the hearth, Jane sitting nearby, her sewing on her lap, and my eager anticipation mounted with me. I entered the solar to find the scene confronting me not dissimilar to my fantasy, except that while Harri was playing on the hearthrug, Jane was sitting at a table and she was not alone. Seated beside her, their heads close together over a manuscript, was the poet Lewys Glyn Cothi and something about the intimacy of their position rang alarm bells in my head.

As soon as they heard me enter the room they sprang apart but there was nothing bashful or guilty about Jane's reaction to my arrival. She leapt to her feet crying, 'Lord Jasper, you are back!' before bending swiftly to scoop up the little boy and bring him to greet me. 'Look who is here, Harri; it is your uncle, home again.'

She offered the baby's smooth cheek for a kiss but Harri took fright at the dust-streaked, bearded man in brigandine and breastplate and his face crumpled. Over the loud wail that ensued I saw Lewys roll up the manuscript and stow it away in his capacious scrip before rising and favouring me with an awkward bow, hugging the bag protectively before him.

'Oh, do you not remember your uncle, poppet?' Jane gave

the little boy a consoling hug and attempted to make excuses for him. 'Three months is a long time in a baby's life, my lord. Never mind, Harri, you go back to your toys. It is nearly bedtime.'

When he had been returned to the rug and his pile of coloured bricks the infant wails subsided. 'At least *you* do not cry at the sight of a returning soldier, Jane,' I said, deterred from giving her the usual friendly kiss by the presence of another. 'But you have company I see.' I swung my gaze to the poet, who was hovering between the table and the door. 'How are you, Lewys? Still able to place yourself in the way of a meal I see,' I added dryly, gesturing to the unfinished bowl of bread and milk on the other end of the table, which I deduced was actually Harri's unfinished supper.

Lewys shook his head in denial. Though only in his thirties the beard that brushed the front of his old-fashioned brown côte was already threaded with silver. 'I am grateful for all hospitality, my lord,' he said. 'Yours in particular. I hope your stay in London was fruitful.'

'Time will tell – but I think not. What were you doing when I came in?'

Jane and Lewys exchanged glances and it was she who spoke. 'I was helping Lewys to translate a poem from Welsh into English. He has written a *brwd* to Lord Edmund but it is not yet ready for you to hear.'

'Ah. I am glad someone praises Edmund. There was little mention of him at court. It is almost as if he never existed.'

'That is not how it will be in Wales,' said Lewys. 'The name Tudor finds favour in many houses.'

'Well let us drink to that at least,' I said, crossing to a

sideboard where I had spotted a flagon and cups. 'What is in here, Jane?' I asked, touching the jug.

'Some of your Rennish wine, my lord. Let me pour you a measure and then I will take Harri off to bed.'

As she poured I told her I had bidden Maredudd to sup with us, which seemed to please her. She picked Harri up again and a few dark curls were revealed where his coif had slipped. 'He has his father's hair,' I remarked. 'Do you remember Edmund's dark mane, Jane?'

'Of course, my lord, I remember everything about the time your father brought you and your brother to Tŷ Cerrig.' Her expression was bland, unreadable, as she added, 'One of you was handsome and the other was kind.'

I raised an eyebrow. 'Is that what you thought? Which one was I?'

She gave me an enigmatic smile and turned towards the door. Over her shoulder she threw a parting reply. 'You cannot expect me to answer that, my lord.'

Harri waved a chubby hand at me and I waved back. 'Good night, Harri,' I said, grateful for his change of mood. Perhaps I was not entirely the ogre-soldier after all. The door closed behind them and the poet and I raised our cups in salute and drank. 'What do you say of Edmund in your song, Lewys? Handsome or kind?'

Lewys wiped his mouth on his sleeve. 'I only present his deeds and reputation, my lord. I call him fearless but many people spoke of him as handsome.'

I took another gulp of wine and sat down in Jane's vacated chair, gesturing Lewys back to the other. 'So Jane must think I am kind,' I sighed, stretching out my legs and feeling the wine's effect flowing into my weary limbs.

'I do not know many earls who would welcome that description.'

'There are worse words,' remarked Lewys. 'For instance, tyrannous, or lecherous . . .'

'You would not use such words in a praise-song though, surely?'

'There are other types of poetry, my lord – but they are not the sort that earn food and drink.' Lewys had shed his anxious look and his eyes were now twinkling. 'And I get hungry.'

I laughed and slapped my thigh. 'You are always hungry, Lewys. And by God now I am too. Where is Maredudd with the supper? And I need him to help me out of this armour.'

By the time Jane returned, having settled her charge in his cot, no doubt with a nursemaid to rock him to sleep, Maredudd had ushered in a procession of kitchen varlets with all the elements of a substantial evening meal, relieved me of my breastplate and heavy brigandine and provided a clean doublet in which to take my ease. Meanwhile Lewys and I had quaffed another cup of wine and I had picked his brains for local political developments. In his wanderings from house to house, reciting his poems and filling his purse and belly, he seemed able to absorb an abundance of useful information and, encouraged by the knowledge that he had written a praise-song to Edmund, I began to consider luring him onto my confidential payroll. However, along with his talent as a bard, I knew Lewys had also acquired a reputation for womanizing and before I did so I needed to discover if there was more to his relationship with Jane Hywel than getting a little help with translation.

19

Jane

Pembroke Castle

Lord jasper sat with Harri on the floor of the nursery building a castle with shaped wooden bricks. The little boy was watching him patiently, blue eyes glued to the growing pile, waiting for his uncle to give him a sign. The earl smiled and slipped the last brick onto the battlements. 'There you are, Harri, now you can attack!'

With a shout his nephew swept his arm across the castle and sent its walls tumbling to the ground. 'Ha! Ha!' he cried triumphantly, his four baby front teeth bared in a delighted grin.

'Yes, Harri, good boy, you knocked it down!' Jasper looked at me and winked. 'If only it were so easy in real life,' he remarked, beginning to gather up the scattered bricks to start again. 'You seem very friendly with Lewys, Jane. Are you?'

I bent to collect a wayward brick from under my chair, nonplussed.

'Well, are you going to tell me?'

'Tell you what, my lord?'

'How friendly you are with Lewys Glyn Cothi?' He began to build a new wall.

I turned the wooden brick in my fingers, feeling its smooth surfaces. It was shaped for the battlements, in a line of crenellations. The set had been made from scrap oak by one of the carpenters who had worked on the panelling in the hall and painted red, green and blue with vegetable dyes that had no poisons in them. Margaret had been delighted when Jasper presented them to Harri, but that was before she knew Jasper had custody of her son. I resented Lord Jasper's inquisition but at length I said, 'He has been to Pembroke a few times on his travels.'

'A few times? As far as I know he has only been twice.'

'Oh no, he has a regular route around the county. He visits St David's and all the lordships – Wiston and Picton, Haverford and Carew. Sometimes even goes as far as Dale, he tells me. But he always calls in here and stays a night or two to sing us his latest compositions. You are away a good deal but the steward says you like to encourage the bards.'

'Does he indeed? I shall have a word with Steward Dŵnn. I also hear that Lewys likes the ladies. He has quite a reputation. Did you know that, Jane?'

The bricks had reached enough height to add the battlements and I handed over the one I had rescued. 'We talk only of poetry and stories,' I said. 'I do not ask about his love life.'

Harri could wait no longer and jabbed his fist at the unfinished walls, causing a collapse. Lord Jasper raised a fist in salute. 'Aha! You sent in the sappers, Harri! Good strategy.' He turned his gaze back to me. 'But is Lewys a harmless wandering minstrel or is he a roving rogue? You should be careful, Jane. He is hardly the marrying kind and you do not want him boasting of his conquest at Pembroke Castle.'

I was incredulous. If anyone was not the marrying kind it was Jasper Tudor. Had he not told me so outright? Yet he thought he had the right to lecture me on preserving my reputation. I stood up. 'I crave your pardon, my lord. I thought you only employed me in your household. I did not realize that included the right to appoint yourself my moral guardian.'

He was still sitting cross-legged on the blanket, hardly a position of dominance, but he glared up at me, eyes blazing. 'You are my nephew's governess, Jane, and as such I demand a certain moral standard.'

My regrettable temper flared. 'You have no need to worry on that score, my lord. I would never do anything to harm my charge – and that includes upsetting him in any way.'

Harri was sensitive to atmosphere and I could see his chin beginning to tremble. I bent to gather him up and give him a reassuring hug, feeling dampness around his nether regions that demanded attention. 'Come on, Harri,' I said, adjusting my voice to a soothing tone. 'It is time we got some fresh air. Shall we change your napkin, find your warm jacket and go and visit the horses? Say goodbye to your Uncle Jasper.'

The earl scrambled to his feet, as anxious as I was to forestall any baby tears. 'No, we will all go to the stables,' he said, smiling beguilingly at his nephew and squeezing his little hand. 'I need to speak to my Master of Horse and you can stroke my big friendly courser, Harri. You would like that, would you not?' Too young to understand what his uncle had said, the little boy had nevertheless gauged the gentler tone of his voice his chin stopped trembling; he gurgled happily, meaning yes he would.

Over Harri's head Lord Jasper and I exchanged glances. The moment of conflict had passed. Any unfinished business would have to be resolved at some other time. However, no early opportunity offered itself because, no matter what he thought of the poet's attitude towards the ladies, a few days later the earl set off with Lewys as his guide to visit one of the farthest-flung Pembroke manors.

Dale was a remote coastal lordship at the mouth of the great Milford Haven estuary. Getting there involved a complicated journey with many rivers and streams to cross and since Lord Jasper could hardly be expected to walk, Lewys was required to ride. I could not help laughing as Harri and I watched the small band of horsemen set off on their journey. Lewys sat his mount with tense deliberation, holding the reins like a basket of eggs and giving the impression that he was unlikely to remain in contact with the saddle much beyond the Pembroke River. I recalled that he had been less than keen when Jasper had proposed the expedition over supper on the night of his return.

'Why would you want to go there?' the poet had protested. 'Dale Castle is a grim place in the direct path of every gale that sweeps in from the Western Ocean and its lord is a cantankerous old bastard for whom I will never compose a praise poem.'

Lord Jasper had dismissed his objections. 'Never mind your bardish sensitivities, Lewys. Pembroke is a royal domain and I need to inspect Dale's capacity to confront an enemy landing. I will pay you well to guide me to this wind-blasted corner of my territory. Has this cantankerous chieftain adopted the English tongue, or will I have to bribe you further to interpret as well?' It was at that moment I realized that the two men were developing an unlikely friendship whatever the earl's opinion of the poet's lax morals.

Lord Jasper returned from his foray to the western edge a week later, having left the poet en route to make his way on foot towards Gruffydd ap Nicholas's territory, no doubt with a mission to gather information for his new patron. Then Geoffrey and Edith Pole had joined the earl's retinue at the Milford ferry and brought along their own baby son, Richard.

Rich was only a few weeks older than Harri and the two little boys quickly reestablished a relationship they had begun as babies, when Rich took away any toy Harri was playing with and Harri devised distraction tactics to get it back. I thought this very clever of Harri. He did not get angry as my little brothers always had in such circumstances and I hoped such a carrot-rather-than-stick strategy might prove useful to him throughout life.

Edith had seen nothing of Margaret while in England. 'No, she has not left Maxstoke since her wedding. I believe her mother-in-law, the Duchess of Buckingham, is rather a dragon – but do not tell anyone I said so. I just hope she is being kind to Margaret.'

I could imagine Margaret tip-toeing around the duchess while working out the quickest way of getting free of her. I wondered how much support she would get from her new husband, but Edith had only met him at the wedding and then they did not speak much. 'It will be good when he and Margaret can set up their own household but the duchess apparently thinks Margaret is too young yet.'

'And what the duchess says goes as far as her son is concerned, is that it?'

Edith shrugged, more concerned to stay her own son's threatening advance on Harri's building work. 'No, Rich – do not knock the wall down!'

I assured her that Lord Jasper encouraged Harri to do exactly that. 'And he says that the Duchess of Buckingham is a favourite of Queen Marguerite's,' I added. 'Perhaps she will soon be called back to court and the newlyweds will be able to take flight.' I caught Edith's eye and we both erupted into giggles at this prospect just at the moment Lord Jasper and Geoffrey entered the nursery, having concluded their business.

I had last encountered Geoffrey Pole during the tense post-Christmas gathering at Haverford when Margaret had handed Harri over. I thought him a shrewd man, tall and dark, with a high brow and a thin face with twinkling hazel eyes, which I discovered indicated a ready sense of humour.

'Hello, what gossip amuses the ladies while the babies do battle on the floor?' he asked. Swooping on his son who was waving a toy mangonel perilously close to Harri's face, he told the boy, 'That is meant for hurling missiles at castle walls, my boisterous son, not for battering your little friend's brains out!' He swung Rich up above his head and tossed him in the air, causing the boy to shriek with laughter. 'You will not be invited again if you damage your cousin's good looks.'

'They have been playing together beautifully, have they

not, Jane?' Edith declared, defending her son's behaviour. 'And we were laughing at Jane's idea that Margaret and Sir Henry might be able to escape from under his mother's thumb if the queen were to call the duchess to court.'

I squirmed slightly at her frank admission that we had been discussing Lady Margaret and glanced at Lord Jasper to gauge his reaction. He was instantly alert at the mention of her name, asking, 'Why? Is Margaret not happy in her marriage?'

Edith hastened to reassure him. 'Oh yes, she is full of praise for Sir Henry. It is his mother she finds difficult to please. She complains that she escaped our own mother's authority only to encounter one even more restricting in her mother-in-law. Margaret may be young but she has a strong independent streak, as you know, my lord.'

The earl pursed his lips. 'Hmm. I expect the duchess means well but I suppose I might seek the queen's help to loosen the chains a little. It is Sir Henry Margaret should answer to, not his mother.'

'Indeed,' Geoffrey said, casting a teasing glance at his wife, 'just as Edith is entirely answerable to me, of course.' He ignored her indignant 'Huh!' and squatted down to put his son back on the floor. 'Play nicely now, Rich. Here is your mangonel, Harri. Your uncle is going to hold an eisteddfod, is that not a splendid idea?'

Harri took back his siege weapon with alacrity and Lord Jasper hastily interjected, 'Not exactly an eisteddfod, just a gathering of some of the local bards and their patrons. I thought it might provide an opportunity to combine negotiation with entertainment. Lewys Glyn Cothi is arranging it for me, starting with Gruffydd ap Nicholas and his sons.

They all compose a little I am told. What do you think, Jane?'

Flustered by his direct appeal for my opinion, I could not instantly summon a suitable reply. 'I ask you because you know the Welsh mind,' he persisted. 'Will the chiefs of the local lordships find it acceptable to come to Pembroke for poetry, feasting and talking or will they be suspicious of an English conspiracy? I thought I would get my father to help things along. He could perfect a bardic battle he started with Lewys at Caldicot during our hunting party.'

'I believe all Welshmen love a bardic battle, my lord,' I said cautiously, 'nearly as much as a real one. I am sure they will flock to the gates of Pembroke.'

In due course they did not exactly flock but about a dozen Welsh chiefs and chieftains attended the festival, along with their wives and sons, to feast and frolic at the earl's expense and perhaps lured as well by the opportunity to air their grievances. Owen Tudor was first to arrive, accompanied by a small posse of armed companions and several packhorses with a selection of harps among the baggage. Lord Jasper had allocated his father to the guest accommodation in his new mansion and showed him proudly around it, including a visit to Harri's nursery, where Owen presented one of the instruments – a suitably junior version – to his grandson.

'He is Welsh enough to have music in his blood,' said Owen, ruffling Harri's hair. 'This will give him a chance to discover it.'

'It is very generous of you to think of Harri,' said Lord Jasper, who then remarked, 'I wondered why you had brought four harps, it seemed a little excessive.'

'I am as competitive as the next bard,' his father declared. 'I do not want my sound to be drowned out by larger instruments. Also I have a duty to show the king how much I appreciate the annual pension he has awarded me – not before time,' he added under his breath. 'So at last I can afford a gift for my grandson.'

'And a squire and two servants, I notice,' commented his son.

But Owen had retrieved the little harp from Harri, in such a way that he plucked a little sweet tune from it as he took it away, to try and avoid any squall of protest. The trick worked and Owen was able to return his attention to Jasper, who was saying, '… there is accommodation in the house for you but I am afraid your retinue will have to sleep in the Old Hall, unless you want a pile of pallets in your chamber.'

Owen reacted with a grimace. 'Perish that thought! Ah, I must tell you my news, I have taken a lovely lady to my home and hearth. She told me over and again we were destined to be together and so in the end I relented. Her name is Myfanwy and I cannot think what took me so long, she is the comeliest and most spirited little widow.'

A quick movement of his head, caught out of the corner of my eye, told me Lord Jasper had glanced in my direction before responding.

'Well, I wish you joy, Father, and I will make a point of coming to Denbigh to meet your Myfanwy. Will you be taking her before the priest?'

Owen gave a bark of laughter. 'Oh no, my lord earl, have no fear that I will shame you in that way. Besides, Myfanwy may be the prettiest woman in North Wales and she loves me well but she cannot compare to my queen. In my heart

I will always be your royal mother's husband and true lover but we men abhor a cold bed, Jasper, do we not?'

There was such an evident desire for understanding in the question that I glanced round to see the wistful smile that accompanied it. Owen's silver hair clustered in thick curls around the brim of his soft felt hat and I felt a surge of sympathy for this still handsome man, who held on to his virility and defiantly challenged the inexorable march of time to shrivel him in spirit.

Lord Jasper's reply intrigued me. 'If the lady is content with your arrangement then you are a lucky man, Father; a clear conscience can make a cold bedfellow, that is certainly true.'

To free up guest accommodation, Lord Jasper had moved into the new mansion for the first time and with him came the bustle of servants and squires rendering service to their Tudor master; confidential meetings were held in the hall.

I found myself with a dual role as governess to the Tudor heir and the earl's interpreter both at the meetings in the mansion and in the Great Hall where I sat behind his chair to assist conversation with chieftains. My position was not understood at first, I was an object of curiosity and even suspicion for many attending the gathering, but after I had brought Harri to the hall to show him off, my duties became clear and the novelty waned. The female guests in particular became friendlier to me once they had beheld Harri's big blue eyes and heard his few charmingly lisped words of Welsh.

Up to that time I had been ignorant of how lavishly the nobility entertained; I was shocked at the number and quantity of the dishes Lord Jasper ordered and the copious supplies of ale, wine and more exotic liquors he provided to lubricate the feasting. Luckily Edith was there to entertain the ladies in the style expected, although several were, like me, over-awed by the scale of the festivities and a few drank too much and became quarrelsome or sick. All the meals went on for hours but the final banquet lasted from noon until after midnight and included the presentation of prizes for the most admired songs and poems and the announcement of the festival's prime objective, which was an alliance sworn between most of the chiefs. The few who felt unable to swear had slipped away by the time a closing joust was held the following day but crucially the Gruffydd clan had stood solidly in allegiance, bringing most others with them.

'I never thought there would come a day when I would be able to raise a toast to the brother of an English king on Welsh soil!' bellowed the elderly Gruffydd, white-headed now but even at the end of an energetic joust and mounted on his prancing charger, he was still able to raise his cup and make his voice echo around the vast outer ward. Having eaten and drunk his way through seven days of feasting and argument, passed judgement on a dozen bards and broken several lances on less expert jousters, the 'old rascal' was finally conceding victory to his host, whose team had scored two more points than his.

'I speak for all the Welsh clans represented here when I thank Lord Jasper for opening his gates and his purse to us and achieving the impossible – that is to say peace between chieftains who have been feuding for years. May the devil take those who have slunk away without swearing but those of us here can all return to our lordships secure in the knowledge of who will stand firmly beside us against our enemies. But before we go, let us drink to Lord Jasper – a true leader of men. As long as he holds the king's castles in South West Wales, we know our lands are safe. May God support his cause!'

Gruffydd's two sons, Owain and Thomas, led the cheering that followed this speech and I watched Lord Jasper remove his helm and acknowledge the shouts with raised sword and pride-flushed cheeks. Seeing him receive this acclaim, like a knight from my mother's illuminated book of romances, stirred feelings of admiration in me that had lately been lying dormant and lit a fresh spark of courage.

'A clear conscience makes a cold bedfellow,' he had said when Owen first revealed the existence of his Myfanwy. Did that mean he now regretted putting honour before inclination? If I made a new effort to break through his stifling sense of obligation to his royal brother, would he abandon his scruples of betraying the king and admit that he longed for the warmth of human flesh and the joy of love and companionship? I resolved to take a cue from the bold Myfanwy and try again. But I told myself that if I was rejected this time I would no longer remain at Pembroke to care for Lady Margaret's son and feign indifference to the man I loved. I would go home to Tŷ Cerrig and run my father's house and look after my stepmother and her children.

20

Jasper

Pembroke Castle

THE SUCCESS OF MY Easter festival meant I now had a substantial alliance of tenants and landholders on whom I could rely for advice, assistance and military support. What is more I had won important friends for the Lancastrian throne. However, with the Duke of York and his allies still controlling most of the crucial March lordships between England and Wales, there remained an awkward swathe of hostile territory separating us from the Lancastrian heartland and I did not doubt that sooner or later I would be called on to do something about it.

When most of the Welsh guests had ridden off home and the Great Hall had become an echoing void, I was able to relax over dinner in the mansion with my father, Lewys Glyn Cothi, and Thomas ap Gruffydd, the 'old rascal's' son who remained as a guest in the castle. I wished to quiz him about the ever-present threat from his aggressive neighbour William Herbert of Raglan, the Duke of York's main man in South Wales. Before sitting down at table the four of us gathered around the hearth in the oak-panelled hall, beneath the painted ceiling depicting the heraldic symbols of my extended family.

Thomas was gazing upwards, in imminent danger of tipping his cup of wine over the expensive Turkish hearthrug. 'No mistaking whose side you are on, is there, Lord Jasper,' he observed.

I reached out to straighten his cup for him. 'I will not be on *your* side, my friend, if you tip wine over my expensive Ottoman import.'

'We are not used to treading on wool this side of Offa's Dyke, Jasper,' my father remarked, his foot tapping the thick pile of the carpet. 'Perhaps you should hang it on the wall.'

Thomas took a large gulp from the offending cup, lowering the risk of a spill, then immediately raised it again in making me an effusive bow. 'Pray accept my humble apologies, my lord. The decor of this hall is such a feast for the eyes it is hard to know whether to look up or down. You have shown us all how to live like lords.'

Thomas was the youngest of Gruffydd's sons, born to his third wife some twenty years after the eldest, Owain had been born to his first. Of about my age, Thomas was dark haired, broad-shouldered and stocky, a fine archer and swordsman and a competent jouster. Like many Welshmen he spilled words rather than spoke them, often without giving sufficient thought to their order and meaning, but I could easily forgive him this because of his willingness to stand up for his friends and fight as hard for their causes as for his own. I knew he would be among the first I would look to for support in time of need.

'My pleasure in it so far has mostly been to provide a comfortable refuge for my bereaved sister-in-law until her re-marriage earlier this year,' I said.

'Yes, your brother's death was very unfortunate. The plague I understand.'

Thomas knew that the true cause of Edmund's demise was uncertain and looked uncomfortable as he spoke of it. 'So William Herbert would have us believe,' I responded. 'And my royal brother's commission of enquiry hit a Yorkist wall of silence. Another reason to strengthen our mutual defences. However, I am now at liberty to use my new house for its intended purpose – entertaining my friends and neighbours; or at least those I can trust.'

'That is all very well but it lacks the feminine touch,' Owen interjected. 'I have never been one for exclusively male company. Why do you not invite that cousin of ours to join us? The one who is looking after Harri – Jane, is it not? She is a lovely girl and holds her own in conversation. Go on, lad, call her in.'

I could feel the heat rising in my cheeks. 'I will not,' I said. 'You are the one for the ladies, Father. You call her if you want to.'

Owen made an impatient noise. 'Bah! It is not an old man she wants it is you, you blind mole. Who would have thought that I could sire such a lame goose?' He laid a gnarled hand on Lewys's shoulder. 'If you are not careful, Jasper, this skirt-lifting poet here will talk his way into her favour and you will regret it for the rest of your life – well, for a few months anyway!'

'I have no intention of doing anything of the kind,' protested Lewys, shrugging off my father's hand.

'Because you see as well as I do that she only has eyes for Jasper,' Owen retorted with a chuckle. 'Like me, Lewys, you woo where you know you can win.'

'Perhaps the bard could pen a few lines on Lord Jasper's behalf that might win the lady's approval,' suggested Thomas raising an eyebrow in my direction. 'All females are susceptible to verse are they not?'

'Stop this, all of you!' I cried, relieved to see the hall door open to admit a posse of kitchen porters carrying an array of dishes, which they began to lay out on the table. 'I am hungry, even if you are not. Come, my friends, take your places and let us talk of more important things. Which of you will join me at the hunt tomorrow for instance? The Pembroke parks are loaded with game.'

The smell of roasted meat and steaming puddings drew them to the board. Pages arrived with bowls of warm water and we washed our hands, the rush of blood subsiding from my cheeks as I wielded a crisp white napkin, meantime distracting my tormentors with descriptions of the various covers that were available to us for sport on the following day. But as the meal progressed I could not entirely erase their teasing comments from my mind. A blind mole. A lame goose. Was that me? Often I longed for the softness of a woman and the thrill of a warm embrace, but I still woke in the night from dreams of Margaret bent low over her galloping palfrey's neck, skirts flying and a smile of exaltation on her Madonna face. Could Jane – could any woman – match that vision?

The question lingered with me after the dishes were emptied and the wine jugs ran dry and four tipsy comrades bade each other goodnight, swaying from the hall, lit to their quarters by yawning servants. My own duty squire helped me out of my doublet and hose, showed me the piss pot and left me to get myself into bed.

I seemed hardly to have laid my head on the pillow when I was woken by a thunderous rapping on the chamber door. 'Lord Japer, Lord Jasper, come quickly! It is Harri. He has fallen from his cot and I cannot rouse him.' Jane's voice was shrill with panic. I fought to clear the fog of sleep and wine, rolled from my bed, snatched up my chamber robe and staggered to the door. When I pulled it open Jane stood wild-eyed, on the other side, clad only in her chemise. Despite her knocking and shouting, the young squire who had been sleeping in the anteroom had not stirred. Small use he was as a guard, I thought.

'I am sorry to wake you, my lord, but I did not know what else to do.' Jane's tangled brown hair was tumbling around her chalk-white face. 'Please come to Harri. I think he is dead!'

She held a lantern in a violently shaking hand and immediately turned to retrace her steps. I followed the swinging light, half running through the solar and up the spiral stair to the nursery. Harri was lying on the rush floor in a crumpled heap, next to the new cot-bed he had been so excited to move into only a few days before. One of the moveable side-rails was still in place but the higher rail, the one that should have stopped him falling out, was missing from its slots, partly visible on the floor beneath his out-flung body. I threw myself down beside him, putting my ear to his face. Relief flooded through me when I heard the faint sound of snuffling breaths.

'He is not dead,' I said, laying my hand against his neck.

'But he is very cold. How long has he lain here?' I tugged a blanket from the cot and tucked it around him, taking care not to move his head.

Jane shook her head. 'I do not know. Not long I think.' She waved her hand in the direction of a snivelling girl who stood in the shadows, wringing her hands. 'Cerys here was sleeping in his chamber. She said she heard a bang but thought it was a door slamming somewhere. It was a few minutes before she got up to check on Harri and came straight to wake me.'

I glanced at the girl and wondered how few those minutes had really been, for the little boy was very cold. 'Perhaps she could go and find a hot brick. There may be one beside the hall fire, or in the kitchen.'

Jane nodded and sent Cerys off on her errand. 'She is a good girl,' she said, putting the lantern down on a chest before returning to my side. 'But obviously a sound sleeper.' The light settled into a steady pool.

'Many are, when young and hard-worked,' I remarked, thinking of my slumbering squire. 'We need to get Harri warm. I think he may wake up then and we can find out if any bones are broken.'

I heard Jane's gasp of anguish. 'Oh dear God, I pray not!'

'Amen to that,' I said and we both made the sign of the cross. Feeling suddenly dizzy, I put a hand to my forehead and felt the cold sweat on my brow. 'Is there any water here in the nursery?' I asked.

Beside the lantern stood a covered jug and a horn cup. 'We keep spring water here for Harri.' Jane brought me a cupful and watched me gulp it down. 'That will clear your head. I heard you carousing with your friends.'

I began to protest indignantly, 'We were not carousing –' but broke off. Harri was stirring and making little moaning sounds.

Soon Jane was kneeling beside him, her soft voice calling 'Harri. Harri. Can you hear me, sweetheart?' The little boy's eyes slowly opened and tried to focus, then he gave a groan, beginning to cry. 'Sssh. You are all right, Harri,' Jane told him and I marvelled at the calm tone she managed to summon in such a crisis. Gently she held him still, saying, 'Do not move, Harri. You have fallen out of bed. Just lie still and try not to cry. It will make your head hurt.' She placed her hand on his forehead and stroked the hair back, crooning a little tune. It must have been familiar to him because the crying stopped and Harri's blue eyes fixed intently on Jane's face.

She stopped singing and glanced up at me then began probing carefully around his neck and shoulders. 'I think he is not badly hurt, my lord. Surely if he had cracked his skull his gaze would not be so intense.' Harri did not wince as she probed and I felt the fear in me subsiding.

Cerys returned with something heavy wrapped in a thick cloth. 'A firestone,' she said. 'The cooks use them to balance the big cauldrons. But the fire is banked and so the stone is not too hot now.'

'Put it in the cot,' Jane instructed. 'I think we can risk lifting him back to bed.'

When she glanced at me for confirmation I nodded and she gathered Harri up, cradling him against her breast and supporting his head in her hand. Caught in the halo of the lantern-light the pair reminded me vividly of the wall painting of the Madonna and Child in St Mary's Church at the castle gate. It was not an image of groomed and coiffed nobility but of natural, tousled, maternal care; not Margaret but Jane.

My fingers circled her upper arm as I helped her to rise. She had rushed to Harri's aid without thought for herself and through the thin fabric of her linen shift I could feel the deep chill of her flesh. As she laid the little boy gently in the cot I pulled off my chamber robe and wrapped it around her shoulders. 'You are freezing, Jane. You will catch an ague.'

'Let us hope Harri has not caught one,' she said, pulling the robe gratefully around her body. When I saw the garment on her I realized how small she was, almost swamped. She bent to tuck the covers around her charge, saying, 'I thank the Virgin and St Nicholas for protecting you.' Harri's eyes closed. 'Look, the warmth comforts already. He is almost asleep.' She busied herself placing the rails in their slots to prevent another fall and called the nursemaid over to point out how important it was to make sure they were properly fixed under their swivelling security-pegs. 'We have been very lucky, Cerys,' she said sternly. 'There must be no repetition of this accident.' She had recovered her practical self now that her charge was apparently unharmed. Turning to me she said, 'I will fetch my cloak before you catch an ague yourself, my lord.'

Her chamber was a small one off the passage that led to the nursery. I waited outside until she returned, wrapped in her own cloak, and handed me my robe. We had left the lantern with Cerys and the only light came now from the first rays of dawn filtering through an unshuttered arrow-slit. Jane watched me shrug on my robe. We were both shivering, whether from cold or delayed reaction to the shock we had felt seeing Harri lying apparently lifeless on the floor.

'He could have died, Jasper,' Jane said through chattering teeth, her deep brown eyes wide, almost black in the dim light. 'Dear God, supposing Harri had died?'

For the first time in years she had used my name without deference or title and instinctively I put my arms around her and drew her into a tight embrace. I said nothing because there was nothing to say. She was right, Harri could have died but this time luckily he would just have a bump somewhere on his head – I prayed that would be all.

We hugged silently for a long time, sharing each other's warmth and as we did so a message seemed to pass between us, unspoken but heartfelt. I think it was an apology on my part, an acknowledgement that I had failed to understand the deep feelings she had for me and completely failed to comprehend that I had only to recognize my own aching need in order to reciprocate them. Now I was swamped by that need. I felt it so fiercely that I almost crushed the breath from her. She pulled loose but not away, gasping, her mouth slightly open, her eyes gazing into mine and her head almost imperceptibly nodding in answer to the question that she saw in them. 'Yes,' she whispered and reached up to kiss me on the lips. I was engulfed by the same powerful response as the last time our lips had met.

I almost carried her along the shadowy passage and we more or less felt our way down the spiral stair, to the door of my chamber. The April night still had its icy fingers on us and the tumbled covers of my tester-bed beckoned us enticingly into their warmth. But alluring though she was,

Jane also looked so sweet and trusting that I hesitated, uncertain if she completely understood what she was doing. With both her hands in mine I summoned all my courage. I did not want to lose her by telling her the truth, yet I knew I must.

'I cannot marry you, Jane, but please believe me when I say that I will always look after you.' I could only hope that my words sounded sincere, for I could not delude her however much I longed at that moment to make love to her.

'I will hold you to that promise,' she said solemnly, then added, with a typically impish smile, 'but remember you are bedding a virgin, my lord, so please be gentle. Oh, and I would be eternally grateful if you tried very hard to be faithful.'

With an appreciative laugh I gathered her back into my arms. 'Oh, Jane, I love you and I cannot imagine deceiving you.'

She flashed me another irresistible smile. 'Well – just to remind you – I also love you and not many married people going to bed for the first time can say that.'

'No they cannot!' In moments we had both shed our clothes and were sinking into the soft mattress, pulling the curtains closed, the covers up and wrapping ourselves in each other. It was everything I had imagined. Virgin she may have been but she gave herself to me with unmistakable joy.

21

Jane

Pembroke Castle

A LETTER FROM LADY Margaret came at last in June, along with some sunny days when the scented herbs and flowers spilled over the neatly hedged knot-garden where I had taken Harri to play. I had made him several pairs of small hosen with leather soles and patches on the knees so that he did not hurt himself if he fell on gravel paths.

'I will watch Harri for a while if you like,' Jasper said, handing me the letter so that I could read it. He swung the little boy up as he always did; Harri squealed with excitement.

I nodded. 'Thank you, but do not throw him around or he will be sick. He has only just eaten.'

I left them and wandered over to a stone bench in the sun, set against the mansion wall. The seal of the letter was broken but before unfolding it I turned it over in my hands several times, wondering what effect the contents might have had on Jasper. He and I were happy but it had been impossible to keep it a secret that I was sharing his bed. Many of the people around us, Steward Dŵnn and other Pembroke counsellors and their wives, such as Edith and Geoffrey Pole, had been positive about the fact that Jasper had taken a mistress, especially as they already knew me well. Set against this, the straight-laced gentry of castle and town were scandalized, but my friends led the way in persuading the more easily-offended folk that since I was already trusted with the upbringing of young Harri Tudor, I could not be an entirely scarlet woman. Harri's great-grandfather had apparently taken his daughters' governess as his mistress and what had been good enough for John of Gaunt should surely be good enough for Lord Jasper. However, Lady Margaret's opinion was another order of concern altogether; without doubt Jasper would be seriously perturbed by any sign that rumour had reached her of the situation at Pembroke.

To the honourable Lord Jasper Tudor, Earl of Pembroke and brother to the puissant and gracious Henry VI, King of England, France and Ireland, greetings.

Trust Margaret to bring Jasper's relationship with the king into her greeting, I thought. Although still only fifteen she was acutely aware of the power of royal connections and the importance of parading them.

I hope this finds you well and I thank you most earnestly for keeping me informed on the progress and state of health of my most precious and dearly loved son Henry, Earl of Richmond.

I felt a jolt of alarm. This was the first I had heard that Jasper had been reporting to her on Harri's progress and presumably on my supervision of it. Had he described Harri's fall from the bed? Had he – God forbid! – told her of the change in our relationship? But reading on, the pounding in my chest eased as I realized that these fears were groundless and that Margaret's attitude towards Jasper had softened.

It is with much relief that I find myself at last able to write to you freely from our home at Colleyweston in Northamptonshire, where my husband brought me very recently, after the Duchess of Buckingham was called to attend the queen at Kenilworth. Until now it has been impossible for me to obtain access to the services of a courier without submitting my private correspondence to the scrutiny of the duchess, a process with which I did not care to comply. From now on I will be able to conduct my correspondence free of censorship, because my dear and enlightened husband does not believe in it.

Colleyweston is a comfortable manor house, which has only a skeleton staff at present but Sir Henry is to help me hire a new household. We also intend to enlarge and improve the house so that we will be in a position to entertain and invite friends and relations for hunting and hawking. I hope you will soon be among those who are able to join us. To my great sadness my beautiful merlin Elaine did not survive the move to Maxstoke, where I fear the falconer did not keep the mews warm enough for her. But I still have the emerald bells that were the gift of my beloved Lord Edmund and Sir Henry has sent to Ireland for another merlin. No one

*could ever wholly replace your beloved brother, but I am
truly blessed in the husband you chose for me. Sir Henry
is kind, considerate and entirely honourable and now
that we are free to establish our home together I believe
our marriage will flourish and we shall become a truly
united couple. The Virgin and St Catherine have
protected me and you have been their chosen implement.
Now I shall pray to be soon reunited with my beloved
son, whom Sir Henry constantly assures me could not be
better cared for than by his highly esteemed and
chivalrous uncle of Pembroke. I beg you to indulge my
maternal anxieties and continue to provide detailed
reports on Henry's progress, and perhaps you would ask
Jane Hywel to include occasional notes of reassurance on
his physical health and development.*

   I am forever your loyal and loving sister,
Margaret, Countess of Richmond.
   *Written this day the twenty-seventh of May at
Colleyweston Castle, Northamptonshire 1458*

I refolded the letter and looked up to find Jasper standing
before me, hand-in-hand with Harri. 'I notice she still signs
herself Countess of Richmond,' I said. 'I thought the king
had recalled Richmond to the crown.'

'But the title was granted to Margaret for life, or until
Harri marries. I thought you took little interest in titles, Jane.'

I handed him the letter. 'No I do not but Lady Margaret
clearly does. Will she ever obtain custody of Harri?'

'No because she would share it with her husband and
fate may give her more than the two she has so far had. It
is possible that Harri might become a tool in our enemy's

hands, so she will never get custody, not while I live and King Henry is on the throne.' Jasper pushed the letter into the front of his doublet, which today was in shimmering azure blue with high collar and silver braid. Since taking his place as the uncrowned prince of West Wales he had begun dressing rather grandly and I had myself almost defied the sumptuary laws by employing the castle seamstress to make me some new summer kirtles in exquisitely patterned fabrics and bright colours. Not only that, gone was my eternal coif for now I wore more elaborate headdresses copied from the fashionable ladies of the town. Jasper had not made any comment but his glances told me that my efforts were appreciated.

'When I have written my reply to Lady Margaret I shall come to you, as she suggests, for an account of Harri's health to include with it,' he went on. 'It will have to be today, Jane. I haven't yet told you, there came by the same courier a summons to a meeting of the Great Council, only this time it has been called by Queen Marguerite, in the name of her son, Prince Édouard, which can only mean that my brother is ill again.'

'When will you go to the king?' I asked, although I already knew the answer for he never delayed responding to his brother's needs.

'Tomorrow.' Jasper made a face. 'Clearly he needs me. But Geoffrey will be coming too so Edith and Rich can come to stay with you and Harri.'

* * *

After a six-week separation, Jasper sent his harbingers to announce his imminent return. I had dressed myself in

my best and Harri in the red and blue worsted gown
Edith had given him, when we heard the trumpet
announce the first sighting of the cavalcade. Harri had
grown independent and refused to let me carry him down
to the outer ward, but we reached it in time to greet Jasper
– not with a passionate kiss as I would dearly have liked
– but with dignity, because among his retinue, as they
poured through the gatehouse arch, I spotted his father
Owen and, riding beside him, a young woman, who I
guessed must be his 'comeliest little widow' Myfanwy. She
was indeed a very pretty girl, looking at least thirty years
Owen's junior and in spite of his mature good looks I
found it hard to believe that so young a female would
have pestered him to take her as his mistress. Owen
claimed she had said they were destined to be together
but I thought it quite possible that she had a motive of
her own; had she been in desperate need of his protection,
perhaps?

Jasper leaned down from his saddle and held out his arms
for Harri, pulling him onto the pommel where the little
boy sat, goggle-eyed at the milling crowd of horses, liveried
servants and men at arms. 'One day you will have a big
horse and a cavalcade like this, young Harri,' said his uncle,
giving him a smacking kiss and passing him down to me
again, before jumping from the saddle and acknowledging
my discreet curtsy with one of his inevitable blushes and a
brief squeeze of my hand, a reaction which disarmed me
and fooled no one, least of all his father.

Owen lifted his companion down from her horse and
escorted her towards us, commenting to Jasper, 'Is that the
best you can do for your lovely lady, after so long a

separation?' Ignoring his son's exasperated grunt, Owen bowed over my hand and presented his companion in Welsh. 'Jane ferch Hywel, may I present Myfanwy ferch Gwilym of Denbigh, who flatly refused to be left behind when told I was coming to Pembroke.'

'I wished so much to meet you, Jane, having heard a great deal about you.' Her voice was soft and her Welsh words warm as she presented her cheek for the kiss of welcome. It was smooth and creamy but I saw close up that there were tiny lines around her striking violet eyes, which added extra years to my initial estimation of her age. Our brief embrace also told me something else; that she and I were in the same condition. At a rough guess Owen and Jasper Tudor were to become fathers within weeks if not days of one another.

It was later that night, after we had retired to bed, that I broke the news to Jasper of our expected child. To my dismay he did not express the delight I had hoped for.

'How long have you known?' he said.

I could feel my heart begin to flutter with alarm. 'I knew before you left but it was too early to tell you, I could have been mistaken. Are you angry? It is frequently the result of a man and a woman sharing a bed I believe.' His apparent indifference had nudged me into sarcasm and he responded vehemently.

'No, no, Jane! How could I be angry?' He put his arms around me and his next words were muffled in my hair. 'I am downcast and worried about the state of the world the babe will enter. I fear there is a real threat of civil war. That is how bad it has become.'

I pulled back from his embrace. 'Babies will still be conceived, war or no war, Jasper.'

He gave a hollow laugh. 'You have a pragmatic view of it, sweetheart. But there is something else that worries me. Did you know my grandfather the King of France was mad, and his country descended into civil war because of it? Well, I left the king recovering from another period of stupor, and just like King Henry, I too may fall into a that state one day, or grow mad like the grandfather I share with him. I may become incapable of raising an army or running my estates or even providing for this child you are carrying. And God forbid but the child may also suffer from the same malady.'

'And what about Harri – your brother's son?' I pointed out. 'Does he not also run that risk? Yet I believe many of your grandfather's descendants have shown no sign of madness. It serves no purpose worrying that you and your children will lose their minds, Jasper. I would even suggest that worrying is the best way of doing exactly that.'

He let me unlace his tight doublet and pull it off. 'You are right,' he said. 'And of course I will be proud to welcome my first offspring. When do you expect it to make an appearance?'

'In the spring; at about the same time as your father's child, I would guess.'

He stared at me, a deep frown creasing his brow. 'What? Did Myfanwy tell you she was pregnant?'

'No, she did not need to.' I tapped my nose and smiled. 'It takes one to know one.' I stepped out of my gown and hung it and his doublet on a clothes-pole. 'Now, let us pretend that I have not told you and you can take pleasure in discovering what changes your son or daughter has already made to my body.' I knelt then to remove his hose and when

I looked up I was happy to see that the creases in Jasper's brow had vanished.

I let him push me gently down onto the bed and he clambered over me to draw the curtains around us. Conversation ceased as his lips claimed mine and I felt his weight pressing me into the feathers. Then there was nothing to be done but celebrate our reunion by succumbing to the demands of our rising passion and the glorious rhythm of its fulfilment.

22

Jane

Pembroke Castle

MYFANWY WAS A WOODLAND nymph, a small, dark secretive creature who would frequently slip away into the forested hills beyond Monkton Priory, a monastery visible from the western battlements of the castle. After several hours she would return with a basket containing what she called 'nature's treasure'; fungi, roots and herbs, many I did not recognize and some which looked quite sinister.

'Do you not worry about her roaming alone?' I asked Owen, who seemed quite relaxed about these excursions. 'The woods are dense and there is no telling who may be lurking in them.'

Owen just shrugged. 'Myfanwy's mother was what some people call a Wise Woman, and in her own right she is a child of the forest. She would detect anyone nearby before they even knew she was there and she carries a knife tucked into her garter.' He grinned lasciviously. 'It was one of the first things I discovered about her. She almost unmanned me when I attempted a kiss!'

Myfanwy and I walked together into Pembroke town a day or so later and I took the opportunity to quiz her. 'Owen told me you were brought up in the forest. Is that why you like to walk in the woods?'

Those mysterious violet eyes of hers regarded me steadily. 'I was born in the king's forest in the valley of the river Clwyd near Denbigh. Only coppicers and charcoal-burners, bodgers and the like live there. My father guards the king's beasts – deer and boar and wolf – and my mother, who was a healer, used the plants that lurk in the undergrowth, as well as those growing out on the high slopes where there are no trees. Tonics and potions are sought after – people travel miles to buy them and they buy charms and spells, too, for ailments of the mind. Folk like us in the deep valleys believe that trees have spirits and faeries live in the streams, but they are not always friendly, and they require understanding.'

She fell silent and I scurried alongside her, choosing my next words as carefully as my footsteps along the refuse-strewn thoroughfare. 'It can sometimes be dangerous for a woman who tries to help people like that,' I hinted. Getting no response, I am ashamed to say that I blurted out, 'What did your mother die from?'

Myfanwy stopped still and shot me a sharp glance. 'Oh she was not accused of witchcraft, if that is what you are thinking. The travelling priests are sympathetic to the country ways and they often used my mother's cures themselves. No – in a way she killed herself. There are many, many different plants and most are kindly, some are helpful, but some are dangerous. One day she made a new potion from a selection of roots and fungi and became very sick. In two days she was dead.'

I made the sign of the cross. 'God rest her soul. Did you discover what it was that caused her death?'

'No, my mother always kept a recipe secret until she had perfected it and tried it herself; then, if she was satisfied, she got me to write it down. She had not yet given me the recipe for the potion that killed her. But I have her book. My father wanted to burn it but I hid it and took it with me when my father arranged a marriage to a widowed farmer, to get rid of me because he was grieving and full of anger.'

'Blessed Marie! How old were you then?'

'Seventeen. I was old enough and my husband much older but he was kind and did not work me too hard on his farm. He did not even mind that I did not conceive. He already had several sons – but unfortunately the eldest took a fancy to me. When my husband learned this they had a fight and the son hit his father on the head with a spade.' She heard my gasp of horror and a bitter smile crossed her face. 'I do not think he meant to kill him but he was drunk and did not know his own strength. It is wild country there, Jane. Then the son dragged me into his bed. He would marry me he said, but I knew it was against the law and besides I hated him. So I slipped a sleeping draught into his ale and ran away.'

The Market Place was too busy for this kind of conversation but near the church we found a quiet corner and I asked her to continue her sad story. 'Where did you go? How did you live?'

'I ran to Denbigh, to an apothecary there who had bought some of my mother's cures. He and his wife took me in, but I had to let them use some of the recipes. My mother would have been furious. Sometimes I think she haunts me because of it.'

'Why would she do that?'

'She said they were more precious than her children. I was the only one who knew them and I have betrayed her.' I could see tears in Myfanwy's eyes.

'How long did you stay with the apothecary?' I asked.

'Almost a year. Owen came to the shop for a cure and – well, at first I kept him at arm's length but he was persistent. Being Parker of Forests for Denbigh he knew about my husband's death. He told me that my stepson had claimed I murdered him and ran away. Then I saw my stepson in the street one day and I panicked, thinking he might set the sheriff's sergeants on me if he found me and that they would never believe a woman over a man. There were no other witnesses to my husband's death you see. The next time Owen came I accepted his invitation to live with him. I thought he would protect me.'

I laughed at that. 'The way he puts it you practically threw yourself at him, the rogue.'

She did not laugh with me. 'I probably did. I was terrified of my stepson. He is not a kind man like his father was – like Owen is.' Then she did give a little laugh. 'Or perhaps I just prefer older men.' She patted her rounded belly. 'And this one has given me a child. Will our babes be born at the same time, Jane?'

I nodded. 'Not far apart I think - before spring anyway. Will you still be here at Pembroke?'

'I hope so. I feel safe here but I will go wherever Owen goes.' Her near-black eyes lit with a fervent glow. 'I owe him that much at least.'

* * *

Our babies were born within a month of one another. I think I was lucky, or else I come from sturdy farming stock, because I was scarcely aware of my pregnancy until after Christmas and suffered only a short labour, delivering my baby girl in early February without any long struggle or lying-in. Jasper defied all the midwife's protests about men in the birthing chamber and came to my bedside almost immediately afterwards.

'She is beautiful,' he declared, cradling his swaddled daughter and gazing into her blurry blue eyes. 'And you were so stoical, Jane, barely a moan I am told. Such a different experience from poor Margaret's.'

'Lady Margaret was thirteen and I am twenty-one,' I pointed out. 'She was amazingly brave but also very tiny. Harri is lucky to be alive.'

'And lucky to have you to mother him – as is this one. What shall we call her?'

'I should like to call her Elin but the English would call her Helen,' I said.

Without a marriage contract he had no legal say in what name I chose. He shot me a sharp glance, aware that his persistence in calling me Jane rather than Sian still rankled. He repeated the name. 'Elin. What do you think, little girl?' he held the baby up to face him, supporting her swathed head in his large, calloused hand. She blinked once or twice and then fell asleep. 'She appears unconcerned. So Elin it is.'

'Elin means bright and shining,' I told him. 'I thought it appropriate. You cannot see it for the swaddling but she has red hair.'

Jasper smiled at that. 'She is definitely mine then,' he said.

'Myfanwy has agreed to be a godmother.' I glanced across the chamber to where Owen's mistress was still clearing up after the delivery. 'Also Edith, if she can get here for the baptism. Who would you like as godfather?'

He frowned, considering carefully. 'I would say my father but he may not be here to guide her as she becomes an adult. So Geoffrey I think if Edith is godmother. I will send to Haverford immediately. As long as the winds remain calm they should be able to cross the haven.'

'Well, Elin is a healthy little thing. I think we can wait a day or so,' I said. 'But not too long or Myfanwy will be giving birth herself.'

I was up and churched before Myfanwy retired to the same chamber but she, poor thing, laboured long and hard to bring her lusty baby boy into the world. I held her hand and felt my fingers crushed painfully together as she struggled not to cry out in her pain. 'Just scream,' I advised. 'No one will hear you and if they do, it is too bad.' But she would not and I believed her ordeal was made worse because of it.

She had prepared her own concoctions to drink and rub on her swollen belly and I burnt willow wands around her bed as she asked me to but her pains remained intense. I feared it might be a grim augury when, on the second night, a gibbous moon rose high in a black, starless sky, while the midwife struggled in vain to turn a babe that seemed determined to arrive feet first. Eventually however, with a single, blood-curdling scream, Myfanwy finally managed to deliver her son, helped by the midwife's desperate tugs on the child's legs. As the Church allowed, if there was a danger of the baby dying unshriven, the midwife hurriedly baptized him Dafydd after the patron saint of Wales, whose Feast Day it was and perhaps it was St Dewi who miraculously blew breath into the infant's lungs, for he took a huge gasp and turned from blue to bright pink in seconds. Myfanwy's wounds were sewn up with the midwife's special needle and silken thread but I would swear it was her mother's herbal wash, used in profusion, which prevented her torn body from developing a fever.

If Jasper had built his mansion to house his family in comfort he had certainly achieved his aim. Three young relatives now filled the nursery with their cries and gurgles – his daughter, his half-brother and his two-year-old nephew. In blood, if not legitimacy, the Tudors were flourishing.

PART THREE

Hostilities

1459–1461

23

Jasper

Pembroke & the northern Welsh March

IN ORDER TO CONFRONT the rebellious Yorkists, Queen Marguerite had imported a new form of recruitment from France called conscription, which enlisted by compulsion rather than allegiance. Across the realm fields remained uncut as every town and village was required, rather than requested, to supply its quota of fighting men in support of the crown. Sending funds in lieu was no longer acceptable. The system was unpopular and many communities failed to comply, while some expressed their displeasure at the queen's assumption of royal power in her son's name by sending their troops to support the Duke of York instead.

York's declared intention was to muster enough men under his white rose banner to pressure the king into addressing their grievances, but unfortunately there had been a clash of arms between the opposing affinities at a place called Blore Heath in the Midlands, in which the royal commander, Lord Audley, had been killed. Determined to quash what she now deemed an armed rebellion, Queen Marguerite had convinced the Council to issue a charge of treason against the Yorkists and send out further commissions of array. In addition to my Welsh force, which we had delayed mustering until after the fields had been scythed, royal armies were gathering in the Midlands, the South West and Cheshire. The kingdom was shuddering under the tramp of marching feet.

Jane came with an anxious question as Maredudd helped me into my armour. 'If you are injured or killed, what should I do? I can take care of Elin but who is responsible for Harri?'

I shrugged my shoulders into the polished links of my new lightweight mail coat and shook my arms so that the sleeves fell to my wrists. I expected to be wearing it under my armour almost constantly over the next few weeks so it needed to be comfortable. 'Geoffrey Pole has instructions regarding all the children,' I told her. 'He is my executor. I rely on you to keep Lady Margaret informed about Harri as usual but ultimately his future will be decided by the king.'

'So if you do not return I should take him to the king?'

'No, Jane,' I replied. 'If I am killed or injured the king will be told and he will liaise with Lady Margaret. Who knows what the future holds?'

'Exactly. Supposing no one tells me anything? I may not even know you are dead.'

'I would tell you, sis,' Maredudd interjected, looking up from buckling my greaves. 'Earls are not killed in battle without anyone knowing.'

'And if I am killed I hope you might grieve for me a little and pray for my soul, if you can find the time,' I added.

Her responding smile was rather forced. 'Of course you may both be killed but I would rather pray for your safety and survival, if that is all right with you.' There was a pause then she added as an afterthought, 'Please try very hard to come back to me, Jasper, if only to acknowledge your next child.'

'You are pregnant, Jane?' I exclaimed. 'How far on?'

'It is early days. This one should be born next spring, but as you said, who knows what the future holds?'

Jane's words lingered in my mind as I led my Welsh army north. My fears had been justified; the country threatened to disintegrate into the worst kind of civil conflict, with brother fighting brother and cousin, cousin. Fathers might even find themselves confronting their sons on the battlefield. I had received orders under the king's seal to take my force to the Duke of Buckingham's castle at Brecon, collect the troops already gathered there from among his tenants, and continue over the mountains to follow the River Wye to Hereford, a route that would largely avoid Herbert territory and the chance of a premature clash with York. Once there we learned that the Earl of Warwick had brought a large troop of crack soldiers across the Channel from Calais and marched through England to join the Duke of York at Ludlow.

We merged with the main royal army at Ludford Bridge, a location confronting the Duke of York's vast castle, which bristled with guns and archers and fluttered with the banners of the participating rebel lords – York's falcon and fetterlock, Salisbury's green spreadeagle and Warwick's bear with ragged staff. We could glean little notion of their strength, but our twenty thousand-strong royal force occupied a host of tents under a forest of multi-coloured battle standards and hoisted high above them all were the royal leopards and lilies, flying beside the king's gold-fringed personal symbol of an antelope. There was no mistaking the presence of the monarch in these Lancastrian lines. It would be treason for any of Henry's subjects to attack.

I found him in his silk-lined tent, seated in state at the head of a polished oak table conferring with his commanders. 'This is a sorry situation, Jasper,' he said dolefully in welcome.

How I wished his squires would call in his armourer because, as usual, he looked swamped by his mail-shirt. However, he appeared a good deal more alert than he had at our last meeting, conscious of the tension among his companions and the knife-edge on which his kingdom was poised.

I knelt to kiss his hand and he motioned me to rise and take a seat beside him. From his distracted expression, encouragement was badly needed. 'Your army looks in good heart, my liege,' I said. 'And your commanders have the duke successfully pinned down. I would call it a satisfactory situation.'

'That is what I keep telling his grace.' The grey-bearded Duke of Buckingham, Constable of England, was seated at the king's other hand, wearing his cuirass, mud-splashed as if fresh from the field. 'The Yorkists are holed up like the rats they are. We have them trapped. They have been dodging about all over the country avoiding us and now they have to come out and fight.'

'That is exactly the problem, Humphrey,' complained the king. 'York, Salisbury and Warwick are all my cousins. I do not wish to fight my own kinsmen and subjects. I want my realm to be at peace. I will offer them one more chance to come and swear allegiance and be pardoned.'

Buckingham's face suffused but he nevertheless spoke in a measured tone. 'Cousin he may be – albeit a distant one – but you cannot pardon Salisbury, my liege. He has already committed treason by crossing swords with a royal army and killing your commander Lord Audley. And there can be no denying that York and Warwick have raised their standards against their king. That is surely rebellion, which requires more punishment than a kiss on the cheek and a smack on the purse.'

'Yet I will offer York and Warwick pardon,' Henry insisted, 'and any of their captains who offer me allegiance, except Salisbury if you insist. Of course they will have to pay hefty fines in land and coin for their rebellion, which will please the Chancellor who tells me constantly that the royal coffers are empty.'

'After you send out your offer of pardon, my liege, perhaps you might then show yourself walking among your troops,' I suggested. 'Many of York's men may not be fully aware that they are being asked to attack the king's person – their sovereign lord, to whom they have all sworn allegiance. If they see you they may refuse to follow the white rose into battle.'

'You are right, Jasper.' King Henry stood up. 'Very well, bring my crown and the sword of state and I will walk among the men in full sight of the rebel army. Anyone who fires an arrow at us after that will be considered a traitor. Then perhaps they will all disperse and I can go back to Kenilworth and be granted a little peace.'

That night, after the king's promenade through his lines, as many as a thousand men crept stealthily across Ludford Bridge to claim his pardon, including the Earl of Warwick's close ally Sir Anthony Trollope with his crack troop of five hundred men brought from Calais. It must have been a bitter blow to the earl and to the Yorkist cause. Soon after dawn the following day I went to the king's tent to celebrate Mass with him and a messenger came to tell us that, far from preparing for battle, half of York's men had vanished from their lines across the river. A little later the Duke of Buckingham brought intelligence that the Duke of York and the Earls of Salisbury, Warwick and March had fled Ludlow during the night, leaving the duchess to surrender the castle.

I was aghast. 'Poor lady! She will be unprotected and terrified.'

Buckingham shrugged, as if the Duchess of York's state of mind was of little importance to him even though she was his wife's sister. 'I have issued orders that the town is not to be sacked, your grace, but our men are angry that the rebels have insulted the crown and may be difficult to control. I will obtain the keys to the castle from the duchess myself and see to her protection but I have also learned that the Duke of York is heading for Ireland through Wales. I think it is Pembroke's job to stop him taking ship.' He glanced from me to the king for confirmation.

King Henry's brow knitted. 'Humphrey is right, Jasper. York must be stopped and this time there will be no pardon. Waste no time, brother.'

It was only after I had rounded up my father and Thomas ap Gruffydd and their choice of trackers and set off hot-foot on York's trail that I realized I had not been able to inform the king privately, as I had intended, that he had a new niece and a new stepbrother. Royal recognition would have to wait. Being illegitimate, the births would not appear in the official court record.

Owen, through his office as a Royal Parker, knew the northern part of the Welsh March well and when we picked up the trail of a small group of horses heading north from Ludlow up the valley of the River Onny he was certain this must be York and his band of followers heading for the duke's favourite embarkation port for Ireland at Penrhyn. It was a small harbour on the estate of one of York's faithful followers and it was also close to Anglesey or Ynys Môn as Owen called it, the seat of our Tudor ancestors and a good source of reliable information, should we need it. We thought the York party could not have more than ten hours' start and, being fugitives, would probably move cautiously, avoiding the towns and villages and keeping to any cover available. But even the deep valleys were peppered with farmsteads and pockets of population where people would be bound to notice a group of armed men on well-bred horses. If we asked questions, cut corners and kept up a good pace we believed we might just catch them up.

At the end of the first day the trail branched off into the trough of an ancient earthwork, the great ditch and rampart built to mark the border between the old territories of the Welsh Britons and the insurgent Anglo-Saxons. Although its origins were unknown, on maps I had seen it marked as Offa's Dyke, named after a mysterious Saxon lord or king. We followed it north, skirting the settlement of Welshpool and hugging the western foot of a steep, bare-topped hill, which our trackers called Long Mountain. I took a diversion with Owen to the summit of this mount, hoping it might prove a useful viewpoint from which to scan the surrounding countryside. To the east it offered a panorama over the rolling hills and forests of England through which we had just ridden and to the north-west, the direction we expected York to be taking, a commanding vista towards the high peaks of Gwynedd, but it did not grant us any sight of horsemen; the foothills were thickly wooded and the bleak summits too distant. All that the climb had afforded me was a vivid impression of the empty wilderness confronting us and a depressing hint of how small was our chance of finding anyone in it that did not wish to be found.

Over the next night and day, with only a few hours' rest, we pursued our quarry all the way to Penrhyn but, when we got there we found the harbour empty and the gates of the fortified manor house firmly barred against us. Owen questioned a boatman of his acquaintance who operated a ferry between the mainland and Anglesey and he confirmed that a small ship had sailed from Penrhyn that morning but claimed to be ignorant of its destination. I was satisfied that its passengers must have been the Duke of York and his group of retainers and decided that even if we crossed to Anglesey and commandeered a ship from the royal castle of Beaumaris it would be impossible to locate and board a lone vessel on the rolling expanse of the Irish Sea. I sent the trackers back to the king with a letter admitting our failure and Owen, Maredudd and I decided to pay a family visit to Tŷ Cerrig on our way back to Pembroke. Whatever treasonous schemes the Duke of York might hope to devise while trapped in the wilderness of Ireland, he remained at liberty to do so.

24

Jasper

Pembroke Castle, Coventry & Northampton

I WAS RELIEVED NOT to have witnessed the dreadful
ravaging and ransacking that occurred at Ludlow after
my departure in pursuit of York. The lust for plunder among
the conscripted soldiers of the king's army had inevitably
led to the looting of the duke's castle but it was the extent
of pillaging and burning in the town and the dreadful
violence inflicted on its women and children that horrified
me when I learned of it in November.

I was attending an emergency session of Parliament at
Coventry, which was officially opened by the king. But
Henry then immediately absented himself and all the subse-
quent legislation bore the hallmark of an implacable Queen
Marguerite, whose comprehensive revenge on the Duke of
York and his allies was pushed through the legislature by
the young lords whose fathers had been killed at St Albans.
York, Salisbury and Warwick were attainted for treason, to
be beheaded without trial should they ever be apprehended

on English soil, and their extensive properties, offices and revenues were all forfeit to the crown or granted to those who had supported the king. Among other titles, I and not the Duke of York was now the Constable of Denbigh Castle. Of greatest value to me though were grants of a substantial house in the London suburb of Stepney and the use of a tower in the palace of Westminster. These would provide much-needed bases from which to administer the daunting number of royal offices and lordships I now held.

However, of more personal consequence during the Parliament was the fact that the queen had taken complete control of access to the king, preventing any private audiences with him, even for his brother. 'He simply cannot take the stress at present, Jasper,' Marguerite maintained when I questioned her fierce protection of her husband. 'But I consult him about all policy-making and I will convey any private concerns you may have to him. I reminded him of your father's efforts on behalf of the crown and it was his idea to invite Master Tudor to attend Council and be dubbed a knight bannaret. I hope you are content with his reward of an annuity of one hundred pounds. I suggested to his grace that the world thought it strange for his stepfather to be without title or income commensurate with his standing.' She placed her ring-laden hand on my arm in a gesture of concern. 'It was a – what is the English word? – a blunder, was it not, Jasper? That the son should be made an earl, a Privy Councillor and a Knight of the Garter, while the father remained common Master Tudor. But I want no thanks for righting a wrong that was due to oversight rather than intention.'

Of course I thanked her profusely and she permitted the

newly dubbed Sir Owen to lead her out to dance at that evening's entertainment, after which she revealed that he had told her of his pride in recently fathering another son. 'You did not tell me that you had a new brother, Jasper,' she admonished me. 'I think your father was a little surprised that you had kept the news to yourself.'

I was so grateful that Owen had refrained from disclosing details of my own family affairs that I only managed some lame excuse that the king's state of health had dismissed all other matters from my mind.

Christmas was almost upon us by the time Parliament rose and Owen and I travelled hastily back to Pembroke. We discovered that Jane and Myfanwy had developed a close friendship and I agreed with their suggestion that Myfanwy should stay and take charge of the nursery during Jane's spring confinement. In any case Owen would not be returning immediately to North Wales because the Duke of York's deputy at Denbigh Castle refused to surrender the command and military action would be needed to oust him. My father now had the power as a knight banneret to command in battle, and he undertook to assist me in recruiting the necessary siege force. Despite his advance towards sixty, Owen still retained his youthful zest for the military life and we became quite a team, travelling together all over the southwest, collecting oaths of loyalty and promises of arms, artillery and men whenever the muster might be called.

We rode back into Pembroke on the last day of March and my second daughter Sian, as we called her after her mother, arrived two days later. Proudly I arranged a special churching ceremony and Mass at St Mary's and a subsequent feast, which was held in the Great Hall of the castle. In the presence of the entire household Jane was feted and praised, even in a poem by Lewys Glyn Cothi, and I sat at her side taking pleasure in her delight at being granted public recognition as the mother of my children. But only two weeks later, a letter came from Margaret that I was reluctant to show to Jane.

To Jasper, Earl of Pembroke from Margaret, Countess of Richmond, greetings.

I write to congratulate you on the birth of your second daughter, who Jane Hywel tells me has been baptized Sian. Jane intimated that had I still been living in the vicinity of Pembroke, she would have begged the honour of my standing at the font as the little girl's godmother. But I wonder why you did not tell me yourself of your daughters' existence and of your relationship with Jane Hywel? Could it be because you feared my disapproval? As you know, as nurse to my son I have always held Jane in high regard but had I still been at Pembroke I would certainly have advised you to seek the sanctity of marriage with someone of your own status. However, I find it difficult to deny the joy of children to anyone, and send a gift of silver cups for both your daughters, and my hopes for their future welfare. I am happy that Henry is not alone at this young age but shares his nursery with other children, whether true or baseborn. Jane tells me Henry has been using the wax tablet and stylus I sent. I am also content with the arrangement you have made for Henry to begin lessons with the monks at the Priory of St Mary and receive religious instruction.

During the coming summer, if the kingdom remains peaceful, Sir Henry and I intend to tour our estates in Somerset and the southwest and I would greatly appreciate a meeting with you and Henry at Caldicot or somewhere convenient during that time. I feel the separation from my son acutely, especially since it seems it is unlikely I will conceive again. It is a special child you have in your care, my lord Jasper.

I am, as ever, your friend and sister,

Margaret, Countess of Richmond.

Written at Colleyweston this twenty-fifth day of April 1460, the Feast of St Mark the Evangelist.

I finished reading this letter from Margaret with mixed emotions, reflecting on its reproachful tone and the fact that my brother the king still knew nothing of the birth of my children while Margaret did. I felt had to show Jane the letter, even though it would point out her folly in revealing the existence of the children to a lady who, although not one of Queen Marguerite's official ladies in waiting, was nevertheless becoming a regular visitor to court.

'Lady Margaret will inevitably tell the queen,' I said, having found Jane alone in the herb garden.

'What if she does?' she demanded. 'I cannot see the problem in the birth of our children being public knowledge. It is known in Pembroke, why not in Kenilworth? I am not ashamed of them, even if you are.'

'You know very well that I am not ashamed of them but I am concerned that the queen will tell King Henry before I have been able to do so myself and he will not be pleased.

It will not enhance the chances of our daughters receiving favourable royal treatment.'

'This would not be so if you had written to tell the king of the girls' births. Look at your father, who proudly tells the queen of Davy's birth and receives a knighthood and an annuity for his honesty and candour.'

She was steely-eyed and formidable in defence of her children but while I admired her for it, I could not let her think that I had deliberately withheld the information from the king.

'I had every intention of telling Henry face to face, with my head held high, but Queen Marguerite prevented it. You took it upon yourself to tell the one woman most likely to reproach us.'

Jane peered again at the letter. 'Of course she has to reproach us for our "sins" because she is so pious, but we have not lost her support have we? She says she holds me in high regard and does not think his baseborn nursery companions will contaminate her precious son. How noble of her!' Her tone had become scathing. 'I know what is really troubling you, Jasper – losing Lady Margaret's esteem. Because she is your ideal of womanhood, is that not the truth? What is it you really want, my lord? Is it genuine affection, the gift of children, or do you want the cold, sexless admiration of this perfect patron?' She thrust the letter back into my hands and turned away, taking a few strides down the garden path before turning to deliver her parting shot. 'You might note that Lady Margaret at least says she is sending our children silver cups. So far you have not offered them or me any form of security for our future. Have you thought where we would live if you were to die or be killed, Jasper? Am I supposed to go crawling back to my father, who I have more or less abandoned at your behest, to present him with two extra mouths to feed? While you think about this, I think it better that I sleep in the nursery with the children. At least that will please Lady Margaret!'

I had thought this was just a brief display of female pique and that relations would be restored between us within hours but as her absence from my bed extended into days I began to give more serious consideration to her words. Did I truly see Margaret with her lofty titles and petite femininity as the ideal woman? So that others like Jane, more earthy and practical, with curves at hip and breast, who embodied motherhood and empathy over grace and intellect, were less admirable? Perhaps I did, or at least perhaps I had at one time held this view, but I did not believe it to be true now. I realized that I had never felt so content as when contemplating Jane with our two little maids and reflecting on the fulfilment their threefold presence gave me. After a week of pride-driven loneliness, during which I made a visit to Tenby, I sent Maredudd to call Jane officially to my business chamber, the room where I conducted my correspondence and met with petitioners. It was a summons, which out of fealty she could not refuse.

When she arrived I dismissed my two clerks, one of whom had been working on a document, which now lay before me on the desk. Jane appeared, plainly dressed for the nursery and wearing a grim expression. She looked wary as she obeyed my signal to take a chair, perhaps anticipating reprimand, especially as I began by presenting a facade of business-like gravity.

'Jane, you are right, I should before now have made

provision for your and our children's future security,' I began. 'Also, I realize that I have been taking your services too much for granted, the governess of a nursery such as Pembroke now boasts should command more recompense than you have received, for which I apologize. And aside from that, your extended absence from my bed has brought home to me how profoundly I would regret it should you wish to leave it permanently. With these factors in mind, I have had deeds to a house in Tenby drawn up in your name, to provide you with some independence.' I pushed the document across the desk towards her. 'Included in this deed is a pension for life from my Pembroke revenues, should you need or choose to take our children to live there.'

She made no move to take the document and I thought that she could not have heard me. I said, 'Please do not think for a moment that I want you to leave.'

She looked up at me then and there was an expression of deep concern in her eyes. 'I thought you were casting me off,' she said. 'I have been cursing my runaway tongue and now you confound me with this.' She picked up the deed and stared down at it. 'I have misjudged you. Forgive me.'

I stood up and pulled her to her feet to kiss her on her lips. 'Do not ask my forgiveness, Jane,' I begged. 'What you said was right, I have for many years placed Margaret on a pedestal but at least her letter showed me that I have not afforded you enough credit for the skill and kindness you show in your role as Harri's governess. And now that we have our own two children I realize that our love is worth more than any ideal, more than gold coin.'

Our visit to Tenby to view the house was the last day we

spent together for several weeks. It was well furnished, tucked away in a quiet alley off the main thoroughfare and boasted two floors above a vaulted undercroft, which had previously been used as a workshop. There were even latrines on each of the upper floors, which made it one of the most luxurious houses in the town. I could see that Jane was impressed.

We climbed up onto the roof turret and took in the view across the harbour and the sweep of sand where the fishing boats were pulled up. With a sideways glance, Jane commented, 'There would be plenty of room here for more than just our present two children,' which was when I knew I was forgiven. Our lovemaking that night was poignant – gentle and memorable.

The following day Owen and I left for Carmarthen, where we had arranged to muster our siege army for Denbigh. He was as keen as I was to regain control of this particular castle and town, not only to fulfil our royal commission to do so but because Myfanwy wanted to return there.

As far as I was concerned Denbigh was a Yorkist lair and I had for too long neglected my duty to bring it back under crown control. The name meant 'rocky fortress' in Welsh and it certainly lived up to it. The castle was perched high on a prominence and surrounded by the town, which made attacking its walls practically impossible, even with the guns I had managed to acquire from the Tower of London. I was relying on my father to use contacts acquired during his sojourn there to winkle out informants who might enable us to enter the castle by subterfuge and I was not disappointed. In his absence York's local support was declining and towards the end of May we managed to get the gates opened to us and install a new deputy constable with a substantial garrison loyal to the king.

However, jubilation at our achievement was short-lived. When we rode to Kenilworth to report to King Henry we discovered the royal family and their army had departed suddenly to confront a Yorkist invasion from Calais led by Warwick, Salisbury and York's eighteen-year-old son Edward, Earl of March. First they seized and garrisoned the port of Sandwich; then, after recruiting substantial support in Kent, they moved on to a rousing welcome in London. We rode south to find that the royal army had dug defensive ditches on the banks of the River Nene at Northampton and were lying in wait for the invaders to make a move. A battle was inevitable. Meanwhile the queen and the prince had taken up residence at Northampton Castle with the constable, Duke Humphrey of Buckingham, but the king had taken refuge with the nuns of Delapré Abbey and, as usual was 'not to be disturbed'.

'Take your men back to Pembroke, Jasper,' Buckingham ordered with his usual gruff authority. 'Lord Grey of Ruthin brought a force from North Wales to join us a few days ago and we need you to keep watch on Herbert in the south. We do not want him creeping up on us without being confronted. The king will be delighted with your news about Denbigh and I will keep you informed of developments here. We will have no trouble trouncing these rebel Yorkists and if any survive the battle I have no doubt the rebel earls will soon be awaiting their trial for treason in the Tower.'

Being outranked, I had no choice but to comply. Once again I was denied any personal contact with my brother and had no opportunity to assess his state of mind or confide my family news to him. Henry was becoming a phantom king; I sometimes wondered if he was still alive.

We were back in Pembroke before news of the battle of Northampton caught up with us. Far from trouncing the Yorkist insurgents, the royal army had themselves been trounced, primarily due to the battlefield treachery of Lord Grey of Ruthin whose troops, by some devious arrangement, actually stood aside as Warwick's men attacked, leaving the royal camp wide open to enemy incursion. The veteran Duke of Buckingham had been killed trying to protect his sovereign. King Henry had been taken captive and was now in the Tower of London. The queen and Prince Édouard had fled with the remnant of their army. Furious that I had not been there to defend my ailing brother, I railed against the turncoat Lord Grey but most of all I feared for the future of England.

25

Jasper

Pembroke Castle & The Welsh Marches

MYFANWY WOULD NOT BE moved. She was determined to follow Owen to war, even if he categorically forbade it, which he did during our last supper together in the mansion at Pembroke.

'You cannot stop me,' she retorted. 'Fighting men need their women more than they think, especially women who have healing skills, like I do. I will ride with the baggage train and many a trooper may be glad of my salves and potions if it comes to a battle.'

'There is not much *if* about it, Myfanwy,' I told her, attempting to support my father's ban. 'We are marching to confront Edward of York. He is not recruiting in Hereford for a Holy Day picnic. He has revenge on his mind.'

Edward's father, Richard Duke of York, had crossed from Ireland following the Yorkist victory at Northampton and defiantly re-claimed his vast Mortimer estates around Ludlow and Hereford. After commissioning William Herbert to raise a Welsh force and hold the March, he and his duchess then made a quasi-regal progress through England to London where, and no doubt to his fury, the Lords had refused to acknowledge his attempt to claim the throne. However, a hastily summoned pro-York Parliament did eventually pass an Act of Accord, which reversed the previous session's attainders and duly appointed the duke Lord Protector of the Realm and Prince of Wales, heir to King Henry. With my brother still confined in the Tower, by the end of October Richard of York had made himself ruler of England, in fact if not in name.

Queen Marguerite and her seven-year-old son were in North Wales, where they had taken refuge after fleeing the Northampton defeat. I rushed to meet them there and guided them to the safety of Harlech Castle where a ship was found for them to sail to Scotland. Once there, Marguerite had acquired the sympathy of its Regent, the recently widowed Queen Marie of Guelders and obtained substantial financial and military support. As her part of the bargain Marguerite had betrothed Prince Édouard to a Scottish princess and promised to return the border town and castle of Berwick to Scotland, perhaps unaware that this was a move that would be as unpopular among the English people as the loss of France had been.

Meanwhile disaster had overwhelmed the Yorkist cause. While Marguerite was still marching her Scottish force south, an English Lancastrian army led by the Duke of Somerset had headed north and caught up with and confronted the Duke of York at Wakefield in Yorkshire. In the ensuing battle York had been killed, his second son Edmund, Earl of Rutland, cut down while fleeing the field and the following day Warwick's father, the Earl of Salisbury, had been captured and beheaded in Pontefract Castle.

While this twenty-four hours of bloodletting was going on in Yorkshire, Queen Marguerite's uncontrollable army of Scottish mercenaries had been looting and committing acts of violence across the far north. Undaunted, the Duke of Somerset united with them and they marched on London together, jubilant at the destruction of York and determined to release King Henry from the Tower and return him to his throne. But accounts of the rampaging Scots had travelled before them to London and prompted its rich merchant-citizens to close the city down.

Warwick's men defended London, while Edward of York combined forces with William Herbert to raise the white rose in the Marches. Bombarded by reports of armies wreaking havoc across the kingdom, in my worst dreams I pictured the crown of England being kicked around the realm like a football, with no telling on whose head it might finally land.

Committed to defending my own and Prince Édouard's Welsh territories, I had recalled my men and artillery from Denbigh to my standard and hired a mercenary contingent from my cousin, King Charles of France. Unfortunately James Butler, Earl of Wiltshire, had been appointed to command it; the former favourite of Queen Marguerite and the man who had deserted me at St Albans. Whether I liked it or not, by rank he would be my second in command when we confronted Edward, now calling himself Duke of York, who was waiting on the Welsh border like a crouching lion, daring me to defy his right to be there.

'Think of your son, Myfanwy,' Jane told her friend sternly. 'Davy is not yet a year old. He needs his mother.'

Fixing Jane with her violet eyes, Myfanwy clasped her hands in a pleading gesture. 'But I know Davy will be safe here, Jane. I cannot look after him better than you but I can look after both Owen and Jasper if I go with them. Denbigh was just a siege but this conflict could decide who wears the crown. It will be more than a skirmish and there will be wounds a-plenty. No, I will be needed by our men and I *will* go with them.'

As if to illustrate her determination a log fell in the hearth, emitting a shower of sparks. Owen slammed down his cup and shoved back his chair 'There is no more time to discuss this. Jasper and I have much to do. If you are among the camp followers when we depart tomorrow then you are there and you will have to fend for yourself, Myfanwy.'

My father was right; with men and armaments to organize we did not have time for domestic squabbles. However, true to her word, when my retinue and Owen's troop gathered in the Outer Ward at dawn the following day, Myfanwy was there among the carts and cannons, mounted astride a sturdy palfrey with stuffed saddlebags, her slight body armed against injury and the winter cold by a padded gambeson and a fur-lined cloak. Where she had acquired all this at such short notice I did not like to ask but I had to admire her resourcefulness.

'She is a brave woman,' Jane said, following the direction of my gaze. 'I loaned her my cloak. I pray she will be safe.'

'She will not be going into battle, Jane.' I bit back a protest that the cloak, lined with costly minerva, had been my New Year gift to her.

'For a female there are other forms of danger.' Jane's expression was grim.

I put my arms around her, not wishing the subject to sour our farewell.

We took the high route through Brecon once more, marching fast, mostly because our task was urgent but also to keep warm. Winter had come to the peaks and snow was lying on the high passes but even so we reached the River Wye in only five days. Keeping to Buckingham's Lancastrian lordship and following the Welsh bank below the long bluff at Hay we cut east towards Leominster, thus far encountering no opposition. But we had now entered York territory; in the afternoon, as we approached a village called Kingston from the south, our scouts brought back reports of a large troop encampment a few miles beyond it to the north. Edward of York had brought his army out from his castle of Wigmore and chosen his battleground beside the River Lugg.

Owen urged that we camp near Kingston where there was good flat ground with fresh water in the river. Lord Wiltshire was not a happy man. 'We need meat,' he complained. If I judged it right he was scornful of the mercenaries he commanded, who would not move unless they were paid every day and who spoke languages he did not understand. I could only hope that when it came to a battle his captains would correctly and speedily interpret his orders into Irish, Breton and French but it was not a situation I relished. 'There were deer in the woods behind us.'

'York deer,' I said grimly. 'You run the risk of losing men in a skirmish if Edward's soldiers get wind of a foraging party.'

'It is either that or commandeering the farmers' oxen.' Wiltshire gestured across the wide valley, which was dotted with farmsteads set in pastures that would be lush with grass in summer. 'There must be some fat ploughing teams around here. Will your men not also demand meat?'

'Our men are locals,' Owen said gruffly. 'They fend for themselves. I have seen a good number of fresh hares and rabbits slung from their belts. All they need is fire and sleep.'

'And what will you eat tonight, *Sir* Owen?' Wiltshire's contemptuous stress on my father's title made my hackles rise. He was no more than a jumped up bog-Irish peer himself but I held my tongue. I knew the folly of an argument between commanders on the eve of battle.

Owen's teeth gleamed in a smile, although the angry glint in his eye told a different story. 'Heron, I fancy, my lord, it is no problem for a Welsh archer to bring down a slow-flying heron. I expect the innkeeper's wife will cook it for me.'

'I do not doubt it, sir,' I said. I knew it would be Myfanwy roasting the heron over a campfire and keeping her man warm in a bed at the inn that night. Turning to Wiltshire I made a proposal.

'We should go together to the Prior of Leominster, James, and arrange to buy some mutton. The town is famous for its wool, and there will be sheep a-plenty for butchering.'

* * *

Edward of York had chosen his battleground well. He must have ridden these fields and meadows as a boy. Perhaps he had surveyed this spot when he was a young squire learning military strategy from his governor Sir Richard Croft, whose castle I could see from my chamber window at the inn, where I too was staying. The young heir of York was powerfully at home among his friends and allies in this lush and fertile valley.

There was something else I could see in the frosty light of dawn on that second day of February. A cold mist clung to the surrounding hills and in the east the sun was rising through its icy haze. As I watched, an awesome and alarming sight dazzled my eyes. Instead of a single sun climbing into the heavens there were three; one central golden sphere with rays of silver streaming out from its circumference, attended by two smaller orbs standing sentinel on either side. I had heard tell of such a phenomenon but never seen it for myself and those who had described it to me had not done justice to its power or conveyed the sense of fear and wonder it evoked. There was no denying the trembling of my limbs and the sheer terror that set my heart pumping like a smith's bellows. Surely God was sending a portent but what message did it convey on this dawn of battle? Was it victory for one side or the other, and if so which? Or was it a sign of the Almighty's disapproval of the brotherly blood that would be spilled that day? I made several panicky signs of the cross to fend off any evil omen but found I was unable to tear my gaze from the miraculous spectacle on the horizon.

The three suns remained suspended for as long as the mist lasted, which seemed like hours but could only have been minutes. When it lifted it took the two attendant sundogs with it and the world was left with one brilliant sun in a clear blue sky and what could only be described as perfect fighting weather. I blinked my eyes repeatedly but it was as if the image had seared itself on my eyelids and every time they closed I saw that portentous triumvirate burning fiercely before me again. Then my ears picked up the sound of singing; male voices raised in a familiar hymn, which seemed to be coming from an invisible choir. Almost blindly I pulled on my hose and brigandine and stumbled to the door where I could hear urgent hammering on the planking.

It was Maredudd, lugging the leather bag containing my armour. 'Quick, my lord! You must arm and away to the camp. The enemy is making battle lines and our men need rallying. Some of the French are threatening to leave!'

I shook my head to clear it. 'Did you see the three suns, Maredudd? Is that why they are leaving? Are they frightened?' I watched him tip the armour parts onto the floor and sort through them for the first piece.

He glanced up at me, puzzled. 'Frightened, my lord? No. They are complaining about their commander, their food and their conditions. They say they cannot fight in these circumstances.'

I think my eyebrows must have knitted together, so fiercely did I frown at hearing this. 'Tell me, did any of them mention the three suns in the sky?'

Maredudd buckled a greave to my left calf. 'No. What three suns?'

'You mean you did not see them?'

'Obviously not, my lord.'

'It was a sign from God, although I do not know what it signified. But I will visit the camp as soon as you have tacked me up. I have things to say to those Frenchmen!'

By the time I reached Wiltshire's camp it was in chaos. The French and Breton mercenaries were muttering together, while the Irish had seen the three suns and were on their knees singing psalms, convinced it was a sign of God's displeasure. Their commander was making no effort to address their fears. 'You have to reassure them, James,' I urged, keeping my voice low to prevent it carrying through the fabric of his tent.

Wiltshire raised a sceptical eyebrow. 'And what language do you suggest I use?'

I could see that his heart was not in the battle ahead, let alone in quelling the present uproar in his camp. 'Sign language for all I care,' I retorted. 'Promise the French and Irish an extra groat for the day and show the Bretons that you believe the suns were sent by God to encourage them. Surely you can do that.'

He stared at me in bewilderment. 'Do you really believe that yourself, Jasper?'

I threw up my hands. 'It does not matter what I believe! It is what they believe that counts. That is what I am going to tell my camp and then we shall form our battle lines and deploy to confront York. There is no time to lose.'

A year ago, after York had fled to Ireland, Wiltshire had returned from his exile in Burgundy and, like me, been made a Knight of the Garter and as I raced to rally my own men I raged inwardly that he had woefully failed to grasp the motto of that august order of chivalry; *Honi soit qui mal y pense* – Evil be to him who thinks it. My army assembled beside the River Lugg, I turned to find Owen as agreed on my right – and I sent up a prayer of thanks when Wiltshire and his mercenaries lined up on the left flank as arranged, so that we presented a united front to the Yorkist ranks. Everyone was on foot, cavalry was too vulnerable to artillery and arrow-fire. Some commanders chose to order the battle from horseback but I believed that gave the infantry the impression that we were not all in it together and had vetoed Wiltshire's suggestion that we did so. It was immediately obvious that our enemy had done the same, for as we waited for the heralds' last minute parley the two sides began to hurl a barrage of taunts and threats, promising each other death and the fires of hell in all manner of violent ways, and our men aimed most of their vitriol at the lofty youth in the van of the opposing army who was standing, hand on sword, defiant.

I had never before encountered the eighteen-year-old who now called himself Duke of York. Edward had been too young to attend court while I lived in my brother's royal household and, at an early age, had been sent to Ludlow to get his education and training on his own rich Mortimer estates in the Welsh borderlands. Now that I was close enough to study him, gleaming in his polished armour and still helmetless before the battle began, I was surprised to see that he was not thick-set and dark-haired like the father for whose death he was seeking revenge but lean and outstandingly tall, his flaxen-hair blowing in the breeze as he stood head and shoulders above his men, like a crane among chickens. Even when a helmet covered his hair there would be no hiding this giant among his soldiers. I wondered how I would have felt at his age and in his position, leading an army into the maelstrom of all-out battle, concluding that I would have been exceedingly nervous and at the same time extremely anxious not to show it; much the same as I felt now, facing my first full battle command, just as he was.

I had sent my heralds to parley with his but it was only a formality. Whatever his frame of mind, there was little chance that Edward would let us melt away into the land-scape because for him it was fight, or lose everything, either in battle or with his head on the block. I could not suppress a secret admiration for an eighteen-year-old facing up to such a choice.

It took a few tense minutes for the parley to fail and the heralds walked back to their respective lines hurling their warders high into the air. Roars arose from the opposing lines, closely followed by opening salvos from both batteries and immediately the agonized cries of the wounded began to merge with the blood-curdling yells of the hale. Swords were raised and pole-arms lowered for the charge.

What none of us on the Lancastrian side had noticed was that during the hiatus of the parley, Yorkist longbowmen had covertly taken up positions at the edge of a tree-belt on the other side of the River Lugg. They had begun firing their armour-piercing war-arrows almost before the heralds' warders had landed and although Owen's Welsh archers quickly returned their fire a number of his company had fallen before Wiltshire's French arbalesters had wound up their first crossbow bolts. Meanwhile my men braced them-selves for the onslaught from Edward's infantry advance, saving their energy and allowing the Yorkist hotheads to expend theirs by charging at us pell-mell over the rough, frost-hardened ground. We held them off successfully, although the fighting was intense. Meanwhile the guns were exchanging fire to deafening effect and the enemy artillery found an unfortunate number of casualties amongst my men. We were soon tripping over fallen comrades, our feet slipping in their blood.

At first I and my retinue were too busy fighting off

Edward's knights to notice anything except what was in the immediate range of our visors but when the Yorkists strategically backed off to re-group I took the opportunity to survey the battleground. Owen's men had not moved in to surround the Yorkist advance as we had intended and looking to the right I saw with a shock the depletion of his ranks. The Yorkists meanwhile seemed as many as ever; I could not see that our guns had damaged them. But looking to my left I felt my stomach lurch with shock. No one was firing our guns and Wiltshire and his fifteen hundred mercenaries, who should have been fighting in a wing formation, were nowhere to be seen; they had simply disappeared, as if the ground had swallowed them up. A clue to their line of escape came to my attention; a significant pack of the Yorkist right wing heading in hot pursuit, past the main core of the fighting and towards our camp, where no doubt Wiltshire had been first to get to his horse and make his getaway at the gallop. A string of violent oaths echoed within the confines of my helmet as I had a sickening realization that this was a replay of St Albans; the same man, the same disappearing act. Only this one was to have a more devastating effect.

The enemy, on witnessing the departure of our left wing, redoubled the force of their attack. It was obvious that our position was rapidly becoming hopeless. I saw my father still fighting valiantly, keeping his footing but being forced back towards the steep riverbank. In a fortuitous gap in the almost constant blast of enemy cannon fire I yelled at Maredudd, who was close by me, viciously hacking away at the enemy.

'Get to the herald, squire! Tell him to sound the retreat. This battle is over for us.'

I hoped the formal signal might achieve an organized

retreat but no sooner had my herald's trumpet sounded and the men put up their shields and began to back off, than Edward of York waived all control of his force, which immediately became a horde of snarling, vengeful demons, intent on cutting down as many Lancastrians as each of them could individually manage. What should have been acknowledged as a military surrender became not a retreat but a rout of the bloodiest kind. There was no time to think, let alone regroup and defend; suddenly it was every man for himself, in a terrifying race for survival.

I flung up my visor, the better to see my way over the dead and wounded and the ridges and tussocks of the uneven ground and I set my course as best I could in the direction I had last seen my father but to my distress he was no longer anywhere in sight. I was discovering that there were no rules when it came to a rout. No one appeared to be taking prisoners; mere survival required deft footwork, stamina and an ability to sense when to turn and slash at an oncoming foe in order to buy enough time to sprint the next few yards, before repeating the procedure. It was only when we finally reached the camp and there was a moment to catch our breath, that I glanced around to see that a number of my close retinue had gratifyingly bunched around me, including the standard bearer who doggedly held aloft the blue and silver bordered lions and lilies that distinguished my banner.

'Unhook it and stuff it in a saddlebag, lad,' I told him hastily. 'Identification now means death.' With desperate urgency I raised my arm and signalled west. 'Mount up men and head for the hills. We must ride into the sun until darkness falls and if we have not lost them by then, Heaven help us!'

Obeying military foresight we had left our horses saddled and as I mounted I noticed that Owen's horse was gone, along with Myfanwy's, the only slight reassurance I could glean before oncoming Yorkist marauders were clambering over the carts we had upturned behind us, yelling obscene oaths and hurling any missiles they could find as we galloped away towards Wales.

26

Jane

Pembroke Castle

The death in battle of Sir Henry Stafford's brother Humphrey, Duke of Buckingham, at Northampton had put paid to the tour of their Somerset estates Margaret had planned, and the longed-for reunion with her son. Her latest communication, with its terse demands, showed me for the first time the extent of her anxiety.

> *To Mistress Jane Hywel, governess to Henry, Earl of Richmond at Pembroke Castle.*
> *It is some weeks now since I received any communication from my lord Jasper, Earl of Pembroke, and I only risk the life of my loyal courier in order to ascertain what danger to my son there exists in the present tumult. I rely on Lord Pembroke to ensure Henry's future security and noble upbringing. I must demand that you supply by a return letter any information you may have regarding the status and*

whereabouts of your lord, which you should write
immediately and entrust to my waiting courier.

I pray that you will be able to reassure me of Lord
Jasper's continued good health and ability to care for and
protect his nephew and ward.

Please pass to Henry my eternal love and maternal
blessing.

Margaret, Countess of Richmond.

Written this day, the twenty-first of January 1461, the
Feast Day of St Agnes the Martyr.

Of course I hastily penned all I knew, which was worryingly little, assured her of Harri's health and promised I would write again as soon as I received any news myself. Although somewhat resentful of the dictatorial tone of her letter, I understood her anxiety for her son and totally shared the agony of not knowing whether Jasper was alive or dead.

Pembroke had been eerily quiet in the days since Jasper and Owen had led their men away to war with Myfanwy among the camp followers, and if it had not been for the children needing my attention, I believe I might have spent my time on my knees in the chapel, praying for divine intervention on Jasper's behalf. He had not said so but I knew he had been extremely nervous setting out on his first battle command. Although he was the king's brother and recognized as the most powerful nobleman in Wales, he had little experience in the art and conduct of war and while there was no doubting his ability to wield a sword, his ability as a commander was untested.

It was Lewys Glyn Cothi who brought the first report. He had marched out with the army, wearing one of Jasper's old brigandines and equipped with pike and poniard. When a page came to the nursery to say that Lewys was waiting to see me my heart began to thud. 'Is he alone?' I asked the messenger, beckoning one of my assistants to take over the task of supervising the older children's evening meal.

'He walked in with a few companions,' the boy replied. 'But only he awaits you in the hall. He looks very tired.'

That was no exaggeration. I had once encountered the bard soaked and shivering after walking from Carmarthen to Pembroke in a winter storm but I had never seen his shoulders so slumped or his face so grey as it was when I found him crouched over the hall fire.

'Lewys, I pray you do not tell me Jasper is dead!'

The words sprang from my mouth without preamble and he straightened instantly. 'No, no, Mistress Jane, not Jasper – but Owen. Owen is dead, God take his soul.'

I felt myself swaying and he rushed forward to steady me and steer me to a chair. I shook my head to clear it and made the sign of the cross, uncertain whether it was in gratitude for Jasper's life or prayer for his father's death. 'God have mercy – Owen! Was he killed in battle? How did he die? And where is Myfanwy?'

Lewys stepped over to the buffet, poured two cups of wine from a jug, then pulled another chair close to mine. 'Here, drink this. I will tell you everything in the right order.'

I stared at him over the rim of the cup – it was then that I noticed he was no longer wearing the Pembroke livery of red and green in which Jasper's retinue had marched away but his old bard's tunic and hooded cloak.

'There was a battle, as we expected,' he began, his dark

eyes studying my face intently. They were blood-shot and heavy-lidded, as if he had not slept for days. 'Edward Mortimer lay in wait for us near his castle of Wigmore, beside the River Lugg.' By Edward Mortimer I knew he meant Edward of York, calling him in bardic fashion after the Mortimer estates on the Welsh March, over which he had held sway since a boy. 'We camped overnight and at dawn there was a fearful omen. We saw three suns rise in the sky and no one knew if it was a sign for good or evil. The French troops threatened to leave and all the men were unsettled, hardly ready for what was to come. I was no different. In the Yorkist lines banners were flying that were brought from the halls of Raglan, Hergerst and Tretower, in which I had often sung my poems. We were to fight friends and patrons. It was . . . distressing.'

His eyes filled with tears and I felt my own begin to sting in response. 'Civil war is an uncivilized business,' he said, steadying himself by taking a deep gulp of wine and clearing his throat. 'Mortimer had more men than we did but Lord Jasper had deployed well, and through the first charge we stood our ground and forced the enemy to back off. But Yorkist cannon continued to cut down our men and we saw there was no answering fire, Lord Wiltshire had simply vanished, his company of foreigners had scattered and run, even abandoning their artillery. Owen surged forward to attack Mortimer with the men he had left but it was useless and now they outnumbered us two to one. Lord Jasper was forced to call a retreat.

'Within minutes it was a rout and I was running for my life, along with Lord Jasper and his retinue. Your brother Maredudd was with him. Brave Owen rallied his men to the horse lines and they began a fighting retreat towards Hereford, taking Myfanwy with them, of course.'

Lewys paused to take a gulp of wine before continuing. 'Lord Jasper headed west for the hills but riding was not for me, I do not ride well, as you know, I decided to rely on disguise for my protection. I had my bard's scrip and my tunic and cloak hidden in a cart and I lay in a ditch for a few hours before seeking shelter with a fellow poet at Hay, though not for long as it put him in danger with Yorkists swarming everywhere, seeking the blood of our fleeing soldiers, boasting what they would do to Lord Jasper when they caught him – but I am sure they will not, never fear. At nightfall I made my escape from the town and headed across the mountains. It has only taken me six days to get here.'

Six days was scarcely possible. He could hardly have rested. I jumped to my feet, calling for a servant and ordering food and ale immediately. I was shamefaced. 'What can I have been thinking?' I said. 'Forgive me. I am so shocked by your news and worried for Lord Jasper. And Owen? Poor gallant Owen; you say he was killed. May God have mercy on his soul.' I made the sign of the cross and sat down again. 'How? Was it in the rout?'

He shook his head. 'I am confused and horrified by his death. Passing through Brecon, near the castle garrison there, I witnessed the arrival of a Lancastrian courier and I eavesdropped as he told people the news that Owen Tudor had been executed in Hereford Market Place.'

'Executed!' I could hardly believe my ears. 'But he was a knight banneret. As a prisoner he was worth a good ransom . . .'

Lewys shrugged. 'We will have to wait to find the truth. Revenge for York's death, I imagine, who knows.'

'Poor Myfanwy! Did you glean any news of her?'

The bard opened his scrip-bag and pulled out a grubby scrap of paper covered with scratched and spattered writing. 'I think I did,' he said, strangely. 'I transcribed a story the courier told.' Then he read what he had written, deciphering his own scrawled words with deliberation.

> 'Owen Tudur's head was stuck on the market cross for the crowd to mock. But when a madwoman climbed up to take it down they all fell silent. She wept and crooned as she wiped the blood from the face and kissed the lips of the dead man and placed his head on the steps of the cross. Then she set it about with lighted candles and began to sing. People who had muttered that she should be arrested became quiet because her voice rang out clear and beautiful and the song was a psalm. A breeze stirred the candle-flames and moved through the silver hair on the severed head so that it seemed to float above the steps.'

By the time he finished, tears were pouring down my cheeks. 'Oh, Myfanwy!' I whispered. 'What happened to her, Lewys, do you know?'

He hung his head, perhaps attempting to hide his own tears from me. 'I know nothing more, Mistress Jane. But I think I would have heard if she had been taken or harmed. She will come back to Pembroke somehow, to her son, that is what I believe.'

'If she is mad with grief, who knows? We can only hope.'

I wiped my tears on my sleeve. 'You are the first to return, Lewys. Will Lord Jasper come back here, do you think?'

'For certain.' The bard nodded emphatically. 'He will come back to you and to his children.'

I pressed my fingers to my temples, trying to calm the thudding in my head. 'I pray you are right but I would not want him to risk it if the Yorkists are hot on his heels. If they cut off Owen's head, why should they not take Jasper's as well?'

Lewys made no comment but his silence acknowledged the truth of my words. Then servants arrived with the food and he fell on it like a starving animal, causing me to wonder how Jasper and his retinue were faring in the winter wilderness of the mountains.

27

Jasper

Tŷ Cerrig, Gwynedd

BEFORE WE REACHED GWYNEDD we learned from a well-informed driver of a mule-train that Edward of York had turned to march east at double speed to meet a fresh challenge, recalling his troops from our pursuit, for it seemed that our cause might not be entirely lost.

Queen Marguerite had made a successful rendezvous with the Duke of Somerset and together they had marched their armies towards London, prompting the Earl of Warwick to bring King Henry out of the Tower to confront them, doubtless hoping that the queen's men would baulk at attacking the king's person, although that had not stopped them at St Albans six years before. Ironically this confrontation also occurred near St Albans but this time Warwick had been caught with his guns facing in the wrong direction, forcing him under fire to abandon the battle and hasten west with his army to meet Edward of York. In doing so he inadvertently left King Henry behind, who sat calmly waiting under a tree for his queen to collect him. Although I was heartily relieved to hear that my brother was once more with his family and not languishing alone in the Tower, I could not help laughing when I heard this story, imagining Edward's anger. The king he thought he had dethroned was once more at large with an army and I greatly enjoyed the thought of Warwick's embarrassment at losing him.

Not that I had any right to crow. My own defeat at the hands of young Edward of York rankled bitterly, mainly because I should have known better than to trust the craven Wiltshire and cursed my failure of judgement for relying on him to take any form of command. From Gwynedd I sent word of our safety to Pembroke, and of my intention to make a tour of the castles I still controlled in North Wales, to check their defences and reinforce their garrisons from my retinue if necessary. But before tackling this task we made a detour through Abermaw and trotted up the road from the seashore to call in at Tŷ Cerrig.

Instead of the usual winter bustle around the farmyard there was an unnatural silence, a complete and uncanny absence of activity. As we passed through the gate I noticed with alarm that a sinister laurel wreath hung over the farmhouse door, an indication that someone had died. Maredudd's urgent hammering on the door brought his brother Dai to meet us. He was now a grown man with a full beard, wearing a black jacket over his working tunic and an expression that was far from welcoming.

'If you have come here to hide from the Yorkists you have come to the wrong house,' he growled, fixing his eyes on Maredudd. 'We are in mourning here for our father, killed by your men at the battle in the March.'

'Hywel is dead? Fighting with the Yorkists?' I made the sign of the cross, astonished by the circumstances of this tragedy.

Maredudd flung the reins of his horse at one of the other mounted men. His face was suffused with anger. 'Father died in support of the Yorkists you say? Even though he has been taking money from Lord Jasper for five years? I cannot believe it. When did he lose his mind?'

Dai's fists clenched, as if he was on the verge of using them. 'As far as I am concerned he was in perfectly sound mind. If you come here expecting to receive the fatted calf it is you who are mad, because there is nothing here for you.'

I swung down from the saddle and stepped between the two brothers, worried that fists might begin to fly. 'Where is Hywel's body, Dai? Every son has a right to pay his respects to his father. Have you brought him home from the battlefield?' I kept my voice quiet and measured, hoping to prevent violence exploding.

'Of course we brought him home,' the young man snarled. 'His guts were spilling out and we buried him quickly in the churchyard on the shore. You can go down there if you want to spit on his grave, *Lord* Jasper.' His stress on the title spoke eloquently, along with the sneer in his voice. 'You wasted your guilt-gold here.'

'Not entirely.' This quiet comment came from a sturdy youth with cropped brown hair who had appeared in the house entrance and who I barely recognized as Evan, the youngest member of Hywel's first family. I remembered him best as the eight-year-old boy who had never seemed to stop running when we first came to Tŷ Cerrig with Owen.

Now he had his father's lean face and the body of an archer, with wide muscular shoulders and slim hips, on which his knife-belt sat low over a black sheepskin jerkin. 'I will give you God's greeting, Lord Jasper, even if Dai my brother will not.' He made a small bow in my direction before moving towards Maredudd, arms open. 'And a welcome to you, big brother, who are now head of the family.'

Mixed feelings of relief and distress showed on my squire's face as he returned Evan's embrace, realizing that his family's loyalties had become dangerously split.

'We will not come in if it is awkward,' he said, hands resting on his younger brother's shoulders. 'But tell me the situation. Where is Bethan?'

Evan shook his head sadly. 'She died before Christmas, along with her infant son. Her mother looks after the girls, poor little orphans.' He turned to me and pointed to a new tower which had been added to one end of the farmhouse. 'As you see, my lord, your gold has been put to good use. There was scant room for the family before that was built.'

'It was raised by the sweat of men, not by the charity of Lancaster.' Dai folded his arms across his chest belligerently, his brow still balefully knitted.

I could not help a note of indignation creeping into my response. 'I owe my allegiance to my royal brother,' I told him. 'To the crown, not to the House of Lancaster, of which I am not a member; just as you are not members of the House of York.'

Dai shrugged. 'If we must have an English king, I support the man more up the task. And so I bid you farewell, Jasper Tudor. There is no welcome for you here.'

'On the contrary, it would seem you are outvoted, Dai,'

Maredudd retorted, gesturing towards the open door. 'My house is at your disposal, my lord. We will find refreshment and then I will go and kneel at my father's grave. But I do not expect you to do the same.'

I gave him a rueful smile. 'He was my father's cousin. I will come with you. My father would wish it.'

'Is he not also dead?' Dai's words fell on my ears like a cannon-shot.

I shot him a piercing glance. 'What do you know that I do not?' I demanded.

His grin was ghastly to behold. 'He was beheaded. Executed as a traitor in Hereford Market Place.'

By his grim pleasure in telling me I knew he was not lying. A surge of uncontrollable anger sent my hand to my sword hilt. Only Maredudd's gasp and his arm across my chest stopped me drawing it from its sheath.

Through a red mist I heard Maredudd ask, 'How do you know this, Dai? It cannot be true. Sir Owen was no traitor. He was fighting for his king.'

'A monk from the Leominster priory told me: Owen Tudor was captured by the Vaughans a mile from the battle-field and taken to Hereford. They said he was executed in retaliation for the deaths of Edward of York's father and brother at Wakefield.'

'They were killed in battle!' I protested. 'Vaughans – which Vaughans?' I asked.

'Roger Vaughan of Tretower and his men the monk said it was.'

Before that moment I had not considered myself a vengeful man but I became one in an instant as the name seared itself on my brain like a brand. I took my hand off my sword and stepped back from my squire's restraint. 'Let us go to the church, Maredudd,' I said in as calm a tone as I could muster. 'I have a vow to make.'

The little stone church on the seashore served the inhabitants of a number of farms scattered on the lower slopes that led up into the mountains of Gwynedd. Its churchyard contained only one fresh grave. I spent a few minutes offering prayers for Hywel's soul; prayers unavoidably tainted by regret that he had accepted my annual purses and then betrayed my trust by turning his coat. It came to me that his action might have been in retaliation for me taking Jane as my mistress, which only made things worse.

I left Maredudd at the graveside and entered the church, shivering in the chill of an interior that the sun's rays never reached in winter. It lacked the wall-art of English churches and was dim and stark but a beautifully carved crucifix adorned the bare altar and I knelt before it, removing my gauntlet and putting my hand on the cold stone table. My voice echoed around the pillars of the empty nave and up into the timbers of the roof.

'I Jasper, Earl of Pembroke, swear by Almighty God that I shall not rest until the man responsible for the murder of my father, Owen Tudor, on the block at Hereford, is dead at my hand, and I name him as Roger Vaughan of Tretower.'

I rose to my feet and pulled two gold coins from the purse on my belt, tucking them under the wooden foot of the crucifix. I hoped that the next time the priest said Mass he would catch their gleam and I hoped he would not spend the money in the local alehouse but use it to embellish his plain little church in some way, to the glory of God. Out in the churchyard Maredudd was standing beside his father's grave, staring over the churchyard wall at the restless waves that washed the pebbles on the shore.

I walked up behind him. 'I will release you from your fealty, Maredudd, if that is what you want. You are your father's heir and your place is now here.'

When he did not turn I knew he was going to accept my offer. His voice was gruff as he replied. 'I do not want to leave your service, my lord, but my duty lies here, especially as Dai has become a Yorkist.' He did turn then and his eyes were moist. 'But I would be grateful if you would take Evan into your retinue in my place. He is young and obviously fit and he learns fast. I will be able to deal with Dai more easily if Evan is not here.'

He did not expand on his last remark, nor did I wish him to do so. How he tackled the rift in his family was his affair. 'I will take Evan if he is willing to swear allegiance,' I said. 'And the pension will remain the same.'

We rode back to Tŷ Cerrig in meditative silence.

28

Jane

Pembroke Castle & Tenby

After the disaster of Jasper's defeat in the Marches there was a false peace. Bereaved families mourned their dead, tended the injured, welcomed home the living and then went back to their tasks in home, field and workshop. Meanwhile we heard that Edward of York had consolidated his flimsy grasp on power at a place called Towton in North Yorkshire, snatching a desperately fought victory in a long and bloody moorland battle, which was reported to have claimed over twenty thousand lives. My mind could not envisage fatalities on that scale. It was said that the streams ran red with blood for days. Scarcely a village in England can have been spared casualties. King Henry, Queen Marguerite and their young son fled from the field on horseback, struggling for days over snow-covered hills until they reached Scotland; forced into exile from their kingdom. As for their scattered forces – those men from the towns and villages who had fought under their royal standard and survived – they had no choice but to swear allegiance to a new and unknown king or face a short and brutal existence as outlaws.

Jasper had not yet had to make that choice, were he indeed to be offered anything other than the scaffold. By early April he had completed his reinforcement of the Welsh strongholds that still held for his brother and returned to Pembroke, depressed and exhausted. I was profoundly shocked at the change in him. He had ridden out of the castle at the head of his liveried retinue, magnificent in shining armour, his father beside him and their banners flying proudly overhead. A thousand men had left that day; many of those who outran the rout returned directly to their homes and buried their weapons, some now served in the loyal castle garrisons and only seven rode back under the gatehouse. I was startled to see Evan among them rather than Maredudd and amazed at the transformation in my younger brother, now a man when I had left him a boy.

Jasper had written to tell me about my father's death in the battle but he had not wished to burden me with Hywel's defection to York and Dai's hostility at Tŷ Cerrig. These he confided at our first opportunity for private conversation, his tone subdued, the voice of a defeated man, which wrenched at my heart, even more than the anger and hurt I felt at my father's betrayal.

Not for the first time I blessed the forethought that had included a bath chamber in the design for Jasper's mansion. Servants had filled the stone tub almost to the brim with hot water and steam rose around us as I scrubbed the ingrained dirt from his skin, horrified by the sight of him, haggard and filthy and covered in insect bites after weeks living rough in barns and bothies. The clothes he had been wearing I had ordered consigned to the fire, hoping to prevent the bloodsuckers they sheltered migrating to the rest of us.

'Is it likely you will be forced to flee Wales?' I asked. 'So far we have not received any attention from the Yorkists.'

'Edward of York will soon turn his attention west now the king is fled. And believe me, Jane, I will be at the top of his reprisal list. For him my father's head will not be enough revenge for the deaths of Wakefield.'

I refused to let the tears rise, those for the deaths of both our fathers and the tears provoked by my dread that Jasper might soon follow them to the grave. It had not escaped me that he was now the only member of King Henry's family still at large in the kingdom and surely a prime target for extermination by York. Despite Pembroke's three portcullises being permanently lowered and a twenty-four-hour watch posted at all corners of the battlements, from now on I knew we would live in constant fear of an attack on the castle. However, I was also aware that I must for the sake of our children give serious thought to every future possibility.

*　*　*

As he recovered his strength and returned to his former vigour, Jasper became more than ever determined that his brother's cause should not be considered lost. 'There are still many supporters of the Lancastrian throne,' he declared, 'particularly in West Wales. It only needs one show of strength to bring them all flocking back to King Henry's standard.'

Edward of York did not wait to be crowned before commissioning his faithful lieutenant in Wales, William Herbert of Raglan, to seize all Jasper's lands and castles. A proclamation to this effect was even posted in the Pembroke Market Place, until Jasper sent a posse from the garrison to rip it down.

'What man dared to post Yorkist propaganda under my nose!' he stormed. 'I am still lord of Pembroke. Let Herbert show himself powerful enough to take it from me!'

At the beginning of July, news came that the Duke of Exeter was preparing to embark from Flanders with an army of mercenaries, supplied as a result of Queen Marguerite's personal plea to the Duke of Burgundy. They were expected to arrive before the end of the month at Harlech, a coastal castle on the shores of Tremadog Bay, north of Tŷ Cerrig, which still held for King Henry and which contained its own walled harbour. Jasper immediately began to muster a new force, in order to march north from Pembroke to rendezvous with them.

'This is a risky venture, Jane,' he confided, taking me in his arms. 'Who knows when I may return this time, if at all.' But I could not feel downcast or afraid because the face I so loved was restored, the red beard close-clipped, the cheeks filled out, the intense blue eyes smiling into mine, and he said, 'We deserve a little peace before we are consumed by war, do we not?'

He suggested we spend a few days together at the house in Tenby. The Yorkists would not look for him there and we would be only a few miles away if Herbert made a move.

At four-and-a-half Harri was of an age to detect changes

in the emotional atmosphere. He had been fretful during Jasper's absence in the spring and ecstatic on his return and now he was very aware of his uncle's renewed restlessness. When he learned that we were both going away he grew distressed and tearful. 'What will happen if you do not come back, Mistress Jane? Who will look after me? Where would I live?'

These were questions fundamental to any child's existence and I had no definite answers to give him. Harri's future was a conundrum without Jasper and he sensed the insecurity. He was right to be anxious, I reflected. Of all the children, the biggest question mark hung over Harri's future.

We rode to Tenby with a small escort, which included Evan, with whom I had so far found no opportunity to talk privately. On entering the town the first thing Jasper wanted to do was to inspect the work that had been done on its walls, for which he had contributed a considerable slice of the finance. There was now a stout tower overlooking the harbour and I noticed that cannon were already in place on its battlements, even though the roof was not yet complete. Precautions had also been taken against imminent attack from the sea, and all these new defences cast a shadow over my spirits – until we dismounted outside the timbered facade of my house, where I proudly wielded the big iron key that turned the lock on the heavy oak door. Jasper handed the reins of our horses to our escort and then they trotted away and we were alone together.

Once inside, to my delight Jasper seemed to shed the cares of the world. He kissed me and I smiled and kissed him back. Wordlessly, he took my hand and we ran, laughing, up to the next floor two steps at a time. By the time we found the main bedchamber we were both breathless and the shadow of imminent danger seemed to spike our love-making with extra zest. Knowing our time together might be short inspired a fresh and eager passion between us and before long the fear of what might be to come vanished in a summer storm of sensuous pleasure.

We hardly left the house for three days, but I spent some welcome time with Evan, walking and talking by the shore, while Jasper wrote letters to his supporters in North Wales, seeking recruits to swell the Flemish force that was due at Harlech. It was then that my brother told me the truth behind our father's defection to the Yorkist cause.

'He accused Lord Jasper of using you, Sian.' Evan's cheeks grew pink under his dark stubble when he said this. 'Like the Norman conqueror claiming *droit de seigneur*. He said he felt ashamed that he had taken gold for the kind of service you were providing. I'm sorry, Sian, it's best you hear it from me rather than find out later from wicked tongues. Had you come to Tŷ Cerrig he might well have refused you entry.'

I felt as if someone had punched me hard in the stomach. 'But, Evan, you have sworn fealty to Lord Jasper. What do you think?'

My brother kicked a stone on the beach and sent it spinning into the water. 'I liked Lord Jasper the first time I met him – same as you did. And he did not change when he became a lord. Our father did not read him right.'

'So you would not betray him?'

He shook his head. 'I wanted to enlist in Owen Tudor's archers but Father would not let me. Even so I could not believe it when he marched off to join William Herbert's muster.'

'He was an old fool,' I said bitterly. 'Too old to fight. Why did he not send Dai?'

'Because Dai is no soldier. Besides Father said that if Owen Tudor was fit to fight then so was he.' Evan shrugged and made a hapless gesture. 'It turned out neither of them was.'

'At least Hywel died on the battlefield and could not have been involved in Owen's execution. That would have been terrible indeed.'

'I hope he would have refused to be party to that. What will you do, Sian, if Lord Jasper is captured?'

Evan's blunt question took me by surprise. Since we had come to Tenby, Jasper and I had avoided this topic, but he had told me when he first returned to Pembroke that he wanted me to take our children to Tŷ Cerrig and if Myfanwy does not come back, Davvy too. With Maredudd now head of the household I supposed he believed we would be safe there. But I could not bring myself to confide, even to Evan my own entirely different intentions. I had learned that in general men became dictatorial if a woman showed any sign of defiance.

'And little Harri? What will happen to him?' Evan asked.

I frowned. 'Since Lord Jasper is attainted, I think wardship of Harri reverts to the crown and no doubt some noble person will be granted his custody. I hope it might be his mother but I think it unlikely, sad to say. One thing is certain though, I will never be permitted to remove King Henry's nephew to a rustic farmhouse in Gwynedd. Even one that has a grand new tower!' I gave Evan a rueful smile. I had a suspicion that Harri might rather like to grow up on a farm.

On the way back to the house I stopped at a baker's shop and bought a mutton pie for our dinner, fresh bread and ale and some strawberries, picked fresh that morning and lying like polished rubies in a woven rush basket. I found a young courier in the hall, waiting for Jasper's letters and recognized him as one of the brave messengers who still made rounds of the lordships and families of north and West Wales remaining loyal to King Henry.

'Any news, Jenkin?' I asked him. These couriers were our chief source of information from outside the earldom.

'Carmarthen has opened its gates to Herbert's men,' he replied glumly. 'I only just got out in time or I might be a prisoner now.'

I gave him a sympathetic glance before climbing the stairs. The present hostilities doubled the risks he faced and his narrow escape set my mind racing. If the Yorkists were in Carmarthen they were only thirty miles from Pembroke. The net was closing on Jasper.

Jenkin had delivered a letter from Lady Margaret, which Jasper showed me in our private chamber, and I could see from his expression that our idyll was coming to an end. It was little more than a note, ink-spattered and in her own handwriting, with no formal greeting.

Jasper,

Despite my pleading and my husband's decision to take the royal pardon, the usurper Edward has dismissed my petition for custody of Henry and sold it to William Herbert for a thousand pounds, placing financial gain above a mother's love. How can a common Welshman afford such a price? I am appalled that Henry thus falls

into the hands of the man who ordered the death of his
father. I imagine you know that William Herbert also
has a royal commission to seize your lands and take
Pembroke castle? I am torn between begging you to
surrender without exposing my son to the dangers of a
siege and urging you to blow the murderer's head off
with one of your cannons. If Henry is still in your
hands, Jasper, and if you are in any position to steer his
future, then I beg you to remember how precious he is to
me, my only son, the only child I will ever have. I have
no choice but to put my trust in you and although I
cannot condone your relationship with her, if Jane
Hywel is able to remain as his nurse and governess it
would have my approval, and she should continue to
write to me about my son's activities and well being.

In great haste,
Margaret, Countess of Richmond

I folded the letter and handed it back to Jasper with a
grimace but this was no time to be offended by her haughty
tone.

'She has given you a terrible choice to make, Jasper,' I
said. 'What will you do?'

'I have already decided,' he replied. 'I must go to Harlech
to meet Exeter. With his Flemish mercenaries and my Welsh
recruits we have a chance to secure the principality for King
Henry – I cannot put Pembroke before that necessity. I can
no longer protect Harri, and he is too young to be taken
on campaign, so I have instructed Constable Skydmore to
surrender the castle and little Harri to Herbert when he
comes. As for Margaret's hope that you will stay with the

boy, I want you and our children to come north with me when I go, Jane. I want to know you are safe at Tŷ Cerrig, rather than being Herbert's hostage.'

I stared at him in horror. 'And leave Harri at Pembroke? I would be neglecting my duty. Lady Margaret more or less ordered me to stay with her son. Besides, from what Evan tells me I do not know that we would be welcome at Tŷ Cerrig. No, Jasper, I cannot come with you. Lady Margaret would never forgive me – or you.'

Jasper was on the verge of contesting this refusal but my final remark – the prospect of giving offence to his honoured lady – proved too much for him to contemplate.

When Jasper left for the north a few days later I remained at Pembroke with the children, waiting for fate to play its hand.

29

Jasper

The wilderness of Gwynedd;
Caernarfon & Harlech Castles

I HAD WAITED IMPATIENTLY for a fortnight, expecting him to arrive at Harlech, only to receive a message from the Duke of Exeter that, inexplicably, he had landed further round the coast at Mostyn in Flintshire, the estate of a Lancastrian family loyal to King Henry. Unfortunately it was surrounded by Yorkist lordships; his Flemish army would have to fight its way across North Wales. In fury, I disbanded my men. Why should they kick their heels, waiting for a duke who gave no thought to an agreed rendezvous?

Herbert's men were everywhere but Maredudd then brought me where none would think to search now winter was coming. Evan stayed with me while I waited, showing me how to survive in the hostile, bracken-smothered territory where our ancestor Owen Glyn Dŵr had sheltered from the English sixty years before. In a small stone hut where a shepherd sheltered in summer, all I had to occupy me, apart from playing cards with Evan, was keeping watch, keeping warm and cursing the Duke of Exeter. Occasionally we heard Jenkin's signal whistle and stepped out to receive the latest communications and fresh supplies. In the second week of October a letter reached me from Jane, addressed via her brother at Tŷ Cerrig. The letter was unsigned, undated, neither of our names was written – but her greeting was warm and loving. Every day when I re-read it to remind myself how different life had been only a few weeks ago, I was shaken once more by the momentous news it contained.

My best beloved I kiss your lips.

I pray that our courier will deliver this safely. I write it on the eve of leaving Pembroke for Raglan. Yes, I am entering the lion's den and so are all the children.

William Herbert came to Pembroke three days ago with a large armed force and a terrifying battery of guns. His arrival caused great consternation in both town and castle. On the second day his herald approached the walls to offer terms. As you instructed, Constable Skydmore was intending to surrender the castle without conditions but I asked for time to prepare the children. When I told Harri that he would be going to a new home he begged me to go with him. I said I would have to ask his new guardian.

When the herald returned next day the constable asked if I might speak personally with Lord Herbert and I was escorted to his tent in the siege camp across the river. Instead of the rough-mannered, tough-talking soldier I had expected, I found a gentleman who listened politely to my proposal that I be allowed to accompany

Harri to his new home and bring his present nursery companions with him. I explained that I had been his nurse and governess all his life and that separation from us would cause serious problems in the young boy's behaviour and his health, a matter of paramount importance to his mother. I do not know whether Lord Herbert has ever encountered Lady M but the mere mention of her name gave him pause. After some thought he said it would be up to his wife to decide whether her household could accommodate four extra youngsters and their nurse.

I now have agreed to go with all the children to Raglan and then see if Lady Herbert approves a longer-term arrangement. If she does, I fear it will mean that any future meetings between you and me may not be easy – perhaps impossible – but I am doing what I feel I must and rest assured that I will always do my utmost to keep all the children safe. I remain forever,

Your very loving friend.

I hoped against hope that Jane would write again, although I knew it would be next to impossible to send a missive from a Yorkist castle to a hunted Lancastrian outlaw. I had written a brief note in reply but I doubted it would reach her. Meanwhile the man who I believed had killed my brother now had custody of my lover, nephew, half-brother and daughters and was hunting me. The demon of despair haunted me during this time and only a burning ambition to destroy the Yorkist usurper and restore King Henry to his rightful throne kept it at bay.

As I tucked the letter away I suddenly heard the alarming

sound of harness jingling. To preserve our security Jenkin always came the last mile on foot so I knew it could not be him; besides this was too much noise for just one horse's trappings. My instinctive reaction was to reach for my cuirass and as I did so Evan came slipping through the door of the hut. He had been up on our lookout rock and was panting from the run.

'A column of horses and men is approaching up the valley under a wheatsheaf banner. That is the Duke of Exeter's badge, is it not, my lord? He has brought his whole thundering army into the hills!'

I let out a roar of anger. 'Arrgh! Jesu, he will have every Yorkist in Gwynedd on our trail. How in Heaven's name did he discover my whereabouts? We must have been betrayed.' Evan looked deeply troubled and I read his thoughts: Maredudd would never have revealed our whereabouts but perhaps Dai guessed where we had gone. However, I said no more as my squire fitted the back plate of my armour.

I looked less like a scruffy shepherd and more like a knight of the realm as we left the hut and descended the slope to meet the approaching army. The duke and I had both been attainted in the recent Yorkist Parliament but no Lancastrian would ever acknowledge its right to remove his title. 'His grace of Exeter I presume?' I said, bending my knee to the leading knight whose helmet had its visor up and a fox's tail attached to its crest. Exeter's nickname was 'The Fox', one I chose not to use because I had a sneaking admiration for the animal. 'It is a long way to bring a whole army just to find two men.'

Exeter swung one leg over the front of his saddle and jumped down from his horse. 'They will not let me out of their sight, Pembroke. Not until I pay them.' He removed the helmet and threw it blindly back to his squire, who had to lean so far from his horse to catch it that he almost toppled off. I wondered what the penalty would have been had he missed it.

'Pembroke by name but at present no longer by estate,' I remarked dryly. 'Although the sight of your men gives me hope of regaining it.'

In a guttural language I took to be Flemish, their captains were ordering the foot soldiers to fall out. Exeter moved closer to me so that his next words would not carry to the troops. 'Do not hold your breath, my lord. This is the surliest herd of bullocks I have ever had the misfortune to command. The Duke of Burgundy emptied his prisons into my ships. If I had my way I would march them all straight to the slaughterhouse.'

This attitude stirred unfortunate echoes of Wiltshire's sour view of the force he had abandoned in the Welsh March and I sent up a silent prayer to St Michael that I had not drawn a short military straw again. 'Perhaps they realize you have marched them all across North Wales for no good reason. Why did you not make landfall at Harlech as planned, duke?' I gave him his title but not the deference that should have gone with it.

He scowled and his lip curled in a snarl. 'I had business in Mostyn that is not any business of yours.' He turned his back and surveyed the wild, brown landscape. 'And what a dump we have marched into. This country is Hades without the warmth.'

I ignored his attempt to avoid my question. 'It is my business, sir, since our plan was to attack Caernarfon Castle and your delay has given the Yorkist Constable time to strengthen his garrison and unmask the man I had planted inside to open the gates to us. A week ago he was thrown from the battlements with a noose around his neck.'

'You did not choose a very skilful agent then, did you?' With a shrug Exeter turned to his squire, a youth with the misfortune to have buckteeth. 'Bring out the wineskin coney-face. I could drain a cask and our host does not appear to be offering any refreshment.'

Everything I had heard of Exeter's unpleasant character had surfaced in the last few minutes but I swallowed the indignant riposte that was on the tip of my tongue and turned to Evan with a wink the foxy duke could not see.

'Fetch his grace a draught of our best Welsh ale, Evan. That will quench his thirst better than wine.'

It was no surprise when the duke spat out his first gulp and emptied the rest on the ground. 'Ugh - water! A man can die from drinking that.'

I shook my head. 'No, my lord duke, not here in the Welsh mountains, unless your men have already peed in our stream.'

'Well you are right there for once, Pembroke. Their Flemish piss would poison a man in seconds.' Exeter grabbed the wineskin off his squire and tipped it high to suck a long draught.

I watched with distaste, summoning my patience with difficulty. 'Nevertheless we need them if we are to have any hope of getting into Caernarfon Castle, so I advise you to order them to drink their fill upstream, urinate downstream and then march straight back down the hill to the coast in hope that we get there before William Herbert does.'

Unfortunately we did not. The march to Caernarfon took two days and as we drew close to the first King Edward's massive grey fortress, Exeter and I climbed to a highpoint to reconnoitre the surroundings, only to spy a large force approaching from the east with banners fluttering. High over them all flew the three white lions of 'Black William', the standard of the new Lord Herbert.

I was instantly seized with the desire to attack. Exeter however was not of the same mind. 'They have numbers, Jasper,' he said. He had taken to calling me by my given name, although I had not invited the intimacy. 'We should retreat to Harlech and wait for your Welsh recruits to join us.'

On Exeter's arrival I had sent out a new call to arms to the northern Welsh families who remained loyal to the Lancastrian cause but there had not yet been sufficient time for them to respond. 'That will give Herbert the chance to acquire more men and artillery from Caernarfon,' I protested. 'Then we will be truly outnumbered. No – it is now or never.'

Exeter scowled, an expression with which I had become very familiar. 'Queen Marguerite gave me the command here and I say we retreat to Harlech. If we keep our men to the west side of the hill the approaching army may not see us until we are well out of range.'

I had a sudden vision of the Earl of Wiltshire's vanishing-acts, which I feared Exeter was highly likely to emulate; but in reality I had no choice. The Flemish mercenaries would only take orders from Exeter and when he announced the retreat he told their captains that the gold to pay them was at Harlech Castle. Then his elbow nudged my arm and in a low voice he added, 'They will move at a good pace when they hear that, eh Jasper?'

'And where actually is the gold, my lord?' I muttered in reply.

He gave me a sideways glance. 'It is safely lodged at Mostyn, of course. Edward of York has granted all my revenues to my witch of a wife and I need funds to live on. You will learn to milk the system too if he stays in power for long.'

Exeter had been married to Anne Plantagenet as a youth, one of the more toxic unions between Lancaster and York. She was the elder sister of the Yorkist usurper, who had much earlier managed to negotiate a deed of separation and when Edward took the throne she also persuaded him to grant the attainted Exeter estates to her, rather than taking them back to the crown. If the duke had hated the House of York before, this action had made him loathe it even more.

I should have guessed there was more to Exeter's wish to retreat than met the eye. He and his entourage were all mounted, whereas the Flemish mercenaries were on foot and when Herbert sent his cavalry out to harry our rear, the Flemish infantry broke ranks and began to run to escape the thundering hooves. It was some time before word of the chaos behind us reached the van and my first instinct was to gallop to the rear-guard's aid but Exeter was having none of it, manoeuvring his horse to block my way. 'If you do not get to Harlech first, Jasper, they will not open the gates and the Yorkist army will be all over ours. We have to ride on, that is an order!'

This was another bitter choice for me. I prayed that one

day I might fight alongside truly honourable commanders, who would have only the welfare of their men and victory over York at the forefront of their minds.

The weather deteriorated fast as we galloped towards Harlech and our first sight of the castle was shrouded in a sea wrack, its pale stone towers seeming to float on a swirling white cushion, while below it Tremadog Bay had become an invisible roaring fiend. Through wind-hurled spray from the waves crashing on the rocks below we climbed to the gatehouse entrance, shouting for admittance, but our voices were no match for the pounding surf and I think it was luck that a head appeared over the battlements above us and I was recognized.

Exeter muttered darkly as we stood before the first in a succession of drawbridges and portcullises. Having been admitted across two lowered bridges, at the first gatehouse portcullis we were asked to dismount and inspected at close quarters through the grille; arrows were trained on us through slits in the walls on either side and the guard growled, 'Names and business, if you please.'

Exeter was on the verge of exploding. 'Jesu, man, you know the Earl of Pembroke and I am the Duke of Exeter. Now get this gridiron lifted and let us escape this accursed wind.'

I had endured this tight security many times and approved its thoroughness. The garrison commander was a man I knew well and admired. Dafydd ab Einion was a stern and stolid Welshman whose loyalty to the Lancastrian cause was well ingrained. He knew every man of fighting age in West Wales and constantly rotated his force from families selected for their trustworthiness. Exeter might try but he would not defeat the constable's rules of defence with bluster. There was a predictably fiery encounter with the garrison commander himself before, eventually, the second portcullis was lifted, followed by a third and then at last we were permitted to emerge into the fading daylight of the inner ward.

A plump woman of a certain age stood waiting inside and made a suitably deep curtsy to the duke. 'My wife, your grace,' said Dafydd curtly. 'She will show you to the guest quarters. I will be at your disposal in the great hall when you are ready.'

Then Exeter landed a cannonball in our midst. 'There are a thousand Flemish mercenaries moving in this direction with Herbert's army hot on their heels. My orders are not to admit them.'

Dafydd's eyes rolled in astonishment. 'It is true that there is not room for a thousand men in the inner ward, your grace, but they can make camp in the outer ward. The curtain wall will at least give them protection from their pursuers.'

'No!' Exeter's voice rose to a shout. 'They are not even to be admitted into the ditch. Herbert can deal with them as he will.' He turned abruptly to the constable's wife and added in a slightly milder tone, 'Now, madam, lead me to my chamber.'

The Harlech gatehouse also served as a keep and we were each given a spacious room on the top floor. My chamber had a narrow window overlooking the castle entrance and provided a view of the small settlement nestling under its walls. I saw a number of shadowy figures creeping around these buildings and assumed them to be some of Exeter's Flemish soldiers looking for shelter and perhaps somewhere to hide. A large crowd of them had already gathered on the far side of the ditch shouting for admittance, a demand that was clearly being ignored.

Going to speak with Exeter I found him doing as I had done, looking out of his chamber window at the scene below. Torches had been lit on the battlements of the drawbridge towers, throwing an eerie, dancing light onto the growing mob of Flemings. The wind had dropped and their shouts carried clearly up to us, the voices full of anger and fear.

'What are they saying, my lord duke?' I asked him. 'You must have enough of their language to understand their curses.'

Exeter turned; to my shock and amazement he was smiling. 'They can curse all they like. I am rid of them now.'

'So you have thrown them to the wolves,' I said. 'They will never get home from here.'

'I told you, they came out of the Flemish prisons. They do not wish to go home. Scum like them will find their own level. There are plenty of outlaw bands in this country that will be glad of their throat-slitting skills – those that survive. Do not waste your sympathy on them.'

'And where do you intend to go now? Or do I need to ask?'

Exeter approached me, leaning aggressively close. 'First I am going back to Mostyn, to collect my gold. Then I am going to France. I dare say you can provide me with a ship.'

I gave a hollow laugh. 'How many Burgundian vessels did you leave unpaid at Mostyn, duke? I have no intention of asking the constable to risk one of his supply ships taking you into hostile territory. We were due to meet at Harlech and here we are. You ordered a retreat from Caernarfon and we retreated. Now you have abandoned your army and so I am no longer under your command, for which I thank Almighty God.'

I did not wait for his response but turned on my heel and left, making my way down to Dafydd's hall and more congenial company. The constable confided that there was only one small ship in the harbour at the foot of the castle cliffs. 'I fear it may have sustained some damage today, due to the rough seas,' he said with a conspiratorial smile.

I clapped him on the back. 'That is what we will tell Exeter. He won't risk a leaking ship. Tomorrow I will take your "damaged" vessel down to Abermaw for repairs.'

Dafydd frowned. 'Are you leaving Wales, my lord? That will disappoint my men. They see you as their only hope.'

'I am not leaving for long,' I assured him, 'but I must meet with King Henry who is in Scotland. I need his written authority to negotiate with our European allies. My uncle Charles has recently died and the new king of France is my cousin Louis. I have never met either of them but whereas King Charles was pro York, I believe King Louis to be on our side, so I have high hopes of obtaining men and funds from him. That is why it is essential that you hold Harlech for us, Dafydd, so that we have a safe landfall for another campaign – next time I promise without the dubious assistance of my lord of Exeter!' Unfortunately I had to raise my voice over the desperate shouts of the men at the gate.

'Did I hear my name?' The duke strode across the hall to the hearth where Dafydd and I were standing before a crackling fire. 'Not plotting secretly I hope?' His tone was light but his eyes were cold.

The constable bowed deeply and indicated a cloth-covered trestle, laid out ready for a meal. 'Lord Jasper was just saying we should wait for your grace before eating. Will you take a seat, my lord?'

'Jesu yes!' Exeter advanced to the chair placed in the middle of the board. 'My belly thinks my throat has been cut. And let there be wine. I could drain a cask!'

It was not until he had consumed several dishes and sunk a flagon of wine that he brought up the subject of a ship. 'We have not been able to see this famous harbour of yours, Constable,' he began, his voice slurring noticeably. 'Are there any ships in it right now?'

'Only one, your grace,' replied the constable, casting a swift glance at me, which did not go unnoticed by the duke.

'Ah - one is enough. I hereby commandeer it in the name of Queen Marguerite. I need to return to her court in France immediately.'

'I fear that will not be possible, my lord.' Dafydd avoided eye contact and wrung his hands as if mortified.

Exeter's chair went flying as he leapt out of it and flung himself at the Welshman, who instantly ceased looking humble and pulled out his dagger. I grabbed at the collar of Exeter's brigandine and pulled as hard as I could, dragging him off balance and flinging him across the table. Dishes and cups went crashing to the floor and he turned his fury on me but I was ready for him and not drunk. Before he could recover his equilibrium I had him in a headlock, my left arm across his throat.

'Lose the blade,' I hissed at Dafydd, then yelled in Exeter's ear, 'Calm down, duke! The ship is damaged by the storm. It is not seaworthy. Unless you want to risk being drowned.'

Still half-strangling him I reached with my other arm and righted the chair he had overset then I pushed him down into it and held him there.

He stared up at me, eyes popping. 'That Welsh bastard pulled a knife on me. I will have him strung up.'

At this point Evan made an appearance, pausing at the hall entrance to assess the situation before crossing the room at a run. 'My lord! What has happened?'

I stood back, releasing my captive. 'His grace of Exeter is retiring, Evan. The wine does not agree with him.'

Dafydd had retreated out of reach and returned the dagger to wherever he kept it. I was aware that Exeter had had a lucky escape; Welsh soldiers were famous for their skill with a blade at close quarters.

'There was a misunderstanding,' I said calmly, wandering casually over to join the constable by the hearth where the fire had died to embers. 'A seaworthy ship will be acquired with all possible speed, your grace. Meanwhile the constable's excellent food and wine have done their work and I for one am going to get some much-needed sleep. I suggest you do the same.'

To my surprise and relief Exeter heaved himself to his feet, shook his head as if to clear it and lurched over to clap me on the shoulder. His temper tantrum seemed to have vanished like that of a small child but the slur in his voice had not. 'Good idea, Pembroke, show me the way.'

Between us Evan and I managed to get him up the spiral stair to his chamber where his squire took over without comment, as if this was a regular occurrence. I then returned to tell Dafydd I would be down at the harbour at first light.

'Tell the captain we will take the ship to Abermaw. It will be just me and my squire and two horses. His grace of Exeter will not be joining us. I will send another ship to pick him up but he will have to pay the captain himself.'

Dafydd nodded. 'As you wish, my lord, but I would be grateful if you leave written instructions for his grace; if I tell him there could be another incident and I would not guarantee his survival.'

Later, before allowing myself to sleep, I wrote three letters.

To the Duke of Exeter from Jasper Tudor, Earl of Pembroke

I have taken the damaged ship to Abermaw for repairs. From there I will send a ship and a captain of my acquaintance to convey you to the destination of your choice. I hold it your responsibility to pay the captain for his services, which should afford you no difficulty once you have recovered that which you left behind on landing at Mostyn. If you should shirk this payment I will learn of it and ensure that justice is done at a time of my choosing.

I did not give this letter the distinction of a signature but merely used my Pembroke seal. Then I wrote two private letters, which I hoped the resourceful constable might find some way of conveying to the first recipient.

To my lady Margaret, Countess of Richmond, from Jasper Tudor, Earl of Pembroke, brotherly greetings.

I write this on the eve of taking ship to a destination I will not disclose for the security of us both. I beg you not to think that I am abandoning England and the

326

Lancastrian cause, which I swear on the Virgin's robe I will never do as long as there is breath in my body. We still have many allies both in this kingdom and in our neighbouring realms and it is my intention to seek aid from them all. It would be helpful if we could establish some form of courier service to carry our continued correspondence, men who are known to us both and unremarkable to the present regime. Perhaps you could give some thought to this matter, as will I.

I cannot tell you how deeply I regret that the custody of my nephew, your beloved son Henry, has been forcibly removed from me and awarded to my sworn enemy, William Herbert. I hope you are at least a little reassured that he is still in the immediate care of Jane Hywel, who I dare to hope will continue sending you regular reports regarding his upbringing and progress. I give heartfelt thanks to Almighty God that the violence that brings so much sorrow and loss has so far not been inflicted on the heirs and children of the warring factions and pray that this situation continues.

I am and will always remain, your loyal friend and devoted brother-in-law,

Jasper Tudor

Written at Harlech Castle this seventeenth day of October 1461

P.S. I hope that you can find a way to deliver the enclosed note.

I folded the second letter inside this one and inscribed Jane's initials on the front. Writing its content brought tears to my tired eyes.

To the beloved and neglected lady of my heart,

*This short message is a greeting, a farewell and a
heartfelt apology. I left you to face my enemies alone
and I cannot praise highly enough the bravery and
steadfast loyalty you displayed in keeping faith with all
your charges, risking your own life and freedom to
accompany them into what you so accurately call the
lion's den. I dearly wish I could convey to you in person
my deep love and profound admiration but my own
duty to those I have sworn to serve now takes me even
further away from you and for a length of time I
cannot calculate. I assume that the lack of any
communication from you means you have all remained
together in the same restrictive custody and I will try to
find some secret way to send and receive news. At the
same time I will be working constantly towards
restoring the true king to his rightful throne and our
life and love to their proper course.*

*Until that comes to pass, I send you my solemn
promise to find a way to visit you and our children
before you forget an ardent friend and they a loving
father.*

I neither signed it nor used my signet ring but pressed
my lips to the soft wax that sealed it, hoping their imprint
would convey its own message.

PART FOUR

Two Crowned Kings

1467–1470

30

Jane

Raglan Castle

'WHEN WILL THEY EVER come?' Harri's forlorn question was accompanied by a sigh. 'I thought it would be today.'

I lowered my sewing to look across the room to where the boy was sitting cross-legged on a cushioned window seat. Diamond-paned glass gave him a rain-blurred view over the rolling hills to the southeast and the road that led up to Raglan Castle. He was anxiously awaiting an arrival of enormous importance to him, but clearly Maud Herbert had no patience with such preoccupation. She approached Harri with an exasperated expression on her pretty round face. 'Why not stop staring out of the window and come and play ninepins with me?' she suggested.

A steady downpour had put a stop to any of their normal outdoor afternoon activities, so the children were confined to an upper chamber of the Great Tower at Raglan Castle trying to entertain themselves, some with more success than others. The younger members of the household had been temporarily moved into the old moated tower because Lord and Lady Herbert were expecting important visitors, who would be occupying all the new apartments clustered around the recently completed Grand Court extension. It was these guests who were the object of Harri's nervous anticipation.

'Why not go and play with Maud, Harri?' I suggested. 'It will distract you.'

The boy still found it hard to tear his gaze from the view. Harri Tudor was now a gangly lad of ten with a neat mop of thick brown hair, keen blue eyes and a ready smile and he was about to meet the mother he had not seen since he was a toddler and could not remember at all. 'Do you think she will recognize me, Mistress Jane?' he asked, for what must have been the tenth time that week. 'I have no idea what she looks like.'

I smiled at him fondly. 'You hardly resemble the baby you were when she was obliged to leave you, Harri, but you know each other's minds from all the letters you have exchanged. You know that she is a great lady who loves and cares for you and is proud of all your achievements. And when she sees what a handsome and well-mannered boy you have become she will be even prouder. Is that not so, Maud?'

The girl still stood with her hands on her hips, frowning. A little older than him, Maud was a lively, practical young lady who was good for sharing games and jokes but these worries of Harri's, with which I could sympathize, were merely irritating to her.

'Everyone likes you, Harri, so I suppose your mother will

as well,' she said, taking his hand. 'Come on, the pins are set up and I am going to beat you this time.'

As they set off to begin their game young Davy Owen suddenly sprang from behind a wall hanging and leaped onto Harri's back. 'Ha ha! Made you jump!' he crowed, clinging tightly to the bigger boy's neck.

Harri wrested his hand from Maud's and shook him off with an amiable grin. 'Get away, Davy! You are too heavy.'

The other boy pouted. 'It was a good ambush though, was it not?'

Harri tweaked his ear. 'Yes, Davy, it was well planned; I give you that. Now let me get on with my game.'

'Stop being a nuisance, Davy, and go and bother someone else. Harri is playing with me.' Maud's brow creased and she flounced the skirt of her green kirtle to express her annoyance before bending to pick up two wooden balls and handing one to Harri.

Harri took it and turned to catch the attention of Cicely Herbert, sitting beside me. She was supposed to be getting on with her embroidery but it was lying idle in her lap and she was watching the others enviously. He called across to her, 'Cis, why do we not play doubles? You could partner Walter and Maud and I will take you on.'

I hid a smile. Maud was always jealous of anyone else claiming Harri's attention and the inclusion of others in the game would avoid Maud getting too possessive of his company. I often thought it remarkable how Harri was able to steer a situation the way he wanted it and it did not surprise me in the least when Cicely eagerly laid down her embroidery and, with big-sisterly determination, dragged her brother Walter across the room with her. Maud sulked for a few minutes but it was not long before her strong competitive spirit overcame her resentment. The elaborate carving of the chamber's ceiling vault was soon echoing to the rolling sound of wood on stone, the clack of falling pins and the cries of youthful triumph and frustration.

I was particularly glad to see Harri draw Walter Herbert into the game, because although they were quite close in age and shared lessons together, there was no real camaraderie between them. Walter was still suffering from the abrupt departure of his older brother William – now married to Mary Woodville, the queen's younger sister, and become a member of the royal household – and had so far spurned all Harri's efforts to replace his older brother in his affections. Walter's acceptance of an apparently casual offer of a game of ninepins was therefore a minor coup on Harri's part.

A big tester bed occupied one side of the large chamber and Isabel Herbert and my own two girls, Elin and Sian, had commandeered the cosy private space within the half-drawn drapes to play with their dolls, away from the teasing interference of the boys. Having been dismissed by the older children, young Davy had crept up with a hobbyhorse he had collected from somewhere and poked its head quietly through the opening in the curtains. He then started making horsey sounds and nodding the head up and down, which inspired hysterical girlish giggles. I finally abandoned my sewing completely and dumped the chemise I had been mending in the basket at my feet.

Approaching silently behind Davy I demanded, 'Exactly what do you think you are doing, young Master Owen?' By now I had perfected the art of imitating the voice and intonation of Lady Anne, chatelaine of Raglan and mother of all the Herbert children. 'I shall be obliged to report your behaviour to Lord Herbert,' I went on, 'and he sends naughty little boys like you to the dungeon for days and days and days.'

Unfortunately I had chosen to stage my performance at the exact moment that the lady herself entered the chamber unannounced. To my consternation, from behind me I heard the real voice of the lady concerned. 'Only for days and days, Mistress Jane? Actually I think it might be for years and years.'

My heart began to thump in alarm, for she was my employer and also the woman who had been kind enough to allow me to bring my own two little girls and their orphaned cousin into her household. We all now looked upon Raglan Castle as our home and those children had made lasting friendships with the lady's own children. For a few agonizing seconds I feared I had just brought an end to all that and then the words she had uttered and the way she had uttered them filtered into my frozen brain, for although her lips were snapped shut, her striking green eyes were dancing.

'That was a very good impression,' Lady Anne said. 'Have you had a lot of practice, Mistress Jane?' Behind her the older children had stopped their game and were casting gleeful glances at each other.

'No, of c-course not, my lady,' I stuttered. 'I was just playing a joke on Davy.' I felt rather like a naughty novice nun being reprimanded by the Mother Superior.

'I knew it was not you, Lady Anne.' Davy had withdrawn the hobbyhorse and stood with it held between his knees, like an angelic page practising at the quintain.

The baroness favoured him with a stern look. 'Did you indeed, Davy Owen?' Lady Anne came from the class of Anglo-Welsh Marcher gentry who scorned to use the Welsh language and traditions. At Raglan Davy had become known as plain Davy Owen in the English fashion, without the 'son of' Welsh patronymic and as yet he remained unaware that it had been Herbert allies who had murderously executed his father without trial.

'And you were not attempting to disturb the girls' games at all?'

The boy's deep brown eyes grew large and round and he pushed the head of the hobbyhorse forward. 'No, my lady; Dobbin just wanted to see what they were doing.'

Lady Anne waved a finger at him to indicate that she was not charmed by his little pleasantry, although she probably was, and turned back to me. 'I have not come to exchange foolish remarks with a silly boy, or to listen to their governess attempting to imitate me, amusing though you all apparently find both.' This at least was true because by now the rest of the children were sniggering. 'I have come to tell you that our guests have been delayed and will not get here until tomorrow at the earliest. All this rain has swelled the Severn and closed the Chepstow ferry crossing.' She put a sympathetic arm around Harri's shoulders. 'I know you will be very disappointed by this. But the Severn is a fickle river and not to be trifled with. No doubt the Countess is just as frustrated as you are.'

'My mother said in her letter that she had to wait for royal permission to visit me.' Harri blushed, clearly building up to an awkward question. 'Why has it taken so long, my lady?'

I bit my lip, hoping the query would not annoy his guardian, but also very curious how she would answer it.

She took her time but then explained quite simply. 'Your mother and her husband are relatives of the old king, Harri. It has taken some time for the new king to trust them but now he does. You should be very grateful to King Edward.'

It took even longer for Harri to deliver his response, his eyes flicking about as he carefully considered how to word it. 'I am very grateful to have an opportunity to get to know my mother, my lady.' He made no mention of the Yorkist king who had deposed his uncle and namesake.

Lady Anne's dark brows knitted under her elegantly wired gauze veil but she gave only a brief nod, removed her arm from Harri's shoulder and moved towards the door. I could not help admiring a woman who managed to keep tabs on every aspect of her large household in addition to producing a child almost every year. The Herberts' ninth child was due before Christmas.

As she swept out, leaving a waft of flowery scent behind her, I dropped a curtsy and hoped she was out of earshot when I heard Walter's voice raised in anger behind me.

'You refused to acknowledge the king's kindness, Harry Tudor. That is treason in this house. You are lucky my lady mother does not have you locked in the prison tower.'

Harri had gone pink. 'I did not refuse. It was not the king who moved mountains to grant my mother permission to visit me; it was the queen, the lady Elizabeth, who sympathizes with my mother's long separation from her only son.'

I sighed, hopes of a rapprochement fading. Harri wanted to be friends with Walter but he was also staunchly loyal to his Lancastrian roots and tried never to mention King

Edward's name, a provocative stance in this Yorkist family. Equally, Harri had never spoken of his uncle Jasper or his grandfather Owen, nor mentioned them in his letters to his mother, which were carefully vetted by his tutors. He had been obliged to learn at an early age the enormous value of being able to keep secrets. I myself had never revealed the true father of my children but told the Herberts that I had been married to a Pembroke Castle cook and widowed soon after the birth of Sian. Luckily when we left Pembroke both my girls and Davy had been too young to be aware of their fathers' names. Only Harri knew who they were and he was not telling: he and I shared this secret and also some of the information which reached me in Jasper's infrequent letters that were smuggled to me.

Later that night, I read again the most recent one, squinting in the flickering light of a single taper. At Pembroke Jasper had been used to relying on clerks to pen his correspondence but now that he was an outlaw and an exile he did not trust others to write for him and he had crammed the words onto a single sheet of paper in his characteristically quirky hand.

My dearly beloved and woefully neglected lady, it seems so long since I kissed your lips that my own are sadly withering and my heart is sorely aching. But I write to tell you that I have made plans, which I hope and pray will bring us briefly together again. My sailing skills have improved and I am now confident of steering my own ship towards a rendezvous with those that I love most in the world. I cannot say where or when I will make landfall but God willing I will see you soon and

hold you in my arms, my sweetest Jane. I trust that you
are not too closely watched and that you are able to make
excursions outside the castle walls without arousing
suspicion. In the hope that this is so I will send word of
my arrival in the vicinity. It may be that a certain
other person, well known to us both, will also be visiting
your hosts and I hope you will be able to liaise with each
other. I dare write no more on this and have only space
to assure you of my unending devotion to you and to our
children. If you think it safe, please assure the boy that I
think of him constantly also and please, my sweeting,
burn this after you have read it and taken from it this
ardent kiss, which I make in lieu of signing.

There was a slight smudge on the last words, which I
assumed to have been made by his lips. I pressed the paper
to mine, tasting ink and persuading myself it held the flavour
of Jasper. I had found the letter earlier in the day pushed
into a crack in the retaining wall of the moat. It was only
a matter of casually leaning over the parapet to look at the
fish kept there ready for the kitchen and slipping my hand
in, hidden by the folds of my skirt. That was how I knew
that an undercover Lancastrian agent either worked in the
castle or made frequent visits but I had no idea who it might
be. The location of the secret cache had been delivered to
me anonymously in a note slipped into a pile of Harri's
clean laundry, which I alone handled.

This letter was only the sixth I had received in as many
years since coming to Raglan and I had read each a dozen
times before forcing myself to destroy them. Apart from my
two little girls they were now the only link between Jasper

and me, and with each letter I felt our relationship hanging by an ever-weaker thread but this latest letter and the possibility of a reunion had drawn all my feelings for him back to the surface.

At that moment, lying on the lumpy straw mattress of my truckle bed, I would have given anything to feel his arms around me and to surrender to the soaring sensations that his kisses and caresses had always inspired. In my distress I almost imagined that he was there with me, wiping the tears away and coaxing me into the healing release of mutual passion. I flung myself onto the pillow to stifle my sudden sobs. If I am honest it had always been his ability to stir my blood to fever heat that had nourished our union and fed my love for him. I missed him physically, emotionally and in every way – hardly feelings of a kind I could share with the children or admit to my Yorkist hosts. Swamped with loneliness, I cried out my pain and frustration in smothered anguish. Then I forced myself to hold the crumpled letter to the taper-flame. My latest link with Jasper vanished into ash and smoke, but the faint hope it had inspired would not die.

31

Jane

Raglan Castle

HARRI WAS PERMITTED TO sit beside his mother at the banquet provided to welcome the Countess of Richmond and her husband Sir Henry Stafford to Raglan. Earlier in the day I had watched their arrival in the new Grand Court, where Harri had lined up with all the Herbert children considered old enough for ceremonial. His impatient shifting from one foot to the other was halted by a frown from Lady Anne while Lord Herbert made a long florid speech of welcome. Then the formality of the introductions: Lord Herbert started with his wife and proceeded down the line; Anne, Maud, Cicely, Walter and then finally Harri.

Standing at last in front of her son Lady Margaret solemnly studied him from head to toe. They met as strangers and yet the likeness between them was striking; the same delicate build, the same straight aristocratic nose, the same fine features and proud stance and, until Harri made his growth spurt into manhood, almost the same height, for she remained tiny. The only pronounced difference was in the eyes; whereas Lady Margaret's were a speckled slate grey, his were deep blue and full of curiosity and empathy; eyes that Jasper maintained were, like his own, inherited from his mother Queen Catherine, Harri's grandmother.

Harri withstood his mother's scrutiny for several long moments before suddenly remembering his manners, snatching off his soft cap and dropping to his knee to do her honour. His greeting was whispered and I could not hear the words but they inspired a beaming smile from his mother, which transformed her whole appearance and wiped years off her apparent age. Suddenly I recognized the girl I had attended at Pembroke, the girl who had blossomed as she recovered from her widow's grief and found the energy and zest to take pleasure once more in the world around her and the new life growing within her. With a joyful laugh she bent to grasp Harri's upper arms and urge him to rise so that she could embrace him properly. Enfolded in that warm embrace Harri's bright eyes shone with love, and all at once I saw in him a look I had seen in Jasper's eyes. It seemed that Lady Margaret still had the ability to pull a Tudor male into her web with a single smile.

The banquet had been long and formal but I noticed that Harri and Lady Margaret did manage some private conversation between courses, despite the plethora of entertainments provided. The most interesting and controversial of these was a performance by the bard Lewys Glyn Cothi, who had often sung at Pembroke in praise of Lord Jasper but now, like the cunning creature he was, he had crafted a long poem to Lord Herbert in which he hailed him as the new *Y Mab Daragon*, the Son of Prophecy, though I noticed he did not mention exactly who he would be saving his people from. This change of allegiance puzzled me and certainly, when word of it spread, Lewys's defection taking *Y Mab Daragon* with him, would undoubtedly affect Jasper's power to stir Welsh followers to the Lancastrian cause. Lord Herbert looked proud and pleased with the homage Lewys paid him and no doubt he rewarded the poet with a handsome purse. However, I wondered how welcome the praise-song would sound to Lady Margaret, who must have last heard the legendary title applied by the very same bard to Lord Edmund, the father of her son.

I was soon to find out. At the end of the banquet the lady herself called me to her side on the dais and informed me that she wished Harri to be moved from the children's accommodation in the Great Tower into her own chamber off the Grand Stair. 'Lady Herbert agrees with me that I should enjoy as much of my son's company as possible for the short period of my stay and that you, who know his daily routine and habits, should place yourself temporarily among my servants as well. I am telling you now so that a bed can be made available for Henry and his belongings moved immediately.'

I bobbed a curtsy. 'Yes, my lady. I will see to it.'

Lady Margaret glanced around before speaking again in a more confidential tone. 'You are familiar with Welsh traditions, Jane. Do these praise poems carry much weight with the people? Their loyalties seem sadly fickle. I can remember when Lewys Glyn Cothi hailed Lord Edmund as the Son of Prophecy before Henry was born.'

'The title certainly captures people's imagination, my lady;

Y Mab Daragon is a powerful symbol of Welsh pride.' I dropped my voice to a whisper and my eyes subserviently to the floor. 'Perhaps we might discuss this when we are among your own people.'

She raised her head and her voice reverted to noble authority. 'Yes, well thank you, Mistress Jane. Let me know when you have made the arrangements. I would like to retire with Henry as soon as possible.'

I hurried away to do her bidding, this new arrangement playing into my schemes, and the sooner I could warn her that the Herberts were not aware who was my children's real father the better. The custom of wealthy nobility to occupy individual bedchambers, though married, added to the convenience of the arrangement and I would be able to liaise with Lady Margaret as Jasper hoped.

Sir Henry Stafford cheerfully escorted his wife and Harri to the door of the chamber they would share. He was a good deal older than Lady Margaret and not robust; close up, an angry red rash could be detected behind his full beard. Nevertheless they seemed a fond pair as they exchanged kisses and blessings for the night to come. For Harri to sleep on, I had caused my own small truckle to be placed beside his mother's velvet-hung tester and procured some finer sheets and covers for it than those I was permitted to use. I had arranged to sleep myself on a palliasse in the separate ante-room allocated to Lady Margaret's servants, but she instructed me to bring this into her chamber.

'I think it would reassure my son to see a familiar face, should he wake from a nightmare,' she announced in front of her own attendants, to counter any jealousy that she was favouring a stranger. I hoped it meant that she was making it possible for some private conversation with me.

With maternal thoroughness she observed Harri's bedtime routine and listened particularly intently to his prayers, smiling with satisfaction when he included one for the soul of his dead father. When the tired boy had fallen deeply asleep she settled herself, silk skirts rustling extravagantly, in the high cushioned armchair beside the fire, which I had stoked to burn brightly and ward off the autumn chill. A footstool lay nearby and she gestured me to sit on it. I felt a little like a lowly handmaiden sinking down before a queen.

'At last I have an opportunity to thank you, Jane, for your admirable care of Henry and, most especially, for your remarkable loyalty in remaining at his side for so long. As you can imagine the enforced separation from my son has been extremely painful for me but that pain has been some-what eased by the knowledge that he has been able to rely on you for his comfort and security. I will not forget that.'

I shook my head sorrowfully. 'Harri has never for one second failed to regard and honour you as his true and loving mother, my lady.'

Lady Margaret favoured me with one of her winning smiles and made an affable gesture. 'Yet it must be admitted that Lady Herbert is an intelligent and gracious lady; indeed your letters telling me of her treatment of my son, and his Oxford-trained tutors and priestly confessor, gave me much needed reassurance, Jane.'

'I must tell you though, my lady, that it has been neces-sary for me to conceal the true identity of my children's father from the Herberts and beg you not to disclose it.'

Lady Margaret raised a reassuring hand in pledge and I rushed on. 'In a letter to me Lord Jasper hinted that he had written to you regarding a possible meeting during your visit here. I am sure you will understand that I am eager to know if it is true that I may see him again after all this time.'

Lady Margaret frowned but then seemed to put her disapproval of me aside and instinctively bent closer. 'Keeping your secret at least assures me that I can trust you enough to keep mine, Jane, which allows me to tell you that I have established a courier system in order to maintain a correspondence with key Lancastrians who uphold their allegiance to King Henry. Lord Jasper intends to sail into Tenby very soon. In fact he may already be there.'

My heart began jumping in my breast but I tried not to show it. 'Is a rendezvous arranged?' I asked. 'It may be difficult to leave the castle without an escort. The Herberts are very security conscious.'

Lady Margaret made a dismissive gesture. 'That will be no problem. My own escort will serve me and we can lose them when I choose. I have already told Lord Herbert that I wish to make a private pilgrimage to a shrine near here, where Lord Edmund made a vow shortly before he died. You shall accompany me. I will not tell you more until we are on the way there. Lord Jasper will send a note here to confirm his arrival via the usual route.'

I nodded. 'I will check the letter drop tomorrow morning. But I believe Lord Herbert has plans for your further entertainment so I hope there is no clash.'

Lady Margaret did not seem concerned. 'Jasper will lay low and wait. He knows I will be kept busy.'

I was awed by her self-confidence. It was hard to find any trace of the desperate girl I had found on my arrival at Pembroke and nursed through a traumatic childbed.

The following day Harri was eager to show his mother his skill with arms and she was keen to meet his tutors so I found it easy to slip away to the letter drop in the wall of the moat. The note I found there was brief and enticing. *'The swift has landed.'*

Jasper's personal emblem was a golden martlet, or swift. Clearly the wandering outlaw had made port and was on his way even now to the pre-arranged meeting place. I ached to know where it was and felt as if, had I known it, I would already be riding at a gallop to meet him.

Only after I had shown the note to Lady Margaret did I remember having to wait to retrieve it until after someone passing by on the other side of the moat had waved at me. It was the bard, Lewys Glyn Cothi.

32

Jasper

St Aedan's Church, Bettws Newydd

I HAD KNELT WHERE my brother had knelt when he made his sacred oath to St Aedan ten years before. Edmund had never confided the gist of his vow but he had not long discovered that Margaret was expecting a child and so I had always assumed it was a prayer for a son, with some sort of promise attached. An heir would secure his Richmond title and estates and it was a bitter circumstance that he never knew the son that was born to him, nor lived to defend the Richmond estates against theft by a usurper king. Ours had been an erratic relationship in our adult years but I nevertheless felt Edmund's absence acutely. I had welcomed the opportunity to confess deep regret for his passing and to pray for his soul.

The church was a Christian shrine, dedicated to St Aedan, a travelling preacher who had converted heathen Celts and performed miracles all over South Wales a thousand years ago.

'What kind of miracles?' Evan had wanted to know. At first he would not enter the little church but had halted further up the hillside on which it nestled in its yard, to look out above the mist, a thin mist that swirled and gave the impression of ghosts rising from the ancient graves.

I shot the squire an impatient glance. 'You are more Welsh than I, Evan, you tell me.'

He shrugged and grinned back. 'I am probably one of the heathen Celts he missed, my lord. Is this where we are meeting the ladies? What a spooky place!'

'I hope so, if they received my message. We will have to wait and see whether Lewys managed to deliver it. After Lord Edmund came here he told me Bettws Newydd must be the loneliest spot in South Wales. He said that people avoided it like the plague. It was his idea of a joke because the Great Pestilence had wiped out the whole village a hundred years ago. But at least those ghosts you find so spooky should preserve us from prying eyes.'

'Did your brother not die of the plague?' Evan asked anxiously. 'He might have caught it here.'

A hollow laugh escaped me. It was an irony that people believed my brother died of the plague. I did not believe he died of plague at all; he was Black Herbert's prisoner and was murdered.

For two days and nights we had waited, sleeping in the bare nave beneath its only ornaments, the large wooden cross and reliquary on the stone altar. A vast semi-circular cope chest sat abandoned in the lean-to vestry, mouldering and too big to move, like the empty houses left behind when the village was abandoned.

Then in the bright light of the third morning, they came.

Margaret's smile caused my heart to perform its accustomed flip and I revelled in the blaze of her fine scarlet gown with its gold clasps and glossy fur trim, evoking the days of courtly show I had once relished and now lost. Then my eyes turned to Jane, sweet Jane in a dull brown cloak and a peaked linen coif, her expression a confusion of joy and uncertainty and I could see the effort she made to control her emotion. She bobbed a shaky curtsy and whispered something inaudible.

With unexpected consideration Margaret turned away and approached the dusty altar, making the sign of the cross as she approached, then she dropped to her knees before it and began to murmur a Latin prayer.

I took Jane's hand and led her into the vestry. After she had greeted Evan with a sisterly hug, I shooed him out and shut the door. Freed from constraint she threw herself into my arms with a little cry. 'Jasper – my dearest lord!'

I pulled her close so that she could feel the sudden urgency of my desire for her.

'I still want you as much as ever, Jane,' I said. 'In other circumstances we could love each other here and now in God's house and I am sure the Almighty would understand our need. But I need Margaret too.'

Jane nipped my ear painfully. 'You worship the ground she walks on,' she hissed, moving her hips against me. 'She winds you round her little finger. I hate her. And I want this.'

She pressed the hard evidence of my desire in her hand and I forced myself to pull away from her while I still had control. I cupped her face in my hands. 'You are the mother of my children and the treasure of my loins. We are a pair.

Please believe me when I say that I love you and one day very soon we will be together again. But Margaret is my link to King Henry's loyal followers, my conduit back to power. Until I achieve that, all I am is a roving outlaw without hearth or home. I must have access to her connections and her couriers.'

Breaking free, Jane stepped back and tucked her hands demurely away under her cloak, her expression calm, as if lust had never lit its flame there. 'I understand that, my lord. I also know that you have feelings for her that are deep and enduring, but they will never be reciprocated. I believe her entire capacity for love is reserved for the boy whose birth nearly killed her – her ambition for Harri is all consuming and she will use you and anyone else of influence to secure what she considers his rightful place beside the throne, whoever may occupy it. Although she serves the new queen and at the same time schemes with you, her loyalty does not swither between York and Lancaster as it might appear. It is focused solely on Henry Tudor and the drop of royal blood she has passed to him.'

I gazed at her, shaking my head in wonder. 'You have more in common with Margaret than I realized.'

'Except that *I* love you, Jasper Tudor, as much as, and more perhaps, than I love our children, which some may find unforgiveable.'

A sudden sense of guilt sent the blood rushing to my cheeks. 'My little Elin and Sian! How are they? They must be growing beautiful, like their mother.'

She gave an indignant laugh. 'It is too late to start flattering me like a sweet-tongued sailor, my lord! The girls are fine – they are happy within the routine of the Herbert brood, and they share their education. Elin takes after you, with her flame-red hair and her striking blue eyes but she has a temper to go with it. Sian is more like me, mouse brown and a little shy.'

I raised an eyebrow. 'Huh! Not like you at all then. Perhaps she will be a late blossom. I like the sound of our flame-haired temptress though. How I wish I could see them! Perhaps I soon will. I sense the Wheel of Fortune turning.'

Jane wrung her hands awkwardly. 'I am afraid their father is dead to them. As I told you, the name Tudor is best never mentioned in the Herbert household.'

She had written in one of her letters that she had lied about the identity of the girls' father and although I knew it was wise, nevertheless it rankled, and one day soon I hoped to ram the fact down William Herbert's throat, on the tip of a sword . . .

Jane gestured towards the closed door. 'Is the lady aware of the wheel turning?'

Anxiously I ran my fingers through my hair once more. Margaret's startled scrutiny had made me acutely aware of my dishevelled appearance. 'I need to speak to her on that topic. That is part of the reason for this meeting. I am sorry, Jane, but I will have to have some private conversation with her.'

'Oh dear, what a penance for you.' Although her tone was sarcastic, she pulled a bone comb from her sleeve pocket. 'Fingers will not tame that fiery mane, my love. Bend down and let me tidy you up.'

The feel of her hands in my hair almost had me pressing her into a close embrace once more but I bit my lip and resisted. I made myself a silent promise that the next time

Jane and I were together it would be in less frustrating circumstances. Whatever she said about my feelings for Margaret, it was Jane's joyful pleasure in the act of union that kept her persistently in my mind, even when the demon lust drove me to the stews.

'Did you know that Lord Herbert has petitioned King Edward for a marriage between Harri and his daughter Maud?' she asked, tugging at a stubborn tangle.

I winced, as much at the notion of the marriage as the pain induced by Jane's combing. The very notion of Harri tied to a Yorkist wife, especially a Herbert, was anathema. 'Does Lady Margaret know this?'

'If she does she has not told me. Hold still.'

Under her fresh attention to my beard, my cheeks were soon burning and tight red curls were beginning to mingle with the dust on the flagstones. 'Thank you, Jane,' I said firmly, moving away. 'I will be sure to mention it to her.'

'Did you also know that the bards are beginning to hail Lord Herbert as *Y Mab Daragon*? Even Lewys Glyn Cothi was singing in his praise at Raglan the other day.'

I shrugged. 'Lewys will do anything for a fat purse. Besides it is in our interests that he continues to be made welcome at Raglan. Who do you think gets the notes to you?'

Jane did not look surprised. 'I had more or less guessed it was him. So he is playing a double game like everyone else . . . '

At that moment Evan burst into the vestry without knocking. 'Riders approaching, my lord! They have seen the ladies' horses but fortunately ours are too well hidden.'

'We should take cover,' I decided. 'The ladies are here legitimately, even if their presence is unusual.'

With an effort Evan hauled open the lid of the vast wooden cope chest that stood against one wall of the vestry. 'If we get in here Jane can use her skirt to sweep away the prints. If she and Lady Margaret are found in the church the men may not come in here at all but if they do they are unlikely to lift this lid. I only did in case it would serve this very purpose. After you, my lord.'

The squire indicated the dark, cobwebbed interior of the chest. Apart from the spiders at least it was empty but its present occupants hardly made it inviting. 'This had better be necessary, Evan,' I said, swinging my leg over the side and breaking down the intricate silk network. 'Get rid of them quickly, Jane, please!'

'I will do my best,' she said, remaining commendably calm. 'But suppose they are thugs or bandits?'

'If you shout we will come with weapons drawn,' I assured her. 'Let us hope you will not have to.'

Evan followed me into the chest and we heard Jane grunt with effort as she lowered the lid, plunging us into darkness. There were shuffling sounds as Jane dragged her skirts over the footprints on the vestry floor followed by the noise of the door closing behind her as she joined Margaret in the church; then silence – dreadful, chilling silence. In a sliver of light I saw the whites of Evan's eyes only two feet away, wide with alarm. I could see his hands, white-knuckled and clasped chin-high over his knees. A spider scuttled across them, black, long legged and gone in a flash. To shift my position I put my own hand to the floor and felt something squish under my palm. For several minutes my heart thudded like a drum in my chest, as I tried not to let my thoughts dwell on our claustrophobic confinement by concentrating on who might be approaching and what would happen if we were discovered.

Fortunately Jane soon reported back. 'A couple of monks from the local priory. Once they discovered we were pilgrims they did not stay long. I believe they are still genuinely frightened of the plague.'

Lady Margaret had followed Jane into the vestry holding her costly skirts high off the floor but dust devils already clung to the gleaming fabric. She watched us clamber out of the chest, frantically brushing cobwebs and creatures off our clothes and hair.

'I have little time left, my lord,' she said, backing off in distaste. 'Shall we discuss our business now? I should like to go outside where the air is sweeter. Jane and your squire can keep a watch.'

33

Jasper

St Aedan's Church, Bettws Newydd

L ADY MARGARET SPOKE LIKE the noblewoman she was, accustomed to giving orders. I made a courtly bow. 'As you wish, my lady.' The flourish must have looked absurd coming from a dishevelled soldier because she shot me a look of wry amusement before leading the way out into the daylight.

Jane and Evan left the enclosure and began climbing the hill to acquire the all-round view offered from its crest, while Margaret and I took a precautionary position in the deep shadows of one of several venerable yew trees that flourished on the high side of the sloping churchyard. Their gnarled trunks looked as if they had weathered at least a thousand winters and I wondered if they had been planted in some Druids' grove, before St Aedan had converted the heathens.

Margaret plunged straight into her chief concern. 'King Edward has been wooing me with gifts,' she began. 'Yet he refuses me the only one I really want – my son.'

'Yes, I heard he had granted you the manor and palace of Woking. That must have been hard to resist.'

She ignored the irony in my voice. 'Why should I resist?' she retorted. 'I can play the grateful Yorkist with the best of them. Besides it is convenient for my duties as lady in waiting to the queen.'

'My lady of Richmond dancing attendance on a girl from Grafton; that must take some swallowing.' I was trying to rile her.

She shrugged. 'They call Elizabeth a commoner but her mother was a duchess – your royal brother's aunt. She is as noble as you are, Jasper.'

'Touché.' I grinned. 'And she is ennobling her family at the gallop I gather.' Then in hope of an honest answer I sprang it on her:

'And how do you like the notion of Maud Herbert marrying Harri?'

Margaret's brow darkened. 'About as much as I like Henry being called Harri,' she snapped. 'His drop of royal blood does not need diluting, although I fancy that is Edward's plan. If he is to build a York dynasty he wants no hint of competition.'

'Can Harri – your pardon, Henry; there are so many Henrys that it becomes confusing! – can he really be considered a contender for the throne?'

Her grey eyes turned glacial. 'I have a blood claim to the succession and therefore so does he. And his claim grows all the stronger while Edward's queen continues giving birth to girls. Perhaps Elizabeth should consider making a pilgrimage here to St Aedan. He certainly granted your brother's prayers.'

'Ah, you confirm my guess that Edmund came here to pray for a son.'

'Indeed he did – and I come here now to seek the saint's intercession for that son. Even though you do call him Harri, if *I* cannot have custody of my Henry I pray for you, his uncle, to restore your brother to his throne and regain wardship of my son.' She laid her hand urgently on my arm. 'And I have reason to think that day may not be far off.'

'You have a great deal of faith in a long dead Irish saint, Margaret.' Irony had not left me.

She laughed. 'I do not rely solely on St Aedan. In fact I put much of my trust in a more worldly champion; the Earl of Warwick.'

'Warwick!' Now I was incredulous. 'He boasts that he put Edward on the throne in the first place! Why on earth should he want him off it now?'

'You are out of touch, Jasper. The cub king has become a lion and no longer does Warwick's bidding. First Edward made a commoner his queen and let her appropriate all the best manors and marriages for her kin and now he offends even further by refusing to allow Warwick's daughter to marry the Duke of Clarence.'

'Is *everyone* building dynasties around the Yorkist throne?' My mind was racing.

Margaret pursed her lips. 'Not if Edward can help it. That is why Warwick will be lured to our cause. We need to conjure a meeting between him and Queen Marguerite.'

My reaction to this notion was utter disbelief. 'Impossible! Marguerite hates, no loathes, the Earl of Warwick – has done for years. They will never be allies.'

'It seems unlikely, I agree, but consider this; Warwick is

on the verge of rebelling against Edward and Marguerite is desperate for her son to sit on the throne of England. All it would take is an alliance between them to achieve what they both want. It will not happen overnight but I want you to go to Marguerite in France and start a process of gentle persuasion. She listens to you. And I will work on Warwick.'

The sheer audacity of her idea amazed me. I thought it through. The great Richard Neville, Earl of Warwick, who had risked his life and fortune to put his cousin Edward of York on the throne of England, was now considering rebelling against him and Margaret honestly thought he could be brought to kneel at the old queen's feet? I was not so sure; if Warwick wished to marry his daughter to Edward's brother George of Clarence, was it not more likely that he really wanted to put George on the throne and make his daughter queen? Warwick did not call himself 'Kingmaker' for nothing.

I said to Margaret, 'I will go to Anjou to see the queen but I do not hold out much hope. Marguerite is living off her father who squandered his wealth trying to make himself King of Sicily. Her gowns are patched and her courtiers get only bed and board. And I am sorry to say that my cousin, Louis of France, is completely unreliable. He makes grandiose promises of aid but when it comes to the pay-out you find his purse strings are suddenly tied.'

Margaret's brow knitted. 'I thought he had granted you a pension.'

I laughed bitterly. 'He gives me a hundred livres a year but I spend all of that traipsing around Europe on his missions.' I ran my hands eloquently over my battered brigandine. 'As you see I am hardly dressed in silk and satin.'

She shrugged. 'Well I have money but not enough to fund a rebellion. However, if Warwick joins our party I am sure Louis will open his coffers. Let us work on that.'

'Very well, I am prepared to do anything to get my brother out of the Tower. Is there any chance you might be allowed to visit him?'

It was Margaret's turn to laugh bitterly. 'Absolutely none! But my doctor has a colleague who tends him and he tells me King Henry is well treated. He lives in his own royal apartments and spends most of his time on his knees in the oratory. I think if he were to be restored to his throne it would only be as a puppet king.'

'An anointed puppet of true royal blood is better than an upstart usurper,' I retorted. 'And at least he has a son and heir.'

'Yes, what of the prince, who I believe his mother insists on calling Édouard? I imagine she must regret having chosen that Yorkist name now.'

'Perhaps, but Marguerite is not one to admit it. He is nearly fourteen and greatly impressed King Louis when they met. I would say that her son is the only reason Marguerite gets any money at all from the French exchequer. Louis called him a "promising prince".'

'That is something I suppose.'

I guessed Margaret's half-hearted response was due to a maternal bias towards her own son.

She added slyly, 'Since Yorkist Edward has been on the throne, rumour about Édouard's conception has been less active but that does not mean to say it has gone away. What is your opinion, Jasper – is he truly your brother's son?'

I answered her emphatically. 'If you saw the prince you would have no doubt who his sire was.'

'Good.' She gave a brisk nod, apparently satisfied. 'Let us walk towards our horses. Jane and your squire should see us and come down. I really must get back to Raglan.' We had walked several paces out of the shadows when she suddenly tucked her hand into the crook of my elbow and drew me to her. Then to my utter surprise I felt her lips on mine.

There was nothing casual or brief about her kiss, or the way she caressed my neck as she granted it. 'Thank you, Jasper,' she said, drawing back with apparent reluctance. 'You have given me encouragement to pursue my plan. Send me word when you are with Marguerite and I will write with the latest news for you to collect there. And let us thank the angel Gabriel that our courier service still operates without incident.'

I was bewildered. There had been many times when, as a younger man, I might have fantasized about a kiss from Margaret such as the one she had just bestowed but now my feelings were mixed. Rather than being thrilled to the core, I was more concerned that Jane might have seen the incident. I even wondered if Margaret had intended that she should, although I could not fathom her motive.

Meanwhile she was casually chattering on as if nothing had happened. 'I am very impressed with my Henry's skill with the bow and Lord Herbert has all the young boys practising at the quintain as well, though as yet only on foot. On my return to Woking I think I will send Henry a pony. He is not tall but it is not too early for him to begin jousting at the ring, is it?'

'Not if the pony is well trained.' Ungallantly I pulled away from Margaret's attached hand, left her beside her horse and went to meet Jane and Evan as they approached. I told Evan, 'We will escort the ladies until we come near where their guards are waiting, but we cannot afford to let them see us. And Jane, I must speak with you before you go.' Her gimlet gaze alarmed me.

'Do not be long,' Margaret called, seeing us move back within the churchyard, where Jane hissed, 'I saw you kiss her,' before I could open my mouth.

'No, sweeting, she kissed *me*. I have no idea why.'

'Because I was looking,' Jane retorted. 'She is jealous of our relationship. She does not want you but she wants you to want her.'

'Jane, we love each other. Surely that is what matters. Margaret has changed and I am no longer the romantic youth that put her on a pedestal. It is you I love.'

'I am glad, Jasper, but I am realistic and it often puzzles me that you do love me, when you mix with glamorous, powerful women like Lady Margaret, who dress in silk, read the works of Aristotle and can organize a spy network.'

I laughed. 'If I do mix with such paragons, few of them have time for a penniless exile . . .'

Reaching up she planted her lips on mine. Our kiss was brief but intense and bore no resemblance to the one Margaret had so mystifyingly planted on me. When she broke away she said breathlessly: 'Hurry up then, Jasper Tudor, and win the throne back for your brother so that we can love each other to sleep again. Of such simple pleasures is the world made wonderful.'

I nodded emphatically. 'I will,' I said. 'I swear I will.'

34

Jane

Raglan Castle

'SLOWER MASTER HENRY! DO not let your mount dictate the pace. Lean back, rein him in!'

The roar from the Master at Arms was so loud that it hurt my eardrums but Harri, galloping towards the quintain with the visor of his helmet pulled down, probably hardly heard him. He was wielding a half-size lance but it was clear that he was having difficulty controlling the long white-painted pole and at the last minute his horse swerved, the lance tipped upwards and the point missed the board of the quintain. There were disappointed groans from some of the spectators but whoops of joy from others, who were not supporting his team.

Harri pulled up the pony his mother had sent him after her visit to Raglan. The Welsh gelding was called Cirrus after the wispy white clouds seen high in the sky on a sunny day and Harri loved him. Even though he had swerved offline and caused his rider to miss the target he still received a pat on the neck as Harri brought him to a halt beside Walter's bay cob. An attendant took the unwieldy lance off the boy.

'Sorry, Walter,' Harri said quietly so that I barely caught the words. 'I lost control of the lance.'

Walter blew out his cheeks and made a rude noise. 'No, you lost control of the horse, Harri, which is why you should not pat him like that. He should know that you are displeased with him.'

There was still no love lost between Walter and Harri. The older Herbert girls had both gone off to their marriages with wealthy barons, but Maud was still waiting and hoping that the king would approve her marriage to the future Earl of Richmond. I had heard her boasting once to my girls that she would be Harri's countess one day but so far there had been no betrothal and, knowing Lady Margaret's opposition to the match, I wondered if there ever would be. Harri himself kept very quiet on the subject, ensuring that no one discovered his opinion on the matter, least of all Maud.

At the end of the morning's joust-training Lord Herbert joined the spectators. There had been a call to arms to quell an uprising in Yorkshire and meanwhile another rebel force landed in Kent. Herbert along with the Earl of Devon had been ordered to intercept it. 'I do not expect it to be a difficult task,' he told the two boys. 'So I have decided to take you both with me in my retinue to give you experience of a campaign. You will be assigned to a minder, who will tell you what is going on at every stage and I want you to pay strict attention to everything he says and does. The muster will take place here at Raglan and we will march east at the start of next week. Meanwhile you will each be fitted with body armour. The Master at Arms will call you to the armoury tomorrow. Is that understood?'

Predictably the boys responded enthusiastically in the affirmative but as they passed by on the way to the stables I heard Walter remark to Harri, 'My lord father is only taking you in order to keep an eye on you. He thinks your uncle might try to abduct you if he leaves you here.'

I did not hear Harri's reply but I could imagine that he was thinking exactly as I was. Did Walter know something we did not – that perhaps among the so-called rebels who had landed in Kent was Jasper Tudor?

Since our meeting at St Aedan's shrine I made a point of going to the moat-wall letter drop whenever the bard Lewys made a visit to Raglan and I was rarely disappointed. That was how I learned that Jasper had managed to land a French army at Harlech the previous year and led an attempt to recapture Denbigh Castle, which had fallen back into Yorkist hands. When his raid failed he had made a 'slash and burn' expedition through North Wales and caused untold damage to the forest and farms of much Yorkist territory. A furious Lord Herbert had marched to confront him but Jasper and his followers had managed to escape by sea, whereupon Herbert had turned his army and artillery against Harlech Castle, which was finally forced to surrender. For ridding his kingdom of this last Lancastrian stronghold, King Edward had rewarded his faithful Welsh Lieutenant by granting him Jasper's earldom, an act both Harri and I found hard to stomach.

'It sticks in my throat to call Lord Herbert by Uncle

Jasper's title,' Harri admitted during a rare moment when we were alone together in the small chamber he now shared with Davy Owen.

'And mine,' I confessed. 'But it would not be sensible to offend him, Harri. We have to bide our time until King Henry is restored and Lord Jasper gets his earldom back.'

'I fear it is too late for that, Mistress Jane,' he said sadly, 'and we will never see Pembroke again.'

'Never say never, Harri, and do not tell anyone else how you feel. The Herberts have treated you well. It would spoil all Lord Jasper's plans if you were suddenly to be considered a hostage rather than as you are now, a member of the family.'

His alarmed expression told me I had touched a raw nerve. 'Do family members threaten each other?' he asked. 'Walter says if there is a battle he will hold a knife to my throat. I think he imagines I can somehow assist his father's enemies.'

'But there will be a knight with orders to protect you both,' I reminded him. 'Do you know who he will be yet?'

'Yes,' replied Harri with an ironic twist of his lips. 'We are to have Lady Anne's nephew to watch over us, Richard Corbet.'

I frowned, trying to fit the name to a face. 'But he is not a knight, is he? He is only eighteen, a mere squire.'

'Yes, he is a squire but also a close family member. There will be just him and Walter and me on some hilltop viewpoint, watching and waiting to see who wins.'

I stared at him, a knot forming in the pit of my stomach. There was a fraught silence, as if neither of us could actually voice the fear that was uppermost in our minds.

'Will you have any weapon about you, Harri?' I asked faintly.

'Walter and I have been issued with daggers but Richard Corbet will also have a sword.'

I drew him into a tight hug and for once he did not resist. He is twelve years old, I thought, too young to find himself in such a potentially perilous position.

We sprang apart at the sound of footsteps approaching the chamber door. It was Davy, nursing a cut lip, the neck of his chemise smeared with blood. 'Have you been fighting again?' I asked him, as I pulled a clean shirt from a clothing chest and Davy sounded off about 'That lying snake Walter' who had claimed that Harri 'was only going on the muster because my father does not trust him enough to leave him behind.'

'Thank you for defending me, Davy,' Harri said with a grin. 'I can always rely on you.'

Over the next few days Raglan Castle changed from a nobleman's palace into a military headquarters, gradually filling with the knights, troops, heralds, craftsmen, artillery, oxen, horses, carts and the mass of supplies needed to support a campaign army. Men marched in from all directions, pitched their tents or were allocated lodgings, and the waggons, guns, animals and fodder were marshalled in the outer baileys under the walls of the new towers. Pennants and banners bearing the arms of scores of Marcher families flew from tents and turrets and the great blue and red Herbert battle standard with its three rampant white lions was hauled down from its place of honour over the dais in the Great Hall and raised at the top of the Great Tower.

Any knights and foot soldiers approaching the castle for

the first time must have marvelled at the size and splendour of the magnificent fortress that William Herbert had built over the last eight years on the skeleton of his father's more modest stronghold. The enormous gatehouse was particularly impressive, with its soaring twin towers and alongside it, the mighty Treasury Tower. As well as providing a demonstration of his rapid rise to pre-eminence in South Wales, Raglan Castle had also become the seat of justice and the focus of authority in this hitherto unruly part of King Edward's realm.

From the wall-walk at the top of the Grand Stair I watched with the younger children as the new earl's retinue gathered in the court below. His phalanx of household knights was resplendent in armour, over which they wore uniform red and blue tunics bearing the Herbert white lion badge, their horses covered in matching heraldic trappings. Behind them their liveried squires lined up, bearing their knights' shields and helmets, and at the rear, on their smaller ponies, came Walter and Harri mounted either side of their minder, Richard Corbet, a sturdy-looking young man on a bay cob laden with bulky saddlebags. I thought he looked as if the task he had been allocated was not much to his liking but he did smile at Harri when the boy spoke to him, although I could not hear their exchange.

'My lord father says that the Earl of Warwick is leading the rebels,' said Maud. 'But I thought he was a Yorkist. Why would he be fighting us, Mistress Jane?'

I knew the answer to that from Jasper's letters but I was not going to reveal my knowledge. 'The motives of lords are a mystery to me, Maud,' I replied, 'you should ask your tutor.'

It took several hours for the column of fighting men, waggons, guns, and camp followers to clear the castle precincts, heading northeast on the Gloucester road. The image of Harri almost lost among them lingered in my mind's eye, so small and vulnerable on his white pony. For once I found myself hoping that a Yorkist army would return victorious and with the lord's two young pages safely among them.

35

Jane

Raglan & Weobley Castles

ON THE SECOND DAY of August a small party of armoured knights on lathered horses cantered through the castle gatehouse and news spread like wildfire from the Kitchen Tower to the Great Tower that Lord Herbert had been defeated in battle. The worst had happened. Then a little later, seeing Lady Anne, her inflamed eyes instantly told us, worse than the worst.

Eventually she was able to speak. 'I have to tell you my children that your beloved father is dead.' For the moment she could say no more but simply held out her arms and gathered all her children to her. I stood wordlessly by, desperate to ask after Walter and Harri – for Harri's welfare and his very life I now feared more than ever.

One of Lady Anne's companions offered kerchiefs, and along with their mother the children made forlorn gestures of comfort to each other until all at once, the chatelaine drew breath. 'We must be brave and we must help each other,' she told the children firmly, then raised her head and caught my eye. 'It will be necessary to pack their things as soon as possible, Mistress Jane. My lord's retinue is scattered and it is no longer safe for us here. I am going to take all the children to my brother's castle at Weobley. We will leave at dawn tomorrow.'

I bobbed a curtsy. 'Yes, my lady. May I ask if there is any news of Master Walter and Harri. Are they safe?'

She shook her head, frowning. 'I do not know. I wish to take the children to the chapel now, Jane, but please come back to me later, when we will speak some more.'

Judging by her expression there were things she wished not to say in front of the young ones and I made another curtsy in acknowledgement before taking my leave. Not long after their return, when I had already made good progress filling two travelling chests with their essentials, I was once more summoned to Lady Anne's chamber, dreading what additional bad news I might be about to hear.

Her young lady companions were absent and she invited me to sit on a stool beside her armchair. Although her face was still puffy from weeping, she was composed and tearless and had taken time to change her usual white gauze veil for a sombre black one. I was grateful when she addressed my chief concern straight away.

'I know you will be anxious about Harri, Jane, as I am about Walter, but I am sure we will soon hear news from my nephew Richard, who was charged with their care. Unfortunately I do not know what instructions he had in the event of this outcome but he is a sensible and trustworthy young man and he will have kept the boys safe, I am certain of that.'

'Let us pray that is so, my lady, and may I say how sorry I am for your loss.' They were trite words but it was all I could think of to say. Because he was Lord Jasper's sworn enemy, Lord Herbert had not stood high in my estimation but I knew Lady Anne's mourning would be more heartfelt than social convention required.

Her eyes instantly filled with fresh tears but her voice was harsh and fierce. 'It is more than just a loss it is a desecration! My lord was not killed in the battle, he was captured and the next day he was taken before the Earl of Warwick in Northampton. There was no trial, no reference to a higher authority. It seems that not only has Warwick invaded the king's peace, he has wickedly taken the law of the kingdom into his own hands. He arbitrarily sentenced my lord to death for treason, along with his younger brother Richard, his second in command.'

There was a pause while she drew several deep breaths to steady herself. 'I am told that Lord William pleaded on his knees for his brother's life, saying that only he was responsible for any perceived offence, but Richard was marched out there and then to the scaffold. He was only twenty-eight. William was given time to write a codicil to his will and then he, too, met the axe. I can imagine King Edward's fury and despair when he heard of these deeds, for my lord and his brother were his most faithful servants.'

Shocked and horrified by what Lady Anne told me, I was at a loss for words. Finally, after a long silence she reached out and clutched my hand, whether to offer comfort or express her anger I could not tell. Her eyes were screwed tight shut as she added, 'I cannot think how I am going to tell my children of this terrible deed and I do not know who to go to for help or redress.'

At length I found my tongue. 'Does anyone know where King Edward is, my lady? Will he bring a force against Warwick perhaps?' I was clutching at straws, hoping as well that Jasper had not been involved in these executions and hardly believing that it would be possible.

With an effort Lady Anne removed her hand from mine and resumed her composure. There were nail marks in my skin where her fingers had gripped me painfully. 'The king has been detained by Warwick's brother, the Archbishop of York, and taken to Middleham Castle. He was apprehended a few miles from Northampton, heading to London with a small escort, and was overpowered.' She shook her head in bemusement. 'At present it would seem that England has no king, or else the Kingmaker has usurped the role himself, an uninvited and unanointed tyrant.'

'And two young boys are wandering somewhere in a country that is in a state of anarchy!' My exclamation was an involuntary cry of despair.

She silenced me with a grim stare. 'We must maintain control, Jane. Let us hope we hear some news soon. Richard's family has many branches living in the March and he could have sought shelter with any one of them. I have despatched a message, asking my brother to send out men from Weobley to enquire. All we can do is wait and pray there is news when we get there.'

As I completed the packing and supervised the loading of the chests onto a cart I could not rid my mind of the spectre of Harri lying with his throat cut at Walter's feet. I repeatedly told myself that they were only boys and that

Walter's threats had been mere bravado but the vivid image kept returning and my desolate mood deepened.

We were all melancholy during the two day journey from Raglan to Weobley. A couple of Raglan servants drove the baggage carts, with a nursemaid looking after baby Katherine in one and little Philip, Elin and Sian up beside the driver of the other. There were two grooms to help with the horses and ponies ridden by the rest of us but that was hardly protection, should we run into any trouble. It was safe around the villages where field-workers were out labouring to bring in the harvest but every empty moor or common we crossed and every wood or forest we entered we dreaded being confronted by rebel soldiers hunting for fleeing royal troops. However we arrived at Weobley without incident in the late afternoon, the younger children hot, tired and tetchy and the rest of us simply grateful to stretch our legs after dismounting in the extensive outer bailey, while we waited for admission to the inner precinct.

Compared with Raglan, Weobley Castle was an old-fashioned fortification, located high on a motte, its grey stone walls built in a classic square with four round towers at each corner, perched over banks that fell steeply into a dry ditch. The stables and other wooden outbuildings were located all around us in the outer bailey and the single entrance to the fortress itself was via a raised drawbridge and narrow wooden stairway, which traversed the ditch and ran up the steep side of the motte to an arched pedestrian gateway. The heavy oak gate was soon opened, the draw-bridge was lowered and we were able to climb into the shelter of the thick walls. Inside, in the busy courtyard, Lady

Anne's brother Sir Walter Devereux, created Lord Ferrers by King Edward, was waiting to greet us and beside him stood his nephew and namesake Walter Herbert. And next to him, the Virgin be praised, stood Harri Tudor. My heart seemed to bounce off my ribs in relief.

Lady Anne was embraced and welcomed by her glowering brother. 'It is a black day that brings you here, sister,' he said, his angry words loud and echoing off the surrounding buildings. 'But I thank God you and your children have reached the safety of my walls.'

'We thank you for their refuge, brother,' she replied in softer tones. 'And I thank God you have Walter and Harri here also. Their safety has been an added burden on my mind. Come, let me bless you, my son,' and Walter stepped forward to kneel for his mother's blessing.

From the expression on Harri's face in that moment I knew that I had a story to hear from him, but at this time of crisis Weobley was a closed and congested castle, with archers patrolling the battlements, troops camped in the courtyard and busy officials and servants crowding every passage and stairway. Finding somewhere to speak alone with him would not be easy and then fate intervened . . .

Lady Anne had wisely dispatched all but one of her female companions to their homes and she had been allocated only a small chamber for herself and the single female companion she had brought with her. The morning following our arrival she sent for me. Somehow she had acquired black mourning apparel and sat on the only seat the tiny room possessed, a deep stone shelf under the narrow glazed window.

Her hands were folded tightly in her lap and she fixed

me with an accusing stare I soon learned the cause of it. 'My brother tells me that you have been Jasper Tudor's mistress and that your little girls are his bastards.' I saw her lip curl in distaste and felt anger surge, only with difficulty stopping myself from crying out in defence of my children. She pursued her complaint. 'You have taken advantage of my generosity and, under false pretences, brought the children of my husband's enemy into my household. You have utterly abused my kindness by lying to me over an extended period.'

I could contain my indignation no longer. 'I do not believe you can accuse me of taking advantage, my lady, when I have given you eight years of faithful and unpaid service and cared for your children as if they were my own.'

'Silence, jade!' The lady's calm demeanour had vanished entirely. 'I have not brought you here to plead your cause. I wish you to take your children and leave my employ and that includes removing young Davy Owen, whose true parentage I hardly dare to guess at. Take the three of them and go from this place. I do not wish to see your face again.'

'But what about Harri?' I cried. 'He will be left alone among his father's enemies.'

'Harri is still my husband's ward and will remain here. I will write to inform his mother where he is and that he is safe with us. Collect your things together and take only what you can carry. I do not care where you go but wherever it is you will have to walk and I urge you to consider your sins along the way.'

I was flabbergasted, suddenly seeing a side of her I had not known existed. 'But – but my children! You brought us here – miles from anyone we know. I have no money. You cannot in all Christian decency throw us out into unknown

376

territory without transport, money or protection!' There was no question of avoiding her gaze now; my eyes were drilling into hers and she met them without flinching.

'Do not speak to me of decency! You came to us in the guise of a decent widow, who had been entrusted with the care of a wealthy nobleman's heir. Now I discover you are neither decent nor widowed. Worse than that, you are the leman of my husband's enemy and have probably been his spy all the time you have been under my roof. If you were a man you would be under arrest and clapped in irons. Think yourself lucky I do not bring charges against you. The servant who showed you here has orders to stay with you while you gather your belongings and your children and ensure that you leave my brother's castle. Now go.'

The anger raging inside me sustained me through the difficult task of rounding up the girls and Davy and encouraging them to wrap their most precious and necessary possessions in a blanket and knot the corners so that they could each carry their own. I had no compunction in taking the blankets, considering it a challenge to the woman I had until so recently thought of as compassionate.

'But where are we going and why can I not say goodbye to Harri?' Davy asked fretfully. 'He will come out of his Latin lesson and look for me. We always go to dinner together.'

'We would all like to say goodbye to Harri, Davy, but the armed man outside the chamber door will not let us near him,' I replied. 'He and several others are ready this moment to escort us out of the castle.'

'I do not understand,' wailed Elin, her cheeks wet with tears. 'What have we done?'

'None of us has done anything. Everything has changed as a result of Lord Herbert's death and we have to leave. That is all.'

'But why is Harri not coming with us?' Even Sian had found her voice to protest. 'He is one of us – our family!'

'You all know that Harri was Lord Herbert's ward. The king is in charge of him now. Perhaps he will go to his mother. He would like that.' I wanted at all costs to avoid telling them the bitter truth, that with King Edward a captive and the Earl of Warwick playing his own despotic game, Harri's future was possibly even more uncertain than ours.

I thought of packing paper, pens and ink so that I could write to Lady Margaret but how would I get a letter to her now? She could never have dreamed that Harri's guardian would take her precious son to a battle, only to lose it along with his head. I had never imagined that my small deception at the start of our life with the Herberts would result in being cast out into enemy territory, miles away from friends or family. As we hauled our bundles down the steps from Weobley Castle it felt as if we were walking into a nightmare.

36

Jane

The Welsh March

FROM RAGLAN IT HAD taken us two days to ride to
Weobley but I had no idea how long it would take to
walk to safety, if such a thing existed for a woman and three
children alone in a hostile world. In the village outside the
castle we were already unwelcome strangers. Fists were
shaken at us, insults shouted and doors slammed on every
side as the street emptied of people. It was as if we had F
for felon stamped on our foreheads and it made me suspect
that during the short time it had taken to pack our bundles
Lady Herbert had had a cryer declare us outcasts.

'What is the matter?' Elin shouted furiously at a ranting
gossip, who was hurling refuse at us from the doorway of
her house. 'Why do you hate us? We have done nothing
to you.'

Davy pulled her away. 'Leave it, Elin. We should go *now*.'
Apparently sure of which direction to take, he marched her
purposefully along the rutted road that led downhill out of

the village, heading into a forested wilderness. Above us a blazing sun shone down from an azure sky. In any other circumstances it would have been a beautiful day.

Sian and I had to run to catch them up. 'When we clear the village I think we should aim southwest,' I told Davy. 'Following the sun. I remember Lord Jasper saying that the lordship of Hay belongs to the Duke of Buckingham; he is a ward of Harri's mother. We must try to reach it before nightfall.'

It was a stab in the dark, something to say. I did not even know how far it was. Our chosen path took us along forest trails, which climbed uphill and down, the valleys cut by fast-running streams. In a clearing by one of them, as the sun set, we sank down exhausted, ate apples, drank water from our cupped hands and rolled ourselves in the blankets in which we had wrapped our belongings. Fearful, I lay long awake, my ears straining for any sound but finally I slept and when I woke at first light it was to find that some unknown thief had crept up on us and made off with whatever he or she could carry, including Sian's favourite doll and the few groats I had managed to squirrel away. Davy and Elin had taken the precaution of tucking all their belongings under their blankets and from them nothing had been taken, for which they earned my praise. Davy revealed the knife he had kept safe. 'I think we might need it soon,' he said seriously, comforting no one. Seeing our faces he added, 'For cutting up any game we catch,' which only prompted Elin to ask scornfully, 'And how would we cook when we have no fire?'

'We will not starve before we get to Hay,' I said as cheerfully as I could.

After an hour or so we came to a major river, much too wide and deep to cross and we followed it upstream, looking for a bridge or a ford. I guessed this was the Wye. We followed it against the flow to take us deeper into the Welsh hills and, I hoped, into friendly territory. We hid from some soldiers as they tramped past our concealing thicket and something caught my eye when I peered through the bushes. The badge on their jackets was a white rose. If these were men from the garrison at Hay Castle it meant that Hay was no longer Lancastrian; it was in the hands of York. It was only then I remembered, with a jolt, that the Duke of Buckingham's custody had been taken from Lady Margaret and granted to Edward's queen, Elizabeth Woodville. It was no place for us.

And yet we needed food and we needed directions. Now I had to hope we could find a priory or a monastery, which might take pity on us and give us a meal at least. Davy took on the role of advance scout and eventually came running back from a bend in the river to tell me that a woman was kneeling beside the stream doing her washing. St Christopher must have been watching over us because the washerwoman was kindness itself; she directed us to cross a nearby ford and told us how to find the closest priory. 'If it is charity you are looking for,' as she put it, eyeing our makeshift bundles. Meanwhile she gave the children the loaf she had presumably planned to eat herself. And she restored some of my faith in humankind.

The monks at Clifford Priory, when we found them, were few and mostly elderly but true to their calling they served us a simple meal and accommodated us in a small guest dorter. The prior advised me against travelling alone with the children in these troubled times but I explained that I had no choice and asked directions to Carmarthen.

After two nights and a day of the monks' warmly given charity we left. However, I had overheard talk of a travelling bard and was inspired to ask the prior if Lewys Glyn Cothi was known to him. When told he was in the vicinity I asked for a message to be given to him should he appear; my name and the direction I had taken with the three children.

Davvy had begged a fishing-net from one of the monks and learned how to make a cord snare-trap to catch hares. He also discovered how to make fire with two sticks and some dry grass and for several days I thought we were doing well as travellers. Then, while sitting by our fire after dusk, two men carrying sickles suddenly emerged from the shadows to challenge us as vagrants. Before long we were being marched to the nearby castle, which loomed over us, dark and menacing against the night sky; all the more so when we were told this was the lordship of Sir Roger Vaughan.

I had barely time to recall that this was the man who had led Owen Tudor to his execution before we were pushed through the gatehouse and then through an iron-hinged oak door straight into the castle's hall, where a dozen men and women sat at their supper. We were lined up before a large grey-haired man who tore the last shred of meat from a mutton bone before hurling it to the two hounds waiting expectantly at his back. Had my own teeth not been chattering with fear I might have been impressed at the strength of his, considering his years. His voice was also apparently unaffected by age.

'What have we here, Meurig?' he bellowed. 'Some entertainment for us?'

'Vagrants, sir,' began the chief of our captors. 'Lit a fire in the hayfield. Danger to your second crop.'

'It was not!' cried Davy. 'It was on the packed mud near the stream. I made sure it was safe.'

'Silence!' shouted the lord. 'I will not be shouted at by a filthy vagrant in my own hall. Shut his gob, Sim.'

I swung round to see the second guard clamp his spare hand over Davy's mouth. The boy's eyes rolled in anger, which turned to alarm as the sickle blade flashed before them.

'I do not wish to deal with this now, Meurig.' The grey-haired man waved his hand dismissively. 'Take them away and lock them in the cellar. I will come down there when I have finished my supper.'

My arm was grabbed and I was being pulled away when a familiar voice spoke up from the far end of the trestle. 'Sir Roger, I know these people. They are not vagrants.' It was Lewys Glyn Cothi.

I did not know whether to rejoice at seeing a friend or tremble at the possibility that he might expose me as Jasper's mistress. I could not bear to think what Sir Roger Vaughan would choose to do with me if he discovered that.

The knight raised his eyebrows at Lewys and grinned. 'Great Heaven! Not another of your doxys, Lewys?'

The bard bridled. 'You flatter me, Sir Roger. No, this is my cousin Sian and her three children. I do not know why they were camping in your field but I guarantee it would not be with the intention of burning your hay crop.'

I took courage and wrenched my arm from my captor, deciding it was time to drop a curtsy. 'No indeed, Sir Roger,' I said. 'We were merely intending to rest in your byre for the night on our way home. I apologize for causing you distress.'

Sir Roger cleared his throat loudly. 'Harrumph. You should have made yourself known at the gate, Mistress. Where is your home?'

He waved back the men with sickles and I felt a surge of relief but at the same time I also scrabbled mentally for a reply to his question. The wrong answer could land us in even hotter water than we had been hitherto. 'Like Lewys, my family is from the west, sir, but my husband is a mason and we have been in Hereford. He has travelled on to find new work and will send for us again when he has found it.'

Sir Roger glared at his man with the sickle. 'So not a vagrant, Meurig?'

'She said she had no money, sir.' The man scowled fiercely at me.

'It is hard to explain at the point of a blade,' I retorted. 'We were set upon by thieves the other night and all our money was stolen.'

'Well, Mistress Sian, when the trestles are cleared you are welcome to sleep here in the hall but meanwhile you can go to the kitchen for some supper. Now let me get on with my meal!'

Lewys came out to greet us while we ate and his cheeks grew pink as he received our grateful thanks. When I told him of our eviction from Weobley and our travels so far he was indignant. Then I revealed that Tenby was our destination, which I had not told the children, in case they let it slip.

'You cannot go that far alone, Mistress Jane,' he said. 'You will become lost or worse. I will guide you to Tenby and see you safely to your house,' adding in a whisper. 'Lord Jasper would expect no less.'

'I cannot let you do that, Lewys,' I protested . . . but Davy was thrilled, especially at the prospect of learning how to lift a trout from a pool with his bare hands, which Lewys had once boasted he knew how to do.

I laughed and gave him a hug. 'Oh, Davy, we could not have got this far without you. I look forward to your first trout!'

We all had cause to thank Davy and his net and snare over the next ten days as, weary and footsore but rarely hungry, we followed the bard over mountain, river and moor. And I blessed the boy and his sharp knife for another reason, because he slept beside the girls. Lewys was a good guide and friend but I knew his reputation and I did not like the way he looked at Elin.

37

Jasper

Chateau Chinon, Touraine, France

CALLED 'THE PRUDENT KING' by his courtiers, Louis XI of France was known among his detractors as 'The Universal Spider', because he ruled through a complex web of spies and diplomats rather than maintaining order, as sovereigns were wont to do, by the power of edict and sword. Chateau Chinon was the hub of his web, located on the River Vienne in Touraine, which had been his personal dukedom as Dauphin and to which he had frequently withdrawn in anger when his father, my mother's brother, had been alive. On the family tree we were first cousins, but we were hardly the kissing kind. Louis had been crowned King of France around the time my brother was usurped but not until recently had he shown any interest in assisting King Henry's restoration, despite my consistent efforts to gain his support. He had granted me a meagre pension but one that he considered gave him *carte blanche* to harness my diplomatic services around the courts of Europe; and since becoming stateless I had been forced to accept that beggars could not be choosers.

At least I had been allotted a small but private chamber at Chinon and a letter from Lady Margaret had been waiting there for several weeks when I arrived back at the start of November. I was surprised to receive it at all, considering the political upheaval in England and the disruption it must have caused to our courier network. Some of what she wrote I already knew through other sources but the terse and cryptic nature of the letter vividly conveyed her anxiety about Harri, whom she referred to as R – for Richmond I presumed.

To my very good friend.

You have no doubt heard that Herbert's hubris led him to believe he could not lose the battle at Banbury and Warwick's hubris sent his defeated rival to the scaffold. Both events put R in the greatest possible danger. I lived in fear that he had been killed or captured, then at last I learned that he lived and had been taken to a place in Shropshire, where Herbert's widow and children had taken refuge. I have received assurances of R's safety and good health but since his appointed guardian is dead, I wish to petition the crown for his legal custody. However, I am told Warwick has the king under house arrest in Middleham and, not content with Herbert's head, has ordered the execution of the queen's captured father and brother. The queen herself has fled to sanctuary at Westminster Abbey. England is in the invidious position of having two living, consecrated kings who are both confined, Henry in the

Tower and Edward at Middleham, while uncrowned
Warwick is ruling despotically and without authority. I
fear Fortune's Wheel may have turned against us
entirely. The future is in God's hands, to Whom I pray
hourly for mercy and guidance. MR
   Written on the twenty-ninth day of August, 1469

I folded Margaret's letter and added it to what I called
the Conspiracy Casket, which I kept double-locked among
my belongings. But of Jane and the children I had no news.
Thinking of her practicality and praying hard, I told myself
that no news was good news and tried not to speculate
whether they, too, had gone to Shropshire. Or if not, where
were they and how did they fare?

A royal summons came. Once arrayed in the, admittedly somewhat crumpled, fur-trimmed doublet and gold
Lancastrian collar that I kept for court appearances, I passed
swiftly through King Louis' crowded Audience Chamber,
exchanging brief pleasantries with those of his courtiers I
knew, many of whom were obliged to wait hours gossiping
and conspiring while awaiting admittance to The Presence.
I had often had to do so myself and heaved a sigh of relief
when, without any delay, the duty chamberlain threw open
the door to the inner sanctum.

'The most noble and puissant Lord Jasper, Earl of
Pembroke, your grace.'

It was pleasant to hear my title used, having been officially
but illegally stripped of it eight years ago. Louis advanced
with his hand out to greet me; I kissed it with a low bow.

'Jasper!' He said my name in French, sounding as if he
was desperately hoping for something – *J'espère!* 'I have been

expecting you. The news from England is more promising I think.'

'Indeed, your grace?' I could not help the question in my voice, for it seemed less than promising to me.

'Yes, yes.' Louis rubbed his hands. 'Edward is back on the throne, he has generously forgiven his brother Clarence and the Earl of Warwick for rebelling against him and now he has made his other brother Gloucester, Constable of England. The situation is ripening nicely, ready for us to pounce!'

This was news indeed but his was not the way I would have looked at it. 'If you say so, sire. I cannot see it myself.'

He wagged a majestic finger at me. 'Ah, but you see only the obvious and do not detect the undercurrents. Warwick tried and failed to depose Edward and put Clarence on the throne, yes? He held Edward prisoner and executed his favourites, the Woodvilles, father and brother, yes? And yet Edward does not cut off Warwick's head in retaliation, as you might expect, but instead makes Gloucester, his youngest brother, Constable of England, in charge of defending his kingdom, though a mere boy of seventeen. What does that say to the world?' Louis lowered his voice and spoke into my ear. 'It says that Warwick and Clarence are finished. Edward fears them about as much as two drunks at a Midsummer revel. That he considers them not worth his trust and not even worth executing.'

Louis patted my cheek and moved away, face aglow, magnificent rings flashing in the blaze of a twenty-candle chandelier as he made his next pronouncement. 'The Earl of Warwick is a man with an overblown opinion of himself.'

And he is not the only one, I thought. Keeping my face straight while Louis continued his polemic was not easy.

'That fact has not changed. He will not stomach further disparagement by the king he once considered his puppet. He will not tolerate being outranked by the boy Richard of Gloucester. Believe me, it will not be long before Warwick and Clarence return to the fray and however great Lord Warwick thinks himself, he still needs allies. I predict that he will be knocking at my door within weeks.' In his element, the king's smile was smug.

I responded with an upward twist of my eyebrow. 'And how will you react, your grace?'

I could swear that Louis's long, warty Valois nose actually twitched, but he stilled it by laying his forefinger against it, gazing at me through narrowed bloodshot eyes. 'I will send him to Queen Marguerite.'

I blew air noisily from my cheeks. 'I would suggest that you prepare the ground first, sire, or she will never receive him. There is no love between those two.'

He waved his hand airily. 'Perhaps not but Marguerite wants her son on the throne of England and Warwick wants his daughter as queen. Having failed with the elder daughter Isabel's marriage to the dissolute Clarence, he will embrace the prospect of succeeding with the younger, little Anne Neville – for whom we will arrange a betrothal. A good dynastic marriage will always seal an alliance and I am very impressed with young Édouard of Lancaster, a fierce lion cub.'

'Unlike his father, who lives yet,' I reminded him. 'I hope you do not expect King Henry to make way for his son?'

'No, no,' Louis said impatiently, as if his English cousin were a mere inconvenience. 'It will happen, all in God's good time. And fortunately Édouard takes after his mother, who is a formidable woman. She and Warwick will make sparks enough to light a conflagration, from which, God willing, a phoenix will arise.'

'Or a dragon,' I suggested dryly. 'After all Édouard is the Prince of Wales.'

Clearly irritated by this mild pleasantry King Louis paused and stroked his chin, his full lips pursed in thought. 'We made a mistake sending you to Wales last year, Jasper,' he observed. 'It achieved nothing and cost too much – and it led to the loss of that dragon's lair of yours with the unpronounceable name – Ar-leck is it?'

It was not the first time he had brought up the subject of my recent attempt to bolster Lancaster's Welsh standing by re-capturing Denbigh, an expedition badly under-funded at the last minute by Louis's Exchequer. My siege on the castle had failed as a result but I had followed it with a devastating chevauchée through the Yorkist Vale of Clwyd and a furious William Herbert had taken revenge for this by throwing a vast siege army at Harlech Castle. Lancaster had lost its last toehold in Wales and Herbert had been granted my earldom of Pembroke as a reward, both humiliating events for me.

'At least Herbert will not be staging any more revenge raids. We have Warwick to thank for that,' I reminded him.'

'Yes, so we do. The earl is rather prone to cutting off heads is he not?' Louis observed tartly.

'Does that bother you?' I asked in surprise.

'No, but I thought it might concern you, or will you hope to return to England on good terms with Monsieur le "Kingmaker"?'

I made an ambivalent gesture. 'I share his scorn for the

men whose heads he removed but I am not sure I think him any more honourable than them. I wonder if he would have sent them to the scaffold had they been old nobility, as he considers himself, instead of what you French call *arrivistes*. However, there is no doubt that Warwick has done us a favour by removing a few Herberts and Woodvilles from the political scene.'

Louis raised an eyebrow. 'Hm. You consider yourself a match for Lord Warwick then?'

I recalled my series of contentious meetings in Anjou with the exiled Marguerite and shot him a thin smile. 'Whether I am or not, I can assure you of one thing your grace; Queen Marguerite definitely is!'

38

Jasper

Chateau Angers, Anjou, France

LOCATED IN THE WEST of Northern France, close to
the border with Brittany, Angers was known as the
Black City due to the sombre colour of its roofs, tiled with
slate from the quarries that surrounded it. It was also a
city built on two thousand years of history; in its walls
and cobbled streets were signs of the ancient Celts, Roman
settlers and Germanic invaders, while above me loomed
the legacy of the Christian missionaries, the twin spires of
the cathedral of St Maurice and the massive bell-tower
of the Benedictine Abbey of St Aubin. Dropping down to
the banks of the River Maine, I stared up at the vast bulk
of Angers Castle and could almost count the civilizations
layered in the rock on which it stood. It was a fortress
buttressed by no less than seventeen towers, each startlingly
banded with alternating rows of black and white stone,
defended by the fast-flowing river and, to landward, by a
deep dry moat inhabited by a menagerie of man-eating

lions and tigers. It was both spectacular and daunting, an awesome castle, not one that extended a visual welcome or the promise of comfort and luxury.

I was there at the behest of King Louis but also as a guest of Queen Marguerite's ageing father, King René. Cynics dubbed him 'the king with many crowns but no kingdom', for René clung to his long-defunct ancestral claim to the kingdom of Jerusalem, and had bankrupted himself trying to regain his father's kingdom of Naples and Sicily, lost to his rival claimant, King Alfonso of Aragon. In a way, he might be compared to my brother Henry who had also lost two kingdoms, but at least King René still presided over vast swathes of rich French territory in the form of his duchy of Anjou and his counties of Provence and Piedmont.

As he grew older people had started calling him 'Good King René' and whenever I was invited into his company I greatly enjoyed it, for he was a cultured man, a poet and painter of miniatures and, to my delight, a great enthusiast for chivalry in all its manifestations. He had even written a book on the subject, which on this visit I had been encouraged to borrow, whiling away a few fascinating hours absorbing his detailed instructions on the staging of a tournament; the ceremonial, the weapons and armour and the layout of the lists, even the costumes of the heralds and judges and the prizes to be awarded. Time which I might otherwise have found tedious as I waited for developments in the matter I had really come to Angers to pursue, namely the return of my brother to the throne of England.

I had been there for a week before letters caught up

with me, of which the most welcome was from Jane, which told me of her shameful eviction from Lady Anne's presence with the children, and her precarious journey to Tenby. My relief at knowing they were safe was intense. Lady Margaret had sent thirty crowns to Jane when she learned of her plight and for this she had my gratitude. I hoped they would find a safe home among the folk of Tenby, many of who remained among my greatest supporters.

Lady Margaret's epistle, the latest of many that had reached me during my sojourn in France, was without preamble, crudely encoded and considerably shorter than Jane's but in contrast to her last anxious and dejected communication, it left me in no doubt of her renewed determination not only to regain control of her son's birthright but also to restore the Lancastrian throne.

> *It is time to strike. E is back in action but R is still in the hands of the widow and I despair of ever reclaiming him while E remains in power. My own people have suffered his deadly wrath following a failed uprising in Lincolnshire, which W secretly backed. Now he too fears for his head and has taken ship to Calais with his entire family, including C. You must summon all your diplomatic skills, because my sources tell me that L is prepared to help W to reinstate H through an alliance with M. To secure L's help, it is more than ever your task to bring W and M together and force them to collaborate. If you can turn the Wheel of Fortune to achieve this, we can end E's bloodthirsty regime and restore H to his rightful status. As soon as I hear positive news I will send funds. MR*

I had heard of the Lincolnshire rebellion she referred to; news had spread through Europe of its violent suppression by King Edward. Margaret's stepbrother, Lord Richard Welles, had been arrested for a breach of the peace over a property dispute, which had infuriated his only son Sir Robert, prompting him to offer Warwick and Clarence help by raising a rebellion in his Lincolnshire lands. Believing Warwick to be loyal, Edward had commissioned him to put down the rising but when he realized that the army Warwick had raised had been handed over to Sir Robert's command and was actually moving against his smaller royal force, Edward had Lord Welles brought to the battlefield and gave Sir Robert an ultimatum to lay down his arms or see his father executed. Believing it an empty threat, Sir Robert refused to surrender and he and his rebel army had watched in horror as Lord Welles's head was immediately lopped from his body. His anguished son launched an instant attack but at the first barrage of royal cannon fire he was abandoned by most of his troops. Captured in the rout, he was executed a week later. Clearly Lady Margaret was enraged by this ferocious Yorkist revenge on her mother's kin and anti-Yorkist feeling in England needed only to find a leader. Warwick was perfectly fitted for this role but he needed French ships and men and King Louis would only grant them if his Lancastrian cousins were returned to power. The Spider wished to extend his web across the Channel.

No sooner had I absorbed the content of this letter than a page knocked on my chamber door with an urgent summons to attend King René in his chamber. He greeted me graciously, bending down from his throne to raise me from my knees. Even in private His Highness displayed the trappings of royalty, sitting beneath a blue brocade canopy hung with silver tassels and wearing one of his many gem-encrusted crowns – a gold circlet with trefoils, which admirably set off his thick silver hair. Beneath it his bulldog countenance was relieved by a genial expression, his dark brown eyes twinkling conspiratorially while his thin lips curved deeply downwards into ample jowls. I liked him and I believed he liked me.

'There is news from Louis, Lord Jasper,' he said, cutting straight to the point. 'He has had word from the Earl of Warwick. The Calais garrison remained loyal to Edward's crown and prevented Warwick's ships from entering harbour, even in a fierce storm, so they were blown around Cap Griz Nez. *Voilá* – the Warwick is in France, whether he likes it or not.' He gave me the briefest of smiles, revealing brown-streaked teeth. 'He has his whole family with him and Louis wishes you to go to Boulogne and greet them. It seems there was some drama on board during the voyage and they need help.'

I frowned, wondering what was behind this request. Louis's 'wishes' were never straightforward and I doubted if Warwick had specifically asked for me because I knew he considered me to have been among the first of the '*arrivistes*' at Henry's court, even before it had disintegrated entirely into factions. 'It will take me a week to get to Boulogne,' I pointed out, 'so I hope their need is not urgent. Would it not have been quicker for his grace to send someone from Paris?'

King René looked sardonically down his nose at me. 'Perhaps you would like to call at the French court on your way and say that to Louis's face?' he suggested.

I shrugged. 'I think I will take a shorter route,' I said. When The Spider gave an order there was little point in querying it.

'Will you leave at once?'

It was not really a question but an assumption. I tugged gently at my Lancastrian SS collar. 'As soon as I have packed away the court finery and had my horse saddled, sire.'

He nodded. 'Good. I wish you a safe journey.' It sounded like a dismissal and I made to leave but King René held up a restraining hand. 'You are to bring Warwick and his family here to Angers, Jasper,' he added. 'Louis will also be here by then. He and Marguerite are to meet next week for what he called "consultations".'

I immediately understood King Louis's reason for sending me to meet Warwick. He intended to start working on the stubborn Marguerite and the quicker I got to the earl, the sooner I could begin a campaign of persuasion with him. Predictably neither of them would readily stomach the idea of an alliance and it would take all the pressure and arm-twisting we could each employ.

I made my well-practised court bow but King René was still not quite finished with me. 'One more thing, Jasper – Boulogne is dangerously close to the Flemish border. Take care you do not stray over it. I know you reckon to travel faster with just your squire but on this occasion you are to take six of my men as an escort. King Louis and Duke Charles of Burgundy are arguing over a question of homage and the duke might consider you a very useful hostage.'

39

Jasper

Chateau Angers, Anjou, France

QUEEN MARGUERITE CAST A scornful eye over my well-worn court doublet. Undeniably its once-glossy fur trimming was matted in places and the silver lace showed signs of tarnish but I stared pointedly back at the faded ribbons tying the crimson satin sleeves to the bodice of her pink gown and the ragged patch of embroidered swans on its skirt. She had asked to see me prior to her crucial meeting with the Earl of Warwick.

'Royalty and poverty do not fit comfortably together, do they, Jasper?' she observed, her lips curling in a thin smile. 'I imagine Lord Warwick's apparel is immaculate.'

I shrugged. 'A little salt-stained, your grace. Their crossing from England was perilous.'

Her smile widened and her deep violet eyes flashed wickedly. 'So I heard. How unfortunate.'

Her gleeful expression belied the sympathy of her words. Unsurprisingly, after eight years in exile she had become cynical. We had been born in the same year, but if my mirror did not lie, Marguerite showed her age more than I did. She had suffered much tribulation since my brother had been forced from his throne and was living in relative penury. Fine lines traced the contours of her face and there were no funds for costly new gowns to draw attention away from them.

'Unfortunate indeed,' I echoed, 'especially for the young Duchess of Clarence, who lost her first child at sea, during the height of the storm. It must have been a terrifying experience for her.'

Marguerite's face fell. 'King Louis did not tell me that,' she said, creditably shamefaced and making the sign of the cross. 'Poor Isabel, may God sustain her.

'Has Louis convinced you to make a deal then?' I asked.

The queen bridled. 'I have agreed to hear Warwick's proposal, that is all. And he will have to crawl to me on his knees to make it.'

This statement startled me into incredulous laughter. 'Ha! You cannot mean to humiliate the man so?'

'Can I not?' she responded coldly. 'Watch me.'

*　*　*

At high noon the great hall of Chateau Angers was bright with sunlight, streaming in through the parade of long, mullioned windows that afforded a panoramic view over the River Maine. Alive with dust motes, the sunbeams brilliantly illuminated the spectacular scenes on the hangings, which lined two of the other three walls. When he had heard where the meeting between Queen Marguerite and the Earl of Warwick was to take place, King René had ordered a section of his father's famous Apocalypse Tapestry to be brought from storage in the cathedral crypt and hastily hung where it might act as a backdrop to the crucial encounter. Under the warmth of the sun it exuded a musty aroma of damp canvas, which mingled with the earthy scent rising from the new rush matting covering the uneven stones of the hall floor and the flowery herbs strewn about to disguise it.

In its entirety the one hundred and sixty foot length of the complete tapestry was far too much even for the considerable capacity of the great hall walls, so René had selected only the last of its six panels, which showed the concluding triumph of Good over Evil, progressing from left to right in a double row of fourteen framed scenes of unfolding narrative. Predominant colours of blue, red and gold glowed in the sunlight and caused the fantastic figures of angels, beasts, dragons and saints almost to leap from the canvas. The crowd of courtiers attending this historic occasion could hardly fail to draw sense and significance from such vivid imagery.

As I waited for the arrival of the two main parties, I took the opportunity of examining the tapestry in detail and formed the fanciful notion that King René might be seen as the scholarly observer depicted reading from St John's gospel at the start of the panel, whereas secretly and probably heretically, I compared King Louis to the figure in the final scenes where God in his Heaven, previously invisible, ultimately revealed his face to the Christian Elect as they received their reward of admittance to Paradise in the New Jerusalem. At the final trump Good did prevail over Evil but I could not help noticing that the weavers had not made the Righteous look very joyful about it. I wondered how favourable a portent it offered for the outcome of the day's events.

Queen Marguerite arrived first, accompanied by her entourage, which included her loyal and venerable counsellor and Chancellor, Sir John Fortescue, a number of her other faithful courtiers and ladies and her beloved son, Prince Édouard. During the six years that the young prince had been in exile in France he had matured from a skinny boy into a muscular youth, obviously well acquainted with the arms practice-yard. Whether Sir John, as his governor, had managed to develop his intellect to a similar extent had yet to be demonstrated but as he took his place behind his mother's throne the arrogant expression on his beardless face did not give me substantial grounds for hope.

Warwick timed his arrival perfectly to allow Marguerite to settle herself in her father's velvet-draped throne and exchange greetings with Louis's representative and me. The French king had made a point of departing Angers the previous day, leaving one of his closest advisers to witness and report on the meeting. I assumed that by absenting himself he hoped to ensure that if necessary the French crown could deny all involvement in any resulting English insurgency. With similar intent, I made a point of moving some distance away from Marguerite as a flurry of activity at the hall entrance indicated the approach of her protagonist.

The Earl of Warwick took three long paces into the hall and paused, allowing his family members to file in behind him. His Countess, Lady Anne, stepped swiftly up to her husband's left shoulder, closely followed by her younger daughter and namesake and to his right hand came nineteen-year-old George, Duke of Clarence, advancing alone, his countess having yet fully to recover from the nightmare stillbirth of their first child during the storm in the Channel.

None of the Warwick party displayed any outward sign of their close encounter with shipwreck but their apparel on this occasion gave a good idea of just how much treasure would have gone with them to the seabed, had their vessel sunk. All were extravagantly clad in rich silks and satins and bedecked with jewellery of blinding magnificence, in keeping I supposed with the extreme wealth that the vast Warwick estates afforded them – or had done until they had been forced to flee England's shores. Despite having made an extraordinary effort to dress like the queen she was, Marguerite appeared dowdy by comparison.

Perhaps annoyed by her sartorial disadvantage, when Warwick took his next step forward the queen immediately raised her right hand and uttered one word with sharp authority.

'Stop!'

Having brought him to an abrupt halt she added, 'If you wish to acknowledge me as your queen, my lord of Warwick, you will do so on your knees.'

Warwick's countess gasped in disbelief and the earl's brow creased into a deep scowl. He opened his mouth to protest then thought better of it and snapped it shut like a trapdoor. There was a pause and a collective holding of breath, then slowly and with athletic deliberation, despite the copious silver streaks that now featured in the earl's long, dark hair and carefully barbered beard, he lowered his knees to the rush matting, never removing his narrowed gaze from Marguerite's face.

She nodded slowly. 'Good. Now you may approach but . . .' she continued hastily as he made to get to his feet, 'you may not rise.'

Warwick's eyes scanned the thirty-foot distance between them; his frown deepened and his lips compressed but the queen's expression was implacable. At her shoulder Prince Édouard licked his lips, relishing the prospect of seeing the man crawl to his mother's feet who, five years ago, had led his royal father through the streets of London to imprisonment in the Tower, bareheaded on a spavined mule. I thought for a moment that the earl might baulk and spring indignantly to his feet, thus inevitably destroying all the hours of hard negotiation Louis and I had expended over the past week. I did not know what threats and promises the King of France had laid on Marguerite's table but I crossed my fingers and hoped that the stubborn Warwick would remember the baits I had offered him, dangling the prospect of a regency while my brother lived and the vision of his daughter as Queen Consort of England, his descendants its kings.

To my intense relief the earl forced his lips into a smile, waved acknowledgement of the order with a flourish worthy of my father Owen, and began his long and awkward progress along the coarse matting. Freshly laid and tightly woven though it was, within moments his dazzling white hose had become mired with brown dust and his knees must have felt the painful bite of sharp rush-stems. I had to admire his fortitude in nonetheless keeping his smile fixed and his eyes pinned to Queen Marguerite's. Behind him with measured footsteps followed his countess, his daughter and his son-in-law, all stony-faced at this humiliation of the exalted head of the House of Warwick.

Queen Marguerite's throne had been placed on her father's stepped dais covered in blue velvet and as Warwick drew near she thrust out her right foot in its red Cordovan leather shoe. The implication was obvious and, taking a deep, steadying breath, Warwick all but prostrated himself, bending to kiss the high vamp with its gleaming jewelled buckle. When he lifted his head I could almost feel his desire to wipe his mouth clean but instead he spoke loudly and clearly.

'I am your grace's most humble servant.'

The queen withdrew her foot. 'That is a violent change of tune from the traitor who dethroned his rightful king and set a lecherous Yorkist puppet in his place. What has happened to bring you crawling to my feet, my lord of Warwick? Has the puppet cut his strings? Does he no longer march to the rhythm of your drum? Has he disparaged your rank and set unworthy commoners above you?' Her voice grew strident as she warmed to her tirade. 'Let me hear you admit it. You have been betrayed and denigrated, just as you betrayed and humiliated King Henry, your true sovereign.'

Warwick bowed his head, concealing his expression. 'Indeed, your grace, we suffer the same pain.'

'We do no such thing!' she snapped. 'I suffer a queen's agony at the crimes committed against her lord and king. You suffer a villain's bruised ego at the failure of his own heinous schemes. We have nothing in common.'

He spread his hands in supplication. 'We have the interests of our children, Madame. Surely that is enough to bring us – and them – together.'

Her laugh rang harshly into the rafters. 'Ha! My son is the true-blooded Lancastrian heir to the English throne.' She reached out to grasp Prince Édouard's hand in a fierce grip. 'Your daughter's ancestry is tainted with bastardy. We need no upstart Neville blood to boost our royal claim.'

The young prince flushed with pride and moved closer to his mother's side, breaking his silence with his shrill tenor. 'Let combat demonstrate whose cause is Heaven-blessed! False Edward is a cowardly pretender who consorts with commoners and criminals and will flee before the divine right when I confront him in the field. God will restore my father to his rightful throne.'

The earl nodded enthusiastic approval of this bellicose rant. 'I am certain the Almighty will favour your cause, Prince, but you will need men to stand beside you on this field of combat and any Englishman will tell you that the Warwick bear commands the greatest number of loyal followers in the kingdom. Together we will bring Edward of York to his knees.' He gave an ingratiating laugh. 'And perhaps you will graciously advise your royal mother to allow me to rise from mine.'

'No!' Marguerite's strident denial made her son jump. 'Not until I have heard Lord Warwick plead for forgiveness – until we have all heard him do so.' She lifted her chin and cast her gaze over the other occupants of the hall, letting it linger on each face until one after another they allowed their lids to drop before the challenge. Only fourteen-year-old Anne, arrayed in sumptuous white brocade embellished with gold lace, her dark hair flowing down her back like the bridal offering she was, locked eyes with her potential mother-in-law and refused to avert her gaze. I saw the queen's eyes narrow with pique and her head tip to one side, as if she was on the verge of pointing out this evidence of defiance to her son, only to find that he too was studying Anne's small, heart-shaped face, his downy upper lip lifted in a sneer.

Anxious to deflect attention back to him, Warwick hastened to pursue his persuasion. 'I fully understand your grace's hesitation. I myself have cursed men who broke the vow of fealty. When Sir Anthony Trollope crossed the line at Ludford Bridge, it felt like a dagger in my heart. It goes against the very principle of the code of chivalry.'

'I am surprised you can recall chivalry's strictures, my lord,' remarked the queen acidly. 'And should I conclude that you consider loyalty a male prerogative, pertaining only to warfare?'

'Far from it, Madame, let ladies embrace it too, as I am sure you do. But when faithful service is ignored and society's rubrics violated, as they have been under Edward of York, then we are bound to consider ourselves released from fidelity's bond, are we not? After much searching of my soul I have come to this conclusion and so has his grace of Clarence.'

Marguerite made a derisive noise and shot a dismissive glance at the young duke. 'Having been forgiven once for rebelling against the crown, your son-in-law has now deserted his brother for a second time, a sad example of the deplorable perfidy of our times.' Heated blood rushed to Clarence's cheeks but before he could protest she ploughed relentlessly on. 'I do not wish to be twice betrayed as Edward has been and have yet to be convinced of the wisdom of forgiving you even once, my lord of Warwick. Because of your treachery King Henry has suffered extended periods of exile and imprisonment. For nigh on ten years the rightful King of England has been denied his throne, his realm has descended into violence and anarchy and Prince Édouard and I have been deprived of a husband and father's loving company. Blame for much of that can be laid directly at your feet, for had you not supported Richard of York's arrogant lust for power and his unworthy son's vainglorious ambition, England would have been spared a decade of ungodly misrule. It goes without saying that my son and I wish to restore King Henry to his rightful place as England's sovereign lord, but the burning question before us is whether to put our trust in a proven traitor in order to do so?'

By this time the Duke of Clarence had turned away and was pacing the floor behind the countess and her daughter, apparently fighting the urge to intervene in this war of words but, by fair means or foul, Warwick must have extracted a vow of silence from his young ally as his lips remained angrily compressed. With his clasped hands now extended in entreaty and his gaze deferentially fixed on the floor, when Marguerite asked her question and fell silent, the earl put his case in a speech that indicated careful rehearsal.

'Honoured lady, it is inscribed in Holy Writ that our Lord Jesu urged a man to forgive his brother not merely seven times but seventy times seven. So I pray that forgiveness once, or even twice over, is not an impossible favour for a pious and God-fearing queen to grant a humble subject, who comes to her in true contrition and on bended knee. In return for your gracious clemency I would become your loyal liegeman in life and limb and pledge my sword and strength to you and the Lancastrian cause. I am, Madame, a man who earnestly recognizes the error of his ways and begs to be readmitted to your good offices and to the service of King Henry.'

For the length of an Ave, Queen Marguerite studied the top of the earl's head in silence, her mouth working in such agitation that it seemed she might bite her lip clean through. At length Warwick lifted his head and raised his eyebrows in mute enquiry, while the rest of us began to shift about, swapping anxious glances and nervously clearing our throats but no one spoke. I watched Prince Édouard catch Sir John Fortescue's eye, but the old knight laid his finger on his lips, making the youth scowl and let whatever it was he had thought of saying remain unvoiced. Finally his mother spoke again.

'You have much English blood on your hands, my lord of Warwick. Thousands of loyal Lancastrians have died under the onslaught of your traitorous armies at St Albans, Northampton, Ferrybridge, Towton – so many battlefields. How should we manage to work together with the bodies of all these men lying between us in bloody reproach? What can you do to atone for so many widows, so many orphaned children?'

Warwick lifted his shoulders and made a hapless gesture. 'Every battle has its casualties, your grace, and it is true that I have seen many victories and some defeats while honing my skills of generalship. And now all this experience – this expertise – is at your command, if you will accept it. Together, if God wills it, we can restore your husband to his throne and secure a glorious future for your son.' He paused, before adding as if on an afterthought, 'And my daughter.'

Marguerite leapt on this final comment. 'Oh yes! We are none of us unaware of what truly drives this about-turn of yours, Lord Warwick. Not content with catching a royal duke for your elder daughter, you now demand a prince for the younger.' Her eyes roved over the figure of Anne Neville still at her mother's shoulder, her face as pale as her gown. 'Have you asked for her consent, I wonder? Although I hardly think she would refuse!'

Warwick turned around as best he could while still kneeling, and beckoned Anne forward. 'Of course she consents. She is an obedient and dutiful daughter, are you not, Anne?'

The girl made a deep curtsy before the queen, keeping her eyes downcast and her expression veiled, but there was no great enthusiasm in her answer. 'Yes, my lord father,' she whispered.

I had a sudden thought of my own daughters; I hardly knew them any more. Would either of them have been as self-contained and compliant as this child gave the impression of being? And how did she really feel about the prospect of being used as a bargaining tool for this unholy political alliance?

Irritated by what he perceived to be Anne's indifference to his charms, Prince Édouard could restrain himself no longer. 'I am no keener on the marriage than you, my lady, believe me! I would much prefer to share a battlefield with a renowned knight such as your father without being obliged to share a bed with his milk-sop daughter.'

'Silence!' Queen Marguerite erupted into anger at her son. 'No gentleman ever slights a lady in public, Édouard. I banished the Duke of Exeter from my court for just such a display of bad manners. When Lord Warwick and I have concluded our business I order you to apologize personally to the Lady Anne. Meanwhile hold your tongue and keep your insults for the battlefield.'

Warwick leapt on the implication of this outburst like a cat on a mouse. 'Then you do intend to treat with me, Madame? Indeed, how else will you gain the support of King Louis and the men and ships required for your army?'

As Édouard dropped back, glowering, his mother turned her accusative gaze on the earl. 'Do not make too many assumptions, my lord Warwick,' she snapped. 'I invite you to rise now and I agree to a military alliance on the basis of a legal treaty but that does not mean that forgiveness is granted. That will only occur when King Henry is back on the throne and I will expect you to achieve that before my son and I set foot back in England.'

Wincing, Warwick rose to his feet, the knees of his hose soiled and bloody – then my attention was drawn back to the prince, who had made a loud exclamation of protest. 'No! I wish to accompany Lord Warwick, to fight for the throne. It is my right!'

Marguerite's response was surprisingly conciliating, revealing her deep and protective love for her only son. 'It will be your right when you are of age, Édouard. But we need proof of the earl's commitment before I am prepared to allow you to risk your life in your father's cause. Let my lord of Warwick demonstrate his worth by winning back our throne and then he will have earned the forgiveness he seeks for robbing us of it.'

Pouncing on this challenge, it was Warwick's turn to remonstrate. 'If I am to put my life on the line for King

Henry, I will need a guarantee of your good faith in return, Madame. Before I leave Angers, let our alliance be confirmed by the marriage of the prince and Lady Anne.'

Prince Édouard expressed his opinion of this demand by sniffing loudly and turning his back on the earl. The queen laid a calming hand on his sleeve and slyly proposed a compromise. 'By all means let us celebrate with an alliance between our families, Lord Warwick, but there will be no harm in allowing our children to get to know each other before marriage. I suggest that a betrothal should take place in the cathedral tomorrow and I will take Lady Anne into my household and treat her as a daughter, while you and his grace of Clarence fulfil your side of the bargain. When I hear word that King Henry is restored to his throne, we will joyfully celebrate the marriage and I and the happy couple will embark on our journey to England.'

It was almost as if King Louis had spoken the words himself, so clear was his involvement in this scheme. It bore all the hallmarks of his spider-mind. Effectively Lady Anne was to be held as a hostage against the success or failure of her father's insurgency and I could see from the way the blood rushed to her cheeks that, young though she was, the girl was instantly aware of the invidious position she would be in.

Warwick, too, was hesitant to accept the queen's proposal. Perhaps he also detected a French conspiracy but could not instantly find a way to oppose it. Prince Édouard however detected the possibility of ultimately avoiding this unpalatable marriage and permitted himself a smug smile. The earl turned to look at his family and his glance passed from his countess's face, grim in the frame of her jewelled veiling, to the cornered-coney expression on his daughter's countenance. His reluctance was obvious but eventually, bowing to the inevitable, he offered the queen another of his expansive flourishes.

'It shall be as your grace stipulates,' he said, unsheathing his sword with characteristic bravado and laying it ceremoniously on the velvet-clad step at her feet. 'My sword is at your command, Madame. If King Louis's ships are waiting in the harbour with their coffers full and his promised army on standby, we shall have King Henry crowned again at Westminster before the autumn winds begin to blow.'

Why was it, I wondered, that the vision of Warwick storming Castle England put me in mind of the panel of the Apocalypse Tapestry hanging behind Marguerite's throne, in which the army of Unbelievers was shown attacking the gates of the Heavenly City, led by the seven-headed Beast of Satan, only to be vanquished by holy fire descending from the sky. When I returned my gaze to the group around the throne I noticed that the young Duke of Clarence's eyes were riveted on that very same scene and narrowed in intense thought, as if he was now pondering his own place in this conspiracy of adversaries.

PART FIVE

The Return

1470

40

Jane

Tŷ Gwyn, Tenby, Pembrokeshire

Although it was not signed I knew the message was from Lady Margaret and would have to be burned but first I wanted to commit what it said to memory. The content was cryptic in the extreme.

> *The bear and the daisy have united and our greatest hopes may be realized. Let the portcullis be raised, the red dragon unleashed and the greyhound returned to its dam. The martlet is due to land and then the sun will set.*

I was no expert in heraldry but I knew that the portcullis belonged to Beaufort, the red dragon to Wales and the greyhound was the symbol of Richmond. Margaret was a mother who was desperate to have her son back and Jasper was on his way. King Edward's splendid sun was sinking. As I set the paper to the fire and watched it burn, my spirits rose with the flames. Then I started in sudden fear when Elin's elfin face appeared round the door to announce that a stranger was at the entrance wanting to see me.

Elin was not supposed to answer any knocking; stranger at the door could be a Yorkist agent who had tracked us down. Huw or Eithne should do it, Huw being a local lad hired to help with the heavy chores and Eithne his mother who insisted that I could not manage without her interference. I paid her since she was a great help with cleaning and shopping although she protested that she was only doing me a kindness. I think she wanted to keep tabs on her son and her disciplinary presence in the house was a blessing, when she was there. Where was she now though, when she should have been answering the door?

'She says she knows you,' Elin was saying. I felt a prickling in my spine even before she added, 'Bit witchy, starey black eyes, lots of shiny beads.'

'I will deal with her myself. You go back to your sewing.'

Myfanwy.

The 'shiny beads' were not beads at all but jewels. She looked like a wealthy woman and still a very beautiful one. She fell into my arms when she saw me. 'Sian, thank Jesu I have found you. May I come in? People have been staring at me.'

I ushered her quickly inside.

'How did you find me? I hope you have not been asking for me around the town. They do not know my story here and that is how I want it to stay.'

Myfanwy gave me a scornful look. 'Do you think I would not realize that? Funnily enough I recognized your basket from the Pembroke days. It is very distinctive and it was on the arm of a red-faced woman. I followed her home from the market. Am I not clever?'

'You are indeed.' I gave her a grateful hug, my emotions in turmoil. 'But why have you come here after all this time?'

'Because you have my son of course! He is still with you I take it? How is he?'

'Of course he is with me! Did you think I would abandon him as you did?'

'I did not abandon him. I left him with the person who would best bring him up. I quickly realized, if you did not, that I am not suited for motherhood. May I sit down? I feel quite weary.' She sank onto the window seat with a sigh and looked candidly at me, her gaze absorbing my service-able holland dress, my apron.

A rush of guilt swamped the anger, which until that moment I had not known I felt. I was forgetting that refreshment was the first duty of a host. 'I will have some ale brought. Would you like me to send for Davy too? He is down on the harbour beach annoying the fishermen.'

'No, not yet. I need to talk with you first, Sian.' Myfanwy gave me a smile of entreaty. My Welsh name spoken now in her deep melodious voice inspired a sudden rush of nostalgia for our lost friendship, further banishing the tension the day's events had been arousing in me.

I found Eithne in the storeroom, unpacking her purchases from the distinctive basket. 'I have a visitor, Eithne. Did you not hear the knocking at the door?'

'I did but I thought Huw would go.'

Gone were the days of Pembroke Castle, when the servants had bowed and bobbed to acknowledge orders from the earl's mistress. I told her to find Huw and send him to fetch Davy, after she had brought us some ale. When I returned to the hall Myfanwy had not moved and was staring out of the window watching the cogs and hulks queuing in the bay for their turn to unload on the high tide. 'This must be a prosperous town,' she remarked.

'Jasper certainly thought it worth protecting,' I responded. 'He spent a fortune on its defences.'

'It did not protect him though, did it. Where is he now?'

'If I knew I would not tell you, Myfanwy.' I sat down beside her on the cushioned seat in the oriel. 'What did you want to talk to me about?'

'Davy of course.' Myfanwy curled her legs underneath her in a way that would have horrified Lady Margaret. 'I hope he resembles his father and is not like me.'

'Yes he is very like his father and not at all like you,' I said frankly, thinking that her dark, gypsy looks would not suit Davy's sunny character. 'He is strong and bright and resourceful; by rights he should be trained for knighthood, for he has all the necessary attributes, but the way things are I doubt if the opportunity will be afforded him.'

'But that is exactly why I am here! For although you have this comfortable house and live in a prosperous town it is obvious to me that you do not have much money.'

I felt the blood rush to my cheeks, the way it always did when I was cross or distressed. She laughed and reached out to take my hand. I took it as a placatory gesture and let mine lie in hers. She had changed. Her rustling silk skirts and fashionable beaver hat indicated that she was no longer the wild, carefree child-of-the-forest she had been when she came with Owen to Pembroke.

At this moment Eithne arrived with a tray loaded with a jug, two mugs and a platter of sweetmeats. 'I have sent Huw off to fetch Davy. Shall I bring him in when they get here, Mistress Hywel?'

'No, Eithne, let him wait until I come and get him.'

'Mistress Hywel?' Myfanwy repeated when Eithne had gone. 'I do not remember ever hearing that name before. It always used to be Mistress Jane, did it not?'

I shrugged. 'I needed to give the children some status in the town. I decided to be a widow instead of a paramour. May I ask what you are?'

It was her turn to blush. 'Oh I am just Myfanwy. But I am married again now.'

'To a rich man by the look of you.'

She twisted the eye-catching sapphire ring she wore. 'I married the Denbigh apothecary who took me in when I escaped my first husband's murdering son. His wife died.'

'Before or after you married him?'

Her throaty laugh rippled out, a familiar sound from the old days. 'I had forgotten your wry sense of humour! He is the perfect husband – kind, generous and rich. Apothecaries are much in demand. But he is no Owen Tudor.'

We were still holding hands and I nodded ruefully, giving hers a squeeze. 'The Tudors are a hard act to follow. Was it you who lit candles around Owen's head in the Hereford Market Place, Myfanwy?'

Her eyes instantly filled with tears and she looked away, swallowing hard. Eventually, in a voice hoarse with grief, she asked, 'How could they do that to him? He was so beautiful.'

'You were lucky they did not arrest you.'

'They would not have dared. There is something to be said for being thought a witch.' Myfanwy stood up, pulling her hand from mine and walked across the room to pick up her saddlebag. 'And a lot to be said for having a rich husband.' She took a heavy purse out of the bag and placed it on the seat between us. I picked it up and untied the drawstring. Inside I caught the dull gleam of gold. 'There are twenty crowns,' she said. 'Will it be enough? Ideally I would like Davy to train for knighthood but I realize that Jasper is in no position to take him on. There is money here for him to join some other knight's retinue.'

'I have no idea if it is enough,' I said. 'I will ask Geoffrey Pole when he next visits. He still holds offices in Haverford and Pembroke. Edith – my friend – died giving birth to their daughter Eleanor. Nothing is as it was, as you can imagine. I have no influence without Jasper. It may be that Davy will only ever become a man-at-arms, although I must say that he has the makings of being a very good one.'

'Perhaps things will change,' Myfanwy said, using a kerchief extracted from her sleeve. 'England has been in chaos ever since the Earl of Warwick started stirring up trouble. Now they say he has made an alliance with the old queen. Lord Jasper may be back.'

I bit my lip. I was not about to reveal what I knew to Myfanwy because I had no idea where her loyalties now lay. 'I think it is time you met Davy. I will go and see if he has returned.'

She picked a wafer from the dish and bit into it with her small white teeth. I smiled and left her sitting in the window, gazing out at the harbour and the castle on the headland, which defended it. I could not find Eithne or

Davy, although I searched all the places where I thought they might be. I heard the thud of a closing door and ran up the steps that led to the rear passage. When I reached the hall it was empty but the purse still lay on the window seat. There was no sign of Myfanwy.

Elin appeared, alerted by the slammed door. 'Who was she, Mother?' she asked.

'A ghost from the past,' I replied, quickly pushing the purse into my capacious apron pocket.

I felt a deep sense of regret for my past friendship with Myfanwy. She had been my friend at a vulnerable time when we were first-time mothers together, confiding our hopes and sharing our fears. Her leaving without saying goodbye and without seeing her son had somehow broken that bond.

I put my arm around my daughter's shoulders. 'Come and help me get dinner on the table, Elin. I do not think we shall see her again.'

Davy appeared, loud and complaining, his face hot and cross, his shock of sun-bleached hair tied back with a grubby cord. 'Huw was wheeling me at the quintain in the handcart and I was just beginning to get the hang of it, Mother.'

The natural way he called me 'Mother' made me glad Myfanwy had gone. She had told me she was not the mothering kind; even so I could not imagine any woman liking to hear her son call another one 'Mother'. But what a profound relief I felt that she had not wanted to take Davy from us. He had always been one of the family and his role as provider on our walk from Weobley had reinforced his position in our hearts.

'It was a false alarm, Davy,' I said apologetically. I felt the heavy weight of the purse in the pocket of my apron. Could its contents possibly be enough to provide for the boy's future or would Jasper return to take him in charge and one day see his young brother dubbed knight?

* * *

That evening, when the children were in bed, it gave me a certain acquisitive pleasure just to see the coins spread out on the kitchen table, gleaming in the lamplight. For a moment I contemplated repaying Lady Margaret some of the money she had sent us, but I secretly considered Margaret owed it to me anyway and it did not seem the right way to spend gold intended for Davy's future. These coins were Myfanwy's effort to make amends for abandoning the boy. The money was his and he was ours.

I recited Lady Margaret's message in my head; *The bear and the daisy have united and our greatest hopes may be realized. Let the portcullis be raised, the red dragon unleashed and the greyhound returned to its dam. The martlet is due to land and then the sun will set.*

Feelings of excitement and hope stirred in me with great force. Davy's gold seemed dazzlingly bright where it lay. I contemplated where I could hide it to be safe and then the very idea that anything or anywhere at this precarious moment could be safe made me laugh.

41

Jasper

Tŷ Gwyn, Tenby, Pembrokeshire

I HAD TO HAND it to Warwick, his scheme for outflanking
Edward worked faultlessly. As he had predicted, we landed
on the Devon coast without opposition thanks to a long-
standing local war of attrition between the Courtenay and
Bonville families that kept all the fighting men in that area
occupied in the service of their own liege lords. The royal
coastal garrisons were incapable of confronting even our
relatively small army. King Louis had supplied sixty ships
for our two thousand men and horses and a French admiral
to command the fleet. The wind blew fair for once, landing
us at dusk on various beaches to the south of Dartmouth.

Warwick took the bulk of our French troops and headed
straight for London, while I took a smaller force due north
then west with the aim of collecting men from the Beaufort
estates in Somerset on the way to recruiting in my own
Welsh heartland. Our agents had told us that Warwick's
supporters in Yorkshire had, as planned, staged an uprising

threatening enough to send King Edward rushing north to quell it. By the time my burgeoning army had reached the Severn we received news that Warwick had doubled his force by marching through Kent and then trooped into an undefended London, welcomed once more by the merchant burgesses who pragmatically preferred to preserve the peace and protect their businesses rather than fight Edward's battles for him. Meanwhile Warwick's brother, Lord Montagu, had also turned coat against Edward and brought the large force he had been commissioned to raise against the northern rebellion around to support it. As Warwick marched north from London, Edward found himself in Nottingham, comprehensively betrayed and caught in a Lancastrian vice.

For my part, within a week I had crossed the Black Mountains and made a rendezvous with Gruffydd's grand-sons at Dinefŵr Castle. My friend and ally, Thomas ap Gruffydd and his youngest son Rhys were still in exile in Burgundy but after William Herbert's execution Thomas's four eldest sons, Morgan, Henry, Dafydd and Hopkin had seized Carmarthen and Cardigan Castles from the crown and were still holding them, despite the efforts of young Richard of Gloucester to force them out. I had been in regular correspondence with these four and was gratified to find that they had fulfilled their promise to have a large number of men waiting ready to flock to my standard. In return I guaranteed them all royal pardons for offences against the crown and continued seisin of the two royal castles they already held, to be granted as soon as we had restored King Henry to the throne. Having settled this to everyone's satisfaction I handed my army over to my second in command and Evan and I set off for a much-anticipated family reunion in Tenby.

I had sent prior warning of our arrival and in order to avoid unwanted recognition by the townsfolk we were disguised in common soldiers' sallets and battered leather brigandines. We left our horses at an inn and walked to the house – it was a moment I had been longing for, yet I was unprepared for the rush of emotion I felt on seeing Jane's sweet face. It was three years since our meeting in St Aedan's ghostly churchyard at Bettys Newydd and yet if anything she looked younger and prettier than I remembered. Although I had visited a barber on the way through Carmarthen, I knew that my face had been marked by the uncertain life of a wandering exile; a neatly clipped beard could not disguise the erosion of the years and I was now turned forty. Jane, too, had suffered trials and tribulations enough to leave their stamp on her countenance but I could not see it.

The children were standing beside her in the centre of the hall but I eagerly took Jane in my arms, heedless of the watching household.

As I kissed her mouth and breathed the scent of her skin, I felt her melt into my embrace like a hot flame around a fresh log. Standing back, as dignity dictated, was torture.

'Welcome to Tŷ Gwyn, my lord,' she said, her smile as warm as mulled wine. 'We all so much relish your coming.'

There was a slight emphasis on the 'all', which prompted me guiltily to turn my attention to the children. They stood in order of age, a solemn row of wide-eyed youth, figures that I knew but did not know, with the faces of strangers.

'Elin,' I said, placing my hand on her head where a plaited

427

silk circlet barely restrained her sunburst of copper curls. I gently kissed her forehead. 'My beautiful daughter.'

It was an involuntary remark for she was indeed beautiful, tall for her age and slim with sparkling speedwell blue eyes and a determined curve to her full red lips. She wore a plain green kirtle over a lace-trimmed chemise but there was nothing demure about her response, which caused her mother to frown and pierced my heart like a knife. 'It is good to meet you, my lord father – at long last.'

I hid my pain, gave her a smile and a nod and moved on to Davy. Someone had obviously made a valiant attempt to tidy him up but somehow he still retained a smudge of dirt on his cheek and a cobweb in his hair, as if he had been rummaging in a dark cellar. He had such a look of Owen about him it was uncanny, straight nose, strong shoulders, thick chestnut hair and tawny brown eyes. Time seemed to stand still, so I squeezed his shoulder, man to man. 'You look fit, Davy,' I said.

'And now, last but not least – you must be Joan.' I put my finger under the small child's plump chin and raised her head. Her gaze met mine briefly before dropping to her tightly clasped hands. 'You have lovely long eyelashes, like your mother's.'

A pretty, braid-trimmed coif obscured her hair and she was appealingly plump in a bright blue kirtle laced at the front. 'I am named for my mother,' she confirmed in a little, low voice. 'My name is *Sian*.'

I glanced back at Jane who was eagerly greeting Evan. 'Ah yes. How lucky I am to have two of you.'

Jane broke away from her brother and came to take my arm. She made a face and fingered the studded leather of my brigandine. 'Let Evan relieve you of this before you join us at table.'

Evan unfastened the buckles and Davy watched intently before taking the heavy garment from him. 'I will hang it up, sir,' he said eagerly.

From the oriel window I checked the harbour scene and enquired if there had been any sign of the castle garrison being increased.

'There are no more men there than usual,' Jane replied. 'Why do you ask?'

'If Edward knew we had taken ship he would have strengthened defences at the channel ports,' I replied. 'It means he has moved all his available troops north.'

She looked worried. 'Will he not turn around when he knows you are here?'

I smiled. 'Yes, of course but by now he will have found that he has enemies both behind and in front. He cannot fight them both at once.'

'So what will happen?'

'Warwick thinks Edward will turn and confront him, probably somewhere like Nottingham. But I think he will run.'

She looked horrified. 'Run – where? Not this way?'

'No, without Herbert there is nothing for Edward here in Wales. Even Gloucester has left to join him. He will flee the country – to Flanders is my wager. He made a good move when he married his sister to the Duke of Burgundy.'

I allowed Jane to lead me to a trestle. What she called 'a welcome feast in your honour' was set there and I took my place at the board with her beside me. In the shelter of the cloth her hand strayed to my knee. 'Davy is going to serve us,' she said sedately, beckoning the boy. 'He wants to train for knighthood.' The fingers of her other hand continued to pursue their own agenda. If her aim was to reassure me that her ardour had not dimmed it was certainly succeeding. 'How long can you stay?' she asked softly.

'Well I am certainly here for one night at least,' I replied, avoiding her gaze in order to keep my face straight. 'I need to get to know these children, do I not, Elin?'

I had turned to catch her eye and she blushed, remembering her quip as she had greeted me. 'Yes, my lord father,' she said. 'But one night is not enough.'

I let my gaze swivel to Jane and my thighs closed tightly on her hand. 'She is right,' I said. 'It is not.'

Meanwhile the two girls and Evan sat down together at the other side of the board and while Davy practised his serving skills, I engaged Elin and Joan in conversation. I discovered the distinct difference between them that Jane had described. It reminded me vividly of my own relationship with Edmund, where the older child assumes superiority, which forces the younger to adapt to it even though he or she does not accept it. Intuitively I detected that the meekness with which Sian deferred to Elin's more forceful personality disguised her own inner determination and I wondered how she might blossom if the influence of the elder was removed. Sian enjoyed her dinner quietly, while Elin chattered for them both, addressing me but flashing frequent smiles at Evan. She was a flirt, my little Elin, and her bright hair and dancing blue eyes were enchanting.

Later, when the candles were lit and we settled around the hearth, I related the tale of Warwick's triumphant humiliation at Queen Marguerite's feet. Sian sat sedately in the background while Elin pulled a cushion to the foot of my chair and gazed up at me with her huge blue eyes. She was definitely a Tudor, this flame-haired daughter of mine.

'We shall have to keep a sharp eye on Elin,' I remarked to Jane as we lay in bed that night, satiated by the first urgent slaking of our long-neglected passion. If the truth were known she had probably found my hasty eagerness for her rather less than satisfying and I had every intention of rectifying this after a suitable period of recovery.

'What do you suggest?' Jane asked. 'We cannot lock her away until her body catches up with her feelings.'

'No I would not suggest that. But I have a plan that may have the welcome side effect of keeping Elin out of trouble. I will tell you tomorrow,' I said. 'Not tonight . . .'

The day dawned bright. Jane and I sat on the window seats. 'Here is the matter, then,' I began. 'Everything depends on whether Edward stays and fights or takes flight. All I know so far is that Warwick has secured London for Lancaster and released King Henry from the Tower. I have men ready to support him, should Edward show signs of preparing for a battle; otherwise I will send them to garrison castles around the Welsh March that are presently held by Yorkists. But my prime objective is to go to Weobley, collect Harri and take him to his mother. Margaret deserves to get her son back and I consider it my duty to see it happen. She has been a crucial supporter of our cause and I am greatly in her debt.'

As I spoke I noticed Jane's expression change from open interest to narrow-eyed antipathy. I had forgotten how quick she could be to react when it came to the mention of Margaret. 'So you will leave us, the family you have not seen for years, to go and dance attendance on your honoured lady! Can you not spare us even one more day of your exalted company, my lord?'

'Oh Jane – that hot temper of yours!' I reached up to stroke her cheek but she brushed my hand away and averted her eyes. 'I do not intend to leave you behind but hope you will all come with me. Lady Margaret will be in London. We will go there from Weobley and deliver Harri to her. It is summer and the weather is fine; would Elin and Sian not enjoy the journey and a visit to London?'

She frowned, still avoiding my gaze. 'Perhaps they would but not to stay as unwelcome guests of Lady Margaret's.'

'That will not be necessary. I have a house in Stepney Green, which has been lived in by one of my former councillors, the Yorkist Thomas Vaughan. But he has fled London now and I have written to Geoffrey Pole to ask him to repossess it and hire some servants to prepare it for us. You will not even have to meet Margaret if you do not wish to.' I reached for her chin and this time she let me turn her face to mine. 'I love you, Jane, you must know that, but we are in the midst of restoring my brother's throne. I must keep my army on alert, I must fetch Harri, I must go to my brother in London and I must liaise with Warwick. This is the only way I can devise for us to be together and for me to fulfil my obligations at the same time. Say you will come to London.'

She blinked tears away. 'It is so good to have you back, my lord Jasper. Of course I will come to London.'

42

Jasper

Coldharbour Inn, London, Le Garlek, Stepney Green, & The Bishop's Palace by St Paul's

LADY MARGARET, COUNTESS OF Richmond and her husband Sir Henry Stafford were adept at playing the allegiance game. So successfully had they convinced Edward of York of their loyal support for his reign that not only had Margaret been appointed a lady in waiting to his queen but he had also granted the couple the use of Woking Palace in Surrey and Coldharbour Inn in the City of London. The inn had previously been the property of the Duke of Exeter, the man who had abandoned and defrauded his mercenaries at Harlech Castle and been thrown out of Queen Marguerite's court-in-exile. Exeter remained what might be termed a faithful liability to the Lancastrian cause, attainted and deprived of all his properties in the same Yorkist Parliament as myself. There was little doubt that when King Henry's new Parliament reversed this Act of Attainder, he would claim Coldharbour Inn back, just as I would claim Pembroke

Castle from the Herberts, but in the meantime Margaret still had the use of it and so it was there that I took Harri to be reunited with his mother.

He had been ten when Margaret had last seen him at Raglan Castle. Now approaching fourteen, he was no longer a little boy but a serious youth with a friendly charm, which disguised a keen intelligence. Not having seen him myself since he was taken from my wardship as a small child, I had been impressed during some long conversations on the ride from Weobley by both his physical and intellectual advancement. He had been particularly anxious about earning his mother's good opinion and more than once I had had to assure him that his mother would be as proud of him as I was.

Once we reached London I took rooms at the Kings Head in Cheapside, where Harri and I made ourselves presentable and set off for Coldharbour Lane, while Jane elected to stay behind with the girls. 'Harri needs to spend time alone with Lady Margaret,' Jane reminded me. 'You should not stay too long.'

Coldharbour Inn was the largest and most imposing building in the parade of impressive houses that ran west along the north bank of the Thames above London Bridge. To protect the house from floods it had an extensive walled garden, which led down to a private pier and water gate. We left our horses and Harri's baggage with grooms in the courtyard and were shown to a long high-beamed hall at the centre of the mansion.

Coming into the presence of Lady Margaret always seemed like a special event. She exuded an aura of dainty but dignified grandeur and walked forward to greet us on soft, slippered feet like a swan gliding over a calm lake. Arrayed in a gown of lustrous dark brown silk and brocade and amply adorned with jewellery of gold and costly gems, she greeted Harri with exclamations of such joy and delight that he appeared overwhelmed. Then she led us to seats of carved and polished oak set beside walls hung with bright-coloured tapestries showing scenes of royalty hunting in verdant landscapes. Harri sat quietly lacing and unlacing his fingers while she plied him with refreshments and information, telling him that she would be taking him to court very soon.

'We do not know exactly when. King Henry is staying at the Bishop of London's palace and says he wants to wait until Queen Marguerite comes from France before setting up court at Westminster. But I know he listens to you, Lord Jasper, and you really must try and persuade him otherwise, for now that the Yorkist regime has left there are many loyal Lancastrians returning to London and they all want to pay homage to their king and renew their allegiance. The Bishop's Palace is simply not large enough.'

I gave her a doubtful look. 'I will do my best when I visit him tomorrow but it is six years since I saw him and I do not know his state of mind. He has never liked London, Westminster in particular.'

Margaret nodded glumly. 'I know and it will not help that Elizabeth Woodville has claimed sanctuary at Westminster Abbey with her daughters. Now that Edward has fled to Flanders, Heaven knows if or when she will ever emerge.' She crossed herself and fingered the gold collar she wore at her neck, which had a crystal crucifix hanging from it. Margaret displayed a puzzling meld of wealth and piety.

'Elizabeth is heavy with child so it will likely be born in the abbey precinct. How ironic if it should be a boy. The heir she has long prayed for and which now will have no throne.'

Harri found his voice at this stage. 'What is she like, the commoner queen? The Herberts always said she was beautiful.'

Margaret smiled at her son. 'Yes, she has two of the attributes most needed in a queen, Henry, beauty and fertility. And she has some noble breeding – but only on her mother's side. Unfortunately she also has a trait that made her unpopular with many at court – greed. Every time an estate or a marriage or a lucrative office became available she demanded it for herself or her family and Edward gave it to her. And she is implacable. She will never forgive Warwick for executing her father and brother and for accusing her mother of witchcraft. There is much bad blood between those two. She will not leave sanctuary while he wields any power in the land.'

'So what will happen to her and her family?' Harri sounded genuinely troubled.

Margaret smiled at her son. 'Your concern for the lady does you credit, Henry, but you should not worry on her behalf. Your uncle is a kind and compassionate king and he will not allow any action to be taken against a woman, especially one so close to giving birth. His quarrel is with her husband and entirely justified.' She folded her hands gracefully in her lap and sat back more comfortably in her chair. 'Now let us forget Elizabeth Woodville and talk about you.'

I decided this was my cue to depart and stood up. 'You both have a great deal to catch up on so I will leave you to do so.' Lady Margaret nodded agreement and held out her hand for me to kiss, which I duly did, adding, 'I will leave details of my place of residence and would be grateful if you would keep me informed of events here, my lady. If you or Henry have need of me, I will come directly.'

'I certainly will have need of you. I am relying on you to escort us to court when the day comes. Meanwhile I would be grateful for any news you may have to impart about the king's health. It is of such vital importance to us all.'

Harri rose to bid me farewell, bowing punctiliously before returning my embrace with barely concealed regret. 'I will be back very soon,' I assured him. 'Enjoy some precious time with your mother.'

* * *

'Will we be safe, living outside the city walls? There are so many armed men about.'

Jane was keen to go to our residence in Stepney Green but her question was a fair one. The thoroughfares of London had been relatively free of soldiers, due to the Mayor's restrictive order on the number of retainers incoming nobles were permitted to bring through the gates. But when we exited the city we found large noisy groups of men-at-arms gathered around the taverns at Whitechapel, and there were a number of encampments visible on the wasteland beyond. Jane and little Sian were clearly made nervous by this, being used to living within the relative safety of castle walls or a gated town like Tenby but I noticed that Elin appeared enamoured of the busy road with its procession of traders' carts returning from the London markets to their farms and villages in the flatlands alongside the Thames estuary. She gaily returned the wave aimed at her by a grinning youth in a white hood who was driving one of them, only to be sharply reprimanded by her anxious mother and told to keep her eyes focussed between the ears of her horse, a feat she managed for less than the length of an Ave.

I tried to reassure Jane. 'The house is solidly built and set in a large garden surrounded by high walls. And there are no taverns on the green to attract rogues or vagrants – only market stalls and one very fashionable inn, catering for wealthy travellers. Some of the surrounding houses belong to captains of the ships you can see moored in the docks over there.' I pointed to a forest of masts visible on the river as we traversed the open ground beyond the Mile End crossroads. 'Others are inhabited by rich merchants, who ship their goods in and out on those very ships. These are good, hard-working families who have made their money buying and selling in the Baltic and Flanders. Our closest neighbours are a mercer's family called Gardiner. They trade in luxury fabrics and trimmings.'

Jane gave me a doubtful smile. 'Well, I will be glad to get there anyway. It has been a long journey.'

The house was called Le Garlek, a fanciful notion of the master grocer who had been its first occupant. Geoffrey Pole had arranged the exchange of deeds from Thomas Vaughan, a lawyer with whom I had previously shared the property and who had served on my Pembroke council until I had been attainted; then he had chosen to serve William Herbert and swear allegiance to Edward of York. In the present circumstances he and his family had made a shrewd exit from the London area and taken refuge in one of his properties in the Welsh March, where he doubtless hoped to evade Lancastrian retribution.

Our little procession turned off the main thoroughfare and entered the long tree-lined double row of houses that formed the enclave of Stepney Green. In the shortening October days tall trees were turning russet and yellow above the high garden walls and elders and hawthorns made red and copper splashes around the green. Fallen leaves swirled around our horses' feet causing them to prance and shy. Le Garlek's studded wooden gates were set in a sturdy stone arch and Davy trotted forward, keen to pull the handle he saw in a niche in the wall. A bell rang somewhere inside and a face appeared at the grille set in one of the gates. Almost immediately they began to open.

'Well, you said it was secure,' observed Jane, her smile wider and more confident. 'At least you were recognized.'

'And Master Pole's arrangements appear to be working since the servants are expecting us.' I felt a surge of relief as we all rode under the archway. 'You will be safe and happy here, I promise.'

Early the following day I left Jane in her element, organizing servants, arranging furniture and unpacking the chests, which had come direct from Tenby and arrived before us. We had all slept well in clean linen and she had declared her intention of inspecting the cellars for supplies of ale and wine and walking out to the local market on the green for fresh bread, meat and fish. I smiled as I imagined her loading Elin's basket down with purchases in order to stop her wandering off to explore on her own and looked forward to returning in the evening to a fine dinner. For my own part

I dressed in court apparel and took Evan and Davy with me back to the city to mind the horses while I paid my first visit to the newly restored King Henry VI of England.

It did me good just to hear my brother's title spoken aloud once more in his own realm as I stated my request for an audience to his Chamberlain. Sir Richard Tunstall was a Lancastrian knight well known to me, since we had been dubbed at the same time and served the Lancastrian cause together in battle and siege. Yet Sir Richard, being gentry rather than nobility, had somehow negotiated the dangerous shores of Yorkism, served at King Edward's court and, at Warwick's behest had pledged allegiance once more to his true king. He was a skilled and adaptable courtier.

He conducted me to the Bishop of London's private chapel where I found King Henry exactly where I expected him to be, on his knees before the image of Christ on the Cross. He rose at the mention of my name and turned towards me and I was profoundly shocked by the sight that met my eyes. Henry had never been robust but now nearing fifty his life of fear and imprisonment had told heavily on him and he looked like a man in his dotage. His hair, straggly and grey, still hung down to his shoulders from under his soft-brimmed hat as it had always done, but his eyes were sunk in their sockets, their colour almost indiscernible, and his shrunken body had so little flesh on it that his long robe hung like sacking from a farmer's scarecrow. The skin on the hands he extended to me in greeting was almost transparent, revealing the intricate dark tracery of his veins, and I had to swallow the lump in my throat as I knelt to kiss them.

'Jasper, my beloved brother!' he said, his voice cracking,

his peering eyes doubtful beneath a frown. 'Is it truly you? I feared I might never see you again. Rise, rise, brother, and let me see your face.'

I blinked back tears as I rose to my feet and impulsively drew him into an embrace. 'Henry, your grace, my liege,' I stuttered, hastily drawing back at feeling him stiffen in shock, as if even the grip of a brotherly embrace was too painful for him to bear. 'I crave your pardon. I was overcome to see you again. I bring you my loyal greeting and heartfelt joy at your restoration. England has her rightful king once more.'

'Thanks to you and Lord Warwick and the King of France! I am still trying to come to terms with the situation. To tell you the truth I may never do so; I have become so used to begging the Almighty to grant me acceptance of my lot that I find it hard to remember to thank Him for reversing it.'

Although he spoke lucidly his voice was weak and hesitant and I took the liberty of tucking one hand in his elbow, lest his legs gave way. 'Perhaps the Almighty will forgive us if we find somewhere to sit, your grace, so that we can converse more comfortably. May I hope you have had time to catch up with recent events? I have much to discuss with you.'

He clutched my supporting hand and nodded. 'Yes, yes. My chamber is only a short distance away and there is a fire. I get so cold, even though it is not yet winter.'

'Perhaps you are not eating enough, sire. You must build up your strength so that you can take up the reins of government once more.'

'Oh I shall need your help to rule, Jasper. I have lost touch with events in the outside world and no longer know whom to trust. But I can rely on you to tell me, can I not? I am so happy you have come. The Earl of Warwick frightens me; so forceful, so demanding.'

We walked slowly down a stone-flagged passage to the bishop's chamber where Henry had been accommodated since arriving in London. It was lavishly furnished with heavy embroidered hangings and tapestries, a large crimson-draped tester bed and comfortable cushioned seats and it occurred to me that probably no one wished that the newly returned king would move out to Westminster more than Bishop Thomas Kempe, who was forced meanwhile to use his summer palace at Fulham and travel miles in order to conduct Masses in St Paul's Church.

Henry took the large canopied armchair placed for him beside the hearth. It had been gloomy in the chapel and in the bright light streaming through the chamber windows I became even more alarmed at his frailty and ordered some bread and broth from the duty chamberlain. Had no one noticed my brother's condition, that he was seriously under-nourished? No wonder he was weak and confused.

'What did Lord Warwick say to you before he left, sire?' I asked him, placing a joint-stool close to his. 'Now that Edward of York has fled and taken his household with him, have any arrangements been made regarding the adminis-tration of the country?'

Henry's usual frown deepened. 'I am trying to remember. I think you should ask Sir Richard. He has been handling all that sort of thing. I need to attend to my prayers. There are so many wrongs in the world that need righting and God has given me the duty of bringing them to His notice.'

'But He has also tasked you with ruling England, Henry.

It is the duty of kings to exercise their divine right for the good of their subjects. If you do not then others will usurp your powers again.'

Henry appeared to struggle to grasp my meaning. 'No, no, Jasper, Marguerite always saw to all that. Where is she? She should be here beside me. Why did she not come with Warwick? I cannot rule without her.' In the brighter light tears were visible flooding the faded blue of his eyes.

I could see that any further pursuit of the subject was pointless, and though I had expected this, still I was disappointed. As I had feared, where the government of England was concerned, from now on Henry would merely be a figurehead. The real work of making official appointments, ordering commissions and administering the law would have to be done in his name but not according to his will. I foresaw battles ahead between Warwick and Queen Marguerite and did not relish my role as arbiter. Henry would need me more than ever. Yet Wales would also require my presence. I was going to be busy.

Servants entered the room carrying the meal I had ordered for the king. I felt a sudden rush of emotion and reached out to press the fragile fingers that gripped the arm of his chair. 'Do not worry, Henry,' I murmured gently, as if comforting a child. 'Marguerite will soon be back. Until then I will be here for you. Now you must eat something to regain your strength. Come, let me help you to the table.'

43

Jasper

Westminster Palace & Coldharbour Inn

B Y THE THIRD WEEK of October, Warwick and I had
assumed joint control of the kingdom, appointing
ourselves King's Lieutenants – effectively Regents for Henry
– and the Earl of Oxford Constable of England and Steward
of the King's Household. Warwick had insisted on the appointment of his brother, George Neville, Archbishop of York, as
Lord Chancellor. I had managed to persuade King Henry to
move into Westminster Palace; meanwhile Warwick went
north to reclaim his Yorkshire estates. He would return for
an all-important pre-Christmas Parliament, when the attainders passed on us by Edward would be reversed and our
revenues and titles reinvested. Lancastrians who had escaped
attainder by taking Edward's pardon and pledging him their
loyalty began to gather at court, queuing up to reverse that
vow and renew their oaths to Henry. Invitations were sent
out for a re-coronation ceremony at Westminster Abbey, which
was arranged for the end of the month.

Lady Margaret was anxious to introduce her son to the king as the first step towards recovering his Richmond estates and I arranged an audience but warned them both that Henry's state of mind was unpredictable and they should not expect too much from him. They travelled by barge from Coldharbour to Westminster and I met them on the palace quay. Margaret had excelled even herself in style and presentation and I barely recognized Harri, who seemed to have grown in stature and confidence, standing taller and prouder than I had ever seen him, possibly on account of the splendour of the apparel his mother had procured for him, which had transformed a sometimes-diffident youth into a gleaming figure of nobility on the cusp of manhood.

Even in an audience chamber full of lords and ladies wearing their most sumptuous court dress, the arrival of mother and son caused a ripple of speculative murmuring, then a hush fell upon the assembly as the two made their way towards the throne. The only glaring anachronism was the spectacle of King Henry himself, whose voluminous ermine-trimmed mantle filled more than he did of a seat made to measure for someone of Edward's muscular knight's physique. Despite the crown on his head, he looked like a mad mendicant rather than a monarch and I vowed to have strong words privately with Sir Richard Tunstall, whose responsibility it was to keep the royal household, and particularly its regal head, in magnificent order. As Chamberlain he was hovering behind the throne and announced Lady Margaret as she sank into a curtsy.

Remarkably, King Henry suddenly came to life and straightened up, pulling himself forward on his seat and smiling down at the lady at his feet. She gazed up at him in her turn with an expression of earnest sincerity.

'My gracious sovereign, how good it is to see you here in your rightful place,' she said. 'All your loyal subjects must rejoice to find your standard flying over Westminster Palace, your grace, it has been too long absent.'

'Thank you, my lady,' Henry replied, holding out his bony hand. On the middle finger a magnificent sapphire ring engraved with his personal seal hung precariously on the knuckle. 'And I rejoice to see you back at my side.'

Margaret looked somewhat puzzled by this remark but took his hand and made her declaration. 'I humbly pledge my allegiance to your grace and to your son and heir, Édouard, Prince of Wales.' She pressed her lips to the ring with a fervour that no one could doubt was genuine.

King Henry nodded and shifted his gaze to the youth who knelt at her shoulder. 'How good it is to welcome our admirable prince to court,' he said with enthusiasm, extending his hand to Harri. 'All must surely observe in him the qualities of a worthy successor to my throne.'

There was a fraught silence when Margaret and I exchanged astonished glances, our eyes rolling at the distinct possibility that Henry was confusing Harri with Édouard. Did he actually believe the boy before him to be his own seventeen-year-old son? I considered it entirely possible. After all Harri was about the age Édouard had been when Henry had last seen him, before his mother took him to France for safety. It was quite likely that the years that had passed since had become blank to him, just as the traumatic events they contained had also been wiped from his memory. A swift glance about the room revealed that only a select few, closely gathered around the king, would have heard and construed his unfortunate remark, all of them ostensibly fiercely loyal Lancastrians. I made a mental note of their names with a view to seeking their pledge of silence and thanked the Almighty that the Earl of Warwick was not among them. The question of the succession was a tender subject within Warwick's close affinity, especially for his son-in-law George of Clarence whose loyalty to Lancaster I considered threadbare, and whom Warwick had once encouraged to consider himself a successor to his brother Edward as king.

If Henry thought Harri was Édouard, was it also possible that he believed the woman kneeling before him was his wife, Queen Marguerite? Margaret must have come to this conclusion because after she had watched her son kiss the proffered ring and pledge his allegiance as he had been coached to do, she cast an eloquent glare at Sir Richard Tunstall, who gave her a brief nod of acknowledgement and leaned over to whisper something in his sovereign's ear.

Henry looked up at him in surprise. 'Mass? Is it Sext already? Oh yes indeed, Sir Richard, we must leave immediately.'

He instantly abandoned his throne and the two figures kneeling at his feet, almost stumbling over them in his haste to take his Chamberlain's arm and shuffle on his square-toed shoes towards the privy door leading to the royal apartments and the chapel. Surplus courtiers bowed and backed away, making a passage for his exit and I hastened to make sure of the silence of those who had been standing close enough to notice the king's confusion.

After the audience Sir Richard Tunstall entertained us to dinner in his chamberlain's quarters and apologized for King Henry's unfortunate error. 'His grace's state of mind is unpredictable,' he admitted. 'One moment he can appear alert and rational and the next he loses all recognition of where he is and who is with him. Although he recovered years ago from his complete collapse, he frequently displays a total failure of memory.'

'Even so, can nothing be done to improve his appearance?' I asked impatiently. 'His mantle and his crown were far too large and surely his apparel should be pristine. What are his squires of the body doing for him?'

Sir Richard shook his head despairingly. 'He will not permit anyone to dress him. He insists that God wishes him to attend to himself but of course he cannot. That is why he is so unkempt; his hair and his beard untrimmed. Short of tying him down I do not see what can be done.'

'He cannot appear that way at his coronation!' exclaimed Margaret with alarm. 'He will be a laughing stock and you and his servants likewise.'

'I think if we tell him God has ordained that he wear the garments he wore for his first coronation he may consent,' I suggested. 'Meanwhile we can have a tailor alter them to fit. Perhaps I should make a point of being at the robing. If I word it right he will listen to my advice.'

Sir Richard made me what I took to be a grateful bow. 'Your assistance would be greatly appreciated, my lord.'

As we returned downriver to Coldharbour, Margaret remarked, keeping her voice low so that it would not carry to the oarsmen, 'So our king is not fit to rule. You have a difficult task ahead, Jasper, at least until the queen arrives. Do Marguerite and Warwick get on now? I know their alliance was crucial in restoring the Lancastrian throne but I must tell you that it came as a great surprise.'

'There is still no love lost between them and Queen Marguerite has declared that she will not risk her son's life in England until Warwick can guarantee the throne is securely won. I must warn you that most of my time will have to be spent restoring order to Wales. Warwick will take the lead on English matters, and if you are determined to pursue the restoration of Harri's lands before Parliament meets, it will be Warwick you have to deal with.'

'Yes – the Earl of Warwick, father-in-law to the Duke of Clarence, the greedy turncoat brother to whom Edward granted all the Richmond lands and revenues.' Margaret frowned and sighed. 'What is the likelihood of us getting them back?'

I gave her an encouraging smile. 'For most people, nil – but for the shrewd and charming Countess of Richmond I should think there is every chance.'

She shot me a sideways glance and a wry smile. 'You flatter me, sir. I deduce that the courts of Europe have honed your diplomatic skills.'

'Whereas yours need no sharpening, my lady.' I noticed Harri was following our conversation with great interest and winked at him. 'Listen and learn, young Harri. Listen and learn,' I said.

'Why must you keep calling him Harri?' Margaret complained. 'We are not in Wales now.'

'Truly I do not mind, lady mother,' Harri put in before I could reply. 'I like the Welsh and I speak their language. Not fluently, but enough to converse with them. Besides, when my uncle calls me Harri you know he is not talking about the king.'

'Well, as long as you remember that your name is Henry,'

his mother responded. 'It was your father's wish that you carry the name of the Lancastrian kings.'

'I know.' Harri nodded solemnly. 'I will never forget. You need have no fear of that.'

At Coldharbour Inn that evening Sir Henry Stafford joined us for supper and introduced me to his Steward and Receiver-General, a young man called Reginald Bray. I was immediately impressed by his polite manner and incisive grasp of England's precarious political situation. Margaret and Sir Henry obviously rated him highly because they trusted him not only with the management of their numerous residences scattered about the country and their large household of servants but also as their Receiver General, the official who collected all the revenues from their widespread estates.

'Reginald is my right-hand man,' declared Sir Henry. 'I really do not know what I would do without him, especially since I have been struck with my unfortunate malady.'

At first this malady had been feared to be the dreaded leprosy but later it was diagnosed as St Anthony's fire, which periodically spread a painful red rash over his face and arms. A sudden flare up of this affliction had prevented him coming to Westminster, its effects being only too visible; bearable in a family environment but causing him too much discomfort and embarrassment to expose to the critical eyes of the royal court.

'While we were at court Sir Henry and Master Bray have been devising ways of providing a suitable income for my son, to tide him over until we win back his rightful lands,' Margaret said, taking a seat at the head of the table, a place which her husband seemed perfectly content to concede to her. Turning to Sir Henry, she went on, 'Lord Jasper believes I can persuade my lord of Warwick to agree to strip Clarence of his Richmond estates,' she confided, 'but personally I fear it might incur that young man's easily-stirred wrath.'

'Indeed, my lady.' It was Reginald who spoke. 'It might be more politic at this stage to make provision for Master Tudor from the Somerset estates, at least until he comes of age.' He smiled encouragingly at Harri who sat beside him, washing his hands in a bowl of water held by a kneeling page. 'By then I am sure he will have proved himself more than worthy of them.'

'He is worthy of them simply by birth,' Margaret corrected him, causing her steward's cheeks to flush as red as her husband's. 'But I take your point,' she added graciously. 'And I agree, we should move carefully in these unpredictable times. For that very reason I have not pressed Lord Oxford for an invitation for my son to King Henry's re-coronation at Westminster Abbey. Since at present, even though he is the king's nephew, his noble status has not been confirmed by Parliament and it would mean him being seated on the wrong side of the rood screen, unable to see anything or be seen by anyone, making it hardly worth attending.' Her displeasure at this situation was evident.

I took the opportunity to make a suggestion I had been brooding on for several days. 'In that case, as we will all be at the abbey, it might be an opportunity for Harri to visit his cousins. He has not been in their company since the Herberts ejected them from Weobley Castle over a year ago. I am sure you would like to see them all again, would you not, Harri?'

The boy nodded enthusiastically. 'Yes, Uncle, I would! Are they in London?'

At this point the servants began placing platters and dishes on the table and the conversation paused; fine wine was poured from chased silver flagons into matching cups. Sir Henry and Lady Margaret kept a generous table, even for such a small family gathering. I studied my hostess as these practicalities were completed and noted that her brow had knitted at the mention of Harri's cousins.

It being Friday the meal consisted mainly of fish dishes. I speared a portion of plump roasted eel to place it on my trencher and took a deep breath to pursue my proposal, aiming my remarks at Harri. 'They are not here in the city but I have a house at Stepney Green, a mile or so outside the Aldgate. They are staying there with Mistress Jane and Davy Owen is with them. I know they all very much hope for a visit from you.'

Harri tried not to look too eager as he turned to his mother. 'That would be a good idea, would it not, my lady mother?'

Her brooding expression indicated a negative response but Sir Henry intervened before she could speak. 'That solves the other problem you were fretting about, does it not, Margaret? You were unhappy about leaving Harri to his own devices while we attend on the king. Now he does not need to languish alone but instead enjoy some company of his own age. It is a very good idea, my lord.'

Had we not been at table I would have embraced him. I had always considered Sir Henry an amiable but rather weak character, subordinate to his dynamic and forceful wife but suddenly I found myself admiring his swift appreciation of the situation and his subtle way of ensuring a harmonious outcome.

'Very well, sir.' I beamed a warm smile at him. 'That is settled then. I will return tomorrow and take Harri to Stepney and he can stay as long as you wish to spare him.'

Outwitted, Margaret accepted defeat with commendable good grace. Moreover she had avoided saying anything detrimental about Jane or my family arrangements. Since returning to England and renewing my relationships, I was finding it hard to maintain a balance between the two women who were most important in my life. I badly needed to resolve how to remain close friends with a lady so important to the Lancastrian hierarchy, the mother of my nephew and whom I honoured greatly, while preserving the loyalty, attraction and affection I felt towards the mother of my children.

44

Jane

Le Garlek, Stepney Green & Coldharbour Inn, London

'HARRI! OH, HARRI, IT is so good to see you! We have missed you so much.' Elin rushed in front of us all and threw her arms around her cousin, while over their heads I exchanged rueful smiles with Jasper. I would never be able to suppress the natural affection and exuberance of our eldest daughter, no matter how hard I tried to instil in her the concept of ladylike grace.

When Harri hugged Elin enthusiastically back, I wondered if he might be grateful for some spontaneity, having been treading on eggshells at his mother's house. 'I have missed you too, all of you,' he said, turning to give Sian a warm kiss, which inspired a predictable blush. 'Luckily we never said goodbye so it shall be as if we were never parted.'

It had been raining during their ride from the city and when I removed our young visitor's oiled cape from his shoulders it caused a shower of water.

'Take Lord Jasper's cloak, Davy,' I told the boy, who eagerly complied.

Harri cried, 'God's greeting, Mistress Jane!' and for a moment I saw the essence of Lady Margaret in his well-executed bow and the correct swing of his arm as he removed his smart felt hat. But the upturned brim had filled with rainwater, which flew out in an arc and splashed my face and the front of my dress.

'Oh!' My exclamation was from surprise more than dismay and I quickly brushed the moisture from my face and laughed but Harri clutched at the offending hat and flushed a fiery red.

'How stupid of me – your beautiful gown! I am so sorry, Mistress Jane.' He leaned forward to brush the water from my skirt.

'It is only water, Harri,' I assured him, smiling. 'But thank you for calling my gown beautiful.' It was brown with darker brown collar and cuffs and a black belt with a pretty silver and speckled-agate buckle. I thought it not beautiful, like his mother's unfailingly were, but smart and serviceable. I impulsively emulated my daughter and gave him a hug. 'Now drink some ale and then you can all play an indoor game as you used to in wet weather – and do not let these rascals of ours beat you.'

When rain stopped and the sun had dried the sandy area in the garden, which Davy grandly called his practice ground, Jasper and I wandered out to watch as the two boys squared up, wielding stout staves cut from peeled ash stems. I had insisted that they wear gloves and protective coifs, being unwilling to send Harri back to Lady Margaret with grazed knuckles or a split scalp.

Jasper said nothing in front of the boys but murmured to me as the bout started, 'The staves are quite light and smooth, Jane. It is more a question of tactics than heavy hitting. Anyway I expect Harri has had a few cuts and bruises in the past.'

'No doubt,' I retorted, 'but I have no wish to give Lady Margaret any excuse for calling me a careless hostess. I daresay she is very protective of Harri now she has him back after all this time. I know I would be. It surprises me that she even let you bring him out of London.'

'I have her husband to thank for that. Sir Henry spoke up in favour of the idea before she could think of an excuse to refuse.' He fiddled thoughtfully with his beard, a habit I had noticed him displaying more and more lately as the pressure of his responsibilities increased. 'I shall have to give some thought to Harri's future. Look at him with Davy. He needs the company and rivalry of other boys to spar with. However much I detested the Herberts, they gave him companions of his own age and instruction in the use of arms as well as academic studies. He cannot develop knightly skills in the household of a childless couple. I fear Margaret would turn him into a cleric.'

'Book learning has its points, though. I think you should ask him what he would like himself. He is old enough to know his own skills and preferences.'

Jasper chewed his lip, pondering. 'Yes, I believe I will. This is a good opportunity to let him express his opinion without worrying about hurting his mother's feelings. He is just as protective of her as she is of him. He is so anxious to please her that he does not realize she loves him unconditionally. Whatever he expresses as his wish, I believe she will respect.'

'Even if he says he wants to return to your custody? That is what you want, is it not?' More and more I noticed Jasper had changed in the years he had been in exile. He had become cautious in his dealings with others but at the same time more sensitive to their ideas and opinions, I assumed as a result of the wide variety of people he had been obliged to deal with. Moving from one court to the next, one country to another, he had become more of a diplomat than a soldier.

He beamed at me. 'I believe you can read my mind better than my handwriting, Jane.'

I laughed. 'And it is no wonder! Your handwriting is like snail trails in a garden – all over the place. St Catherine be thanked you have scribes to write for you again now.'

At that moment Davy gave a howl of frustration as his staff flew from his hands and Harri claimed victory by holding his weapon across his opponent's throat. 'My bout I think!' he cried.

Davy dropped to his knees. '*Pace*,' he said, proving that he had learned something in the Raglan Latin lessons.

'But you are very good, Davy Owen,' Harri panted, pulling him to his feet. 'You should put up a pell post here and get one of the girls to shout directions. It would hone your reactions.'

Davy made a face. 'I could not take orders from a girl, Harri. I can beat Will Gardiner easily but you are much better than him.'

'Who is Will Gardiner?'

Davy grinned and pointed at Elin. 'You should ask Elin;

she natters away to him for hours, when he is not sparring with me.'

Elin was not abashed. 'At least he has more to talk about than sword thrusts and vambraces, whatever they are!' she shouted back.

'Who *is* Will Gardiner?' Jasper muttered in my ear.

This was the first Jasper had heard of him but Will had very quickly become a regular in our house. 'His mother brought a basket of eggs to welcome us to Stepney, which I thought very kind, and Will came with her, a pleasant boy who attends a guild grammar school in the city. He is the Gardiners' only son, and Elin, being Elin, seems to think him her particular acquisition.'

Will's father was a Master of one of the city Companies and Jasper thought he would therefore almost certainly be a wealthy merchant. When I told him they had another house in the city but Philippa preferred to live in the fresh air of Stepney, Jasper raised an eyebrow at me.

'Philippa? You are on first name terms then?' He looked at me seriously. 'I am very glad you have found a friend here, Jane. I need to go to Pembroke very soon but perhaps you will be content to remain here while I do? A Parliament has been summoned for the end of November so I will have to be back for that. Then I thought we might all spend Christmas in Wales.'

'All?' I echoed. 'Are you expecting Harri to come as well?'

He made a fluctuating motion with his hand. 'We will have to wait and see. It depends on Harri. After the coronation Lady Margaret is taking him to stay at Woking. We could collect him from there on the way to Wales if he decides to come.'

Will Gardiner arrived for his usual after-school visit but to Elin's consternation her father contrived to engage him in conversation and the rest of the time he was doing archery target practice with Harri and Davy. Elin became ever more sulky and silent as the day wore on.

'What a bright young man Will Gardiner is,' declared Jasper at supper, after the boy had gone home. 'Which of you lads carried the day at archery?'

'He did,' admitted Harri. 'He is a very good shot.'

'Well, he is a bit older than you and stronger. What age is he? Fifteen maybe? He says he is to be indented to his father's business next year.'

'Philippa told me he will be fifteen in January but he is tall for his age,' I said. 'Did you like him, Harri?'

'Yes, I did, Mistress Jane. And he has read some of the books I have enjoyed so I would like to discuss them with him if he comes again.'

Jasper had to ride back into London in the evening. The next day he was required to help the king robe for his coronation ceremony at Westminster.

'Is is true that the Constable, Lord Oxford, will ride into the Abbey on his horse, carrying the sword of state,' Harri asked. 'I would dearly like to see that!'

Jasper smiled. 'I will try and remember all the details to describe the day for you.' He rose. 'But before I leave, Harri, we have matters to discuss together, if you will spare me half an hour? Bring a cup of ale with you and we will go to the solar.'

'And what was his preference?' I asked Jasper before he left. 'Mother or uncle?'

'Both – after a fashion. He wants to become part of my

household and prepare for knighthood under my aegis but he is also a loyal and considerate son who realizes that his mother was only about the age he is now and did not leave him willingly in my care to go to marriage with Sir Henry. So he is torn between filial love and a natural desire for the company and rivalry of other youngsters. He needs to test himself against boys of his own age.'

I became impatient. 'And what conclusion did you both come to?'

'He decided that he would like to live in my household but with the proviso that he spend regular periods with his mother.'

'So who will have the all-important custody?'

'I will, because in the end it will be to King Henry and the Prince of Wales that he will owe his allegiance.'

'Did Harri suggest it should be that way?' I asked, surprised.

'No, I did. I cannot risk his mother's husband playing the custody card if he should ever choose to turn his coat. Harri is the king's nephew and should never again find himself on the wrong side on a battlefield, as he did at Banbury with Herbert.'

'Is Sir Henry not a reliable Lancastrian then?'

'Like so many noblemen who remained in England during Edward's illegal reign, Sir Henry has shown that he bends with the wind and legally he can oblige his wife to bend with him. Besides, he is not in robust health and if he were to die she would inevitably take another husband. Harri will not come of age for another seven years. Anything can happen in that time.'

'Did you explain all this to Harri?'

'No. Clever though he is, he is still too young. We just left it that he would live with me and visit his mother frequently. He was happy with that.' He paused and a shadow seemed to pass over his face. 'The re-coronation tomorrow will put King Henry safely back on the throne but we have not yet secured the kingdom. Warwick and I need to show the people that England can be successfully and peacefully united under Lancaster. And more immediately, I have the unenviable job of telling Margaret that once again I will be taking her son away from her.'

He rubbed at his forehead as if he would erase the lines of worry that were becoming etched there. 'It is not a task I relish, Jane.'

45

Jasper

Westminster Abbey & The House of the Vine, London

ALTHOUGH TRUMPETS SOUNDED A shrill summons
and heralds proclaimed the king's approach in stento-
rian voices, only a sparse crowd gathered to line the
coronation procession as it made its way from Westminster
Palace to the abbey. The troop of liveried royal guards, who
lined the route to keep control, seemed scarcely necessary.

Being occupied in Wales, I had not been present when
Warwick had paraded with King Henry through the city,
on his release from the Tower of London but the Earl of
Oxford had told me that the king had been unable to control
the lively white warhorse on which he had first been mounted
and so it had been necessary to put him on a rather placid
bay palfrey, which had not impressed the spectators. At least
on this, his re-coronation, the short procession from the
palace to the abbey was primarily on foot and I had ensured
that Henry looked the part in a gown of royal ermine and
purple, adorned with gem-studded chains, a jewelled coronet

and gold rings. However, although I tried to persuade him to wear a shoulder brace that would have helped straighten and support his back, he flatly refused and so the prematurely-aged king shuffled rather than strode out confidently to reclaim his throne. The ramrod-straight physique of the youthful and soldierly John de Vere, Earl of Oxford, as Constable of England, made a poignant contrast as, mounted on a prancing black destrier, he bore the great Sword of State before the king and drew most of what acclamation was to be heard. Walking at Henry's shoulders, the Earl of Warwick and I also received our share of approbation and I even heard someone, whom I guessed might be a stray Welshman in London, cry out 'Long live Lord Jasper!' from the steps of the Wardrobe Tower.

As we approached the abbey entrance we passed by St Peter's Sanctuary tucked into the north corner of the precinct, a plain, square stone building with a single fortified door and tiny, shuttered windows piercing the upper floor. Here I imagined the former queen, Elizabeth Woodville, and her three little daughters, enclosed in their shadowy refuge, not knowing when or whether they would be able to emerge. It was certain they could hear the trumpets sounding and the drums beating out the steps of the sumptuously robed column of nobles and prelates escorting the true king back to the throne of St Edward the Confessor.

The abbey church was full, the chancel crowded with barons and their wives who, when asked if they once again accepted Henry as their lawful king, dutifully made the rafters ring with their cheers. Compared to his first coronation the ceremony was brief; there was no need for an anointing because, according to Abbot Millyng who presided, a monarch once blessed with the holy oil remained divinely sanctioned until his death. Nobles and prelates present above the rank of baron renewed their vows of allegiance but those who still espoused the Yorkist cause were strategically absent and so the queue was not over long. As I knelt before my brother and bowed my head to kiss the ring, I feared the heavy crown might slip from his head as he bent to say, 'May God guide me through your good advice, Jasper.' Humbled though I was by his trust, I also felt the weight of responsibility settle like a heavy hauberk on my shoulders. It seemed ironic that the realm, once so firmly ruled by King Henry's renowned and conquering father, should now be under the regency of his mother's secret Tudor son.

* * *

My exile from England had not only separated me from Jane and my children; it had removed me from the orbit of my sister Meg and her family, including old Mette, the Frenchwoman who had so faithfully served my mother, Queen Catherine. News of Mette's death had only reached me several months after it had occurred six years ago.

I had been at Bamburgh Castle, where King Henry had been living in anticipation of marching south for another attempt to reclaim the throne. At that time the Lancastrian cause had plunged to one of its low ebbs and the castle was under a Yorkist siege but a letter from Meg found me, part of a bundle smuggled in for the king. In this particular dark hour God or our patron saints favoured us, for when Bamburgh finally surrendered to heavy bombardment from Edward's formidable new cannons, King Henry and I were permitted to ride out of the gates with the rest of the garrison, under a safe passage back to the Scottish border. It seemed that Edward of York, who would gleefully have taken us both prisoner, had been struck down with measles and handed command to Warwick's brother, Lord Montagu, a rare knight who still played by the rules of chivalry.

However, our good fortune had ended at Berwick where we discovered that England had made a truce with Scotland and King Henry was no longer welcome there. I tried to persuade my brother to take ship with me to France where his wife and son had fled but his fear of the sea overcame him and he chose instead to accept refuge in Lancashire with one of his loyal household servants. A sad mistake as it turned out, because the following year he was betrayed into Edward's hands and confined in the Tower of London.

After the re-coronation ceremony, at the king's request there was to be no grand banquet, with the result that the event I had devoted my life and soul to bringing about ended in a sad anti-climax and I found myself alone. I could have dined with Lady Margaret and Sir Henry at Coldharbour Inn but instead I thought of Mette, or more precisely Mette's death, and I took the opportunity to fling off my court apparel, don some anonymous garb and ride to Tun Lane to see my Tudor sister and her family for the first time in many years.

As I approached The House of the Vine I reflected on the people who had lived there. Even my royal mother had stayed there once, on the occasion of Mette's wedding to Geoffrey Vintner, back in the days when she had run away from the antipathy of the court and lived a secret life with my father. Unexpected emotions surged to the surface as I dismounted beneath the pargetted vine which trailed its bright colours along the plastered frontage of the house. I had experienced war and exile, happiness and despair, love and enmity, while my blood relations who presently inhabited the house, had known nothing of any of it. How different had been their experience of the past ten years. They had not lived like a gypsy as I had done, swapping palaces and castles for ships and mountain hideouts then, across the Channel, riding from one strange European court to another. They had remained in this house, alongside their close neighbours, directing their lives according to the dictates of the Church and the laws of England. Had it mattered to them who sat on the throne or won a particular battle? In short, would we now have anything in common and would they greet me as friend or foe?

In answer to my knock, the door was opened by a youth whose face was vaguely familiar to me but evidently mine was not known to him for he cocked his head on one side and said, 'Give you good day, sir,' with a quizzical look.

'And good day to you also, sir,' I responded. 'I believe I speak with Master Geoffrey Vintner, do I not?' It was a guess. Meg's firstborn had been a son named after his grandfather and, allowing for the difference in age, the similarity of this lad to the Geoffrey Vintner I had known was startling; sturdy build, dark hair, brown eyes and an expression that offered open friendliness.

He shrugged and smiled. 'You have the advantage of me. Perhaps you knew my grandfather. People say that I resemble him.'

'You certainly do,' I agreed. 'Is your mother at home? She

will vouch for me and perhaps even let me bring my horse into your yard. My name is Jasper Tudor.'

Geoffrey's eyes widened to the size of wild plums. 'Lord Jasper! I know that name and I will take your horse myself.' He stepped into the street and took the reins. 'Follow me, my lord.'

The gate to the alley that accessed the rear of the house was open and he led the palfrey down it to the courtyard at the back. Through a side window I glimpsed a room furnished with writing desks, at which sat several clerks busy with quill and ink. In the yard a girl sat on a bench, working vigorously at a churn and a woman in an apron, her hair hidden by a housewife's coif, was taking washing off a clothesline.

'You have a guest, Mother,' said my leader. 'I think you will be pleased to see him.'

The woman dumped the final item of washing in her basket. As she approached me, tucking the last pegs into her apron pocket, recognition struck and her face broke into a dimpled smile. 'Jasper! Oh Jasper, I knew you would come soon!'

Geoffrey and the horse disappeared through an open stable door in the range of outbuildings that lined the yard and I could not resist throwing my arms around my sister, an embrace she returned with enthusiasm and a girlish giggle. 'It has been too long, Meg, I know,' I said, drawing back to gaze down at her fondly. 'But at last I can walk the streets of London again without fear of arrest.'

She took my hands in hers and did a little dance of joy. 'Yes! Yes! It is wonderful. Come in and we will share a jug of something.' Turning to the girl, who had dutifully continued with her churning she said, 'As soon as the butter turns put it in the dairy and follow us in, Catherine – and bring the washing. We will light the fire and hear all Lord Jasper's news.'

The large chamber on the first floor was the beating heart of the house; the hall where nearly twenty years ago Margaret and William Vintner had held their wedding feast and Mette and I had watched Edmund present his cloth of gold wedding gift and almost disclose the truth of Meg's birth. Under the line of casement windows overlooking the street two girls sat sewing and looked up as we entered. One was about the same age as Geoffrey and the other was younger, probably of Elin's years, eleven or twelve.

'Mildred, Alys, this is Lord Jasper, a friend of the family, who we must make welcome. Leave your work and come and greet him.' Meg waved the girls forward and watched proudly as they made their curtsies. Both wore protective aprons over unbleached linen kirtles and white caps over their hair. 'Jasper this is William's niece Mildred and the little one is Alys, our youngest.'

The older girl kept her gaze modestly downcast but the younger one subjected me to a candid inspection with eyes of bright sapphire blue. I returned their curtsies with a solemn bow. 'God's greeting to you both,' I said.

Under Meg's supervision the fire was lit, wine and wafers brought, chairs and benches arranged; she made the promise of a meal later and her firstborn offered me a seat near the fire.

The girl appeared who had been churning the butter. 'This is Catherine, Jasper, whom you met as a small child. I do not think you will remember each other.' This girl was the prettiest of them all, a sweet-faced, pink-cheeked angel, straight from the pages of an illuminated Book of Hours.

I was plied with the refreshments, which I consumed with alacrity. My sister sat beside me and sipped at the good red Bordeaux wine.

I raised my cup appreciatively. 'The other branch of the Vintner family are still importing wine from Gascony then, despite England losing it to France?'

'Indeed they are – busier than ever. Mildy has been living with us for a year now,' she revealed, as her niece refilled my cup. 'Her father is away a great deal. Do you remember her mother and namesake, William's half sister? Unhappily she died quite suddenly last year of a throat quinsy. Mildy was her youngest child, the only one left at home. We are going to find her a good husband, is that not so, sweetheart?'

Mildy blushed and nodded. She offered me more wafers.

'They are excellent and I have consumed more than I should already,' I said politely. There was a question I needed to ask and I put it to the whole room. 'May I ask, did any of you watch the king's procession to the abbey for the re-crowning ceremony?' Everyone stared blankly at me. It seemed there had been no news spread in the city about the event, a task Warwick had undertaken to organize. No wonder the crowd had been minimal. Warwick prided himself on his ability to spread information and I feared his failure in this matter was an indication of his indifference to my brother's cause. For him glory lay in France, where his daughter Anne had now married Prince Édouard and was, he hoped, the future Queen of England.

To steer the conversation elsewhere, I offered my belated condolences for the passing of the children's grandmother

Mette, which were accepted with downcast eyes – then all were gazing at me once more. I said, 'I seem to remember an infant called Jem. Was it short for Jeremiah?'

'Ah yes, Jem is at sea with his cousin Gilbert, Mildy's brother. We think he will make a sailor. It would be good to have a ship's captain in the family now that trade has picked up with the Low Countries.'

I made no comment on this. A declaration of war with Burgundy was part of the agreement Warwick had made with King Louis in return for his ships and men. The 'Spider' wanted to destroy a treaty Edward had made with the Dukes of Burgundy and Brittany. Such a war would once more bring a halt to trade with Flanders and seriously affect London Merchant Venturers like Gilbert Vintner, who so far had backed Warwick. It was going to take some serious palm greasing on the earl's part to keep them sweet. No wonder he had been anxious to collect revenue from his northern estates.

At dusk William climbed the stair from his legal office and the whole household gathered around a long trestle set before the fire, including Martin the legal apprentice, Dolly the housemaid and Jake, who they called the gong boy, suitably scrubbed up from his weekly tasks of mucking out the stables, byres and latrines. I was impressed with the easy relationship evident between the family and their servants; there was no lack of respect given to William and Meg but they encouraged conversation between all occupants of the house. I had come to appreciate such a refectory system during my wandering days in Europe, when most meals on the road had been taken at communal tables in inns and monastery hostels.

My brother Edmund would never have agreed with me but I could not help thinking that of all Queen Catherine's children, fate had dealt Meg the best hand, one where the Wheel of Fortune, whilst it doubtless turned, had nevertheless delivered her less dramatic spins than it had afforded her brothers. And although I should be celebrating Henry's re-crowning, I was acutely aware that the Wheel could yet turn again. Under the guise of countering some spilt salt, I swiftly crossed myself and kissed the reliquary that always hung around my neck, sending up a silent prayer to my patron, St Thomas Becket.

'You seem distracted, Jasper,' murmured Meg, covering my other hand with hers and leaning nearer to keep her words from the others. 'You must have much on your mind now you are the King's Lieutenant. I am doubly grateful that you spared the time to visit us.'

'It is I who am grateful. It does my heart good to see you all.' I turned my wrist and gave her hand a squeeze. 'I have spent years apart from family and friends. It is a joy to find that their love and loyalty have not wavered in my absence.'

After the meal the adults withdrew to the private chamber off the hall, which the late Geoffrey Vintner had called his library. An impressive number of heavy leather-bound volumes still lay stacked on the shelving he had installed to hold them. A brazier had been lit to warm the room and Meg carefully plunged a red-hot poker into a jug of mead to pour as a digestive. Now nearing his fortieth year like me, William had cultivated a fashionable beard, closely trimmed and forked. This and his shrewd grey eyes gave him an air of wisdom and dependability. Seeing him and my sister sitting side by side, she looking as I had heard so like our mother, I was struck by the closeness of our family connection and an urge to seek their advice. As yet they were unaware of the existence of my own children and it seemed obvious that it was time to take them into my confidence.

I raised my cup to them. 'Good health to your close-knit household,' I said. 'Thank you for showing me the rewards of hard work, good discipline and shared love.'

William acknowledged my toast and sipped his drink. 'I think we should add God's will to the mix, my lord. None of it is due to our actions alone.'

I nodded. 'You are right but God does not always reward the worthy. Dame Fortune has a hand in it, I think.'

'She has certainly had a hand in your life, Jasper, and not all for the good,' observed Meg. 'Might she now, at last, grant you the joy of a family?'

'I have a confession to make. I am already father to two daughters.'

William and Meg exchanged a knowing glance.

I went on. 'I hasten to add that although neither God nor the king has sanctioned our union, their mother and I have somehow maintained a relationship, despite a lengthy enforced separation. She and our girls are at present living only two miles away in Stepney Green.' I fortified my courage with another gulp of the warm mead while allowing this news to sink in. 'Secrecy runs in our family, as you know, Meg, and now I need you to keep this information to yourselves. I hope I can rely on you for this.'

'Of course you can.' Meg spoke for them both, it was clear. 'We of all people can assure you of that. But tell us more of these nieces, Jasper, and of their mother. I would love to meet them.'

I shook my head and sighed. 'I think that would not be wise. It would jeopardize both your position and mine if the children were told of their cousins. They are too young yet to be sworn to secrecy and I have never revealed to Jane that I have a living sister. I have been unable to gain permission to marry from my brother the king and circumstances are such now that it will not be possible. Without his permission marriage would offer no security and more likely result in scorn and ignominy. If Jane were of the nobility it might be different but she is the daughter of a Welsh farmer.'

'Was our father not the son of a Welsh yeoman? Yet you were taken into royal favour eventually,' Meg pointed out.

'Yes, because Henry needed brothers who could fight his corner, which I still do. The king is a changed man. He has become reclusive and his mind and memory are not reliable. That is why the Earl of Warwick and I have undertaken to rule in his name. Of course this situation is only temporary. The future lies with his son Prince Édouard, who has been reared and influenced by Queen Marguerite. Who knows what will happen when they come to England for she is a strong and determined lady and not one it would be wise to offend.'

'And your marriage to a commoner would offend her?'

I detected a note of reproach in Meg's voice. 'I do not know. It has not been tested but primarily I have a duty to my brother. He is vulnerable and he needs my advice and presence at court. Secondly, he was reared to believe in the king's right to approve the marriages of his nobles and he would never condone my union with a commoner. Jane understands – at least I hope she does.'

'I wonder if that is so . . .' Meg's murmured response was overridden by William's surprisingly emphatic one.

'Whether she does or not, you are right not to marry her. No good came of King Edward's marriage to Elizabeth Woodville. It has split the nobility even more drastically than it was divided before he usurped the throne and even worse, it has alienated the ordinary citizens. He had seemed a golden-haired, victorious young Galahad when he became king, but he lost all respect when he allowed his lust to override his reason and made a commoner his queen. Many no longer considered him worthy of their loyalty or fit to wear the crown. You might lose the support of your tenants and followers Lord Jasper, if they heard that you took your leman for your wife.'

For a few moments I frowned at William, a commoner who had married a queen's daughter, albeit a secret one. 'Do you speak as a lawyer when you say that?' I asked.

'Yes I do. Marriage is more than just words said before witnesses. It is a legal matter and I have drawn up many a contract for couples who understand its importance in binding our society together. It is as important as the vow a vassal makes to his lord or to his king. Love may come after marriage but it is a hazardous foundation for it.'

'Did we not marry for love, William?' Indignation spiked Meg's interjection.

He leaned from his chair to take her hand, smiling fondly. 'Oh yes, we did, but we had known from childhood that we would and our parents and all our friends and neighbours also knew and approved. Nevertheless I would still say that our marriage is based on more than love. Shared values, mutual respect, loyal friendship – and, thanks be to God, the joy of rearing our children.'

His wife shot him a wicked sideways glance with those devastating blue eyes of hers. 'Are you not forgetting a little something called the marriage debt, husband?'

He gave her a comical look of horror, snatched his hand back and smacked the palm to his forehead. 'How could I forget that? Lust is a terrible thing, Lord Jasper, but at least in marriage it is legal!'

I had to laugh with them but my laughter was edged with guilt.

It was getting late when I collected Evan and my small retinue at the local inn and we set off for Stepney Green but while the men were laughing and joking after their drinking-session, I rode a little ahead of them, taciturn and lost in my thoughts. Witnessing my sister's family life had led me to consider my own. I did not want Elin and Joan to suffer for being illegitimate but more than ever I knew that marriage was not possible with Jane. A way had to be found to solve these two apparently irreconcilable problems and William's polemic on love and marriage had started a hare running in my mind.

46

Jane

Le Garlek, Stepney Green, London

'Elin is not yet twelve, Jasper!' I exclaimed in alarm. 'You of all people know that is much too young for a girl to marry.'

'I am not suggesting marriage right now, Jane, merely that we consider the possibility of a betrothal.' Jasper was using his coaxing, persuasive voice. The one he knew usually won me round in the end. 'Church teaching recognizes that Elin is of an age when many a maid begins to experience the stirrings of desire. She may not know exactly what it is she feels but to me it is obvious that Elin has a great liking for Will Gardiner, and if you are so friendly with his mother it may be sensible for you to discuss, woman to woman, the possibility of a betrothal. He is an only son, likely to inherit his father's business and properties. I am now in a position to provide her with a tempting dowry and his father would almost certainly see the advantage of a close connection to the king's half brother. She would

476

have a good life as the wife of a Merchant Venturer – a secure home and the kind of household she is familiar with. It is not an unthinkable idea.'

I pulled my chamber robe more tightly around me and contemplated the notion of bartering with Philippa Gardiner over my daughter's future. It struck me as being unpleasantly similar to the prospect of a farmer arranging the mating of a prime gilt pig. 'Not unthinkable to you, clearly,' I remarked tartly, 'but then she is not the baby you fed from your breast or the child you nursed through ague and belly-ache. She may be a little madam at the moment but she is my little madam and I love her.'

We were ready for bed but this subject was making me too tense to lie in it. Jasper moved up behind me and put his arms around my rigid shoulders. 'But having reared her through those perilous years, Jane, is it not an act of love to give thought to her future? I am sure she begins to do so herself, or if not yet then very soon she will. Is that not why she contradicts you and kicks against the traces? In noble houses girls are often sent away at Elin's age to live with their betrothed husband's family, while they are still young enough to adapt easily to the ways of a new life. Perhaps you could suggest a trial to Mistress Gardiner? A short stay when they can all discover whether they get on together. You never know, she may already be on the look-out for a suitable bride for her only son. It is as important for a merchant's family to find a good match as it is for landed gentry and you must agree that by any reckoning Elin is a good match.'

'While you are away in Pembroke I will think on it,' I agreed grudgingly, moving out of his embrace and picking up my hairbrush. 'When will you take Harri back to Lady Margaret?'

'Tomorrow afternoon. Would you like to come with us?'

I pulled hard at a tangle in my hair and cast him a sharp glance. 'Has she mentioned repaying the thirty crown loan?'

He shook his head. 'No, and when I asked her she said it was not a loan but a gift. She knows it is your care of Harri that has made him the delightful, well-mannered boy that he is. Evan can stay here with the children and we will be back before dark.'

I nodded, still distracted over Elin. 'Then I will come,' I said, putting down the brush and hauling back the bedcovers.

* * *

The sight of Lady Margaret kissing Jasper in the deserted churchyard at Bettys Newydd had left a scar on my memory. However, three years later I had become confident of Jasper's love for me, and the silk gown and beautiful jewellery he had given me since our coming to London meant I was less intimidated by confronting her refinement and the sumptuousness of her home. Moreover as we all talked together, Harri made it clear to her how important I was to him and the conversation flowed freely. To my surprise, when we parted she expressed a desire to visit me at Stepney Green when we were both next in London. Even the parting with Harri was less poignant than I had expected because it had been agreed that he should join us for Christmas.

On the ride back to Stepney I asked Jasper what could have persuaded Lady Margaret to permit this. He smiled proudly and said, 'Harri did. He has power to charm the birds from the trees that boy. At present his mother can refuse him nothing. After they have spent some time at Woking we can pick him up from there on our way to Pembroke. It should all fit in very well.'

Jasper left the following day to escort the king to Windsor. Now that he had been securely re-crowned, Henry had insisted that he leave his hated Westminster and spend some time in the relative peace and security of the realm's mightiest fortress. Meanwhile I spent several days pondering whether or not to consult with Philippa Gardiner on the matter of Elin and Will. In the end I happened to meet her in the market on the green and decided to reciprocate her earlier hospitality by inviting the Gardiner family to sup with us the following night. While accepting for herself and Will, she revealed that her husband was away and so the opportunity for the private woman to woman talk, which Jasper had suggested, seemed impossible to ignore.

After the cloth was removed we banished the four children to the other end of the hall and remained sitting at the trestle. Over the sound of their noisy game of ninepins we mulled some wine and spices and settled down together like two fountain gossips. As far as I could guess Philippa Gardiner was about my age, slim and dark and prone to wearing elaborately wired headgear, which gave the clever illusion of more height than she possessed. On this occasion her beautifully embroidered hat looked like a short steeple blunted at the tip and was covered by a gauzy veil, wired into a butterfly shape and secured at the front by an amethyst-headed pin. It provided the perfect topic to open the conversation.

'You must give me the name of your headdress-maker, Philippa,' I begged. 'It is spectacular.'

She laughed. 'It is a fashion copied from Bruges. My husband bought the Hennin cap on his last trip there and I wired the veil myself. I am so glad you like it.'

'Very much,' I nodded. 'And I noticed Elin admiring it too – when she could tear her gaze away from your son of course!'

Philippa's eyes gleamed with amusement. 'Yes, they seem to like each other a good deal. It is very sweet.'

'You do not disapprove then?'

'No, not at all – why should I? Elin is a lovely girl and so pretty with her sunburst curls and ready smile.'

'And with a very lively nature,' I added wryly.

'Life then can never be dull with her around,' she said lightly.

'That is true enough.' I paused to take a sip of wine and summon my courage. 'Elin's father was very taken with Will also. He wants me to ask if you thought there might be the basis of a marriage between those two when they are older?'

Observing closely, I thought I detected the gleam in my guest's eyes change from amusement to speculation. 'It might be worth considering,' she said, apparently untroubled by my abrupt proposal. 'Certainly I think it sensible to sort these things out sooner rather than later, before a boy gets too frisky, if you know what I mean?' She cast an eloquent glance in my direction.

'Something girls suffer from too, I assure you,' I remarked.

'I must take your word for that. I have not been blessed with more than my one dear child, but I would have loved to have a daughter; you are lucky to have two.'

'But no son,' I pointed out. 'Which in the circumstances may be a good thing. The stain of bastardy can hamper a boy more than a girl, I think.'

'Do you? Surely any child of an earl – especially one who has no legitimate heir – has only to retain the father's favour to gain advantage from it.'

So Philippa was impressed rather than alarmed by Jasper's status, which boded well but rather than pursue that line I steered the talk on a more pertinent course. 'I am no match-maker but perhaps we should take steps to test this relationship further; Elin and Will have but recently met and have spent only short periods of time together. We leave for Pembroke at the end of the month, as you know. Would you think it presumption if I suggested that we give their friendship a more rigorous test? We would not want Will to miss his schooling in order to take him to Pembroke but . . .' I hesitated.

'If you mean would I welcome Elin as a guest while you are away, then I would say yes, of course,' Philippa cut in, looking pleased. 'I would love the chance to mother a daughter, especially one who may become just that.'

I took a deep breath, wondering if I would be doing the best for Elin by handing her over to another woman? I consoled myself with the reminder that this was only to be for a short time. Besides I had developed respect and admiration for the Gardiner family over the weeks I had known them and could not imagine that they would treat her with anything but kindness. I also thought that Sian might benefit from not being constantly in the shadow of her elder sister. I had a panicky recollection of Lady Margaret putting her baby son into Jasper's arms and then not seeing him again for nine years but told myself firmly that the situation was hardly similar.

'I must talk to Elin about it first, before anything is made final,' I said. 'Although I think I do not need to tell you that I believe she will be thrilled and excited at the prospect.'

'I do hope so.' Philippa lifted her cup to make a toast. 'And I must consult my husband of course, but let us drink to a closer relationship, Jane!'

I touched my horn cup of mulled wine to hers and we both took a sip, eyes smiling at each other across the rim.

At the other end of the hall there was a clatter of ninepins falling and a shout went up from two excited voices. Swivelling to look we saw Will linking elbows with Elin and swinging her around in a victory dance. 'Oh well done, partner!' he carolled. 'We won!'

It seemed a good omen for the future.

47

Jasper

Windsor Castle

IN THE PARLIAMENTARY ROLL King Henry's return to the throne was termed a 'readeption', the Latin word *adeptus* meaning 'having attained', and the first Parliament of the readeption was a busy one, most of the business being to reverse the damage done by the York regime over the previous nine years. The Act changing the Pembroke lands from Herbert back to me was one of the first to be passed but the Richmond lands were another matter. Lady Margaret's best efforts at persuasion had cut no ice with Warwick, who insisted that Edmund's former estates should remain with his son-in-law, the Duke of Clarence. Therefore, with no revenue attached, Harri's custody attracted no contention and eventually it was left to the Regents to decide. I had only to hint to Warwick that I might challenge his declaration of war on Burgundy and he agreed that Harri should return to my care.

Having learned from Jane the arrangement she had made

with Mistress Gardiner I paid another visit to The House of the Vine and asked William Vintner to draw up a betrothal contract, to be used in the event that all parties were in agreement after Elin's stay with the Gardiners. 'If the two families do eventually become united by marriage, then might be the time to take them into our confidence about my relationship to Meg, but that is for the future,' I told him.

When I revealed the sum of the dowry I intended to settle on my daughter he gave a low whistle. 'That amount would compensate a Merchant Venturer for several cargos lost at sea. I should think the Gardiners will snap her up.'

'I hope it will make them aware of her worth, but ultimately it is up to Elin whether she wishes to marry the boy,' I reminded him. 'I am not one to barter my daughter's life away without her consent.'

Consequently, when we left the house in Stepney Green to begin the journey to Pembroke, Elin was not with us. She had been thrilled by the Gardiners' invitation to stay with them for Christmas and seemed unconcerned about missing the celebrations with her own family. Nothing was said to her about a possible betrothal. That would come later, if she proved willing.

'I impressed on her the importance of being dutiful and polite towards Will's parents and helping Mistress Gardiner with household duties but I am not sure whether the message sank in,' Jane admitted as we rode towards the city at first light. 'Philippa may find she has taken a whirlwind into her home.' She then broached a subject that had been troubling me rather more than Elin's behaviour. 'Will the queen be here in time for Christmas? Surely she must be satisfied since King Henry has been crowned again. That was more than a month ago; she should know about it by now.'

'We are waiting to hear from her. King Henry may have word when I see him.'

We crossed London Bridge and made our way through the busy suburbs on the Thames' southern bank, passing the Bishop of Winchester's palace at Southwark and the Archbishop of Canterbury's at Lambeth before cutting across the great commons of Wandsworth and Wimbledon and following the River Mole into the downlands of Surrey. Woking Palace could be reached in a day from London, even when the days were winter short, and we arrived at the torchlit gatehouse at dusk. Although it had meant making a detour, I wanted to collect Harri from Lady Margaret before going to Windsor, as I thought my brother would appreciate a visit from us both before Christmas. I also hoped Queen Marguerite and Prince Édouard would cross the Channel in time to be reunited with King Henry for the festivities, because the restoration of God's rightful anointed monarch to the throne of England was surely something for them to celebrate together.

We were lavishly accommodated and entertained by Lady Margaret and Sir Henry and they were both graciously kind to Jane and Sian and very interested to hear about Elin's friendship and stay with the Gardiners in Stepney. Sian remembered to thank Margaret for the silver cup she had sent her at birth and revealed that she drank from it every day, which had pleased Margaret immensely.

'It was not strictly true,' Jane confessed once we were on the road again, 'but I told Sian to cross her fingers when she said it. The girls do use them on feast days, though.

Can you believe, when I thanked her for the money gift she actually pressed her finger to my lips and told me there was no need for thanks?'

'Noble ladies do like to feel they have distributed a certain amount of their wealth among the poor and needy in order to ensure their souls make it to heaven,' I said, straight-faced.

'Oh, so I am a charity case to Lady Margaret am I?' Jane cried, rising nicely to the bait. 'How does that make you look in her eyes then, my lord Jasper?'

'Up to now I believe she has considered us both in need of her charity. Perhaps one day there may come a time when we are able to return her favours and earn ourselves some heavenly approval.'

We were riding through the river meadows towards Windsor and Jane glanced behind to check that Sian and Harri were looking at the scenery and not us before giving me a wallop on the thigh – the highest she could reach from the back of her small palfrey. 'You are teasing me, Jasper Tudor. I cannot imagine there ever being a time when I will be able to do anything more saintly than she can.'

I rubbed my thigh ruefully. 'When you come to think about it you might find that you already have, sweetheart,' I said, glancing back at Harri. 'There is a boy back there who would not show the promise he does if it were not for you.'

Jane looked at me in surprise before giving a little nod. 'You may be right,' she said thoughtfully. 'Thank you.'

'For what?' It was my turn to be surprised.

'For making me an independent woman. I realize that I never would have been if you had not refused to marry me.'

It was my turn to be thoughtful.

486

The next day I left Jane and Sian exploring the sights of Windsor together and went with Harri to the king's apartments in St George's Hall. We found King Henry in a sorry state of melancholy, huddled over a Prie Dieu in his private chapel, passing the beads of his rosary frantically through his fingers and murmuring indecipherable prayers.

'His grace is fretting about the queen and the prince, my lord,' Sir Richard Tunstall whispered as we stood at the chapel door. 'Today he received a letter from Rouen, telling him that they would soon travel by barge to the mouth of the Seine, where the ships and the army King Louis promised them are preparing to sail to England. The king is terrified of the sea, ever since they were all nearly shipwrecked on their first flight to Scotland.'

'So will the queen be here for Christmas?' I asked.

The Chamberlain shrugged. 'It is in God's hands. I do not think his grace can decide whether to pray for them to sail as soon as possible or to wait until the threat of winter storms has passed.'

'It is so long since they were together.' I made the sign of the cross. 'May the Virgin of the Sea grant the queen and the prince safe passage and bring the king cheer at Christ's Nativity.'

Henry must have heard our voices, for at the end of his rosary he heaved himself to his feet, genuflected to the altar and backed away. When he saw me his face broke into a smile. 'Jasper! It is you. You are very well come.'

I snatched off my hat, bent my knee and kissed his ring. 'God's greetings, your grace, I hope I find you well?' Behind me Harri dropped to his knees but Henry did not notice him.

He took my hand to make me rise. I thought his skin looked less transparent than at the coronation. 'I am well enough thank you, Jasper, well enough. Sir Richard, what can we do to make Lord Pembroke welcome? I know, some hippocras perhaps.' Henry suddenly became quite animated. 'Do you remember when we drank too much of it at Christmas? So many years ago, so many years . . .'

'At least eighteen, sire,' I said with a grin. 'We made merry, did we not?' We began walking slowly down the passage that led to the king's chamber. 'I hope you will do the same this year, when the queen and the prince join you.'

Henry stopped suddenly and looked up at me. 'Sir Richard told me it was Édouard's birthday a few weeks ago. How old was he Jasper? I could not remember.'

I had to think quickly. 'By my reckoning he is seventeen, sire.'

'Seventeen!' My brother's face crumpled and, to my great concern, tears began to run down his hollow cheeks. 'I do not know what he looks like any more,' he moaned and his cry echoed in the empty passage. 'I can only see him as he was when he left. He was a boy and now he is a man.'

I did not know what to say and I was worried about Harri seeing the king in such a state. I turned and saw that he was following at a discreet distance, studiously keeping his eyes on his feet. In silence, punctuated by Henry's occasional sniffs and Sir Richard's embarrassed coughs, we made our way to a guarded entrance, where two sentries came to attention and raised their halberds. One of them rapped on the door and it was opened from within.

'I will take your nephew for some refreshment, Lord Pembroke,' said Sir Richard quietly.

I nodded and beckoned Harri forward. 'Go with the Chamberlain, Harri. I will come and find you in a little while.'

Once we were inside King Henry's chamber I put my arm around my brother and led him to his canopied chair, motioning the duty squire, who was hovering awkwardly, to leave the room.

'You have been lonely for too long, Henry,' I said, pulling my kerchief from my sleeve pocket and handing it to him. 'But soon now you will be able to enjoy being a father to your son again.'

'Do you think he is my son, Jasper?' he whispered, blowing his nose and peering about the room to check for listening ears. 'I know dreadful rumours were spread at his birth but I have always believed Marguerite to be a faithful wife. I took the advice you gave me on that Christmas night and so I can believe it.'

My memories of that awkward encounter were still vivid but I was astonished that his were equally sharp. 'Of course he is your son,' I assured him. 'Those rumours were spread by Yorkists to discredit you. God and his holy angels know that Prince Édouard is the trueborn heir to the throne of England. Your blood runs in his veins and now that you wear the crown again no one can doubt it.'

The king pulled himself up against the carved back of his chair, the moisture drying on his cheeks. 'You should have a son of your own, Jasper. Why have you not married? Is it my fault? I have not found a suitable bride for you.'

'That is your prerogative, sire,' I said with a smile I did not feel.

'Yes, yes. I will pray on it. You should not be left unmarried like our mother was. It can only lead to trouble.' He waved at a nearby stool and I pulled it up. 'Do you know I saw our mother the other day – a picture of her, on the wall. I found it when I climbed a turret to get a view of the weather to the south. I am so worried that the queen and prince will be hit by storms in the Channel.'

I had to close my eyes on the burst of stars that exploded in my mind. Every time I had visited Windsor Castle during my life at court I had tried to find the portrait of Queen Catherine, which I had been told was somewhere in the Great Round Tower, but to no avail. Now Henry was telling me I had been looking in the wrong place. It was somewhere in the royal apartments after all. I tried not to show my excitement because I did not want to add to Henry's agitation but this time I had to know where the portrait was.

'I would like to see that picture, Henry. Which turret did you climb?' I asked him gently.

He waved the kerchief in a vague gesture. 'Oh, I cannot remember. The weather at the time was fair. That was all I needed to know.'

I resolved to change the subject. I would pursue the portrait later with Harri. Another pair of eyes would be useful. 'I have brought my nephew with me today, sire. Would you like him to visit you?'

Henry frowned at me. 'Your nephew, Jasper? Did I know you had a nephew? Who's son is he?'

'My brother Edmund's son. He married Lady Margaret Beaufort, do you remember?'

His expression darkened further. 'No, I do not remember. Why have I not met him? You know I like to meet all members of my family.'

I opened my mouth to tell him that he had met Harri and not long ago but suddenly had second thoughts. I decided it would not be wise to suggest that when they had come to court at Westminster he had mistaken Harri for his own son and Lady Margaret for his wife. He might not believe me, and it might even make him angry. He was still head of the House of Lancaster but more than ever I realized that he was an unreliable and unpredictable head. He might be capable of signing an edict but he was not capable of generating its content, just as he was not capable of remembering quite recent events.

'I will go now and fetch him, sire,' I said. 'He is not far away.'

Henry's squire was waiting outside the door and after he had told me where Harri had gone with Sir Richard Tunstall I sent him back in to attend the king. However, by the time I returned with Harri the opportunity for introducing him to his uncle had passed. King Henry was once more kneeling before a crucifix, praying to the only consistent being in his world.

'We will come again in the New Year, Harri,' I said to the puzzled boy. 'Perhaps the king will meet you then. But I have something else I want you to do while we are here. We are going to look for your grandmother.'

'Lady Welles?' he asked, becoming even more perplexed. 'Is she here at Windsor?'

'No, not your mother's mother but Queen Catherine de Valois, the French Princess who was King Henry's mother and also mother to your father and me. Her father was King of France and she was queen to King Henry the Fifth, the conquering Lancastrian. I have just discovered that her portrait is hanging somewhere here in St George's Hall and I would like to find it before we leave.'

Harri's eyes were round with surprise. 'Mistress Jane told me about Queen Catherine. She said her mother had been one of her ladies in waiting.'

'Yes, Harri, and she was apparently very beautiful so she should not be hard to find.'

The most obvious place to start was the gallery that ran the length of the royal apartments. A succession of portraits hung between the doors that led off this long passage and windows ran along the opposite wall throwing light on many a royal visage but none of them was my mother's, at least not as far as I could tell. Perusing the female portraits one by one I kept telling myself that when I saw her I would recognize her but as one face followed another, painted with artistry of wildly varying skill, I became despondent. I had always regretted having no clear memory of Queen Catherine but I had thought I would instinctively know her, that some forgotten but ingrained image would suddenly make a positive match with a picture before my eyes and there would be no doubt in my mind that it was my mother. When this did not happen Harri urged me to think more carefully about what King Henry had said about seeing his mother on the wall.

'Did he say anything to give you a clue about where it might be? What was he doing when he saw it?'

I told him. 'We were talking about Queen Marguerite and Prince Édouard possibly coming for Christmas. He said he was worried about the weather. He had climbed a tower hoping to be able to see what the weather was like in the

Channel. I thought that was nonsensical, you cannot see that far, even from the highest turret.'

'Let us search the towers, then. All towers have stairs and a stair has to start and end in a room or passage. There might be pictures hanging there.'

'Yes, that is a good idea, Harri. When King Henry's father died his brother Humphrey of Gloucester became Protector and he apparently did not like my mother. He may have hidden her portrait somewhere obscure so that it was not in the public eye. We will ask the Chamberlain.'

It took us some time to find Sir Richard Tunstall who detailed a servant to show us to the hall's four towers. It was like following a labyrinth in three dimensions climbing one tower after another, winding through all their rooms and passages. Then in the last of the four – inevitably! – there was a portrait that set my spine tingling. It hung in such a dark corner at the base of the circular stair that it was almost impossible to discern the features but even in the deep shadows something about the face made me lift it down from its hook with shaking hands.

'Harri, Harri, I think this is it!'

The servant carried the picture through the tower entrance and out into the daylight, where we propped it against the wall.

I do not know how I knew it was my mother but the certainty only grew. Mette had told me that a famous Flemish artist had been brought to Paris to paint it when my mother was sixteen years old, a few years after the fifth King Henry's magnificent victory over the French on the field of Agincourt. Her father, King Charles the Sixth of France, had been suffering one of his terrible episodes of madness and his queen, Isabeau of Bavaria, had assumed the regency with the Duke of Burgundy. Protracted peace negotiations were stalling and the Princess Catherine was being offered as a bride to try and seal the treaty. The portrait was painted to show the English king her outstanding beauty.

She was looking straight out of the painting, as if challenging the viewer to deny the perfection of her countenance. A lump formed in my throat as her two enormous sapphire eyes seemed to instantly claim me, so that I had to make a conscious effort to tear my gaze from them in order to study her other features. Finely arched brows were set above remarkable high cheekbones, the nose was nobly straight and the mouth curved and red as the rubies in her gold coronet, her neck pale, smooth and long like a marble column, set off by a gem-studded collar. She wore a purple velvet mantle trimmed with the tails of winter ermine, over a lavishly embroidered golden gown and yet this glorious royal apparel could not outshine the radiance of its wearer. Never can a princess have been a more tempting prize to a conquering king.

'She looks like you.' Harri's comment took me by surprise. We had both been silent for several minutes.

'Do you really think so?' I was absurdly pleased by his observation. 'But without the beard,' I joked.

Harri laughed, or more accurately, giggled. 'Obviously, Uncle Jasper.'

'It was her idea to call me Jasper,' I remarked. More information relayed by Mette was surfacing, inspired by the picture to which my eyes could not help returning. 'She had a red jasper ring and I was born with bright red hair. Much brighter than it is now.'

'Does jasper have a meaning? Most gems do I am told.'

I turned to look at him again. 'This one was a bloodstone. They say it is the gem of noble sacrifice and brings the bearer passion and courage.'

'Then it suits you,' my nephew said. 'What could be more noble than to have brought your king back to his rightful throne?'

'But I think I have more to prove, Harri, before she is shown to be right. I do not feel my life is over. There is much to do yet.'

He looked a little sheepish. 'I did not mean to make you feel old, Uncle, and I hope I will see you do it.'

I laughed and squeezed his shoulder. 'And I hope I will see you do even more, young man. But come, I want to bring Mistress Jane to see this picture before the light fades.'

* * *

Seeing it, and justifiably overawed, Jane said, 'No wonder my mother adored her.'

'No wonder my father adored her,' I echoed. 'How can I possibly have forgotten that exquisite face? It should surely have engraved itself on my infant mind.' I crossed myself as if saluting a saint. 'May God forgive me.'

I heard rather than saw Jane swirl round to confront me. 'You have nothing to beg forgiveness for, Jasper,' she said indignantly. 'You were a child when she left you. You must have felt abandoned. No wonder you thrust her image from your thoughts. But now you must realize that you see her every time you look in a mirror. If Edmund was your father's son, you are your mother's.'

'But she defied all opposition to marry her love and bring happiness to them both. I have not done that, have I, Jane?'

At first she was silent, her gaze lowered, then out of the blue she said, 'I hear the old queen has had a son in sanctuary.'

My eyes widened in surprise. 'Where did you hear that? I thought it had not been made public.'

She gave a dry little laugh. 'I heard it in Windsor High Street. So do not tell me you have failed, Jasper, not when we, too, have a new life of our own just beginning.'

I stared at her intently. 'Are you telling me you are with child, Jane?'

She met my gaze proudly and nodded. 'Perhaps this time we will also have a boy, to celebrate a fresh start – and a happy life to come, like your mother wanted.'

We shared a kiss then under the intense gaze of the forgotten queen and I felt as if the past with its failures and regrets was a foreign country and the future full of promise . . .

GLOSSARY

Abermaw: the original Welsh name for a seaside town that the Victorians renamed Barmouth, at the mouth of the River Mawddach.

almoner: official in charge of dispensing alms and supervising charitable works.

arrivistes: 'new arrivals' – recently ennobled commoners.

ashlar: squared-off stones worked smooth by masons, used as facing on buildings.

attire: a knight's suit of armour, later used generally for an outfit of clothing.

baldric: shoulder strap to carry a bag or sword sheath. Also a strip of embroidered fabric worn across the body as a male fashion item, sometimes hung with little bells.

banneret: a senior grade of knighthood, having power to command a troop in battle.

barbe: a linen collar covering a woman's chin and neck (*Fr. barbe = beard)* worn with a *wimple as a sign of widowhood.

bard: a poet

barded: heraldic term for decorative horse-trappings (bardings).

bass: a slow processive dance.

Beaufort: a castle town in 14thC Aquitaine, which John of Gaunt gave as a surname to the four children he fathered with Katherine Swynford. They were later legitimized.

Bletsoe Castle: held by Margaret Beauchamp, Margaret Beaufort's mother, located north of Bedford.

bodger: a turner of wood, making bowls and chairs and posts of all kinds and sizes.

bottins: short protective boots – practical rather than fashionable.

bracer: armour for the lower arm – came in pairs, *cf.* a brace of game.

braies: male underwear, worn under hose.

Caldicot: Jasper's castle on the west bank of the Severn estuary.

cariad: a Welsh term of affection – sweetheart, darling, love.

chapman: a travelling salesman or pedlar.

chausses: chain-mail trousers.

chemise: a long linen shirt (French) – worn under *kirtle (women) or *doublet (men)

chevauchée: 'slash and burn' – a string of raids on villages and crops, a strategy of war intended to destroy the enemy's resources and morale.

cog: a sailing ship used mainly for cargo up to 200 tons; some also had passenger accommodation.

coif: tight linen cap, worn by men and women, also by a knight under his helmet.

commission of array: officials sent out to assess men aged 16 - 60 for service in the royal army.

coney: a young rabbit - also its fur.

cope-chest: a large half-moon-shaped chest for storing ceremonial church robes.

coppicer: harvester of regrowth from tree-stumps for brushwood, poles and posts.

Crécy: location in France of 1346 battle when Welsh longbowmen were credited with giving England a glorious victory.

crenellation: the 'gapped teeth' of castle battlements.

cuirass: armour protecting the torso = a breastplate and backplate fastened together.

dagged, dagging: decorative 'ragged' edging, on long sleeves of gowns and doublets, lined with a contrasting colour and often trailing the floor for effect.

damask: an elaborately decorated silk fabric originating in Damascus.

destrier: cavalry horse capable of carrying a knight in full armour – a charger.

Dewisland: area around St David's in Pembrokeshire. Dewi=nickname for David.

Dinefŵr: pron: Dynvoor. A castle in Dyfyd, much fought over in Welsh wars.

divine right: belief that royal blood imbued kings with a God-given right-to-rule.

dorter: a dormitory in a monastery or attached hospice. cf.*reredorter

*doublet: a gentleman's jacket, shorter and more fitted than a gown.

droit de seigneur: the alleged right of a lord to deflower a vassal's bride.

eisteddfod: a festival of the Welsh arts, still held regularly today.

estampie: a vigorous dance from France.

greave: armour protecting the shin.

gauntlet: an armoured glove.

hauberk: chainmail protective tunic.

hippocras: a sweetened and spiced wine-cup.

hogshead: a very large barrel = over 50 gallon capacity.

holland: a coarse unbleached linen fabric, originating in the Lowlands.

honour: a collection of manors held by one lord.

hose, hosen: leg-wear – 15thC gentlemen's hose was tight and joined at the top with a convenience pouch at the front. Women wore separate hosen like today's stockings, held up by garters.

hulk: large medieval cargo ship, crude in design but capable of carrying up to 700 tons.

joint-stool: a collapsible seat joined in the middle which opened as a wide X.

*kirtle: lady's dress, often showing under an outer robe and worn over a *chemise.

Lamphey Palace: summer residence of the Bishops of St. David's located near Pembroke.

*lance: long *pole-weapon used by mounted men at arms, especially in jousting.

livre: French coin similar to the English crown.

malmsey: a type of grape from which a strong, sweet wine was made. Imported from Spain.

limner: an artist, especially of heraldry, miniatures and illuminations.

March: border-lands between England and the old Welsh Principality, held by English noblemen. At times included the southern counties of Gwent, Glamorgan, Carmarthen and Pembroke.

Maxstoke Castle: one of many held by the Duke of Buckingham, located near Coleshill, east of Birmingham.

mews: accommodation for hawks and falcons. Later a garage for carriages and latterly cars.

minerva: fur trimming taken from the red squirrel for court and ceremonial robes of lesser nobles.

misericord: a row of narrow 'ledge' seats in a church choir-stall, allowing support when standing for long periods. (From Latin *miserereor* = 'have pity'.)

mullion: stone division between the lights of windows.

ninepins: medieval game of skittles.

Offa's Dyke: a ditch roughly marking the border between Wales and England, dug in the 8thC.

palfrey: a riding horse, often a mare. Definitely not a warhorse.

pannier: a basket used in a pair, slung over a horse or mule for transporting goods.

pargetting/pargetted: patterned plasterwork often used on timber-framed houses.

park: an enclosed area of land reserved for a lord's hunting.

pattens: wooden or cast iron hooped soles, which could be strapped to the foot. Raised the wearer above snow, mud, puddles and refuse.

Pembroke: town and castle on Milford Haven. Admin. centre of Jasper's earldom.

pike: a long pole-weapon with a sharp metal head used by foot-soldiers.

Placentia: name given to the royal palace at Greenwich – cf. *Pleasance.*

pole-arms: any battle weapon on a long pole – pike*, halberd*, axe etc. Used by infantry. The mounted equivalent was the lance*.

poniard: a small dagger.

Poitiers: location in France of 1356 battle when England was victorious.

portcullis: a defensive iron lattice gate. Also a Beaufort* heraldic symbol.

pottage: a thick soup made with anything available.

psalter: a personal prayer-book, often beautifully illuminated.

readeption: = reattainment (from Latin *adeptus* = having attained)

*reredorter: a monastery latrine. (*rere*=behind *dorter*=dormitory)

quintain: a device for teaching accuracy at jousting.

sabaton: armour for protection of the upper foot.

sallet: a style of helmet not unlike a WW2 'tin hat'.

sapper: one who digs to undermine masonry.

St Alban: a Roman Briton who was executed for refusing to deny his Christian faith. St Albans Abbey (now a cathedral) was founded as his shrine.

sumpter: a packhorse, especially that of a knight, carrying his armour.

sumptuary laws: regulating clothing and diet, to prevent people living 'above their station'. (Nothing to do with 'sumpter'!)

surcôte or surcoat: outer tunic or jacket, often of rich material, worn over armour and bearing the owner's coat of arms.

uterine: 'of the womb', i.e. offspring of one mother by different fathers.

verteagle: heraldic symbol showing a green eagle with wings spread on a yellow ground. Personal badge of Warwick's father Richard Neville, Earl of Salisbury.

vintner: a dealer and importer of wine.

*wimple: woman's headdress covering hair, by mid 15thC becoming restricted to nuns and widows. (see **coif**)

WELSH WORDS AND NAMES

Abermaw: name for the present day town of Barmouth, at the mouth of the River Mawddach.

ab: son of (before a name beginning with a vowel)

ap: son of (before a name beginning with a consonant)

Bethan: a form of the English name Elizabeth.

brwd: praise or enthusiasm – also a poem written in that vein.

Dai: a shortening of Dafydd = David in English

Dewi: an affectionate shortening of Dafydd, often used for St David, patron saint of Wales.

eisteddfod: a festival of music and poetry.

ferch: daughter of

Fychan: Welsh spelling of the English surname Vaughan and pronounced much the same.

Evan: pron. *Evin* A form of the English name John

Emrys: a form of the English name Ambrose

Glyn Dŵr: pron. *Glyn Dour.* Welsh hero of a failed rebellion against the English at the beginning of 15thC. The English called him Glendower. By tradition he was Owen Tudor's godfather and namesake, related through his mother.

Gwyladus: Welsh spelling of English name Gladys and pronounced the same.

Hywel: pronounced *Howell* in English.

Maredudd: a man's name, pronounced *Meredith* in English.

mab: son

merch: daughter

Merlin: legendary bard or wiseman who taught King Arthur.

Sian: equivalent to the English girl's name Jane or Joan. Pronounced *Shaan*.

Tudur: sometimes spelled Tudŵr. A form of the English name Theodore and the basis of the Tudor surname. The Welsh did not use surnames but were known by the name of their fathers and grandfathers. So Owen Tudor was originally Owain ap (son of) Maredudd, which was his father's name, but he was also recorded as Owen ap Maredudd ap Tudŵr (his grandfather's name) and it was this name that stuck, with an English spelling. Otherwise the dynasty would have been the Meredith and not the Tudor dynasty.

Tŷ Cerrig: House of Stone.

Ynys Mon: The Isle of Anglesey.

Yr Wyddfa: The Great Mountain, now known as Snowdon.

Y mab daragon: 'The son of prophecy' in bardic ode, destined to restore Wales to true British rule.

AUTHOR'S NOTES

Jasper has been occupying my thoughts – and often my dreams – ever since I wrote his birth in *The Tudor Bride* back in January 2013, so I'm delighted to be bringing him to prominence at last, believing as I do that he has been sadly neglected as a principal founder of the Tudor dynasty. The name Jasper was given to him by his parents but history does not reveal the reason why it was chosen. It was not a name generally in use in England during the fifteenth century but when I discovered that medieval midwives believed the gemstone jasper could relieve the pain of labour and bring about a safe delivery it seemed a perfect choice for Queen Catherine to make. Her second son by Owen Tudor is on record as having been a redhead and the gem called 'bloodstone', which was popular at the time, is a form of jasper. The fact that I myself was born with bright red hair may also have something to do with my warm affection for my new hero! A minor brush with genetics at university told me that a child with red hair was often the result of a fair-haired mother and a dark-haired father

However, much though I like it, his name and hair-colour were far from being the primary reasons for choosing to write Jasper's story. Sketchy references made to him by historians as Henry VII's uncle and guardian were enough to whet my appetite but extensive further research revealed a hero of the old school, a man who emerged from the shadows of obscurity to become a character honed by adversity, courage, determination and a strong sense of loyalty.

I think of him as the lead in a twentieth century Hollywood blockbuster, to be played by Errol Flynn, Cary Grant or Harrison Ford – so unlike the all-swearing, computer-graphicked anti-heroes of today! Of course in order to give his story authenticity it needed romantic interest but unfortunately in his first forty years history does not give Jasper any kind of female co-star so I have had to extrapolate from a single mention of a name, just as I did in creating Queen Catherine's lifelong companion, Mette, in the *Bride* books. That he had two illegitimate daughters is documented but their mother is unknown. However, when Henry Tudor's second son Henry (later King Henry VIII) was born, Margaret Beaufort brought in a woman called Jane Hywel to be the governess of his nursery. I thought it unlikely that the redoubtable Lady Margaret would have introduced a stranger for such a job and concluded that she must have been very familiar with this woman's skill with children. The rest of Jane Hywel's life, as related in *First of the Tudors*, is entirely fictional, although a Hywel Fychan was one of the relatives brought to England from Wales by Owen Tudor during his marriage to Queen Catherine and appears as a minor character in *The Tudor Bride*.

Owen Tudor's illegitimate son, Sir David (Davy) Owen, lived a real and well-documented life but his mother is unknown, as is the woman who lit candles around Owen's severed head in the Hereford marketplace but I have always liked the name Myfanwy, ever since reading John Betjeman's poem of that name! Except for Jane's family and the farm at Tŷ Cerrig and Jasper's 'secret' sister Meg, her house and family, all other locations and people are drawn directly from historical sources, although their characters are fleshed out from the skimpy recorded detail and some of their actions are fictional, just as ruined buildings are restored and empty rooms refurnished in order to bring history to life. Such is the nature of historical fiction!

Queen Marguerite of Anjou has been well and variously depicted in fiction but I have chosen to use her French name throughout in order to differentiate her from Margaret Beaufort, another essential element of this story and a character who will have plenty more to offer in my next novel. I have also had Marguerite insist that her son be called by the French version of his name so that he is not confused with (King) Edward of York. Besides, I think Marguerite was a stroppy enough character to fly in the face of English bias against the French!

The Earl of Warwick is believed to have revelled in his sobriquet 'The Kingmaker' but I'm afraid I hold to the belief that Jasper performed that task just as ably as Warwick and also, although faced with far greater trials and set-backs, remained steadfastly loyal to the king he served. It was hardly his fault that in combat he was saddled with two notoriously self-serving Lancastrians; Harry Holland, Duke of Exeter and James Butler, the 'Fleeing Earl' of Wiltshire. Readers of my next novel may be happy to discover that Jasper was not always defeated in battle!

Finally, dear reader, if I have omitted to explain any further fictions or anomalies please feel free to tax me with them via my Facebook Page (Joanna Hickson), my Twitter account

(@joannahickson) or on Goodreads, where I will endeavour to respond as soon as possible. Meanwhile if you have enjoyed *First of the Tudors* I hope you will consider reading young Harri Tudor's story in my next novel which, while being very much Harri's story, will pick up where this one finishes; so you will discover more of Jasper, Jane, Elin, Sian, Davvy and Margaret Beaufort, as well as many 'new' historical characters.

Thank you for reading!
Joanna

ACKNOWLEDGEMENTS

When launching into a new writing venture it can be galling if the subject you have been brooding for years suddenly becomes flavour of the moment and other books and articles emerge which cover the same person and period as yours. However I was lucky in that Welsh historian Sara Elin Roberts published her definitive biography *Jasper, The Tudor Kingmaker* a few months before my novel and was kind enough to share with me some of her insight into his life and character over a very convivial lunch in Anglesey, while I was researching in the Tudor heartland where she lives, and in subsequent exchanges of emails. So warmest thanks to her and to Nathan Amin, who writes copiously on the Tudors, in print and on his very informative online blog. Among many others, two research books I found particularly helpful were the recently revised edition of *The Making of the Tudor Dynasty* by Welsh academics Ralph A Griffiths and Roger S Thomas and the definitive biography of *Henry VII* by the late and celebrated Welsh historian, Professor Stanley B Chrimes. These are highly recommended as future reading if you are interested in taking your knowledge of Jasper and the emergence of the Tudors further. And should you wish to go back to (almost) contemporary sources you cannot do better than consult (in translation unless you speak Latin!) the history commissioned by King

Henry VII from Polydore Vergil, an Italian historian who became a naturalized Englishman in 1510 and first published his *Anglia Historia* in print in 1534, during the reign of Henry VIII. Obviously it is biased towards its commissioner's dynasty but nevertheless remains the account that gets nearest to the facts of what brought the Tudors to prominence.

A good deal of Jasper's story is set in Wales and several enjoyable research trips were made there, including one very wild sortie into Snowdonia to view Tŷ Mawr Wybrnant, the 15th Century farmhouse where Bishop William Morgan was born, who first translated the bible into Welsh. It is currently run by the National Trust and well worth a visit, being the building on which I based the fictional Tŷ Cerrig farmhouse. But I advise you to choose fair weather and a full tank of petrol, because on our exit from its remote location in the depths of winter my husband and I found ourselves lost in a snowbound wilderness without a mobile signal and no sign of life for many icy miles. It gave me a very good idea of how lonely and stark was the landscape in which Jasper spent his outcast days in the high mountains. The location of Tŷ Cerrig was based on another place rooted in the 15thC – Cors y Gedol, a house and estate a few miles north of Barmouth (Abermaw), which is privately owned but used for weddings etc. Thanks are due to the owners for not complaining when I lurked around the policies taking notes and photographs. Other fruitful research locations were the castles of Caernarfon, Harlech and Pembroke and Lamphey Palace, all open to the public through Cadw, the Welsh government department responsible for preserving its history. I visited Lamphey on a wildlife evening and was privileged to hold a tame tawny owl throughout the expert's talk, an experience I thoroughly enjoyed. Apart from that it is a beautiful place, full of atmosphere and interest with reference to *First of the Tudors*.

And now to the people who are truly crucial to this book. There would be no meticulously-edited, beautifully-presented, dauntlessly-marketed and purposefully-publicised Joanna Hickson novels without the skilful and friendly team I am so lucky to have behind me at Harper Fiction: my champion and publisher Kimberley Young, fearless and fabulous editor Kate Bradley, charming and capable editorial assistant Charlotte Brabbin and faithful copy editor Joy Chamberlain. All deserve my heartfelt thanks and a special mention should go to Holly Macdonald, who designed the new look for the jacket, which I absolutely love and I am sure readers will too. Katie Moss is still with me on the digital side of publicity - thanks, Katie - and the lovely Jaime Frost continues to handle publicity and public relations without which words do not reach readers.

Penultimate and huge thanks to Jenny Brown, my Scottish friend and literary agent – a doyenne of her ilk and the enthusiastic, well-connected, knowledgeable and stylish lady by whom it is my privilege to be represented.

And finally I am delighted to be publishing a book with HarperCollins in the same year that my friend and mentor Barbara Erskine celebrates the thirtieth anniversary of her ground-breaking dual-period debut novel *Lady of Hay*, which is still very much in print, as are all her sixteen subsequent books. So I congratulate her on a fantastic achievement and thank her for reading the manuscript of *The Agincourt Bride* six years ago and thinking it worth mentioning to her editor over a convivial lunch. The latest result of that serendipity is in your hands, dear reader, and if you haven't read Barbara's books, start now – you will love them!

Joanna

Even the greatest of queens have rules
– to break them would cost her
dearly...

She chose love
over her Kingdom,
but everything
comes at a price ...

THE
TUDOR
BRIDE

JOANNA HICKSON

'Thoroughly engrossing'
The Lady

Torn between the houses of
Lancaster and York.

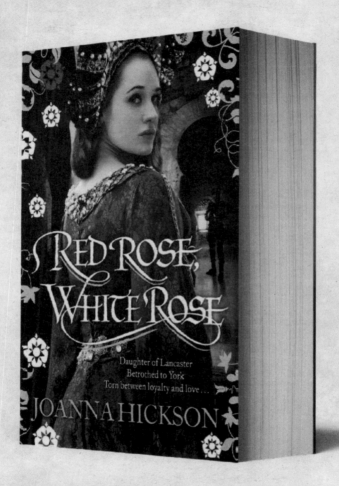

A young woman trying to survive as
the Wars of the Roses tear England
apart...